I'M A STANGER HERE MYSELF

I'M A STRANGER HERE MYSELF

Jean Stubbs

Severn House Large Print
London & New York

This first large print edition published in Great Britain 2005 by
SEVERN HOUSE LARGE PRINT BOOKS LTD of
9-15 High Street, Sutton, Surrey, SM1 1DF.
First world regular print edition published 2004 by
Severn House Publishers, London and New York.
This first large print edition published in the USA 2006 by
SEVERN HOUSE PUBLISHERS INC., of
595 Madison Avenue, New York, NY 10022.

British Library Cataloguing in Publication Data

Stubbs, Jean, 1926 -
    I'm a stranger here myself. - Large print ed.
    1. Businesswomen - Fiction
    2. Friendship - Fiction
    3. Large type books
    I. Title
    823.9'14 [F]

    ISBN-10: 0-7278-7475-6

Except where actual historical events and characters are being described
for the storyline of this novel, all situations in this publication are
fictitious and any resemblance to living persons is purely coincidental.

Printed and bound in Great Britain by
MPG Books Ltd, Bodmin, Cornwall.

To Felix, 1937–2002,
who not only made room for my writing,
but built me a room in which to write.
With my love and thanks, always.

Acknowledgements

These characters and their city do not exist, and the events only happened in my head. But I have acknowledgements to make to the following:

I'm indebted to my friends Joe and Julie Burrows. Julie, upon hearing the synopsis of the unwritten novel, said, 'Your chief characters are all solitary and in search of something.' To which Joe remarked, 'I'm a stranger here, myself!'

To *The City in History* by Lewis Mumford; *Bath and Bristol* by John Britton F.S.A. M.R.S.L., published 1829; *The Old Straight Path* by Alfred Watkins; and *The Secret Country* by Janet and Colin Bord, for research.

To Brilliant Knight Orchestrations, whose classical music concert 'Spirit of the Rebellion' at Pendennis Castle inspired the final chapter.

To Felix, who liked to listen while I read out each novel, and who loved this one.

Finally, to my agent, Laura Longrigg, for her patience, support and encouragement through some hard times. Thank you, Laura.

'I, a stranger and afraid
In a world I never made.'

A.E. Housman

The City

Kate the Child

1976

The Christmas shopping expedition must have been a special occasion because money was tight at Peddleford Flower Farm, and treats usually home-made: probably Grandma had sent a cheque. Whatever the reason, Nora Wing decided that her husband Neville should take the afternoon off and drive the family to the city in the farm truck, there to see Santa Claus and have tea at Mrs Porter's Parlour. Kate was six at the time and being what Nora described as 'an awkward little monkey'.

'She's like my mother,' Nora said. 'Red hair and a nice red temper to match.'

'It isn't! I haven't!'

'No, Nora, her hair's more of a chestnut colour, like yours,' Neville said diplomatically. He winked at Kate. 'And as long as she has her own way she never loses her temper.'

Kate stuck out her bottom lip and considered this. The tone was teasing, kind. She could have responded to it, but Nora had to point out her faults.

'Look at your brother and sister,' she said. 'No trouble at all.'

This was an exaggeration. Nora's maternal generosity was boundless, and having only one child of her own she fostered nature's handicapped. Though they were biddable, the two younger children demanded much of her attention because Reggie was lame and Betsy was retarded.

Kate turned a viper's eye on her siblings.

'Why can't you adopt clever, pretty children that I can play with?' she asked.

'You can play with these two well enough, miss,' Nora replied. 'And if you're so clever yourself then you can teach them! And that's a nasty thing to say.'

So Kate frowned and muttered as she stuffed her arms into the sleeves of her Oxfam coat and struggled to fasten the buttons, watching her mother deal tenderly with Reggie's limbs, which he could not always control, and wipe the dribble from Betsy's chin.

Neville Wing perceived more than his wife did. Seeing Kate's distress beneath her defiance he whispered, 'Give us a smile, then!' and gently pinched her cheek. As she remained mute and obstinate he coaxed her, 'Give us a kiss, then!'

Kate looked at him from under her lashes and saw that he understood. She swallowed a sob. Lavishly, she gave him both smile and kiss. Her heart swelled. She slipped her hand

12

in his and skipped along with him as he escorted Nora and her brood to the van. He loved her best. She was special.

That late December afternoon was stamped on Kate's life. Sitting up on the front seat of the truck, squeezed between her parents, she watched familiar fields flow away, the familiar lane widen into a road, the road become a broad three-lane fast-moving motorway. The speed and aggression of the traffic first intimidated, then thrilled her. Her father's truck battled along in the slow lane while sleeker vehicles soared by. She sat up as tall as she could, watchful and engrossed, until the misty outlines of the horizon sharpened and a mile ahead of them a vision raised the remains of stone walls to the winter sun.

She drummed her heels against the seat in excitement, demanding of her father, 'What's that place, Da? What's that?'

'That's the city, Katie. That's where we're going.'

'What's a city?'

A former university student, he treated each childish question seriously and answered it fully.

'It's a container – you know that word? Something that holds something else?' She nodded. 'Well, a city is a container that holds lots of other containers. Like Grandma's Chinese boxes – you've seen them?' She nodded vehemently. 'The city's containers are houses and shops and business and all the

13

things that people need. If they're ill they can go to the big hospital. If they want to travel they go to the railway station or the bus station. If they want to be educated there are all sorts of schools and a university. If they want to read there's a grand library. If they want to be entertained – to have fun – there's cinemas, a theatre, a concert hall, swimming baths, sports centres. Anything you could name, anything you could want, you'll find in the city.'

Kate turned this information over in her mind for a few moments. 'Not like Peddleford,' she said.

'No, no. The city could snap up Peddleford in one bite and still feel hungry!'

This made her laugh.

'The city's like a big club sandwich, and Peddleford's a slice of tomato.'

This made her laugh still more.

'The city has everything,' said Neville.

He spoke without envy, but his wife was anxious to correct this impression of power and plenty.

'They haven't got space and fresh air and fields full of flowers,' she said. 'Most of them live in a house like a shoebox and when they look out of their windows all they can see is the opposite side of the street. And they hurry to work and hurry back home. Always busy. Always pushed for time. I wouldn't live in a city if you paid me for it!'

'In a house like a *shoebox*?' Kate asked.

But Nora said, 'Now don't start asking

14

questions. We're nearly there!'

The vision grew closer and more distinct. Kate clutched the buttons of her coat in ecstasy. They crossed the river by Southgate Bridge and drove along stately roads, past gracious squares and lofty trees. The buildings were as tall as towers, built of honey-coloured stone, elegantly proportioned. Behind their shining windows must lie beauty, order and tranquillity. Only the noblest people would inhabit them.

Nora's good nature suggested that she had been a little hard on this difficult daughter. She spoke to her intimately, good-naturedly.

'What do you make of all this, then, Katie?'

But her mother had long since betrayed her by wanting other children, and Kate would not answer.

Nosed by glossy cars and roaring motorcycles, the truck trundled doggedly from street to handsome street searching for shelter in all this magnificence.

P said a friendly notice on the side of an archway, and Neville drove through a short grey tunnel that turned into a car park. Beating a BMW to the last space, he grinned to himself.

'Here we are!' he cried, triumphant.

'Here we are!' Nora echoed, relieved.

Neville lifted Kate out and told her not to move, then he unstrapped Betsy and Reggie and fastened their hands in hers, which she hated. But there were compensations.

'Don't move!' Kate ordered them in turn,

15

and felt a thrill of power as the children obeyed her instantly.

Finally Neville helped his wife out. Nora was built on a generous scale in body as well as in heart and spirit, and he steadied her as she gripped the dashboard and felt for the concrete ground with one broad foot.

'That's my lass!' he said encouragingly. Then, turning to Kate, he added in the same tone, 'That's my good girl!'

She thought her father had a lovely face: thin and brown and kind. His humour was pleasant and his voice quiet. She had rarely seen him angry, and then his anger only concerned important matters and they all respected it, whereas Nora flared up half a dozen times a day over trifles, and flickered down again just as quickly. To Kate, her father was safe harbour in that tempestuous household and she wondered if he found the children as intrusive as she did, but his tolerance seemed endless and he spent half an hour every evening teaching four-year-old Reggie how to control his stammer.

Now he said, 'Come on, everybody. Let's see Santa Claus!'

Two-year-old Betsy, denied much vocabulary by reason of years and lack of intelligence, cried, 'Sklaws! Sklaws!'

Kate knew better than to correct her sharply, which she would have liked to do, but she gave the small hand an admonitory shake. Betsy fell silent, her lip trembled for a few seconds, and then she forgot the

16

admonishment as she gaped at the marvels around them.

The little group walked slowly on down Broad Street, pausing at the windows of glittering shops. Betsy flattened her face against one splendid pane and left a dribble of saliva on the glass, to Kate's shame. Neville hoisted Reggie on to his shoulders to give him an overview. Released from his disability the child shouted with joy and patted his foster father's head as wonder succeeded wonder.

Santa Claus was a bitter disappointment for Kate because she perceived a young man's face beneath the foam of white hair, and when he spoke in a voice that was as artificial as his whiskers she ceased to believe in him.

'And what would you like for Christmas, girlie?' he rumbled, slipping a paternal arm round her waist.

She took the measure of him, and unpicked his fingers one by one.

'All the toys in the shop,' she answered sweetly.

Their eyes met. They understood and disliked each other.

'Ho, ho, ho!' he boomed. 'I can't promise you that, but I'll see what I can do.' He gave her a small parcel wrapped in pink tissue paper. 'Here's a pretty present for a pretty little girl,' he said and set her down rather quickly.

Kate opened it at once and, finding a green

17

plastic comb ridged with blue forget-me-nots, she re-wrapped it, said, 'No, thank you,' and put it back in the bin, while Nora hissed a remonstrance that Kate pretended not to hear.

Yet he was an unquestioned success with the younger children, sublime in their ignorance. Betsy mouthed her name and request at him and dribbled on his beard, Reggie fell over his legs and stammered, and they received a beggarly plastic doll and a scurvy plastic whistle with ecstasy.

Outside the store Nora asked, 'So what did you all think of Santa Claus?'

She received an enthusiastic if incoherent response from the younger children, but Kate muttered, 'I just hope that Mrs Porter's Parlour is better than *him*.'

Neville covered this remark by saying, 'Come on, Nora, let's feed and water the livestock!' and hoisted Betsy to his shoulders because it was her turn to survey the universe.

His wife took Reggie's hand and adjusted her pace to his. He limped gamely along, asking her at intervals, 'Is it f-f-f-far?'

Freed from the children, Kate lingered behind.

As the winter afternoon waned the Christmas lights shone like jewels against the dusk. She had never seen so much unattainable splendour and so many different people in her short life, and she became aware that the family that had been her entire world was only a small, shabby fragment of the world itself. Staring into long shimmering windows she compared her reflection to that of other little girls, finding her home-cut hair, second-hand clothes and stout shoes a poor comparison. She was in paradise, but unworthy of it.

'Not far now,' said Neville. 'It's in the medieval quarter of the town.' He could not resist educating. 'That's why the street is called Oldways. Old. Ways. You see?'

Betsy and Reggie remained uninterested and unenlightened, but Kate ran up and clasped his hand so she could listen and question.

'What does that meddy word mean? Is there a real Mrs Porter?' she asked.

'Medieval means the Middle Ages. Between the fifth and the fifteenth centuries. I'll show you in the history book when we get home.'

'There *was* a real Mrs Porter,' Nora chimed in, for she too had been a university student, though her talents were rusting for lack of use. 'She started the tea room in her own front parlour, two hundred years ago. But different people have run it since. When I was a girl the owner was a Mrs Pringle. She and Grandma went to school together, and Grandma used to take my sister and me to the Parlour when we were children.' She paused, remembering, and added, 'But a lot of water's flowed under the bridge since then. I haven't had tea there for donkey's years.'

Nora lived always in the present, so she spoke without regret, merely recording a time that was past. 'Will Mrs Pringle be in the Parlour today?' Kate asked.

'I shouldn't think so. She'll be retired by now.'

'What bridge did the water go under? What donkey do you mean?'

'Never mind that now,' said Nora. 'Here we are.'

Mrs Porter's Parlour in Oldways Street stopped the family in its tracks. They feasted their eyes on the window full of fairy confectionery and gazed into the carpeted room beyond. On spindly chairs before linen-clad tables fashionable ladies drank tea from flowered china cups and chatted. They too had been shopping for Christmas. Glossy carrier bags bearing the names of the city's most prestigious stores stood by them. Their clothes were fine, simple, and very expensive. Their children were well-behaved and well-dressed. One young couple were totally absorbed in each other. Her painted mouth was animated. Her hair shone. Her cashmere coat slid from her shoulders to the floor but she didn't care. She kicked off her high-heeled shoes. He laughed and pretended to be shocked. In smiling complicity the waitress picked up the coat and bore it away.

There was no notice in the window warning them off, but when Neville looked at Nora enquiringly she shook her head.

'No, love. We can't take the children in there. It's not for us.'

The glory of the day had been extinguished.

20

Kate's voice rose in protest.

'But Grandma used to bring you here when you were a little child.'

'Well, that was then and this is now,' said Nora philosophically.

'If Grandma was here this minute,' Kate cried in a childish burst of resentment, 'she'd take me. *I'm* her favourite.'

She might have said she was the only grand-child accepted by either side, but she was too young to understand that. Nora and Neville's parents had long since withdrawn from a way of life that was foreign to them. They lived at a distance that was both physical and emo-tional, and sent cheques at appropriate times.

'Well, Grandma isn't here,' said Nora, 'and it's not our sort of place.'

'But you promised,' Kate accused her.

Nora answered fairly, 'Then I was wrong, and I'm sorry. No, it won't do. We'd best find somewhere else.'

Kate knew that her mother's decision was right. She could imagine the chaos that would result from settling Reggie and Betsy, the fuss of feeding them and keeping them quiet, taking them to the lavatory twice in case they wet the chairs. She envisaged the forbearing smiles and shrewd assessments of other guests, the polite contempt of the waitresses. Worse still, the manageress might refuse to let them in, pretending that the café was full.

'We'll come here another day, Katie-girl,' Neville soothed her. 'I might bring you by yourself one Saturday.'

She knew this was unlikely and it only made her crosser.

'So off we jolly well go!' Nora cried, and the younger children cheered.

But Kate lagged behind, kicking at cracks in the pavement, muttering a long litany about people who broke promises.

Outside the hallowed quarter they found a large, light, noisy tea room full of families where they could spread themselves out, change Betsy's nappy in the mother and baby room, drop crumbs on the tiled floor, mop up the oil-cloth cover with paper serviettes and be comfortable among others of their kind.

Hate it! Hate it! Kate thought, and treated the shocking-pink milkshakes and stolid scones with disgust.

'What's the matter with you *now*?' Nora asked in exasperation. 'This is supposed to be a treat!'

Kate's bottom lip trembled. She could not express what she felt.

'What is it, Katie?' her father asked gently.

She looked up at him, full of tears. 'I want ... I want ... not to be a little child.'

Nora, cutting Betsy's sponge cake into bite-sized pieces, cast up her eyes, but Neville was tender with her.

'Why not, my love?'

She shook her head, unable to explain that children had no power.

'Then what *do* you want to be?' he asked.

22

Kate let her imagination rove through resplendent shops in festive streets, and fixed on an image that would correspond with them.

'I want – I want – to be a grown-up lady – with high-heeled shoes – and lipstick – and shining hair – and kick my best shoes off – and drop my best coat on the floor – and nobody minds.'

Neville and Nora laughed, not unkindly but in genuine amusement. Imitating their parents, Reggie and Betsy laughed immoderately. But Kate cried and cried.

Kate the Woman

From that day on Kate dreamed of something less earthy and noisy and cluttered than Peddleford Farm, where life and work were arduous and basic, though its produce fluttered most beautifully in the wind and clouds of scent drifted across the summer fields. Town dwellers, inhaling the mingled aromas of Nora's cooking and Neville's labours, would have described their life as 'getting away from it all'. But her parents knew that no one got away from or with anything, and accepted hardship as part of a beloved bargain between themselves and the land.

Living according to their principles and having no prospect of further children, they had become foster-parents quite early in Kate's life, and chose those least wanted and most in need, so Kate was never alone, though lonely. But she had no focus for her discontent until she saw the city. Certainly this noble place had rejected her in her present guise, labelled her *Not up to standard*, but she did not accept this rejection as final and looked for a way out of her present situation.

She found it first in the City High School for Girls, but the means of gaining access to this starry place was a scholarship, and this was rarely achieved by pupils of Peddleford Primary School. In the next five years, with Neville as her dedicated personal tutor, she worked for and won it.

Sending her there entailed a family sacrifice. The uniform alone cost her parents' blood. Fares and extras were another burden. They trod their pride underfoot and asked Grandma to help out, which she did. Indeed she did more than that, because when she died a few years later she left the bulk of her small property to Nora, with the request that a certain sum be set aside for Kate's further education. But harsh winters and poor summers had deflowered Peddleford Farm, and the Wings spent all the bequest on freeing the property from mortgage and setting it in bloom again.

They weathered that particular crisis, did

better than before, and kept Kate at the high school until she gained three A-levels with distinction. When she wanted to read art history at the city university, they had to admit that they could not afford to support her any longer and she must begin to earn her own living.

It was a bitter time for Kate. She suffered, and made sure that her family suffered too. In the end common sense overcame her sense of grievance and she assessed her future coolly. A secretarial course seemed the best option, since it gave her a footing in the business world and time to look around. She knew she must make the most of every opportunity, and she had absolute confidence in herself if not in anyone else. She chose a prestigious secretarial college in the city and brought home the brochure.

'If you can *lend* me the money for three months' fees,' she said acidly, 'I'll pay you back when I'm working.'

Her parents hurried to placate her.

'No, no,' said Neville, conscience-stricken. 'You don't have to pay us back. We can manage that much at least, my love. I wish with all my heart we could do more. I do indeed.' For he had imagined his daughter achieving the degree he had left undone.

Holding the brochure out of reach of one demanding child, and stroking the head of another as she read it, Nora observed, 'But it says here that the average length of the course is six months, not three.'

'If you read on you'll find that it adds "according to the student's capabilities",' said Kate, implacable. 'I shall do it in half that time.'

She did.

As if to make up for a wet and windy summer, that autumn was dry, mild and beautiful. Kate made her lunch sandwiches at home and ate them in Adelaide Park, savouring present freedom and dreaming of future independence. Though remaining on amicable terms with her fellow students, she avoided intimacy. They were not of her calibre. None possessed her fierce desire to succeed. Most were learning a skill that would bring in pocket money before they married, and supplement the family income afterwards when the children were at school. Kate, looking for an opening that promised success, thought of them as 'temps' and despised them for lack of vision.

She was given her chance in a small but enterprising business called Celebrations, which specialized in setting up events of all kinds from private garden parties to official occasions. Their owner and director, Hector Mordant, had launched the company a few years previously, backed by a generous legacy from his godmother and the subsequent sale of her property. His CV was impeccable: public school, a creditable arts degree from Cambridge and a well-paid job in advertising.

He was a bright, hard, workaholic who

knew that connections were worth more than achievements, that favours given meant favours returned, and that the best policy was to anticipate trends and be there waiting when the crowd pressed forward, crying, 'We want ...' Add to these gifts good looks, great charm, total selfishness, and an ambition that would bite the hand that fed it if need be, and you beheld a leader of men – and of women, too.

Kate had not the experience to judge his darker side, but instinctively she guessed that he and Celebrations were rising stars, and hitched her aspiring wagon to the pair of them, even at the sacrifice of becoming an overqualified and underpaid junior member of the staff.

Her debut was not encouraging. Hector gave her a cursory glance as he was passing through the general office, and she was interviewed by his assistant and personal secretary, Rachel Benbow. With her severely handsome face and severely smart city suit she seemed to Kate's young eyes the ultimate in sophistication. She was also extremely tough.

Miss Benbow made sure that she had no rivals. She kept her staff at a reverent distance from Hector and a respectful one from herself. And she saw that Kate, who had too much in her favour to be rejected, must be cut down to manageable size before she could be used.

'Your qualifications are quite good,' said Miss Benbow, making light of three distinguished A-levels and the secretarial college's exultant report, 'but you have no experience, so you must expect to begin at the beginning and learn as you go along. Are you prepared to do that?'

She meant, if she had known it, 'Are you prepared to live on a diet of humble pie and thank me for it?'

Kate perceived what the woman was doing, and why, but she intended to triumph, whatever the cost, and answered with enthusiasm, 'Yes, Miss Benbow!'

'You will be on probation for three months, at the end of which – if you prove to be satisfactory – you will be given more responsibility and a pay rise. If not ...' Miss Benbow added, leaving the outcome hanging dreadfully in the air.

'I shall do my best,' said Kate devoutly.

It did not take a vast amount of intelligence to make morning coffee and afternoon tea, to serve it in earthenware mugs for the office staff and fine china for the inner sanctum, to see that supplies were topped up every week, and to balance the petty-cash book. Typing reports that no one else wanted to do, posting letters and running errands for Miss Benbow, were tedious jobs, but Kate achieved all this with good will and good temper. The other girls obeyed their superior implicitly, hurrying for shelter when a storm brewed and keeping their distance. Kate came as close as she dared, made herself indispensable, watched and listened, assessing the woman's strengths and weaknesses.

Miss Benbow was vain, so Kate subtly flattered her. Miss Benbow was ruthless, so Kate learned to be thorough. And Miss Benbow had access to Hector Mordant, but that door remained closed. Still, the woman was in her early thirties, which Kate considered to be elderly. She reckoned that time was on her side. Meanwhile she began her own metamorphosis.

Having paid for lunches and fares and her keep at home, the first thing she did with her first month's wages was to put down a deposit on a stylish suit from Fairfax's. She eschewed grey as being Miss Benbow's favourite colour. Black would be too old for her, brown too dowdy. She recognized that she must tread a fine line in her choice of clothes: to dress well, but not too well. She chose a muted sage-green that complemented her colouring. Still she suffered, standing in one of Broad Street's finest department stores with flushed cheeks, trying to look older than her eighteen years, asking the sales lady if it were possible to pay by instalments. Amazingly, it was. She stinted herself to meet them and collected the suit in time for Easter. From then on her wardrobe progressed steadily. She rinsed her red hair to a glowing chestnut, had it cut into a short, shining bob at Shearers, and went without lunch for two weeks to pay for it.

The probation period over and her wages increased, she stretched her resources to the limit and, despite Nora's aggrieved protests,

29

she found a bedsit in a large house over-looking Adelaide Park. Once a handsome residence, it had come upon hard times, and the land on which it stood was now worth more than the building. While he considered how best to make it pay in the future, the landlord filled the rooms with transient tenants, mostly students, who were powerless to object to its limitations. Grateful for affordable shelter, they hung their stained walls with posters, patched holes in the floor with hardboard and painted crumbling wood in brilliant colours.

Kate's room was let as furnished for the landlord's legal convenience, but the furniture was a ramshackle pretence and so she brought all her personal belongings with her to make it habitable. Her father helped her to move in, leaving Reggie to run the flower farm.

'It's Saturday,' Neville said. 'Nothing much doing at this time of the year. He knows the ropes and it'll make him feel important.'

Kate, being young, was amused by the thought of Reggie feeling important.

The room made habitable, her father took her out for a pub lunch to celebrate this new departure, and kissed her heartily before he left. She knew he was concerned about the state of the house and the perilous condition of the plumbing and wiring, but she could trust him not to confide his doubts to Nora, who would only use this as a reason to bring her back.

He simply said, 'Remember that we're expecting you next Sunday. Your mother will want to see how you are, and give you a good dinner. So don't disappoint us.'

'I'll be there at ten o'clock to help her with the vegetables,' Kate promised.

He hovered, wistful for himself as well as his wife. 'I suppose you wouldn't like to change your mind and come tomorrow as well, would you, Katie?'

To deny him was hard, but she must stand her new ground.

'No, Da, it's too soon. Thank you just the same, but I need time to settle in.'

He capitulated. 'Next Sunday it is, then, – and remember, if things don't work out here, you can always come home.'

She kissed and hugged and thanked him, but had left home for good. She intended to move as far away from fecundity as she could. Untidy animal warmth was to be rejected in favour of cool solitude. To have a room that belonged entirely to her, in which no one else was allowed to enter except by invitation, was the ultimate luxury. Left alone that first afternoon, she felt blessed by silence. Sitting on the side of the dilapidated divan she closed her eyes and experienced peace and tranquillity. Ideas for the future flowed, but she let them go. They would ripen and return. Just now she was savouring the beauty of nothingness.

In Adelaide Park a tall, bespectacled young man with flopping blond hair was sweeping

31

the path. He brushed his way rhythmically through the drifts of bronze leaves, piled them into a barrow and trundled on. As he reached the stretch nearest to Kate's house he stopped and rested on his broom for a few moments, smiling up at the sky and round at the day, at peace with himself. Then once more he lifted the handles of the barrow and trundled away.

She was not romantically interested, not even curious, but at that moment she felt at one with him. His smile reflected the smile within herself. His tranquillity, his being able to stop for a while and look around, to set his own pace and work by himself without hindrance from anyone, echoed her new freedom.

'You get smarter and thinner every time I look at you,' said Nora, who was no fool. 'Are you eating properly?'

'Oh, yes,' Kate lied, 'but they keep me busy running around at work.'

'I don't know why you can't live at home,' Nora said, who knew very well. 'It's only a twenty-minute bus ride away and it'd be a lot cheaper for you. Your father and I don't like to think of you all by yourself in a bedsitter, heating up some tinned rubbish on a gas ring.'

Kate's peaceful room was her personal space. How could she explain that having her own key, knowing that everything would be in the same place when she got back, and being accountable to no one, was bliss?

'Anyway,' said Nora, making the best of the situation, 'I know you eat one decent meal a week here and that's *some* satisfaction.'

A stately goddess, she was presiding over the long black kitchen range, juggling skilfully with pans of potatoes, cabbage and carrots, inspecting a roast of beef, giving the Yorkshire pudding batter a final whisk. A large rice pudding simmered in the bottom oven. In the larder stood a big bowl of stewed apples, a blackcurrant pie and a jug of thick cream.

'Keep you running round, do they?' Nora ruminated. 'Who's in charge of you?'

'Miss Benbow.' Reluctantly.

'You should bring her here for her Sunday dinner,' said Nora.

'I can't ask Miss Benbow...' Kate began, horrified.

'We'd make her welcome,' said Nora, taking no notice, 'and we'd give her a good meal. If she's as thin and smart as you are she probably needs one.'

Kate looked round the kitchen and thought of Miss Benbow in her pearl-grey tailored suit, sitting on the chair with a wobbly leg, jostled by sticky children, faced with Nora's bounty. Her mouth set against her mother's lack of perception.

'I can't do that. I'm not even allowed to *speak* to Miss Benbow except about work.'

Nora woke up from her dream of setting matters right, and scrutinized this difficult daughter. Maternity had not dimmed her intelligence.

'You think we're not good enough for her,' she said flatly.

'I didn't mean that,' she said desperately, 'but she's a very important person in the firm. She's Mr Mordant's personal assistant, and I'm only a new junior. Surely you can understand that?'

'I *hear* it,' said Nora, one hand fixed on her generous hip, the other pointing a fork, 'but what I *understand* is different. It's been like that from the minute you took this job. You won't tell us anything and you won't let us visit you.'

They became locked in a new complaint which covered a far greater and older one. Nora was red-cheeked, Kate tearful.

'All I've got is a room less than half the size of this kitchen, with one little table in it and two chairs and a cupboard where I keep the cooking things. There's a divan bed on one side of the room and a chest of drawers on the other, and the wardrobe is a curtain on a rail. I haven't even *got* a gas ring – as I've told you a hundred times – I've got the use of the kitchen and bathroom, and eight of us share them. Where would I put you all? What would I do with you?'

She could imagine the children jumping up and down on her divan, rummaging in the drawers, Betsy wetting herself because the lavatory was occupied, Nora taking over the communal kitchen and getting in everyone's way, Neville sucking his pipe worriedly and

34

trying to keep the peace. Violation and madness.

'Oh, all right, all right,' Nora said. 'You needn't get worked up about it. If we're not wanted, we shan't come.'

'It's not that I don't want you,' said Kate lamely. But it was.

Betsy, who was laying the table, dropped the cutlery and began to cry. At fourteen years old her body was beginning to govern her emotions.

'And now you've upset that poor girl who thinks the world of you,' said Nora, testing the cabbage and then shaking the fork at her elder daughter.

Kate capitulated and searched for the least stressful form of entertainment.

'Why don't you all come to tea when you've done the Christmas shopping?'

'Oh yes, oh yes!' Betsy cried, dropping spoons and clapping her hands.

The tears were already drying on her cheeks. She was artless and good and loving, trapped in childhood forever, and forever dependent.

Impulsively, Kate said to her, 'And when the weather's warmer – next spring – Mother can put you on the bus one Saturday by yourself, and I'll meet you in Broad Street and take you to tea at Mrs Porter's Parlour. And *that*,' looking meaningfully at Nora, 'is a promise.'

But Nora had long since forgotten a wrong that still rankled with Kate.

35

'That'll be nice. She doesn't get many treats,' she said, mollified, and then in a different tone to Betsy, 'But if you hug Kate to death she won't be able to take you to Mrs Porter's Parlour, so just carry on laying that table!'

As she grew older Betsy took her clamouring woman's body walking in the afternoons. She was collecting wild flowers, she said, to put in an album Kate had given her for Christmas. The reason concealed a cunning no one surmised, and Nora accepted it because she was busy with a new nursling. Normally she would have been more vigilant, but baby Duncan suffered from cystic fibrosis and in keeping him alive and mobile she lost sight of her pubescent daughter.

The furore when Betsy did not return for supper one August evening dragged Kate from her ivory tower and brought her back to her stricken family. It was she, with her new proficiency, who set in motion the tedious process of tracking the girl down. Possible sightings suggested that Betsy had stepped into a red Vauxhall and been whisked away. Her photograph and description were issued to police departments all over the country, and for many months the Wing family was uplifted by false hopes or cast down by false alarms. All that was known in the end was that Betsy, aged sixteen, fair hair, blue eyes, fresh complexion, of medium height and build, dressed in blue jeans, trainers, and a T-shirt sporting a tiger on its front, was last seen on 23rd June, 1990.

Kate had kept her promise. However grudgingly given, she always kept promises. One sunny April Saturday Betsy had arrived on the two o'clock bus from Peddleford and been received into the solitary glamour of Kate's world.

In Betsy's eyes the bedsit took on additional beauty and significance. She translated it into heaven, with Kate as a presiding angel. In the wake of her sister's patronage she was borne round the main sights of the city, and suffered an encyclopaedia of information without blenching once. She revelled in Kate's stories and marvelled at her knowledge, and when her heroine ushered her through the hallowed doorway of Mrs Porter's Parlour, sat her on a spindly chair before a linen-clad table, and ordered the full English afternoon tea, Betsy reached a peak of happiness never before achieved and probably never would be again.

Sometimes, in later years, when she was out of favour with Nora, or with herself, Kate remembered this single act of grace and was glad.

Hector

Later that same year, Miss Benbow, who had been looking drained and old, was taken ill one night and whisked off to the City Hospital.

Hector Mordant, the director of Celebrations, informed the small staff personally. Though pale and evidently disturbed, he spoke with composure. Miss Benbow, he said, had been his right hand from the beginning, dedicating herself to the company and putting its interests before her own. Unhappily, the strain had proved too much, but some weeks of rest and care should restore her to full health. Meanwhile he was sending flowers and a card, which he was sure they would all like to sign.

'No one can take Miss Benbow's place,' he continued, 'but while she's away I shall need a good shorthand typist who is willing to learn much more about Celebrations, so that we can jog along until Miss Benbow returns, and afterwards ease her burden of work.' He put on his most engaging tone. 'Is anyone, I ask myself, brave enough to do all this and put up with me as well?'

Here they all smiled. Hector's fluctuations

of mood were well known and unresented. He was one of those men who was born to be indulged and adored by women, and he exploited his birthright to the full. But there was a problem. Miss Benbow, who discouraged possible rivals, had trained no successor. So though each girl was competent at her particular job, no one was sufficiently qualified to come forward, and the presence of Hector in that small bright office was overpowering.

He was a big, fair man, always immaculately groomed, courteous to underlings, frank with equals, politic with superiors and a shrewd judge of character. He surveyed their young faces.

'I can see that you are all too modest to admit to your excellencies, so we'll start again,' he said humorously, and the girls laughed out of politeness and fear. 'Which of you is the fastest shorthand typist?'

Kate said nothing. The others were eager to report, 'Kate is, Mr Mordant!'

He turned to her – almost turned *on* her, it seemed – speaking abruptly.

'Can you use a computer?'

'Yes I can, Mr Mordant.'

The others said nothing. The computer had been Miss Benbow's province.

Interpreting their suspicions, Kate added, 'I've never used this one but I took two courses in computing at evening classes. I could soon learn.'

In gaining Hector's attention she had lost

the easy companionship of the other girls, but this was a bargain she was prepared to accept.

'What did you say your name was?' he asked.

'Kate, Mr Mordant. Kate Wing.'

'Then come with me, Miss Wing, and bring your shorthand notebook with you. I hope you like hard work and long hours.'

'Oh yes, Mr Mordant,' she answered automatically and entered the sanctum, terrified, but determined to succeed.

The general office, though pleasant, was strictly functional, but Hector needed to impress future clients. His surroundings were as grand as himself, being spacious, gracious and handsomely furnished. The Celebrations floor was in a building on high ground and his windows overlooked the city. He stood by them for an appreciable minute or two, rapping softly on the pane with his knuckles, thinking. Then he settled himself in his chair opposite Kate.

'Sit down and relax, Miss Wing. I'm not going to eat you – yet!'

She smiled, but her stomach continued to tie itself into a knot.

'As we may be working together for some time I need to find out a little more about you.'

He then put her through a short catechism, at the end of which he knew that she was twenty years old, rented a bedsit – 'in a large house overlooking Adelaide Park' – had no regular boyfriend, many acquaintances but no close friends – 'I haven't much time, you see, because I have evening classes three nights a week at Cranborne College,' – and was hampered by family – 'I have to go home every Sunday for lunch. They worry about me.'

He assessed the earnest young face, the fashionable hair cut, the tailored costume and whitest of white blouses, and judged her, rightly, to be self-regarding, intelligent and ambitious.

'You sound very serious-minded, Miss Wing. What courses are you taking at night school?'

'History of Art. Music. Theatre. I take different courses each year, unless they have an advanced course on a subject I've already studied. Then I take that.'

'And you finished your computer course?'

'Yes, Mr Mordant, and I've done advanced courses in French and German.'

He leaned back in his chair, studying her, now amused and interested. 'For what reason?'

For the first time in her life she was dealing with a man who knew how people worked, and how best he could use them.

She answered honestly, 'Because I want to *be* somebody, and I don't know any other way to do it.'

Hector smiled broadly. 'I like that. You sound as though you're doing pretty well so far. If you put the same amount of effort into your work with me you'll do very well

41

indeed.'

She felt as if he had given her permission to become her true self, and from then on Hector stood high in her esteem.

Marriage did not figure in her future plans, and the young men she had met so far did not impress her. She had no wish to exchange her independence for a lifetime of unpaid house-keeping, and she saw no good reason to produce children who would use up her youth and leave her in middle age. She knew, in fact, exactly what she didn't want, but not what she did, and she lacked female role models. Miss Benbow had been the nearest, but having fallen by the wayside she could now only invoke pity. So Kate must en-deavour to find her ideal self unaided, by improving its mind and dressing its body, in order to attain an unknown but desirable end.

Hector became brisk and impersonal. 'Good. Shall we make a start?'

She bent her head over the shorthand book in acknowledgement.

'First of all I want you to order flowers for Miss Benbow and find a suitable card for us all to sign. Go to Charmier's in Broad Street for the flowers. The firm has an account there. Tell them Miss Benbow is ill and leave the choice to them. They have excellent taste and a faultless sense of occasion – the most important sense of all, in my opinion; this firm would be a failure without it. Oh, and don't forget to make a special note of everything I tell you, Miss Wing. I haven't time to take you over the same ground twice. If, for instance, I say "flowers", you should automatically think Charmier's. Understood? I believe that Miss Benbow kept a record of important dates and anniversaries and made sure I was reminded of them. Look through her office diary. I'll give you the key to her desk.'

Kate nodded solemnly. That evening she would write in her private notebook *The sense of occasion is the most important sense of all.* She had found her ideal man in Hector and would learn all she could from and about him.

Before she left his room that first morning she said tentatively, 'About Miss Benbow. Should I – should any of us – visit her?'

She would learn that when Hector dissembled he became light-hearted and offhand. He dissembled now, but she believed him.

'No general visitors allowed at the moment, I'm afraid. Naturally, I shall keep in touch with her progress. Perhaps later on.'

There would be no later on. Her stay in hospital over, Miss Benbow was spirited away to a country nursing home to convalesce. Each week Kate walked into Charmier's in her lunch hour and ordered fresh flowers, and each time the girls penned their modest signatures on the card beneath Hector's lordly flourish.

Meanwhile Kate made herself as indispensable as she could, while dreading her

43

superior's return. She didn't know what would happen. Surely Hector wouldn't send her back to her old post? And yet she couldn't imagine Miss Benbow allowing her one jot or tittle of the responsibility she enjoyed at present. Kate resolved that if he demoted her she would find a better job elsewhere, and ask him for a personal reference. He could hardly refuse. But that solution was second-best. She enjoyed working with him. She enjoyed the work itself. She could understand why Miss Benbow had guarded her province so jealously and kept her subordinates at a distance.

It was a problem she did not have to solve. Three months later she found Hector in his morning stance at the window, softly rapping his knuckles on the pane, surveying the city. She knew him better by this time. The casual quality of his tone told her that he was about to say something important.

'Oh, by the way, Kate, I'm afraid that Miss Benbow won't be coming back after all. She has, fortunately, made a good recovery, but the breakdown affected her nerves and stamina. She won't be able to take the kind of pressures that this job demands. I've enquired into her financial affairs, and naturally she hasn't had time to amass any great savings or buy her own property. So I'm seeing the firm's solicitor and the accountant this afternoon and arranging for her to have a financial gift – not a fortune, but enough to tide her over. I feel it's the least we can do. And I have a business connection in Devon, an elderly gentleman who needs a live-in secretary – nothing too onerous – so she won't be homeless and unoccupied.' He turned from the window to ask humbly, 'Is there anything else you think we might do for her?'

Overwhelmed by his magnanimity, Kate said, 'No, Mr Mordant. I think that's very generous of you.'

'Of the *firm*,' he corrected her gently. 'Of Celebrations.'

Hector *was* Celebrations, but she did not say so.

He continued in a semi-serious tone, watching her, hands in pockets. 'Perhaps you may not think the firm so generous when I tell you what plans we have for you.'

Expectation was quenched in an instant. Downcast, she waited for him to tell her that he was extremely grateful for her help in the previous months, and would see that she had a rise in status and salary, but was appointing some highly qualified outsider to take Miss Benbow's place.

'"Blood, toil, tears and sweat!"' Hector quoted gravely, and chuckled.

The chuckle gave her hope. She glanced up at him.

'I'm offering you Miss Benbow's job, Kate. One moment!' Holding up his hand. 'You've a great deal more to learn before you're up to her standard, though I don't for a moment doubt that you will be. I'll increase your salary immediately, and we must agree a

45

year's contract to begin with. We can sort out details later.'

She could have laughed, danced, cried with delight then, but her cup was literally and metaphorically to overflow when Barbara, the latest member of staff, knocked at the door and brought in Hector's solitary cup of coffee. In Miss Benbow's time she had made two cups of coffee, but did not consider Kate to be in the same category and still offered her a mug in the office with the rest of the girls.

'Your coffee, Mr Mordant,' said Barbara, laying down the tray deferentially.

Hector had a way of staring at people absently, amiably, while observing them closely. Today he gave his full attention to eighteen-year-old Barbara. He had made up his mind about a number of things that fine December morning while he rapped the pane softly, thoughtfully.

'Thank you so much,' he said graciously. 'I wonder, would you bring a cup for Miss Wing, too? She will be working with me from now on.' His smile sweetened the request. He conveyed much.

'Yes, sir,' said Barbara promptly.

No one in Celebrations ever called him sir. The title had been her instinctive response to authority. Now she corrected herself. 'Yes, Mr Mordant,' she said, and hurried out to tell the other girls.

When she returned five minutes later she set down Kate's cup fastidiously.

'Your coffee, Miss Wing,' she said, with the same respect she had used in addressing Miss Benbow.

Kate and Hector

That was eight years ago, Kate reflected, standing by the window of her own house, looking down into Mulberry Street, waiting for Hector. Waiting for or on Hector had occupied her private and professional life since her promotion.

Initial awe had gradually changed to adoration, but so god-like was her image of him that she would never have dared think of love. Yes, she adored, but with the reverence of a disciple, and self-respect prevented her from making a fool of herself. Later she realized that she must have been in love with him, waiting for him to love her, from the beginning.

Hector's commitment was tardier. A man of robust appetites, he admired her pretty face, her trim figure, her slim legs, wondered what she would be like in bed, but valued her ability and her usefulness more than her charms. And she never could pin him down to a time when regard changed to love. Answers ranged from, 'I thought what a

47

lovely girl you were the moment I saw you,' to, 'Oh, I don't know. You grew on me, Kate. You grew on me.' Both comments were true but she found them slightly unsatisfactory.

Her moment came when they were working late one summer evening. Going down in the lift, chatting, laughing, pleased with themselves, they looked at each other and were suddenly silent.

Then Hector took her in his arms and kissed her.

Over the years her living quarters improved with each promotion. As his private secretary the rise in salary enabled her to leave the bedsit and take a small flat. As his fully fledged assistant the flat was newly furnished. But when she became his mistress he moved her to an early Victorian terraced house on the edge of the city's residential area and paid the deposit. And at the same time he gave her six months' notice and the reason for doing so, one evening when the staff had gone home.

'Love and business don't mix, Kate. I'm going outside the firm, this time, for an assistant. I need you to choose her with me, and I want you to train her before you leave.'

Kate protested, 'Oh, but I love my job. And where shall I go?'

He put a finger on her lips to silence her. 'Hear me out.' As she subsided he said, 'I've already thought about it, though with your ability and my references you could get a post equal to this, if not better, anywhere else. You're very, very good, you know.'

'I do know,' said Kate, not boastfully but as a matter of fact. 'I simply don't want to go. Loving you and working with you is everything I want.'

'Nor do I want you to go. We work together perfectly' He brought out his emotional big cannon. 'More importantly, the two of us together *love* perfectly. But believe me, we can't have both,' he beseeched her. 'If you'd rather keep the job, then – however hard it may be – I'll accept that. It's your choice entirely.'

This was no more than a gesture and she knew it, but still Kate cried spontaneously, 'How can you say that? How could I?'

Their embrace, tight and motionless, re-assured them both, but not for the same reason.

He said, calculating, his cheek against hers, 'Whatever I do, your situation won't be easy, but I don't want you to be hurt. There are bound to be conditions. As you know I have a wife and two children and I must think of them, too.'

'I know, I know.' Crying now because she had met his wife, Jocelyn, on brief occasions, calling for Hector at the office to sweep him away to some social function. She had a rich, soft air about her and a way of overlooking Kate that transformed her into a shabby child again, gazing with envy at the elite in Mrs Porter's Parlour.

Hector kissed her eyes and mouth, drew back and looked at her face to face. 'But however responsible I feel for them, you're more precious to me, and I'm going to take care of you. You know that. You believe that, don't you?'

She needed to believe, and so replied as he would have wished. 'Yes, of course.'

He chuckled and spoke lightly. 'Then dry your eyes and come out for a drink before I go home. I have two exciting new proposals for you – and one of them is this.'

With a typically grandiose flourish he drew a set of keys from the pocket of his jacket. They were labelled *No 11 Mulberry Street to be sold by Hussif and Fedor*, the most exclusive estate agents in the city.

'It's the prettiest little place you've ever seen,' said Hector confidently. 'A bijou residence as they say. Such an appalling expression! It's a two-storey terraced house with two rooms on each floor, kitchen and bathroom, a pocket handkerchief of a garden at the front and a man-sized handkerchief of lawn at the back. Window boxes. Mid-Victorian. All the original fittings, apart from rather neat conversions. You'll love it, and it's a good address in a quiet neighbourhood. Similar houses on the park side are selling for thousands more, so it's a bargain as well as beautiful. The best sort of property to buy.'

'Nothing but the best for you,' Kate said between tears and laughter.

'That's why I chose *you*,' said Hector and

kissed her again. 'When we've had a drink we'll go round and inspect it.'

He had one more thing to say, holding her at arms' length, enjoying her reaction. 'The deposit – if you like the house – is a gift from me. I'd buy it outright for you if I could, but I have an expensive family to keep. It won't be much of a mortgage – no more than you're paying in rent for your present flat. It means that we have a secluded place to meet, and you have a measure of security in the future should anything happen to me.'

She put one finger on his lips to signify that he need not explain. He kissed her palm.

'And the other proposal?' Kate asked.

'Oh! Let's talk about that over a drink in Charley's Bar, shall we?'

Hector's suggestions were always commands. Kate fetched her new coat.

No doubt people might suspect that these two were having an affair, but only a private detective could have proved it. They were both excellent dissemblers and always discreet. Sitting opposite each other in the artificial twilight of Charley's Bar, they played the parts of friendly colleagues.

Hector began in a bantering fashion, 'You know Shirley Pringle of Mrs Porter's Parlour, of course?'

And Kate replied in kind, 'Oh yes. Everyone knows Shirley Pringle – which means nobody does. She's the sort of woman who has a hundred acquaintances and no friends.'

51

Hector acknowledged this Wilde-like judgement with an approving nod.

'Well, Shirley – at an age to which she would never admit – has come into her inheritance. She's been the power behind the Parlour chain for years, and at last her worthy but dull parents have decided to retire to the Costa del Sol – of all places! – and hand the business over to her lock, stock and barrel. They're also giving her a considerable sum of money – cutting down on future death duties, I expect – and Shirley has decided to indulge herself.

'She's selling the respectable family home in Coombe Street, and her disreputable little flat in Cornmarket, and buying Melbury Old Hall. I heard the whisper in Hussif and Fedor's a few days ago, when No 11 came up, and I like to know the buzz. So I dropped in on Shirley, asked her to share a bottle of extremely good wine with me at the Swithin Street Wine Bar, and encouraged her to talk.

'It's strange that such a shrewd businesswoman should be such a romantic in the property market. Aesthetically speaking, I revere every crumbling brick of the Old Hall, but I should hate to be saddled with it.'

Kate envisaged the demesne through Shirley Pringle's eyes, and asked, 'Does she see herself as the lady of the manor?'

'Yes, though she puts it differently. She says she's worked hard all these years, and now she wants a lovely home where she can meet people from other walks of life – meaning the

52

county set – and she's prepared to pay for it.'

'They won't accept her,' said Kate. 'They'll eat her oysters and drink her champagne and regard her as a parvenue.'

'That's exactly what I told her, though not in the same words. "Use them, by all means, but don't trust them with money, friendship or confidences!" I said. She won't listen, of course.'

'No,' Kate said, contemplating her glass. 'People with a dream won't listen.' Love had split her into two people: one floating at Hector's will in a sea of emotion, the other watching uneasily from the shore.

'Then, while she was pouring my Margaux down her brawny throat – totally wasted on her! – I had an amazing idea. Well, two of them, to be exact.'

Kate laughed ruefully. The sun of Hector warmed and lit her world, but she knew he would be bound to find a way of profiting through Shirley's move.

'Apart from a talent for supplying the public with delightful English tea shops, the lady has no taste and no sense of occasion,' Hector continued. 'She'll make a harlot of Melbury Old Hall instead of allowing it to be a faded beauty. I thought, while I savoured my wine and she rabbited on, "What a waste of money and opportunity. You need someone to take care of you and organize your social life. Now Kate could do that."'

'Oh yes?' Warily. 'What would I organize? She'll need house and ground staff for the

Old Hall, certainly, but that's not my province. She runs the Porter's Parlour chain herself. She has a secretary and a live-in lady friend. Where would I come in?'

'The secretary and the lady friend are giving her problems.'

Kate answered mockingly, 'What have they done? Eloped together?'

Hector laughed. The idea of women falling in love with women amused him.

Kate laughed too, though she felt she was being manipulated.

'The secretary is leaving in December to marry and live in Ghana or somewhere – which is a nuisance, but bearable. The lady friend is simply clearing off. Shirley was distraught about this. "After all I've done for her!" she kept saying. I sympathized profusely, but was busy gathering facts. Apparently Shirley runs the Porter's Parlours from her parents' home in Coombe Street, so presumably she will do the same at the Hall. She likes to be in control, so the secretarial post is straightforward shorthand-typing-filing. But knowing you, you'll have the entire business at your fingertips in a matter of months. And though she doesn't realize it yet, she also needs a social guide and mentor, and this is a wonderful opportunity for a girl like you. You can literally create your own job at the Hall.' He spoke sincerely. 'You're a first-class organizer. You know your way around. You have taste and social flair. Above all, you know how to use people.' As she opened her mouth to

54

protest he continued quickly, 'How else could you manage *me*? It will be like the work you did for me at Celebrations, only on a more intimate scale.'

Kate noted that her job had moved into the past tense and was afraid, because she had no bargaining power with Hector, who was now in full flow.

'Besides which, you're lovely to look at and to listen to, and Shirley is very susceptible to feminine beauty.'

'So I've heard,' said Kate austerely.

'She'll be disappointed in that direction, of course,' he said, smiling, 'but she can't have everything. She's lucky to be offered so much.'

Kate struggled to stand for a moment against the tide. 'But what precisely *would* I be offering?'

'Officially you'll be her personal assistant,' Hector said. 'Unofficially you'll be her friend and companion. She's a tough cookie where money is concerned, so she's unlikely to pay your present salary, but I'll make up the difference. Then, when you've settled in and made yourself indispensable, we can bargain. Besides, the perks will more than make up for any loss in that direction. Shirley's mean about little things, not big ones. I've heard that she'll spend thousands of pounds refurbishing a parlour and then grumble about replacing a clapped-out old vacuum cleaner. So she'll probably ask you to bring your own tea bags to work and then treat you to a fortnight in the Caribbean!'

Still Kate persisted. 'But in terms of future prospects – where do I go from there?'

Irritated but admiring, for in her position this was the question he would have asked himself, Hector said, 'You're a level-headed, talented and ambitious girl. You'll go far.'

'But *where*?' Kate persisted. 'Where do I go?'

Hector thought seriously. 'Well, dealing with the social side of the Old Hall, you'll be able to make valuable connections – and they're half the battle in the business world. In a few years' time, when you get tired of Shirley, you can go anywhere and do anything in your own field. Start your own company if you want to – but not next door to Celebrations, if you don't mind!'

Kate gave up any hope of restraining him and he surged on.

'Shirley evidently found me sympathetic because she asked me back to the Coombe Street house so that she could show me her plans for the Hall. I've never been there before, and the moment I entered my worst fears were realized. Kate, I went cold with horror. She has a papier-mâché blackamoor seven feet high standing in the hall, holding out a little gold tray for your calling card. I almost put a pound on it and asked where she kept the turnstile!'

He was genuinely outraged, and Kate had to smile.

'The pictures, if pictures they can be called,

56

have been bought by the yard, simply to fill wall-space. And the books, all gilt and leather and presumably bought by the shelf, look conspicuously unopened, let alone unread. God knows what would be inside them, anyway, probably empty whisky bottles...'

Kate began to giggle.

'And a pink bow, Kate, a pink bow from a florist's bouquet, tied round an appalling imitation Chinese vase. And a vast gold clock shaped like the rays of the sun, telling the wrong time – I checked by my Rolex. And, Kate, an electric fire in the drawing room, shaped like the body of a butterfly – and the wings light up.'

She laughed until the tears came to her eyes, and one or two people looked round, smiling to hear such a joyful sound in the dim recesses of Charley's Bar.

'It's not funny,' said Hector, deadly serious, 'it's appalling. Imagine what she could do to Melbury Old Hall. It's a listed building, thank God, so she'll be prevented from ruining it outright, but she'll do her best and we must stop her!' Then he relaxed and grinned and shook his head.

'I know I'm beating the drum, but I really do mind,' he said ruefully. 'Life on the whole is so ugly and chaotic that only art can make sense of it.'

Kate gave a final sniff of laughter, pulled a handkerchief from her bag and wiped her eyes. 'Yes, I know. I feel the same.' She accepted the inevitable. 'So sorting out Shirley

57

Pringle's life is to be my mission, is it?'

His humour had returned.

'Can you think of a better one? I doubt you'll be able to do much for her image. She's too strong-minded and too old to change. But you can help her to spend her money wisely, take care of the Hall, keep the she-wolves at bay and monitor the guest list. If the choice is left to her you'll find city dignitaries jostled by bookmakers, and distinguished public figures accosted by rent boys – or rent girls. Good Lord, is that the time? We must go now if we're to view No 11.'

She felt a familiar chill of fear and jealousy and smiled to conceal it.

Helping her into her new coat, Hector said, 'This is chic. You're clever with your clothes. What excellent taste. So, do I have your permission to approach the scandalous Shirley?'

'I seem to have no option,' she answered as lightly as she could.

They came out into the genuine twilight and walked briskly towards the car park and Hector's Jaguar. The big shops had closed. Flower baskets swung forlornly in the wind. In the slight shelter of their doorways the homeless wrapped themselves in newspapers and blankets against the October night and rolled over to find oblivion.

Hector bought an evening paper at a newsstand.

'By the by,' he said casually, 'to allay any suspicions, this change of job and house should be seen by everyone – office, friends and family – as your personal choice. You're seeking greener fields. Agreed?'

The chill descended again, and stayed. Kate was already finding it troublesome to conceal her present situation from Nora and Neville, who suspected the truth but could not be told. She foresaw years of subterfuge ahead. Still, that was the price to pay for being Hector's mistress.

'Yes, of course.' She remembered something. 'You said you had *two* amazing ideas when you invited Shirley Pringle out – what was the other one?'

His face was frank and open, always a bad sign. 'I was thinking, once you've got the Old Hall shipshape, how useful it will be as a background for some of the local events staged by Celebrations.'

Ah, so that was it. A double coup.

He smiled on her dismay. 'You see, I've thought of everything. Our private life can be established and safeguarded. You're improving your prospects and widening your work experience. Melbury Old Hall will be protected from Shirley. Shirley will be protected from herself. And, finally, Celebrations will have a regular new venue.'

He saw that she could not respond, and caught her hand and squeezed it, to bring her to him again.

'Just promise me one thing,' he said. 'Don't allow her to bring that damnable blackamoor to the Old Hall, even if you've to set fire to it!'

He could always make her laugh.

Jack

On that first day of freedom, years ago, Kate, gazing through the window of her bedsit had seen a tall, bespectacled young man with flopping blond hair, sweeping a path in Adelaide Park. When he stopped briefly, to smile round at the fine October day, his smile had reflected her contentment. In those few moments they had shared a celebration of life, though he did not see her and she had not thought about him since. His name was Jack Almond.

Life had not been particularly kind to Jack. His father, John, was an anxious city clerk in poor health: a lackey at work and an autocrat at home. His mother, Nellie, was a woman who clung instead of supporting, and obeyed rather than form an opinion. So Jack learned early not to antagonize the one nor rely on the other.

As a toddler he was solemn and withdrawn and after much stumbling and clumsiness was discovered to be short-sighted. His appearance was also against him. Nellie Almond trimmed his thick fair hair once a month using a pudding basin as a guide. This, along with his round, wire-rimmed spectacles, gave him an owlish look. In his school years the need to avoid upsetting his teachers and being injured in the playground made him an extremely dull boy. He was generally regarded, when he was regarded at all, as conscientious but not too bright. No one knew that he was a highly intelligent lad, who found life uninspiring and was simply keeping out of harm's way.

At the age of eleven he was shovelled into a comprehensive school and judged to be a midstream pupil, neither clever nor stupid. Paradoxically, this judgement set him free, because nothing marvellous was expected of him and the range of facilities open to him was wide. The school had indoor clubs and outdoor activities in which pupils were encouraged to enrol. Tentatively, padding round his parents' apprehensions, he joined the school ramblers association which put colour in his cheeks and a spring in his step. Then Nellie, who had saved up a vast number of tokens, gave him the result as a Christmas present: a rudimentary camera. Jack had no idea how to use it so he joined the photography club.

Blossoming shyly through the lens of this first acquisition, he became intensely aware of the world around him, and in this new way of seeing lay his real education. He needed knowledge of every kind, and began to read voraciously. Ancient history fascinated him. He studied this and other subjects. He learned to express himself both verbally and vocally. Enlightenment had been a long time coming and his rate of learning was prodigious.

In his sixteenth year he gained eight GSCEs and his teachers reckoned him to be academic material. Jack, consulted for once, chose to read history. He would have liked to roam in new pastures – Brighton or Essex Universities – but as as his mother didn't want him to leave home he agreed to concentrate on a place at the city university.

His father was delighted. He had been subjugated all his working life, and Jack's metamorphosis seemed to promise a time when his son could raise him to great heights. How this was to be achieved he did not enquire, because reality tends to destroy dreams.

In the summer of his final school year Jack gained three shining A-levels and won the school prize for photography, but his father died that winter.

Nellie Almond, as could have been foretold, collapsed. She needed a man around who would exploit her and tell her what to do, and Jack was the nearest man she could lean on. Expelled from his private paradise, he dealt with the facts that she could not face. Two modest pensions, one from the state, the other from the City Hall, would barely keep them. Stunned but stalwart, he gave up all hope of further education and left school to find work, but jobs were scarce and his qualifications inappropriate. Moreover, the shock of finding his present achievements useless and himself unwanted had thrown him back into the limbo of his childhood.

First he tried a plastics factory where the pay was good, the hours long, and the work stultifying. Six weeks later he left. In quick succession he made tea and ran errands in a city office, tried to be a waiter, a shop assistant, and a book-packer, and was consistently fired. His employers found him preoccupied, gauche, forgetful and incompetent. One of them, questioned by Mrs Oddy, a motherly member of the employment bureau, said, 'He's a decent lad, but not very bright.'

Mrs Oddy demurred. 'He's got eight GCSEs and three A-levels!'

'Not in my department, he hasn't.'

And when Jack turned up at the job centre for the seventh time, even Mrs Oddy had to say, 'We do seem to be finding some difficulty in placing you, Mr Almond.'

He hovered before her, a straggling young man whose long limbs impeded his progress. His thick blond hair flopped into his eyes. The arms of his spectacles were mended with adhesive tape. His trousers bagged over bicycle clips.

He gave her a shy smile. Perhaps he *isn't* very bright, she thought, and sighed, but her tone remained optimistic.

'There's a job for a hospital orderly here. You can't expect high pay, but...' Then she had a vision of patients being lost or forgotten in long corridors, tipped out of wheelchairs,

63

taken to the wrong ward, given the wrong medication. 'Better not,' she murmured, looking down the list of find something safer. Her face lightened.

'Now this may be in your line. A sweeper in Adelaide Park. It's the other side of the city from you, but I know you enjoy cycling. A nice healthy job outdoors. And it's a lovely time of year to start. September. How would you like to try that?'

He smiled his charming smile, took the card gingerly, thanked her sincerely, and fell over someone's feet on the way out. Mrs Oddy waited until the swing doors propelled him into the street, and breathed a sigh of relief.

'How long before he's back?' a colleague asked.

Mrs Oddy shrugged. 'It's usually about six weeks. Two months if they've been exceptionally patient.'

Three months later he fought his usual battle with the swing doors and knocked over a chair while trying to sit on it. He was gripping a bunch of flowers which had suffered with him.

'He's back!' The word went round.

Smiles were covert, heads demurely bent. He waited until Mrs Oddy was free.

'Yes, Mr Almond,' she said, smiling hard so that she should not laugh. 'And what can we do for you this time?'

He seemed more aware, more together than before. His hair had been cut by a barber. He was wearing a clean navy sweater and clean navy jeans. He had new spectacles which gave him an academic air.

He said, 'It's all right, Mrs Oddy. I don't need another job. I'm settled, and I enjoy the work, and they're pleased with me. I just wanted to say – thank you!'

He held out the mangled bouquet. Some hard-hearted florist had searched out the worst bunch in the container, and in Jack's great paw the flowers had finally lost hope, but Mrs Oddy was touched.

'Oh, thank you, Mr Almond. How very kind of you.'

The incident had been noticed. There were disbelieving smiles and some tittering. Heads turned as he went out. He had brought an element of surprise, a touch of comedy, a whiff of chivalry to a joyless place.

The women behind the counter were silent for a moment or two.

Then Mrs Oddy said incredulously, 'Fancy someone *thanking* me!'

Sweeping was a meditation in which Jack both found and lost himself. In the rhythmic swish of the brush, the ritual cleansing of paths, the piling and burning of leaves, he contemplated his life. The money was not much, but enough, and the surroundings were serene and beautiful. No one disturbed him. Few spoke to him. There was no tele-phone. If he felt a need for society it was all around him: a constantly changing and mov-ing pattern of people. Only death or disaster could strike through the shield of Adelaide Park. He was even protected by his mother's shame. She felt he had betrayed his father's status as a junior clerk in the City Hall, and endeavoured to ignore his menial post.

They spoke very little, mother and son. They loved each other because of the flesh and blood bond, but were strangers in spirit. When he arrived home she asked whether he had had a good day and told him about hers, then conversation lapsed. She had no friends, just neighbours and acquaintances, and she entertained only relatives, and only when necessary. Jack dared not think of bringing anyone home, even had anyone been interested in him. While his mother was alive Jack could not live.

Then three events changed everything. Nellie, hurrying across Broad Street, head bent, unthinking, was knocked down by an equally absent-minded motorist and taken to the City Hospital. The nurses made her very comfortable, and she died holding Jack's hand. The majesty of death, as of life, totally escaped her. Only her son, standing in the funeral parlour in his new grey suit, staring down at her used husk in wonder, said, 'Did you make any sense of it, Mum?'

Meanwhile he had to find a few answers for himself, and began by spending Saturday evenings in the Lamb and Child, nursing his glass and seeking company that his mother would have described as 'the wrong sort'. Since he could neither cook nor be bothered

66

to learn he bought take-away meals and kept a supply of sliced bread, jars of jam and tinned soups. He had put on weight since her death, and his increasing size and gravity made him appear older than his years. With his fair hair, short-sighted blue eyes and reflective smile, he looked like an amiable Dutchman, and his appearance often opened a casual conversation.

'Excuse me. You English?' asked the girl.

She was cheaply fashionable: spindly, short-skirted, spiky-haired, wearing Dr Martens.

Blushing, he answered, 'Yes.'

'I did wonder. I once knew a Dutch boy what looked like you.'

'Oh,' he said, searching for a topic of discussion.

The girl knew she would have to be direct. She placed her empty glass in front of him and said, 'I'm waiting for a friend, but he's late, and I've run out of change, else I'd buy myself another vodka and tonic.'

Jack was understandably wary. On other occasions he had bought drinks for girls and attempted to come closer, without success. They either told him to fuck off, or took him into the car park, revealed themselves to be knickerless, and asked for the money first. A frustrated, raging virgin, he was terrified of this latest opportunity but unable to refuse.

'Have one on me,' said Jack. 'Until your friend comes.' He did not believe in the friend.

'Actually,' the girl said, 'he's not coming. He's stood me up.'

Her bottom lip trembled: a jilted waif in fashionable guise.

Jack steered her over to a table in the corner and provided her with three successive vodka and tonics and an unused handkerchief which she forgot to return. She cried and confided. He listened and gave advice. The advice was good. He had no direct experience but he was a professional observer and a thoughtful young man, and she was grateful to him.

They walked out together that night and in her misery and gratitude she offered herself to Jack, free of any commitment – moral, emotional or financial. In spite of his physical hunger he made solicitous enquiries about her age first. Eighteen, she said automatically. Her parents? 'Oh, them!' she said. Her state of preparedness? 'I carry them round with me,' she said. So he took her home. As old as Eve, she initiated him in that house of outraged ghosts, and made him ridiculously happy for six weeks, after which she withdrew her favours because her boyfriend had returned. She thanked him and said they'd had fun, hadn't they? She gave him a hug and a kiss and went away.

In his innocence Jack had mistaken gratitude for love. The sorry depths of his heart were known only to himself, and the experience scarred and scared him. After that episode he became many a lost girl's brother, and no girl's lover, and withdrew into himself.

Among the city's historical assets was a rounded hill not far from the east wall, crowned by a grove of small-leaved lime trees. This native species, a rarity nowadays, was growing long before the Romans came because they recorded the site. Later on, early Christians, equating the grove with pagan practices, cut it down, but the trees gradually renewed themselves, and certain rituals were revived and became part of legend. In the twentieth century, as the hold of Christianity weakened and paganism became popular, the grove was recognized once more as an ancient sacred site.

In terms of status it would never rank with the likes of Glastonbury, but scholars considered it worthy of a paragraph or so in their studies, courting couples carved their initials on the bark, interested tourists looked it up if they happened to be in the neighbourhood, and the city cited it in its brochure.

The Grove, Grove Hill, Melbury. Fifteen-minute ride on 75 bus from Eastgate to Melbury Corner. Historically speaking, this sacred pagan site goes further back into the past than anyone can remember. Certain superstitions still persist, and when the setting sun strikes through the trees in a particular spot, you can understand why the grove

69

is still believed to have ancient powers. A delightful, and not too arduous walk to the top of the hill is recommended. Picnicking is allowed, but please use the litter baskets provided or take litter home with you. Do not pick flowers or damage the trees, and keep children and dogs under control. Any infringement of these rules will occasion a heavy fine.

So the city fathers spoke.

Jack Almond had been drawn there in his solitary boyhood, seeking comfort in times of misery, hiding in rare disgrace, even pitching his tent among the trees one midsummer night and being scared out of his wits by something nameless, after which he avoided the place for a while.

Older, braver, possessed of his first camera, he was drawn to Grove Hill once more, mesmerized by its mystery and beauty. Over the period of a year he recorded its moods and seasons at different hours of day and evening. The school photography club gave him the best slot and first prize in their summer exhibition. The collection was much admired, then put away to lie fallow.

One aimless Saturday morning, a year after his mother's death, he was turning out a trunk full of old photographs in the boxroom and came upon this study of the grove. Stimulated, he cleared a space on the parlour carpet and laid out its four seasons. Once more the seductive beauty and ever-present mystery possessed him, obsessed him. A modern man, he was hampered by lack of ritual and the inability to express himself in any but rational terms. There was nothing more he could do for this sacred place by way of photography, but he needed desperately to pay it further homage.

On an impulse he jumped up, pulled on his leather jacket and hurried off to the public library where he passed the morning in the reading room, and returned home with an armful of borrowed books. Fortified by beer, a pork pie and a chocolate eclair, he spent the afternoon making notes. In the evening, needing to see rather than visualize, he cycled to the grove, taking his camera and flash.

Under a frosty moon the lime trees cast long fingers of shadow down the silver hill. Jack's hands trembled a little as he captured the serenity of place and moment, but even in his exaltation he dared not enter its cathedral. Then, realizing that he had become cold and hungry, he cycled back again, ate fish and chips from their newspaper wrapping, piping hot and reeking of vinegar, and fell into his unmade bed with a head full of moonlight.

His father had bought the red-brick terraced house over a twenty-year period. His mother had chosen and cherished each highly varnished article of furniture, and necessities were pinched to pay for all. John Almond was fond of saying, 'An Englishman's home is his castle – and this is ours!' In the state of suspension that had been his life so far, Jack had accepted this judgement without thought or question, but the grove had given him a grander vision.

On the following morning, surveying his inheritance and seeing it as it really was, he said in awe and disbelief, 'What a load of old bollocks!'

Up to her death his mother had allowed him to pursue his hobby under certain conditions at specific times, always to be cleared away before bedtime. Now photography came first and he, who could not organize the simplest domestic arrangements, began a campaign that would have daunted the most experienced housewife. Since his bedroom and the bathroom were functional, and the kitchen did not interest him, he left them as they were, but the miscellaneous contents of the boxroom were tipped on the local dump.

'This,' he said, 'will be my darkroom.'

The parlour had been his mother's pride, used only for ceremonial occasions. Without a morsel of reverence he dismantled it. Heavy furniture, ornate pictures, and oppressive family photographs were crammed into his parents' bedroom on the floor above, and when it could hold no more he locked the door on this sad, marital museum. With much stippling, and three coats of magnolia emulsion, he transformed the red flock parlour wallpaper into a luminous background, and round the walls he mounted his enlarged photographs of the grove, allotting a wall to

72

each season.

'This,' he said, 'will be my study.'

To provide himself with a desk, seat, and shelves he raided the dining room and robbed it of the mahogany table, at which they had eaten many a doleful little Sunday joint and overcooked vegetables. He took the bookcase, minus its books, and removed the glass-fronted doors. He chose the largest and most comfortable dining chair. Then he turned the key on the dining room also.

He brought in a small, curly-legged table from the hall to be used as a refreshment bar, leaving a table-shaped patch of unfaded carpet beneath it. He purchased a powerful electric fire and an efficient electric kettle. At the end of the first day, like the first creator, he looked round and saw that it was good.

His mother would have been appalled.

These labours done, Jack began the happiest time of his life so far. Incapable of demanding anything for himself, he could be ruthless on behalf of his work, and he protected his time, space and requirements for writing. Entering this spare little kingdom he experienced fulfilment. Closing the door behind him he knew peace. The evening that he set biro to paper and printed the title in neat capitals was sheer joy.

THE SACRED GROVE, he wrote, and began its story.

Patrick

Jack's social circle was limited. He lived in an anonymous brick terrace in the outer suburbs, cycled across the city to work in Adelaide Park, shopped on the way home, and drank in the Lamb and Child at weekends. His inner life, far richer, and so far unknown to any but himself, was spent in his study working on the book. The combination of pub and grove brought him his first real friend.

Patrick Hanna, a seasoned journalist, thirteen years older and worldly wise, had recently joined the *City Courier*. A former star on a national newspaper, Patrick was taking a cut in pay and status by applying for this post, a fact registered by the editor, Marcus Bray. Reading Hanna's impressive CV, and wondering why he didn't aim higher, he sought a confidential opinion and was told that the man was brilliant but impossible, and politically speaking could be a liability.

But Marcus was ambitious for the *Courier*. He wanted his worthy provincial newspaper to become a great one, so he prepared to play nursemaid and mentor to this erratic man in order to get the best out of him. Also, being a political animal who played local politics exquisitely and enjoyed the game, he reckoned he could cope with a gifted liability.

Patrick turned up for the meeting drunk and disdainful, ready to ruin his chances. His appearance could be described at best as seedy and at worst as squalid. He had not shaved for three days. His hair needed cutting. His shoes needed mending. His suit needed cleaning. His shirt needed laundering, and his tie should have been thrown in the dustbin. As Hector Mordant would have observed, the damned fellow had no sense of occasion.

Marcus was amused but did not show it. In fact he behaved as if this were a standard interview and the candidate was smart and sober. Impressed, Patrick pulled himself together sufficiently to allow himself to be appointed, whereupon the editor took him out for a celebratory drink, and when Patrick fell asleep with his head on the table Marcus called a taxi and took him home to sleep on the sofa.

Awaking the next morning with an appalling headache, the newly appointed journalist found himself lying in an unfamiliar room, being surveyed by a row of young and interested faces – for the Brays were family people – and realized that he had been outclassed. It could not be said that the experience transformed him, but henceforth he respected the editor and curbed the worst of his excesses.

Marcus was adroit. He held Patrick on a long, easy rein, kept him interested, set him the amusement of ruffling pompous feathers and the challenge of rooting out civic corruption. So Patrick stayed on, lavishing his talents on the *Courier*, and sometimes plunging it into difficulties which Marcus smoothed over. And when he succumbed to the occasional drinking bout and spent the night in a city prison cell, Marcus bailed him out the next morning and saw that he attended the court on time and paid the fine. They suited each other splendidly.

A dark, sardonic man, easy to talk to, difficult to know, Patrick found it hard to relax, and roamed the city at night in search of news, adventure, and something he would never confess even to himself – a friend. For though Marcus was good to him, Patrick knew it was for the sake of the paper, not for himself, and a hundred acquaintances are no substitute for a true companion. Dropping into the Lamb and Child one Saturday evening he spotted Jack hovering hopefully at the end of the bar and adopted him.

Deceived by the young man's shyness, Patrick was inclined to patronize him at first, but Jack was too modest to notice and too generous to take offence if he had. To him the Irishman was as good as a stage play. He watched and listened with admiration and delight, reddening with pleasure, shaking his head from side to side when he laughed, and slapping his hand on the counter when

76

something particularly caught his fancy. As Patrick, encouraged by such an enthusiastic audience, took flight into the realms of fantasy, Jack laughed so much that some regulars were annoyed, and one sour fellow snarled, 'Come on, then, tell us the joke!'

So they found a quiet corner where they wouldn't disturb the clientele, and Jack bought another round of drinks.

'I can tell you're the silent type,' said Patrick kindly, on his fourth double whisky, 'for I've told you me life story and you haven't said a word about yourself.'

Jack hadn't had the chance, though this didn't occur to him, so first he apologized for seeming unfriendly, and then confessed to this gaudy bird of paradise that he was only a lowly sparrow of a park keeper. He gave full details of his school progress, his parents' deaths and his regret at missing university, but said nothing about what he valued most. They ended the evening at Jack's house, with an Indian take-away.

The combination of a stiff lock and fumbling fingers made the key of 44 Markham Terrace doubly difficult to turn, and when at last the door swung open to disclose a dank hall they were assailed by a smell of must and the odours of past meals.

'Jesus, Mary and Joseph,' said Patrick, seeing that someone else lived as he did, from hand to mouth, from day to day, and in dismal discomfort. 'Have you nothing in the world but this and a broom?'

What angel suggested to Jack that he should confide in this exotic stranger? Instinct or alcohol?

'Actually, I do a bit of amateur photography,' Jack admitted. 'Would you like to see it?'

Good-natured, drawn to this childlike man, Patrick said he would, and prepared to praise his work, however commonplace. So Jack unlocked the door to the front room and revealed a miracle.

'Why, in God's holy name,' said Patrick, staring round the walls in awe, 'are you wasting your life sweeping a park?'

'It's a job.' Defensively. 'I have to make a living, like everyone else.'

'There are other ways of earning a crust,' said Patrick, 'and I'm about to suggest one or two of them.'

They opened Jack's personal store of beer then, and talked into the early hours, and Jack woke on the Sunday morning queasy and terrified, for his life was about to change. But Patrick, sleeping in his clothes in the parental double bed, untroubled by their enraged ghosts, was exultant. He always needed a cause for which to fight, and now he had one. And he was, as he often said, a bonnie fighter with the flattened nose to prove it.

'You're a bloody genius,' said Patrick, sneezing into a glass of Alka-Seltzer, 'and I am about to tell the world. But first of all, I have to read your book...'

'Oh, did I mention the book?' Jack asked

pitifully, head in hands.

'You put the manuscript into my very hands. And if it's half as good as the photographs then we've got a winner. Even if it isn't, I know a dozen writers who could shape it up.'

'But I'm not at all sure...' Jack began, afraid of the new.

'Ah, but I am,' said Patrick.

He took the manuscript and a folio of photographs to Marcus, who suggested a local publisher who was ready to take a risk and offer a modest advance and modest royalties. Jack was astounded and grateful, and said so, and shook hands fervently. Fortunately for his bank balance he had Patrick as a self-appointed agent.

'It's a start, but that's all it is!' Patrick counselled in private. 'Don't give him any exclusive rights, hang on to your copyright, and let me see the contract before you sign it. There's a long way to go yet. We've only just started. I've been speaking to the good man Marcus about you, and as I've a gift with the words and you've a gift with the camera he's prepared to let us work together – that is, when the opportunity arises. The pay's not generous – so you can't pack your broom away just yet – but I'm working on that one. I swear that I'll get you out of that bloody park if it's the last thing I do ...'

'It's a very nice park,' said Jack, 'and the sweeping gives me time to think.'

Patrick ignored him.

'You'll have to start freelance. Advertise in the *Courier*. "Have camera. Will travel." That sort of thing. I'll show you how to do it. Then you specialize in something, so that people will say, "Oh, that's a Jack Almond!" Portraits – kids, cats, dogs – any damn thing that'll stand still long enough. Old houses – you move in just ahead of the demolition squad and make it frozen history. Landscapes...'

'I'm not sure I could fit all that in. I'm not—'

'You'll manage. Then when you're established you can start looking round. Find a little shop. Set up a business. Jack Almond, photographer. I'll keep my ear to the ground and my eyes wide open. How's your love life?'

Being friendly with Patrick was hard on the digestion. Jack's stomach clenched. 'I haven't got one,' he said.

Patrick surveyed him with pity and affection. 'You're the only man I know, or have ever known, or ever will know, who would admit to such a thing, but I honour you for it. Well, that's the next step.'

Patrick's love life could not be titled so grandly, being more of a lust life, but he took it upon himself to educate this lost child. He taught Jack how to play. And though the girls to whom Patrick introduced him would never be soulmates, house-mates, or even mates, they were valuable in a different way. Jack didn't find love with them, but he certainly discovered the delights of sex.

In time he also gave up sweeping and learned to take his talents seriously. It was Patrick who found him professional jobs until Jack gained sufficient confidence to find others. As a freelance photographer the pay was not much better, and much of the work mundane, but the experience was invaluable. In the second year of their friendship *The Sacred Grove* was published, to discreet local acclaim, and Jack had the embarrassed pleasure of inscribing copies with a conscientious hand and seeing it displayed in the city bookshops, marked *Signed by the Author*.

By this time Patrick had achieved and bestowed distinction on the *Courier*. People enjoyed reading him, and turned to his page first. The *Courier*, splitting its personality with ease, became known as both guardian of the humble reader and a searchlight on social evils. By race and nature a hater of authority, Patrick pursued his prey with glee and sank his teeth into it with relish. What a good man he must be, readers thought, to expose civic misdeeds so fearlessly. He was not a good man, but a very good journalist. He relished the sweetness of pulling down, of exposing, of degrading, and he did it with such style that his readers laughed even as they deplored, and his enemies were more afraid of his wit than his strength.

Hector Mordant, now high in the city favour and a member of the council, wielded equal authority on the other side of the fence, and it was known that there was no love lost between them. Had Marcus not been a man of power himself, and championed his protegé, Hanna would have lost his job long since. As it was he merely suffered a certain amount of editing and cutting when some story threatened to provoke a member of the city hierarchy to sue the paper. To which his comment was always, and often rightly, 'I expect it's that bastard Mordant again!'

Patrick was a man at the mercy of his own wit. He could never resist a joke even in the most delicate situation. This was one of the many reasons why he had never married. Women were charmed by him, only to find that his sense of humour was unrestrained by sensitive feelings and could puncture the most tender moment. And no woman had ever been admitted to an intimate relationship.

But the main reason for his continued bachelorhood was a passion for personal freedom. True, he was tied like the rest of humanity by the need to abide by certain social rules, but he bucked these when possessed by his personal demon. His only true friend was Jack Almond, because Jack was a man of great kindness and humility and Patrick admired him for qualities he himself did not possess.

Nora and Jack

Eleven years had passed since Kate savoured that first afternoon of freedom, alone in her bedsit. A shy but ambitious girl had become a sophisticated woman who organized Shirley Pringle and the Old Hall and acted as an unofficial agent for Celebrations.

In Jack's case, a great many leaves had fallen in Adelaide Park and been swept up by others. His bicycle stayed in the shed and he now drove a small car. His book had found a London publisher and his local reputation was established.

Making their individual marks in the city, Kate and Jack often met at its various functions, but neither knew that they had experienced those intimate moments on an autumn afternoon, when he rested on his broom and reflected her contentment.

Jack shifted uneasily from foot to foot in the kitchen of Peddleford Farm and wished he had not come. Meeting Kate Wing briefly on civic occasions had been manageable. Meeting her personally at home promised to be an ordeal.

83

No one could deny that she was a hand-some young woman, he thought, and sharp-bright with it. Sitting beautifully erect by the side of the laden farmhouse table, long sun-tanned legs crossed, smiling a social smile, but somehow 'secret, and self-contained, and solitary as an oyster'. Now where did that quotation come from? Oh yes, *A Christmas Carol*. Still, he thought, she's not rock-hard. Something defensive about the eyes. Something vulnerable about the mouth.

There was nothing defensive or vulnerable in the way she greeted him, eyebrows raised, tone edged with amusement.

'Jack Almond. What a surprise!'

There were scuffling sounds in the next room, as of a child trying to escape, and a warm contralto voice crying, 'Harriet, will you stop wriggling?'

Kate lifted her head and turned her chin towards the direction of the voice.

'Mother! You have an important visitor.'

The warm contralto replied to Kate as if Jack were not present.

'Oh dear! Is it Mr Almond? Tell him I'll be there in a minute. I'm just sorting Harriet out. Stop it, Harriet! Have you laid the table, Katie?'

Kate continued to smile, though her brows contracted briefly.

'Yes, and the kettle's boiled. We're ready when you are.'

'Oh good. What would I have done without you? Katie, I meant to say – no, Harriet! –

84

Katie, I haven't had time to explain...'

Annoyance and suspicion flitted across Kate's face. Then she recovered her smile and said, 'Do sit down, Jack. My mother will be with you in a minute. We're always at sixes and sevens in this household. No.' Suddenly serious. 'Not on that chair. The cushion is used by an ancient cat with unfortunate habits.'

'Oh. Right,' said Jack, and chose one more acceptable to her.

The contralto, now relaxed and friendly, said, 'Here we are, Mr Almond!' and a maternal goddess entered, clasping a small girl who was sucking her thumb.

No one ever counted the children who had lain in those feather-bed arms, pillowed their heads against those abundant breasts and been comforted. Nora in her late prime was built on the most generous of scales: deep-bosomed, broad-hipped and soft-footed as a great cat. When she padded forward she swayed, and the floorboards shuddered slightly in homage. Her abundant flesh became her. She was tall and carried her weight well. She wore loose, flowing garments, the uniform of big women, but did not hide behind sombre colours and innocuous patterns. Her smock and skirt were crimson, splashed with orange and white chrysanthemums. Her legs were bare, her feet thrust into old leather sandals. And though the contrast between mother and daughter could not have been greater, Jack saw Kate's likeness to

85

Nora: the fine skin, russet eyes, the same shade of chestnut-brown hair – though Kate's glossy bob was cut by Mr Dennis himself, at Shearers, and Nora's greying mane had simply been twisted into a knot that morning, and speared with a tortoiseshell comb.

In massive splendour she stood there and smiled on him. And in that instant, recognizing the mother figure he had always needed and never known, Jack Almond fell in love with Nora Wing, while she, seeing through the sturdy man to the lost child within, mentally held out her arms to him.

For a moment or so no one spoke. Then Nora, setting Harriet down, began circuitously to explain.

'It went right out of my head, Katie, what with you coming today instead of Sunday, and then Harriet being sick – she will eat grass when my back's turned, Mr Almond, just like a cat. All right then, Harriet, you can go under the table until teatime. Anyway, Katie, you didn't get here until after lunch and you've been out talking to your father, and what with one thing and another I quite forgot. It isn't me that Mr Almond's come to see. It's you.'

Chivalrously, Jack intervened. 'I'm afraid I'm an intruder, Kate. I phoned the Hall this morning and Shirley said you weren't there but as it was business she gave me this number. I'd intended just to leave you a message but your mother,' he said, turning to Nora, who looked distinctly ill at ease, 'very

86

kindly invited me over for tea, and I thought – well, that sounded nice, and – well, I do hope you don't mind.'

Kate was amused.

'So you collared him!' she said to her mother, in a light, dry tone that implied criticism. And graciously to the embarrassed Jack, 'No, of course I don't mind. Why should I?'

But it seemed to him that she minded very much, and Nora knew it.

A tall, thin, weather-beaten man with a likeable face came in then, and seeing they had a visitor held out his hand.

Nora, in disgrace, said, 'This is Mr Almond, Neville.'

'I'm Neville Wing. How are you, sir?'

Nora said, 'I forgot to tell Katie that Mr Almond was coming.'

'You forgot to tell me, too,' he replied. 'But never mind. This is Liberty Hall, Mr Almond. Make yourself at home.'

He was followed by a short dark young fellow with a limp, whose smile seemed permanent, and whose bashfulness kept him hovering on the threshold.

'Ah! Here's our Reggie,' said Neville Wing easily. 'Come forward and shake hands, lad. I think you should know, Mr Almond, that Reggie is the real manager of the flower farm and I'm his assistant.'

Reggie, who found it difficult to manage even himself, liked this introduction very much, but not sufficiently to leave the threshold and shake hands.

'He'll sit down with us when we eat,' Neville assured them.

Nora padded to and fro, brewing tea, toasting crumpets, chatting.

'Mr Almond's come to see Katie on business, Neville. He's a photographer.'

At this stage Kate took over because she was used to introducing people who might not be aware of each other's importance.

'Mr Almond is rather more than a photographer, Mother. He's a local celebrity.'

Nora became flustered and defensive. 'We know that,' she said indignantly. 'We've seen his photographs in the *Courier* many a time.'

'He's not only a distinguished photographer,' Kate pursued implacably, 'he's also an author, and he's written a remarkable book, illustrated with his own photographs, called *The Sacred Grove*.' As this obviously meant nothing to either of her parents, she explained further. 'The book is about *our* grove. The grove on the hill next to Shirley's estate.'

Nora's eyes widened. She improvised. 'Oh, *that* grove!' she cried, as if enlightened. 'Well, sit down everybody and fall to!' She poured tea with an practised hand. She adopted a careless air. 'I know the title, of course,' she lied, 'I just hadn't connected the author's name with this Mr Almond. I've been meaning to read it for ages.'

Annoyed with Kate for exposing her mother, Jack said courteously, 'It will be my pleasure to give you a signed copy, Mrs

Wing.'

'Oh no, I didn't mean to impose on you.' Distressed.

As a photographer she accepted him without question, as a well-known author he troubled her. Fancy Kate saying she'd collared him! Who knows, he might have thought she was celebrity-hunting when she invited him to tea. Reading them both, Kate had to tease.

'Actually, the book is much more than a local success. It's sparked off national interest, and is being translated into other languages. I believe that a paperback is in the offing, isn't it, Jack? You must be delighted!'

He mumbled something about the success being unexpected and not always welcome.

Nora murmured to herself, 'I've got behindhand with my reading, these days. I used to read until my eyes gave out. I was a university student at one time...' She might have expanded on this but her vocation in life did not allow time for personal reflection.

A voice from under the table said, 'I want my tea *here*!'

'Oh, all right,' said Nora, for the meal would be easier without interruptions from Harriet, 'but don't make a mess.'

She passed a mug of tea-coloured milk and a plate of assorted delicacies under the cloth. Two dogs, who had been sleeping by the kitchen range, got up and slunk in with Harriet.

'And don't feed the dogs,' said Nora uselessly.

Kate was talking to her father. 'Jack's book has roused some controversy,' she said mischievously, 'because the grove is becoming well-known and though the city councillors encourage the usual tourists, they don't want it to attract the wrong sort of people. Pagan fringe groups and the like.'

Neville took a pipe from his pocket absent-mindedly, and put it back again, saying, 'Is that so?' And then to his guest, 'I suppose you get a lot of people writing to you, Mr Almond?'

'Quite a few,' said Jack reluctantly. 'Some for, some against.' Here he ventured a mild joke. 'And a few nutters, saying I'm their brother or sister in spirit and can they borrow a tenner or come and live with me!'

This made them laugh.

He took a deep breath and threw off Kate's invisible yoke. 'Let's drop the *Mr Almond*, shall we? I don't like formalities. My name's Jack.'

Delighted, relieved, Kate's parents introduced themselves all over again while she sat forgotten.

'Has this success changed you, Jack?' Neville asked.

'It's changed my life, but not me. Oh, I'm grateful for the money, but I could do without the fuss. It means I'm invited to official functions, and I hate dressing up and talking banalities to people I don't want to know. On the other hand, the book's brought me into contact with others who think along the same lines as myself, and that's a privilege. And it's a relief not to have to worry about money.'

Here Nora and Neville nodded sagely, though that was a blessing they had never experienced.

Jack shrugged it all away, saying, 'Success – as you call it – comes to pluses and minuses, like everything else in life.'

Nora was drinking her final cup of tea before she remembered the reason for his visit.

'Anyway, we mustn't keep you talking, Jack. You're here on business.' She addressed her difficult daughter. 'Would you like to take him into the sitting room, Kate?' Adding quickly, 'It *is* tidy.'

'Oh, there's no need for that,' Jack replied, equally quickly. 'This isn't a private matter.' He addressed Kate, who was watching him coolly. 'Celebrations left a message on my answering service, asking me to contact you as soon as possible. They want me to take photographs of the Old Hall for their brochure. For the summer concert next year.'

Her expression changed subtly. Why the hurry? it asked. The query hung on the air and he stumbled into explanations.

'I've been away on a job all week, you see, and I didn't get back until last night. And as I wasn't sure what day they phoned, and it sounded urgent, and my engagement book's pretty full, I thought I'd better sort it out at once.'

She answered in her genial professional tone. 'Fine! But I don't carry our engagement book around with me, and Shirley and I are away tomorrow – which is why I'm here today. So may I ring you on Monday?'

Nora, sensing too much peace and quiet underneath the table, asked, 'Where's that child gone?'

The dogs emerged, licking their chops, followed by a sticky four-year-old who crawled out at Jack's feet and planted both hands on his knees. 'Boh!' she cried, smiling up at him, and clambered on to his lap.

'Oh, you're a favourite already!' Nora said. 'Do you like children, Jack?'

'Love them,' said Jack, 'as long as they *are* children.'

His vision of the ideal child stopped short nowadays at ten years old. Until then they could be delightful. Afterwards boys tended to patronize him and girls started using make-up, sipping alcoholic lemonade and painting their nails black.

He amended his statement. 'I'm old-fashioned, I'm afraid. I think kids grow up too quickly nowadays, and know too much, too early.'

Kate, around whose Italian sandals the dogs were snuffling for crumbs, said, 'Then you'll certainly feel at home here. My mother keeps a constant supply of children and creates a Christopher Robin world for them.'

She spoke breezily. No one could have called it criticism but Nora flushed up and looked hurt, which prompted Neville Wing to say loyally, 'And a good thing, too!' which Jack amplified with, 'Now I do like the sound of that.'

Nora wound up her hair afresh and anchored it with the comb, restored.

'For the last few months I've been looking after a little group of...' Here she whispered lest Harriet be offended, 'Down's syndrome children.' Her voice returned to its usual dark-velvet level. 'Dear little souls. Harriet helps me with the other children, don't you, Harriet? Usually it's five mornings a week – isn't it, Neville?'

He removed the pipe and said wryly to the curl of smoke in front of him, 'Which can turn into afternoons and weekends and overnight as well.'

Nora defended herself. 'Harriet's only here today because her mummy had to go shopping. Isn't that right, Harri?' Nods and smiles on Harriet's part. Again, Nora defended herself to her daughter. 'And it was Kate's idea that I started this group in the first place, as an interim measure. Now wasn't it? You can't deny that, Kate!'

Father and daughter exchanged an amused look.

'I suggested a small, straightforward nursery group, to come and go at fixed times,' Kate said. 'It was you who introduced the D.S. element and allowed them to take advantage of you. "Let your afflicted ones come unto to me," you cried, and were

93

immediately – and to your eternal surprise – besieged by takers!'

There was a short silence. Nora decided to let this remark go, and turned to the supportive member of her audience.

'You see, I'd been having, and still have, a lot of trouble and grief, Jack – not with these dear children – with the authorities...' Her fingers fluttered momentarily, like a distress signal. She clasped her hands together to quieten them, checked herself and said, 'But that's a long story...'

Kate pursed her lips, moved her chair out of range of the dogs, swung one foot, and glanced at her wristwatch.

'Too long to tell you now,' said Nora, noticing. Her voice trembled. 'Some other time, perhaps.'

'I'd like to hear it now,' said Jack, turning his shoulder on Kate's impatience.

'Only don't go upsetting yourself, Mother,' Neville warned.

But Nora had been given permission, and the dam burst forth. Her husband took out his pipe and sucked it thoughtfully.

'Neville and I have been foster-parents for nearly thirty years, Jack. Just one or two at a time, and as they've grown up and left us, or been adopted or taken back by their families, we've taken one or two more.' She leaned forward, sure of his sympathy. 'A house without a child in it feels empty to me. *I* feel empty. And with Cheryl leaving us last Christmas we were on our own again. So I

94

was looking through a magazine we take. Here, I'll show you.'

She got up clumsily in her haste, nearly knocking her chair over, and her husband again cautioned her with, 'Now don't upset yourself, love.'

Nora took no notice of him, found the magazine and spread it in front of Jack. At first glance it looked like an infantile rogue's gallery – pages of children's photographs with a detailed biography beneath each. This particular portrait had been marked with a cross and under it Nora had printed joyfully, 'She's for us!' and the child named Pearl stared out at Jack in sorrow and bewilderment.

Born into a world with which she was not equipped to deal, her eyes alone told her story. He read her brief history: brain-damaged at birth, infrequent control over limbs, bladder and bowels, some speech sounds, deaf in one ear, mother a single parent unable to cope. He looked up at Nora with awe, and down at the child with compassion, and wondered what purpose could be found in such a life.

Nora said defensively, 'I know she's got serious disabilities, but look at the expression in those eyes. And that little face would be as pretty as a picture if it was happy. I've had children like that before – though not as bad – trapped in a body that handicapped them, and they *can* improve.' She appealed to her husband. 'They *can* be helped, can't they,

95

Neville? Oh, not to be normal. No one can work miracles. But you can reach them, and teach them. Jack, I've set my heart on this child. No one else wants her, and the authorities won't let us have her. They say...' It was hard for her to admit it. 'They say I'm ... overweight.'

Jack guessed that the term had been obese.

'Well, you are, love,' said her husband kindly. 'No doubt about it. But you've got more energy than many a younger woman, and as for wisdom and experience – you stand alone there, love. You stand alone.'

Two fat tears slid down Nora's cheeks and she wiped them away angrily with a tea towel. She turned on Neville as if he were the cause of her misery.

'Haven't I told them, over and over, that I'm prepared to diet?' she demanded.

'Yes, love,' he answered peaceably, 'but it's no good just talking about it. You must do it. If you go to that interview in September, weighing the same as you did in March, they're not going to believe you mean it.'

Kate said suddenly in a voice that was tight with exasperation, 'For heaven's sake, Mother, we've been over this subject again and again and we never get any further. Either diet or forget the whole thing.'

Nora entreated her husband. 'If I started tomorrow I could lose a stone by September,' she offered.

'It'd be a drop in the bucket, love,' said Neville tenderly. 'You need to lose three at least.'

She beseeched Kate, 'If I lost a stone and you did my hair up nicely and I wore my navy-blue costume, wouldn't that make a difference?'

Kate asked, candidly though not unkindly, 'But can you get into your navy-blue costume?'

Nora enlisted Jack's sympathy. 'In my navy-blue costume,' she said, 'I only look about fourteen stones.'

Jack said gallantly, 'Thirteen, surely.'

Nora said, 'You're a good lad. Thank you.' Again she wiped her eyes on the tea towel. 'I can't tell you how much it grieves me. They're feeding and clothing that child and keeping her clean and I don't doubt they're doing their best, but there's a heart and soul and mind in that little body crying out to be noticed and they haven't time for that. And she's in a home where she's one of many, but here she'd be one of us – and special.'

Neville rose from the table and put his pipe away. He looked tired and old. 'Come on, Reggie,' he said, 'there's plenty of daylight left.'

Nora began slowly to stack the tea things on a tray.

Subdued but practical, Kate said, 'I'm sorry, but I must go, Mother. Shirley and I are off at the crack of dawn tomorrow. Let me help you to clear up first.'

Nora did not even look at her. She addressed her daughter by her full name – a mark of disapproval.

'Don't bother,' she said flatly. 'I can manage, thank you, Catriona.'

Silence threatened. Neville hovered on the threshold, uncertain how to help. Jack sensed the basic tension between mother and daughter, and saw that Neville was concerned for them both. He got up and set Harriet carefully on her feet, though she clung to his trouser legs and beseeched him.

'I've had an idea, Nora,' he said, and turned his back on Kate to make it clear that she had no part in this. 'I'd like to take some photographs of you and your nursery group in the farmhouse. I think my friend, Patrick Hanna, at the *Courier*, might write an article about this adoption business. He likes having a go at the authorities and cutting through red tape. We could make people sit up. I can't promise anything, because it isn't front-page news, but at the proper time – just before Christmas, say – readers are open to this sort of story.'

Nora and Neville were transfigured: she with delight, he because she was happy.

'Oh, that *would* be good of you,' Nora cried. 'Bless you, Jack.' She thought of a way to thank him properly. 'Now, why don't you come and have Sunday lunch with us tomorrow? Bring your friend Mr Hanna too, if he'd like to come.'

'I'd love to,' said Jack promptly. 'I can't speak for Pat, but I'll ask him tonight and give you a ring.'

'No need,' said Nora. 'There's always plenty for everybody.'

Kate stood up and took her handbag from the long mantelshelf where she had placed it out of child-reach. 'A good old-fashioned Sunday roast will be a rare treat for Patrick Hanna,' she observed. 'He usually *drinks* his lunch.'

No one listened.

'Sunday lunch is a banquet, Jack,' Neville warned him, grinning. 'Bring your doggie bag!'

Kate kissed her mother's cheek lightly, her father's cheek tenderly.

'Must run!' she said. She addressed Jack, who was still ignoring her. 'Thank you so much for chasing down here, but there was no need. It's worth remembering that Celebrations always panics when a new project hovers on the horizon. I'll ring you on Monday morning and we'll fix an early date.'

'As you please,' he replied, liking her less than ever.

Having put him in his place she turned on her professional charm.

'The grounds of the Hall look truly beautiful at this time of year, and I know you take wonderful photographs.' Smiling. 'Can you arrange fine weather as well?'

'No,' he replied bluntly, 'but I'm sure you can!'

The others burst out laughing, and Harriet and Reggie laughed louder than anyone. To Kate's credit she joined in the joke against herself, though not quite as freely. She kept her tone easy and mocking.

'Oh dear! I see I shall have to do my best!'

'You always do that,' said Nora, and was proud of her, and sad.

Jack swung Harriet high into the air, which made her squeal joyfully, and then he shook hands with Nora and Neville and Reggie.

'I must be going, too, and thanks for the invitation. What time should I – or we – come?'

'Oh, we're easy on a Sunday,' said Nora. 'We don't eat much before half past one or two o'clock.'

'So have a good lie-in and no breakfast,' Neville advised him, 'and then after dinner you can have a good lie-down!'

Jack's old saloon was difficult to start, as usual, and Neville had to assist. While they were getting oiled up Kate's open-topped car swept past them and down the lane. One hand and a scarf fluttered at them, and she was gone.

Jack asked incredulously, 'Who does your daughter take after?'

'Herself, I reckon,' Nora answered, defeated.

But Neville said, 'No. She's us, love. Us when we were young. Us kicking over the traces, jacking in our university education, showing our parents how life ought to be lived. You'd never guess it now, Jack, but Nora and I were flower people back in the sixties, part of a community, sleeping on the beaches in California, smoking hash and talking love and peace. It's the same spirit. It just takes a different shape in different generations. Kate thinks she can do better than us. And perhaps she can. So long as she's happy I don't mind.'

'You were flower people?' Jack asked, intrigued.

'Then as now,' said Neville, indicating the fields. 'It's been flowers all the way, hasn't it, love?'

Simultaneously, each held out a hand to be clasped.

'It was a grand experience,' said Nora, 'but it didn't wear well in the long run.'

'And it was a grand idea,' said Neville, 'but we hadn't thought it through. Dropping out means being dependent in one way or another on those who stay in.'

'Tell Jack what you said to them, Neville, just before we left.'

'I said, "In a world full of flowers, who's going to run the sewage farms?"'

'At which point they threw you out of Eden!' Jack guessed, grinning.

'No, no. There were no hard feelings on either side. Nora was expecting Katie, you see, and we didn't feel we could tramp round with a baby. I know people do. Children are brought up in caravans and old buses and canal barges, but we decided to settle down and work our own land. And I'll say this for our two families – we'd spat in their eye, as you might say, but once they knew we were prepared to make a go of it they put up the

101

money for this place. We saw it as a home and a way of life for us and Katie – and all the other children we were going to have.'

'Only there weren't any others,' Nora confessed, 'and that's how we came to be foster-parents.'

'What a wonderful story!' said Jack, touched, but also entertained.

He liked to think of Kate being conceived on a Californian beach in a haze of hash. Somehow, it served her right. He must tell Patrick. He'd feel the same.

'That's what I mean when I say Kate's us,' Neville explained. 'She's full of ideas about what life ought to be like, and she's trying to change it.'

At this moment Jack's car engine erupted into life and he dared not let it idle.

'Until tomorrow!' he cried.

He could not sweep off between the fields of flowers as Kate had done, but he rattled down the lane at a fair speed. And on the way home he sang the Hallelujah Chrous and beat time with one fist on the steering wheel, because he had found his family.

Shirley

June, 2000

Extract from the *City Guide*'s 'Places of Architectural Interest'.

Melbury Old Hall. Built in Classical style by Venetian architect Giacomo Leoni, c. 1733, for the third Lord Cleydon, a nobleman of exquisite taste, who spared so little expense that he impoverished his heirs unto the fifth generation. The line died out at the end of the nineteenth century, by which time a number of fine pictures and pieces of furniture, and several hundred acres of land had already been sold. In 1899 the house came on the open market, since when the estate has had different owners.

Like some troublesome musical parcel that contained a penalty rather than a prize, Melbury Old Hall had enticed a biscuit manufacturer, a purveyor of popular cough

103

medicine and the inventor of a bicycle pump to reopen it. And each of these entrepreneurs had found the Hall and county society more trouble and expense than they could have anticipated.

During the Second World War it was commandeered by the army and used as a convalescent home for officers.

After that it masqueraded as a private school, without success, and finally languished on the books of three city estate agents, growing cheaper and more dilapidated as the years went by. But as the Old Hall approached the new millennium it found responsive friends in the shape of Hector and Kate, and the past six years had seen its fortunes revive.

The present owner, Miss Shirley Pringle, has tastefully restored much of its former glory, and continues to add to its many attractions.

Elegant on its green knoll, surrounded by trees and still having a sufficient area to afford a landscaped garden, a small park, splendid views and privileged seclusion.

The house is not open to the public, but the gardens may be viewed from April to October on Tuesdays and Thursdays between 10 a.m. and 6 p.m.

The blackamoor who had so deeply offended Hector now stood in the lobby of an Edwardian-style restaurant in the city, where he was much admired. Pictures by the wall-length and books by the shelf-length had been re-sold, and ribbons from florists' bouquets were given to the housekeeper's granddaughters.

Although impossible to restore the house to its original splendour, its present state was both credible and creditable. An aged classical beauty with an air of serene detachment, Melbury Old Hall could once again be viewed with respectful admiration, but her upkeep was prohibitive, and had crippled all its owners so far.

'He's very good, isn't he?' said Shirley Pringle, studying the pack of photographs from Jack Almond.

'No doubt about it,' said Kate.

'I'm thinking I might ask him to do a set of interior photographs as well. It would make a nice album, don't you think? And if we go broke and have to open the house to the public it could be the basis of a brochure.'

'By all means. Do you want me to arrange that?'

Shirley Pringle, who never admitted to being in her late fifties and lied about her weight, was sitting up in Lord Cleydon's four-poster, wearing a man's Regency green and gold brocade dressing gown. She liked to breakfast in bed and to organize her day before she rose. A chameleon, she changed her clothes and appearance to suit different events. At the office she was Pringle the Business Tycoon: tough, but a good guy at heart, with grey cropped hair and a no-nonsense approach. At the Old Hall she became Lady Shirley in a short red wig, tweeds and twinsets. Socially, she flowered according to mood, either with the grey crop and black tailor-made dinner suit or a full red wig, flowing feminine robes, and glittering jewellery that was genuine but on Shirley simply looked vulgar.

Now she peered shrewdly over horn-rimmed spectacles and said to Kate, 'You don't like Jack Almond, do you?'

'I don't dislike him. He's simply not my type.'

'Not a smooth enough laddie?'

This was a dig at Hector which Kate countered by saying, 'Anyway, you do like him, and he's an excellent photographer, so that's all that matters.'

Shirley handed the photographs over to her and said briskly, 'Send him one of your sincere thank you notes, and request that he does the same service for me for the interior – at his own convenience and as he thinks best. Right?'

'Right! Anything else?'

'When I've got a mid-week space on the calendar arrange a private inspection trip for me to the three northern Parlours – and don't tell anybody I'm coming.'

Kate said, 'Certainly not!'

The two women exchanged smiles of complicity.

'Otherwise, that seems to be all for today.' Cool but friendly, Shirley said, 'Tell me, how's Hector?'

His relationship to Kate was long known about and accepted, but not approved of.

'Away with the family. They're in the south of France for a fortnight.'

'Lucky old things. And what about *your* holidays?'

'Not settled yet. Sometime in the early autumn, I expect.'

Holidays were shared with Hector on business trips. A week here, a few days there. Over the past years, at the expense of Celebrations, Kate had travelled widely, stayed in fine hotels, and worked with her lover on his future projects. Always appreciated. Often exhilarated. Occasionally happy. Never content.

'I'll be glad for you to have a break – and glad for me when you get back,' Shirley said and patted Kate's hand. 'Has he said anything more about this outdoor concert that he wants to stage in my park next summer?'

'It's still early days. The only fixture is Melbury Old Hall as a venue. But I gather it will be a very prestigious occasion.'

'Is there anything he's not telling me?'

'I don't think so. He did murmur something about your offering private hospitality

107

to the conductor and soloists.'

'That was to be expected. Nothing more?'

Her loyalties divided, Kate turned the question aside with humour.

'I think that all he's doing at the moment is casting his bread upon the waters and hoping it will return buttered, with jam on it.'

The two women laughed.

Shirley said thoughtfully, 'It's just that I always suspect Hector when he isn't playing the showman. If this concert is as prestigious as he says then he should be boasting about it by now. Anyway, you'll keep me posted, won't you?'

'Of course.'

'Oh, I nearly forgot...'

Oh no, you didn't, Kate thought, 'nearly forgot' means I shan't like what you're going to say.

Shirley's tone was jaunty, her eyes guilty.

'I had a phone call from – guess who? Ingrid, of all people! She's over here for a few weeks, and asked if I could put her up for a night or two.' She added, 'So you two girls will meet again!'

'I should prefer not to meet her at all,' said Kate coolly.

A man of steel where business was concerned, and the silliest of women when love beckoned, Shirley attempted to explain matters to herself as well as Kate.

'It's only for a couple of nights, lovie. Just being civil. Ingrid knows the score.'

'That she does,' said Kate, squaring up

108

papers and clipping them into folders.

'You're so inflexible,' Shirley complained.

'You mean when I make up my mind about someone I stick to it?'

Shirley's expression changed. 'Oh, through thick and thin, and mostly thin, lovie,' she said acidly. 'Look how you've stuck to Hector.'

Kate sorted her folders into two piles. She remained silent long enough to disquiet her employer, then spoke with chilled politeness.

'I'm leaving the northern reports with you. You should have fun with them.'

'Lovie,' Shirley said in a wheedling tone. 'Don't be cross with me about Ingrid.'

'I'm not just cross,' said Kate, 'I'm very angry. Because I can run through this scenario from start to finish, with variations such as the couple of days extending to a couple of months, and you unable to concentrate on anything but the lovely Ingrid, and me making up diplomatic lies to cover your absences – until the good times turn very bad indeed, and I have to see Ingrid off, possibly pay her off, and mop you up afterwards. And I tell you, Shirley, I'm sick to death of it!'

Shirley's eyes, which could strike cold-blue fear into Mrs Porter's Parlour managers, were palely awash. Her voice was troubled.

'Oh, don't be like that, lovie. You know that all I ever wanted was a steady relationship, but it's hard to find. Nobody would be more faithful and loving than me if I ever met the

109

right girl.'

The prospect of that happening was unlikely. Shirley blew her nose with a man's handkerchief and wiped her eyes. She grinned ruefully at Kate.

'Life's a sod, isn't it?'

Kate nodded, relaxed, and smiled back.

'But it has its compensations,' said Shirley honestly, 'and you're one of them. The best friend I've ever had. Well, to be truthful, you're the *only* friend I've ever had.' She came to a difficult conclusion. 'I'll put Ingrid off, if you like. She's probably just broke and doesn't know who to tap next. I'll send her a little cheque, wish her luck, and say I'm sorry but I can't manage to see her.'

Kate's expression matched that of her mother, watching a naughty child abase itself and try to make amends. She hid a smile and spoke with brisk good humour.

'If you're going to give her a cheque you may as well enjoy her company first. Just keep her out of my way until you need me to play the executioner.'

Shirley grinned, shamefaced. 'You're a good lass, Katie. Bless you. I wish you were one of us. What a team you and I would be!'

I'm damned glad we aren't. I'd be swallowed whole, Kate thought. Aloud, she said, 'I'll be in my office if you want me.'

As she went out Shirley called after her, 'You know that there's always room at the Hall if you get tired of being by yourself while Hector's away.' She played with the idea, as

110

she had done many times before. Her eyes narrowed. She was affable in her cunning. 'You could have the Queen's suite, Katie. Your favourite.'

The Queen's suite was a fictitious legend. No royal lady had ever slept there, though perhaps some noble Cleydon had hoped one might.

Kate turned and smiled at her, to show that all was forgiven. 'Thank you. I'll remember that. But I'm perfectly happy at home.'

Shirley looked at her curiously. 'You really love that funny little doll's house of yours, don't you?' she said.

'Yes I do, and for a number of reasons. Oh, it's not Melbury Old Hall, but it's perfect of its kind. And Hector found it for me and made it possible for me to buy it. But mainly I love it because it's mine. That's why.'

Shirley shrugged. Relieved that they were friends once more she did not say that No 11 Mulberry Street was also the place where Hector could find Kate whenever he wanted her, and lay claim to her time by reason of past generosity.

'Let me know when Ingrid arrives,' said Kate with a grin, 'so that we can bare our teeth at each other.'

'Cheeky thing!' Shirley answered, well pleased.

'Miss Wing,' said the manservant as Kate came downstairs, 'there's a person wanting to see Miss Pringle. I didn't quite know where

111

to put him, so I asked him to wait outside.'

His tone and demeanour suggested that the visitor was not acceptable. In her heart Kate prayed that it wasn't a former foster-son of her parents' come to beg money or work – which had happened – but outwardly she exhibited no emotion.

'What kind of person, Walter?'

Shirley was good at acquiring and keeping staff, and this canny middle-aged man, who fulfilled the functions of butler and footman, had been at the Hall since her motley reign began. Privately, he reckoned he had seen them all, but this visitor perplexed even him.

'Very strange, miss. Not your rough sort and not ill-spoken. Quite inoffensive, in fact, but most persistent. Says he's prepared to stay on the front steps all day if he has to, and I know Miss Pringle doesn't like trouble of that sort.'

Neither Walter nor Kate would have said so, but Shirley's desire to play the lady of the manor carried her to ridiculous extremes. Had there been a Melbury Old Hall custom to bathe the feet of beggars on a certain winter's day each year Shirley would have been there at dawn with her wash-bowl, kneeling in the snow, shivering nobly in a spotless white shift.

Walter said, 'I wondered if he might be on drugs, because he's wearing a sort of monk's robe and he doesn't seem to be ... all there.' Here he tapped his forehead and looked significant.

'Did he say what he wanted?'

'Yes, miss. He says that the healer Ezra, the follower Simeon, and the follower Joel, have been summoned to the grove.'

'Oh dear.' She thought for a few moments. 'Show him into my office, Walter, but stay within call in case I need you.'

The manservant held open the door and announced without sarcasm, 'The follower Joel, Miss Wing.'

'Good morning, Mr Joel,' said Kate in her most cordial tones. 'Come in and sit down. I'm sorry Miss Pringle isn't available at the moment but I'm her assistant, and I may be able to help.'

A very small man shuffled in wearing a robe that had been fashioned from a grey blanket and a tasselled bell pull. He was very proud of the robe but not entirely comfortable with it, and judging from the faint odour that accompanied his movements both he and it needed a wash. Worn sandals slipped on bare dusty feet. His scanty beard seemed to have been grown to give an air of maturity to a young face, and his eyes were as round and innocent as those of a child. He folded his hands together and bowed, gazed trustfully at Kate and cleared his throat. He spoke as if he had learned his lines well and was proud of this also.

'I speak for the healer Ezra.'

Kate, twiddling a pencil between her fingers, gave an encouraging murmur of

113

'Ye–es?'

'The healer Ezra, after much wandering, has found the appointed place. The grove is her sacred home.' He paused to allow this information to be absorbed.

'Oh, is Ezra a woman?' Kate enquired, interested.

'Ezra is a healer, whether man or woman it is not important, and she asks the lady to let her stay in the grove,' said Joel.

Kate concealed a smile. He was so earnest, so anxious to play his role well, and withal so ineffectual. She explained fully and carefully, as to a child or an idiot, and perhaps he was both.

'The grove doesn't belong to Miss Pringle, although it borders on her land. It's a municipal property, and the authorities don't allow camping. Nor, I'm afraid, does Miss Pringle allow camping in the grounds of the Old Hall. But as we often get enquiries, particularly in the summer, we've had an information leaflet printed that gives you directions to a municipal site at Marchfield, at the bottom of Grove Hill. I keep them at hand and you're most welcome to have one.' Here she opened the bottom drawer of her desk and picked up a sheet. 'You'll find temporary accommodation there for tents, caravans and other vehicles. The authorities have laid on water and sanitation and access to medical and educational facilities, and they inspect the site at intervals – not in an officious way, just to keep an eye on everything. It's quite comfortable, I believe, Mr Joel.'

He said portentously, 'I am Joel.'

Oh God, Kate thought, drama is all I need. Call me Ishmael. Captain Ahab's round the corner and Moby Dick's outside!

'We have no titles,' the little man explained. 'We have no tents and caravans. We have no possessions. I am Joel.'

This is hard work, Kate thought, and personally I would tell him to get lost, but Shirley has these notions about noblesse oblige.

She tried to be practical. 'Then how are you travelling?'

'We walk. When Ezra stops we find people who will shelter and feed us. Then we walk on. But Ezra is a wise healer who hears of many things, and she heard of the book called *The Sacred Grove*, and she read it. So we came here, and Ezra knew that this was her earthly home and she must stay here to fulfil her destiny. She has heard of the lady at Melbury old Hall, and she knows the lady's heart. The lady will help us.' He leaned forward, having delivered his official message, and confided in a natural tone with a Midlands accent, 'We come here last night and the travellers took us in, and when me and Simeon was scouting round for Ezra we found an empty hut near the grove. We heard it's on the lady's land. It's be just right for us.'

'Ah!' Kate said, understanding the interview at last. 'You want Miss Pringle to allow you live in the shepherd's old hut?' He nodded, relieved. 'And who is *we*?'

'The healer Ezra, and the follower Simeon and me.'

'Just the three of you?' He nodded again. 'And what is Simeon doing at the moment?'

'He's gone to the city to beg for food.'

Evidently he felt that the conversation was becoming too prosaic because he returned to his former exalted tone.

'Simeon has gone forth to the city but Ezra meditates in the grove, which is her sacred home.'

'That hut,' Kate warned him, unimpressed, 'is worse than empty. It's dirty and dilapidated. The roof leaks, the door has been kicked in, and the windows are either broken or boarded-up.'

Joel simply nodded and waited.

'Very well. I'll let Miss Pringle know. But I think it would be advisable for Ezra to come by herself,' said Kate. 'Miss Pringle likes to deal with the top man – or woman, as the case may be.' She opened Shirley's opulent leather engagement book. 'As you have nowhere permanent to stay at the moment we'd better make an early appointment. Miss Pringle is busy all morning. Let's say this afternoon at—'

Joel held up one small grubby hand. 'Ezra will come,' he said. And left.

'Was he a traveller or a beggar, miss?' Walter later asked.

'Both – in a way!' Kate said, and laughed.

116

Ezra

Shirley was moved to heave herself out of bed, light a cigarette, and stride up and down her kingly bedroom.

'And he said that this Ezra had heard of me and *knew my heart*?' she asked, relishing the phrase.

'I shouldn't take that literally. It's part of the spiel. Like gipsies,' said Kate, and quoted in sing-song style, ' "You gotta a lucky face, lady, and a kind 'eart. You gotta fortune coming that you don't know nothing about. There's someone loves you as has kept it secret but it can't be kept secret no more", and so on.'

Shirley looked in her hand mirror and disliked what she saw.

'I'll get dressed,' she said, and reached for her short auburn wig that squatted on its perch near the dressing table. 'But the way you told it,' she persisted, 'this Joel sounded so sincere.'

'Wholly sincere, and completely potty.'

'But what conviction, Kate! *She knows the lady's heart.* And he didn't just ask for shelter, he said that this Ezra *knew* that I would help. Don't you think that's rather remarkable?'

'Not in the least. Word will have gone round by this time that no passing mendicant ever gets turned away,' Kate said flatly. 'Discounting the godly garb and set speeches, he was sent here to tap the lady of the manor for whatever he could get. Personally, I should have nothing to do with this Ezra. Remember what happened when you let that family park their travelling van in the copse? Just for a week, they said, while they sorted their affairs out. We had to call the police in the end, and there was no end of mess and abuse – not forgetting that rascal Patrick Hanna beating the drum at your expense in the *Courier*.'

'That was before I knew the ropes and he knew me. I'm very fond of Patrick now,' said Shirley. 'It was a mistake on his part, which he fully explained.'

'I'm sure he did. He's a plausible rogue.'

'And he made up for it with that lovely interview for the feature on Porter's Parlours. We sat together like old buddies most of the afternoon.'

'The length of time it takes to share a bottle of whisky and a packet of cigarettes?' Kate suggested.

'We happen to like the same brands. He made it perfectly clear to me that he doesn't have the final word in what's published. Some social service was putting pressure on the authorities, and the editor slanted the article to suit them.'

'If you can believe anything that Patrick Hanna tells you then by all means do, but leave fringe charlatans strictly alone.'

Shirley disappeared into her dressing room and conducted the rest of their conversation through the open door.

'Why should they be charlatans? You said that this Joel had honest eyes.'

'My exact words were "a childlike gaze",' Kate replied. 'The follower Joel is retarded. And I should know,' she added tartly. 'I've had personal experience of that particular condition for a number of years.'

Shirley's voice hinted that she possessed hidden depths of wisdom and compassion hitherto unknown to her assistant.

'Ah! But don't they say that fools are closest to God?'

'I think we should leave God out of it. He could only complicate the issue.'

Shirley emerged in an austere navy linen suit with her wig straight. Kate could tell that her employer was displeased because she addressed Kate by her full name and looked past her as she spoke.

'Thank you, Catriona, but I intend to judge for myself. What time did you say this healer was coming?'

'I didn't. I got as far as "this afternoon at" and the follower Joel said, "Ezra will come!" as if she would appear miraculously at the hour of destiny.' Exasperated, she added, 'I never could bear spiritual pretensions. See her by all means but don't fall for that nonsense.'

'I shall be back after lunch,' said Shirley,

very regal. 'Kindly tell Walter that when Ezra arrives she will find me in the rose garden.'

On her free afternoons on summer days the owner of Melbury Old Hall liked to wear a flowered chiffon dress and a shady Italian straw hat. She also carried a little basket of immaculate gardening tools on one stout freckled arm. Luckily, she did not know how to use them – a bonus for which Mr Reeve the head gardener was truly grateful. And today, lest she had to wait long, Shirley also took a folder of plans for opening a Porter's Parlour in the Midlands, and these she was consulting in her rustic arbour when, as she later expressed it, Ezra came to her.

The only child of decent, middle-class Methodists, Shirley had found love a puzzling proposition. Stocky and plain as a child, disturbed in her adolescent years by feelings she was not supposed to have, and treated as a jolly good sort by the male sex, she had been mercifully initiated at the age of twenty by a passing lesbian whereupon all became clear. The difficulty lay with her parents, who would not have understood and certainly not forgiven her. So, pleading late evenings and pressure of work, she rented a flat in the city and lived a life of lies and subterfuge. People whispered or joked about her sexual proclivities, but her parents were liked and respected and not a breath of scandal ever got by that blackamoor in the hall of the Coombe

Street house.

This unsatisfactory state of affairs was relieved by her parents' retirement to Spain, but a deeper dissatisfaction lay in her female lovers, and though Shirley had, as she expressed it, 'a rattling good time', she failed to find lasting love. Still, she had a natural flair for business, and in running the family chain of tea shops, working first for, then with, and finally instead of her mother, she achieved great gratification: envied, admired, successful, and relatively rich. But on this summer afternoon she was to experience a moment of destiny.

Afterwards she could remember no sound, no movement, only the feeling that someone of importance was there, so that she had to look up.

There, at the doorway of the arbour, stood a diminutive woman: black oiled hair drawn tight against her skull and coiling into a knot at the nape of her neck. Her eyes were curiously light against the brown skin. She wore a simple grey robe. As Shirley gaped at her she put two bird-boned hands together and bowed her head in greeting.

Shirley's disorderly mind pecked here and there. Mixed blood. Light eyes, dark skin. I wonder how old she is? I know what that Indian sign means. Can't remember the name. Something like Canasta. Kate would know. What should I do now?

Shirley had been rehearsing this meeting since lunchtime. In the role of benevolent

121

aristocrat, she had meant to extend gracious fingers and deliver kindly words to put the stranger at her ease. The rehearsal had been a waste of time. Both words and gesture were out of place. Slowly, clumsily, she put both plump freckled hands together, and inclined her head.

The eyes looked straight through her, grey and clear. They understood and accepted Shirley's worldly self. They glimpsed another self that Shirley had never suspected, and communed with it.

Why, Shirley thought, it's exactly as if we knew each other already, truly knew each other, that we'd been intended to meet for a long time.

'You are so kind to see me...' Ezra began.

Hypnotized by the voice, Shirley's mind went on pecking. Seems to be of Indian blood. Talks in that pretty, finicky sort of way they do. And there's something else about her. A kind of scent. Not ordinary scent. Something. What do they call it? Kate would know. The ... the ... the odour of sanctity. Yes, that's it. This woman is a saint. I'm meeting a saint.

'...we need very little. Our wants are simple. we would be no trouble. If you would let us live in the shepherd's hut with my followers. There is Joel, whom your assistant has met, and there is...'

Three of them. That'll be a tight squeeze and the hut's in bad condition. I can't possibly let her live in it as it is. I wonder if ... No.

122

If she was by herself I'd offer her a room at the Hall, but the other two...

'... we have no money...'

Shirley recovered. Her voice did not. She should have said benevolently, 'Oh, I would not dream of charging a rent, my dear!' But it came out as a humble, 'No rent, naturally.'

Because – what was it they believed in India? Whoever gave charity to these holy ones was blessed. I'll have the hut repaired. Quickly. She can have whatever she wants. She has only to ask.

Then, being short of words and inspiration, she made namaste again and her world was lit by Ezra's smile.

Avoiding Kate's sceptical eyes, Shirley drew herself up and adopted a friendly but firm approach. To which Kate responded tersely.

'But, as you know, Katie, that hut's not fit to live in. So I must have it repaired and made comfortable as soon as possible. And whatever Ronnie Baxstead and his workmen are doing for us here, tell them to drop it.'

'It's important. They're re-slating part of the Hall roof that leaked all winter and caused so much damage.'

'Well, whatever. They've got all summer to do that. I want them to start work on the hut tomorrow. The roof can wait. In fact we're lucky to have a roof at all. Those poor souls have nowhere to lay their heads.'

'They must be laying their heads some-where.'

'Oh, well, down at Marchfield, I believe. Some travellers have taken them in – heaven knows how, it must be extremely crowded.'

She resolved to have no more interruptions. She spoke with authority.

'And as time is of the essence I intend to inspect the place myself now. I haven't any appointments in the morning, have I? Just the one? Who is it? Oh, *she* doesn't matter. Ring her up and tell her I can't come. Fix another day soon. If you think she'll be offended, send her some flowers. And tell Ronnie that the hut will need a sound roof, door and windows for a start. Then it must be cleaned and decorated. When that's done I'll provide some simple furniture. And they'll need bedding, of course, cutlery, china and so forth...'

She stopped. She left practicalities to take care of themselves. Her voice softened. 'It's an extraordinary thing, Katie, the way she makes you feel. She's so quiet and still. Just a little figure in a long grey dress, very small and pale, with wonderful big grey eyes and a lovely smile. Her voice is quiet, too, and very gentle. She's not pretty, not young, but you can't help looking and looking at her, and feeling at peace.'

Reading Kate's expression correctly, she snapped, 'Don't smile in that superior way, Catriona. I'm telling you that she's a holy person. I've never met one before, but I know one when I see one – and I know what's due to them.'

Then very casually, 'Oh, and by the way,

124

Kate, ring up Ingrid will you? And tell her I shan't be able to put her up after all. She's in some London hotel at the moment. I jotted the telephone number down on my blotter. Tell her I'm sending a cheque to help her out this time, but not to expect anything more from me in the future. In fact, tell her that I don't want to see her again. Yes, I know that's a pretty bald statement, but it's the truth. Wrap it up any way you like, just so long as she gets the message.' Majestically. 'I really can't be bothered with these hangers-on. There are better things to do than carrying the Ingrids of this world.

'And now I'm going to change. Can't plod across that field in flowered chiffon. Oh, and get hold of Ronnie Baxstead right now and tell him to meet me at the hut in three quarters of an hour...'

From that afternoon Shirley marked own Ezra as her private charity, and kept her away from her assistant. But Kate would not have been Kate if she had accepted that state of affairs. Shirley was viewed with wry respect by all her employees, and she reigned over her Parlour kingdom undisputed. But at the Old Hall, Kate was uncrowned queen, and as she was privy to Shirley's business matters as well as Shirley's private life, she knew what was happening at every level. So on the day that the hut was ready for its new occupants, she strolled over to view it for herself.

Shirley had spared no expense. The hut was

sound, white-washed and rather beautiful in its restored simplicity, but that was not all. Shirley had thought, as she would have said, of everything. Seven years ago the results of her generosity would have been appalling, but she had learned much from Kate. The simple furniture had been imported from Heal's, the simple curtain fabric from John Lewis, the simple china and cutlery from Habitat, the simple grey carpet from Axminster. A simple and expensive Swedish stove waited to be fired with wood from an outside lean-to neatly stacked with the finest oak logs. Three very expensive mattresses, and their luxurious bedding, were stacked against one wall.

How to be a saint in discreet opulence! Kate thought, smiling to herself.

Her thought suddenly seemed out of place. Her amusement vanished. Aware of a presence, she turned round and saw a small grey woman standing in the doorway. There was an instant's pause, then Kate recovered her smile and spoke in her cordial professional voice.

'Oh, good afternoon. You must be Ezra. I'm Kate Wing, Miss Pringle's assistant. I came down to see your new quarters. What an excellent job Mr Baxstead has made of them. You must be delighted.'

She held out her hand, but Ezra did not take it. She put both palms together and bowed, and her reply was so gentle that Kate did not register its import for a moment. The accent hinted at Indian parentage and an

126

English upbringing.

'Shirley is very kind, very good, but we do not need all this.'

Joel, and presumably Simeon, who had been following some way behind the healer, now came up and made namaste to Kate. She nodded pleasantly.

'You have met Joel,' said Ezra, 'and this is Simeon. They travel with me. They are my brothers in spirit.'

Yes, Joel is certainly lacking a few essential marbles, Kate thought as she smiled into his innocence, but the other one is streetwise. Now, what brings a big tough man, who looks as if he's done time, into this oddly assorted ménage?

Ezra's followers made namaste again and then their eyes widened as they saw the earthly paradise before them.

'It is very kind of Shirley,' Ezra repeated, 'but we cannot accept all this.'

The followers mimed obedience, but their faces fell.

Oh dear, Kate thought mischievously, every Jesus has his Judas, and in this case two of them. She saw that Ezra was looking at her as if waiting for the uncharitable thought to finish before she spoke. The eyes were very intelligent.

'Kate, will you thank Shirley for these handsome gifts, but explain that we neither want nor need possessions, and would she please take them away?'

Kate was again nonplussed. Then she said,

'Yes, of course. I'm sure she'll understand. Which possessions were you thinking of?' There were so many that she amended the question. 'Or rather, what exactly do you want to *keep*?'

The carpet and curtains and stove were apparently acceptable.

'What about the cutlery and china?' Kate asked.

The followers looked hopeful.

'We have our bowls and spoons,' said Ezra.

'And presumably you're going to sleep on the floor. But what about bedding?'

Ezra said, 'We have our blankets.' In honesty, she added, 'But our blankets are old and thin. Perhaps we shall be glad of these new ones.'

The followers were grateful.

Kate weighed Ezra up. She was impressed, despite her initial prejudice, but even more suspicious. Joel and Simeon she discounted entirely.

'Did you know,' Kate asked, 'that Shirley is sending you a hamper of food?'

From Fortnum & Mason, containing everything delicious.

The followers kept their eyes down lest Kate read their thoughts, but she could guess them.

'No hamper,' said Ezra gently. 'We eat very simply, very little. Rice, vegetables, fruit. Tell Shirley thank you, but no hamper.'

'As you wish, of course,' said Kate, courteous on Shirley's behalf.

Then Ezra smiled beautifully and said, 'But please tell her how grateful we are. She is a generous person. She has a good heart. I knew she would help us.'

'Oh well,' said Shirley, deflated, 'if it's against her way of life, that's that. I was going to do a lot more. I suppose she wouldn't let me give her the food she *does* eat, would she?'

'I imagine that part of her discipline is living on people's charity one day at a time. Regular contributions would rather defeat the purpose.'

'An occasional gift, perhaps?'

'Yes, I'm sure she'd accept that, but don't send a big basket of exotic fruits, just a few apples or whatever.'

Shirley's bright wig was at odds with her downcast face.

'You see,' she said shyly, 'I know she's a special person, and I do so want to help her.'

Kate had work to do and was not enamoured of Ezra, so she merely hugged Shirley and gave her a friendly kiss on the cheek.

'In that case you'll help by not helping too much,' she advised. Then brought her back to the present by adding, 'And as your masseuse comes at three, you'd better get ready for her.'

'But all this seems so wrong,' Shirley cried dramatically, spreading her arms to indicate Melbury Old Hall, 'when you think of that wonderful woman and her simple life.' Her voice throbbed. Her face was exalted.

'Your money enables you to give her a safe

and comfortable shelter.' Crisply.

'I suppose so. It doesn't seem much.'

Kate's patience had run out. She foresaw problems ahead with which she alone would have to deal.

'Shirley, you're not going all spiritual on me, are you?'

'Me? Spiritual?' said Shirley, and laughed.

But her tone lacked the proper degree of scorn, and the laugh was half-hearted.

Paupers Day

September

Extract from the *City Guide*:

The city has always prided itself on its liberal attitude towards the poor and unfortunate: a tradition that dates from the twelfth century, when broken meats from noble and ecclesiastical tables were placed outside the walls in baskets. One of its delightful customs, recorded in *The Festivals of Old England*, is Paupers Day, 'when the good Abbot Ignatius blessed one hundred poor people and sat them meetly in his hall and gave them of beef and bread and ale, and the monks waited on them and saw that each man ate his fill.'

The abbey is now a dignified ruin, but it is well worth a personal visit, or better still, taken as part of the city tour. A timetable of the touring buses may be obtained from the tourist centre in Queen's Square.

Paupers Day is still celebrated in the city.

This custom has changed over the centuries into a form that would be unrecognizable to the charitable Ignatius. Wooden bowls and benches have become tables furnished with fine linen, glass and cutlery. The decorum of the refectory has given way to the grandeur of the Guildhall. And the paupers are city dignitaries who pay dearly for their four-course lunch. It is a very fashionable occasion. To be invited to attend it is an indication of one's status in the city.

As a sop to the good Abbot Ignatius a collection is taken at the end of the meal, and the profits of this banquet maintain a caravan site, originally known as Paupers Ground but later renamed after its location: Marchfield. Here travelling people, circuses and fairs can stay for a while in reasonable comfort and security. Electricity and water are laid on. The authorities provide a wash-house, a bath-house and toilet blocks. There are two telephone kiosks, a postbox and a bus stop at the south end. A community nurse visits on Mondays. Rubbish is collected on Fridays. A glass-fronted notice board carries information of other public services available.

Marchfield is a showcase of its kind and the city had frequently been praised for its community spirit. To balance this munificence, the council keeps close records of visitors, and those who misbehave are not allowed to stay again. In consequence it can boast of having the best-behaved gipsies in England, who never steal openly but make a satisfactory living from crossing palms with pound coins and charging top prices for their handmade baskets, crocheted lace and whittled clothes pegs. Some gipsy families, who have visited the site for three generations, are known by name and regarded as local colour. But in recent months Marchfield has threatened to become a municipal headache.

On Paupers Day, at the top table in the Banqueting Hall, Hector was being especially charming to Shirley, mostly because he needed her and partly because he had been asked by important people to broach this delicate subject.

'I can't help thinking, my dear girl,' he began, 'that your boundless generosity – of which, I freely admit, we all take shocking advantage – may cause you problems you don't foresee.'

Shirley's auburn wig was as vibrant as ever. She had chosen to wear a plain but expensive grey costume for the lunch, and fewer pieces of jewellery than usual. In conversation she was voluble and vivacious, and her laugh rang out over the other tables. Yet in the intervals of silence her florid face looked shyly happy, and from the centre of her inner world she smiled to herself. At the moment she was occupied in demolishing a little sugar basket of sorbet, for her appetite never failed her, but Hector's remark brought her busy spoon to a halt.

'Of what are you speaking?' she asked haughtily, though she guessed.

Hector smiled and broke open his sugar basket. 'Of your household saint, my dear.'

'Do you mean *Ezra*?' Said with emphasis.

'I mean Ezra,' he agreed amiably, spearing a small strawberry and popping it into his mouth, 'who is – forgive my frankness – living on your land under your patronage, whilst using a municipal property, Grove Hill, for private purposes. Her visitors are gradually growing in quantity, if not in quality, and the council is beginning to wonder how many new travellers Marchfield can hold, and what to do when the site is full.'

Shirley chose her ground and stood firm.

'Has anyone complained of loss, theft, damage or trespass?'

'No, they haven't. But the council feels just a mite apprehensive. Half a dozen or so travellers asking to be prayed for – or whatever this person does – are no problem. A horde of them tramping up Grove Hill will mean trouble. This issue is further complicated by the popularity of a certain local author here present. Some quite distinguished and respectable people, having read *The Sacred Grove*, want to visit the site. We welcome them, of course, since they stay in the city and behave themselves properly and swell our coffers, but they won't come if they're to be confronted by a weird woman and jostled by a horde of impecunious and unwashed worshippers. And speaking of that peculiar little book, I'm surprised how much interest it's aroused. He's an odd sort of fellow, isn't he?'

Here he nodded in the direction of Jack Almond, who was enjoying his food and wearing the suit he had bought for his mother's funeral.

Shirley, who had glanced at the book jacket, remembered a quotation on the back.

'What on earth are you talking about, Hector?' she demanded. *'The Sacred Grove* is a fascinating mystery, and a delight to read.'

'Have you read it?' he asked, amused.

'Not right through. Not so's to speak. But I mean to. It's on my coffee table this minute. Anyway, Kate reads all the books that matter, and tells me about them, so I'm quite familiar with it.'

'There's a rumour that *The Sacred Grove* is your household saint's bible.'

'That's rubbish. Ezra is a deeply religious person and wouldn't regard an ordinary book as a bible.'

'But reading it did draw her to the grove, didn't it?'

Shirley could not deny that.

'And her preference for both the book and the grove will draw others,' Hector said seriously. 'Did you know that local sales have increased since she's been here?'

'Oh, shut up, Hector!' Shirley said, dropping hauteur in favour of armed combat. 'Jack Almond's book was a local best-seller long before Ezra arrived, and it had already caused quite a stir nationally – with a particular type of reader.'

'Exactly. His childish fantasy may well become a cult. That could be dangerous. And so could she!'

'Ezra?' Shirley cried, and gave a short, sharp bark of a laugh. 'Dangerous? There's not an atom of harm in her. She wouldn't know what harm was if it jumped out of her porridge.'

'She's dangerous *because* she's unaware.'

'She's a holy person, Hector, not that you'd know what that means!'

'She's a holy fool then.' He turned his attention to Jack. 'And he's a fool, too. Look at the company he keeps, for instance.' He pointed to the Press table, which was in a hilarious mood. 'Any man trying to further his career would cultivate influential people who could help him, instead of hobnobbing with the hoi polloi.'

At that moment Jack threw back his head and fairly shouted with laughter. The others ᴊoined in, but the joker remained solemn. He was a long-faced, curly-haired man with droll blue eyes, a crooked mouth and a broken nose. As the laughter died down he added another line to the tale and set them off again.

'I speak of Patrick Hanna,' said Hector drily, 'our professional troublemaker. Give him one sniff of a good story and he's shot it, skinned it, and hung it out to dry before you know what it's about.' He grinned mischievously at Shirley. 'Just think what he could do for your household saint if she wanted a spot of publicity.'

'Well, she wouldn't. She's not that sort. And Patrick's all right,' said Shirley uncomfortably, because he was currently on her invitation list and she found him entertaining. 'You two just rub each other up the wrong way.'

'What a pair he and Jack Almond make!' Hector continued, mocking them. His tone was lazy but his eyes glinted. 'Hardly an advertisement for the bachelor life. Have they heard of tailors and barbers, I wonder? Or dry-cleaners, for that matter! I notice spots of forgotten sauce on the lapel of Almond's so-called jacket, and the knot of Hanna's tie is halfway round his neck. You couldn't call either of them snappy dressers. You couldn't even call those garments suits!'

'I'm not talking to you in this mood, Hector,' said Shirley, and turned rather pointedly to someone else for conversation.

The private feud between Hector Mordant

and Patrick Hanna was a matter of amusement to everyone but Hector, who did not find his tormentor funny. Patrick, on the other hand, found Hector very funny indeed. Having no pretensions himself he made a butt of Hector, aiming his arrows at the public image and his darts at the private one. In turn, Hector plotted against him. He could not vie with Patrick in wit but he outmatched him in local politics. So they see-sawed up and down, gaining or losing points, and unable to leave each other alone.

Now Jocelyn Mordant, who had been listening to her husband's conversation while smiling and nodding at a loquacious neighbour, leaned forward and touched Shirley's hand to attract her attention. A tall, dark, slender woman, the perfect foil for Hector, she was the mistress of many pretty gestures and phrases while meaning none of them, but for once she seemed genuinely interested.

'Shirley, dear – about your amazing little saint – is it true she's a healer?'

Always glad to talk about Ezra, even to someone she disliked, Shirley replied, 'Oh yes. I'd been on painkillers and physiotherapy for months with this frozen shoulder,' hunching it up proudly, 'but she cured it in three sessions.'

'Does she do miracles?' Jocelyn asked. Reading Shirley's expression, she added quickly, 'I'm not being flippant. Unlike my gifted husband I'm inclined to believe in these things.'

She and Hector bestowed appreciative adjectives on each other as a matter of course. *My lovely wife. My gifted husband.* Social coinage.

Mollified, Shirley said, 'You mean like curing cancer?'

'I wasn't thinking of cancer exactly, but yes – can she cure serious illnesses?'

Hector leaned forward and asked the table at large, 'And can she minister to a mind diseased? Pluck from the heart a rooted sorrow? Oh, what absolute rot! Have you heard the story of the healer who ordered the lame man to throw away his crutches?'

'Yes. Several times,' said Shirley impatiently, and continued to talk to Jocelyn. 'To be honest, I don't know and I've never asked, but I will if you like.'

'An old school friend of mine...' Jocelyn began, and then as Hector showed signs of interrupting again, said quickly, 'You don't know her, darling!' And back to Shirley, 'She lives a long way off and I doubt if she's strong enough to travel. Can your Ezra heal from a distance?'

'My dear girl,' said Hector, amused, 'you sound positively medieval.'

Jocelyn laughed, subsided, and, as if her question were of no importance, began immediately to talk to someone else.

'The woman's either a fraud or as daft as a brush,' Patrick Hanna was saying. 'All that playing to the gallery with the little grey gown

138

and the begging bowl, and the two disciples. And speaking of them, I'd hazard a guess that one's done time and the other's escaped from a loony bin. So I'm inclined to think it's a con trick. Ah well, we'll find out when winter comes. Summer's a grand time to be holy, with the lady of the manor smiling on them as well as the weather, but they'll be up and off at the first cold snap, with everything they can lay their hands on – including the silver spoon from the lady's own mouth.'

The men round the table laughed again, but Jack remained serious.

'No, you're wrong there, Pat,' he said. 'Her followers may be suspect and she may be naive, but I believe she's genuine. Mark my words. She's genuine.'

'Well, you would say so, seeing that your book brought her here, and the sales are going up and up – unless, of course,' with a twinkle, 'you have a fancy for plain little middle-aged Indian women in dingy clothes?'

Jack shook his head and vowed that had nothing to do with it, but did not feel he could defend her further.

'Ah, here we come,' said Patrick, diverted, as the toast-master called for silence and the mayor prepared to give the Paupers Day speech. 'The full belly preaching about empty bellies. How I do love a hypocrite.'

Six months previously the city fathers had proclaimed their public goodwill, and bowed to the inevitable pressure of public opinion,

139

by granting a small group of travellers a semi-permanent place at Marchfield. This idea, floated around for some considerable time, had been clinched by the arrival of a group headed by a man named Mike. Like Neville and Nora Wing in their day, Mike was well-educated and articulate, though he spoke in the language of the road. Like them also, he was living according to his principles and in poverty. He approached the local authority to ask for a place in which the group could settle down, so that their children could be educated and work found for themselves.

The desire was understandable, but this would have counted for nothing in the city had he and his people not stayed in Marchfield before and reports about them been good. A cross between a patriarch and a mascot, Mike's command of the group was impressive. He interviewed well, and though outlandish in appearance seemed frank and intelligent. So they decided to give him a chance.

There were limits to their benevolence. The term *semi-permanent* meant as long as the travellers kept to the rules and unless the council had second thoughts or a new motive. Their site was clearly marked out, being the portion to the right of the main entrance and adjoining the bottom field of the Old Hall. They were warned to stay within these boundaries and, lest they stray further, a notice on Shirley's fence informed them that trespassers would be prosecuted.

Finally, to prevent disputes between Mike's group and those passing through, another notice set out the code of conduct for all itinerants. The tone was one of friendly patronage, but in plain language it meant *Any Fighting And You're Out!*

So far the scheme had been successful, though the atmosphere could be uneasy at times. The gipsies in particular, regarding themselves as the royalty of the road, looked on the new-age travellers as riff-raff and were inclined to be scornful. Still, the facilities were good, and no one wanted to lose a free lodging, so they were all careful not to quarrel.

As the privileged were listening to the Paupers Day speech in the Guildhall, a significant event was taking place in Marchfield, two miles away, where the encampment was swarming with people in transit.

An ancient dusty bus, containing a family of eight, had coughed into the compound and found nowhere to go. As part of the brotherhood of travellers they had a right to stay, but logistics were against them, so the bus stayed half in and half out of the entrance, with its sorry nose pointing hopefully forwards, and gave a despairing rattle followed by a deadly silence.

There is always a leader in every community, however temporary, and now a long cavernous-cheeked fellow with greying dreadlocks and worn jeans stepped forward

141

to assess the newcomers. Children appeared from everywhere and stood at a respectful distance from the man known as Mike, observing and listening. Women with toddlers straddled on their hips or clutching their hands came up behind them – a medley of unwashed faces, curtains of unbrushed hair and bright, cheap clothes. In silence they watched a man, and a woman with a baby in her arms, climb down from the bus, followed by five subdued, ragged children.

'All right, mate?' Mike asked, though it was evident that all was wrong.

'We been on the road since morning,' the man answered in a hoarse voice. 'The old bus cain't go no farther. We cain't go no farther, neither.'

'What's your name, mate? Where've you come from?'

A familiar story emerged in fragments. Unemployed. Behind with the rent. Moved out. Moved on. Police at every turn. No work. No money. No food. Begging. Sometimes, in desperation, stealing. They had heard on the grapevine that this was a good place to come, that they would be looked after. The baby was sick, and the mother, having no nourishment herself, had none to give.

At this his wife began to cry without shame, like a child, mouth open and askew, tears running down her cheeks, sobs coming in gulps. And, because she had broken down at last, her children followed suit, clasping their

142

arms round her waist and knees for comfort. The man stood slightly apart, head bowed, shoulders shaking, taking their grief upon himself, trying to hide his own.

They could not be turned away.

Mike clapped his hands and shouted, 'All right, everybody. They've had a rough time – like the rest of us. How about a mug of tea all round? What about a butty for these here kids? We can rummage up a meal between us, can't we, mates?'

His tall, gaunt woman came up and said quietly in his ear, 'But where are we going to put them, Mike?'

He hesitated, but life had changed since Ezra arrived, and Shirley's adjoining field was lying fallow. Under his orders the men in his group took down the notice, removed part of her fence, and stacked the wood neatly on one side so that it could be remade when necessary. Vehicles were moved together to leave a pathway to the field. Then the new-comer climbed into his bus, which made a final feeble effort and hawked its way into a corner under the trees.

Mike put his arm round the man's shoulders as they walked back to the camp.

'You'll be right, mate,' said Mike. 'Tomorrow I'll see Ezra and she'll have a word with the owner. Ezra can heal the sick kid, too. They told you the truth when they told you to come here, mate. You'll be right, mate. You'll be right.'

Parting

Hector's marriage had died long since, and when he spoke of his family at all these days it was with resentment. Jocelyn's extravagance, the childrens' school fees, the expensive house on Beck Hill sapped him financially and emotionally.

'I get nothing out of it!' he would grumble.

So, Kate reflected, she and No 11 Mulberry Street should have been a source of comfort in contrast to his cold home, but in fact she and Hector now saw less of each other than they had when she was his assistant. Gradually they had drifted into a state that resembled an aging marriage but without its benefits. He would arrive late and be too tired to make love. He would cancel an evening together at the last minute because something else had come up. And she had no redress. Unlike a wife, who could legitimately complain that he neglected her, Kate had to accept the situation with as much grace as she could muster. Their relationship was stagnating. It had begun as a bubbling rill. Now she visualized it as a still pool emanating the odour of death.

Hector must have been thinking along the

144

same lines, because when they next met, over a drink in a wine bar, he began with an apology.

'Sorry I've been so dreary lately, but – quite apart from the problems at home – I've been thinking a lot about us and the future.'

His tone was tender and her spirits revived.

'This present situation isn't satisfactory for either of us, Kate, and it's certainly not fair on you. You deserve far more than part-time attention from me.'

She knew he was selfish and self-seeking, but in his own way he had taken care of her and she never doubted that he loved as well as admired her.

'I blame myself. I must do something about it,' said Hector decisively. 'We can't drift on. Yes, I must do something about it.'

So, perhaps the hurly-burly of the chaise longue was over – not that there had been much hurly-burly recently – and they could seek the deep peace of the marriage bed. Of *their* marriage bed.

Kate was not such a fool as to think he could leave his family easily or cheaply. Jocelyn for one, pretty and acquisitive, would exact a high price. But Hector was tougher and cleverer than his wife at driving a hard bargain. Celebrations was financially sound. Kate earned a good income. They could work something out. And it would be wonderful, after years of secrecy, to come out into the open and be accepted.

She lowered her eyes so that he would not

145

see the hope in them.

'Can't stay any longer, I'm afraid,' said Hector penitently. 'Sorry about that, too, but on top of everything else I've got trouble at Celebrations.' He picked up her hand and kissed it. 'I really shall have to find a new assistant.'

He had hinted at this two or three times in the last few weeks, though Kate's latest successor had seemed to be as dedicated and efficient as the long-forgotten Miss Benbow.

'Why, what's wrong with Paula?' Kate asked.

'Oh, I don't know!' Hector had replied, shrugging his shoulders, dismissing the subject as soon as he had raised it. 'I think she has her eyes on a greener field. But I shan't mind.'

Kate began to fit these pieces together to form a promising new jigsaw. He was making a break with both home and office. Was he thinking of a double partnership? Wife and business assistant?

Smiling, she replied, 'I know you'll sort everything out beautifully.'

Celebrations as a firm had kept in touch with Kate at Melbury Old Hall, and during her years there Kate had acted as go-between, translating Hector's ideas into practical terms and helping the house to pay something towards its upkeep.

At first this had been easy, because Shirley offended Kate's sense of rightness, but as she became aware of the person behind the

146

bombast, Kate had grown to like her new employer and her loyalties were divided. Not that Hector exploited Shirley in terms of money, but he did treat the Old Hall as a company annex and Kate as its organizer, and left her to explain, persuade and smooth down in his wake.

This had succeeded so far because Shirley could not resist playing the county lady. To entertain local and visiting celebrities at the Hall was her delight. To open her park and gardens to the public and walk among the common people, smiling and nodding, and hear someone say, 'Look! That's Miss Pringle!' was balm to her plebeian soul. And Kate was by her side, or lady-in-waiting distance behind her, to make up for any shortcomings.

'I can stay with her until she finds a new assistant. Train the assistant if necessary. My former move in reverse. I shan't have anything on my conscience. I've done my best for Shirley. Now I must look after myself.'

So Kate thought.

Hector finished his drink quickly and stood up.

'Must go. No need for you to hurry. Have another on me. We'll talk seriously at the weekend. How about dinner at Lamprey's on Saturday evening?'

Lamprey's was a country clubhouse some miles outside the city. All their personal venues were out of town, discreet, and possessed of tables in private corners where

147

they were unlikely to be seen. But Kate was tired of hiding and being hidden, so for once she turned down Hector's suggestion. She needed this talk to be on her own ground.

'No, let me cook dinner for us at Mulberry Street.'

Surprisingly he agreed, only stipulating that he brought the wine.

The evening was progressing splendidly, and Kate felt awash with gratitude.

Hector had arrived early for once, laden with delicacies from Fortune's Food Hall and dark-red roses from Charmier's.

'Father Christmas cometh early!' he announced, and proceeded to clutter up Kate's small kitchen and interfere with her arrangements.

Although he knew that she had planned and was cooking their evening meal, he had still wandered pleasurably round the Food Hall, buying anything that caught his fancy: a box of Belgian chocolates, an oblong dish of French paté, a tin of German biscuits, a jar of almonds in honey, a bottle of excellent cognac, and a fine champagne. That he had chosen champagne was a good omen. Champagne is for celebrating.

All these he poured forth on the kitchen table, giving orders as to their destinations, while Kate laughed and protested and tried to clear a space for them.

'We shall need an ice jacket for the champers, and it should be cooled at once. And

148

these,' burdening her with roses, 'need their stems cutting and standing in a bucket of cold water for an hour.'

'I know. I know.' Loving him, exasperated by him.

Hector was wearing a new blue-grey suit and looking exceptionally well and handsome. The years had been kind to him, leaving him little heavier, a little greyer, but upright, fresh-complexioned and flowing with vitality.

'Stop fluttering round and come here!' he commanded.

He gave her a long, full, lingering kiss, such as they had enjoyed in their best and earliest years together. Afterwards they held each other close, and she laid her warm cheek against his cool one and breathed the smoky scent of autumn air.

'My girl!' said Hector softly. 'You've always been my girl, haven't you?'

He gave her a final kiss and released her.

'What a wonderful smell!' was his next comment as he strode into the little passage she called a hall, shrugging off his overcoat.

'One of your favourite dishes, and I must concentrate on it,' she called over her shoulder. 'Why don't you go into the sitting room and pour yourself a drink?'

'No, I'm staying here because we begin with champagne,' he decided, and further hindered her by demanding that the glasses be chilled in the refrigerator, which meant that she had to move their desserts on to a lower shelf.

There would have to be some tactful compromises when they lived together permanently, Kate reflected. Hector had a habit of taking over every situation, which she found increasingly irritating. But their occasions together were so few and precious that she would not challenge his supervision. She even took a certain pleasure in the disruption he caused because it showed that he was involved.

'Here's to the moment!' Hector cried.

She moved the saucepan off the burner for a third time, to clink and drink.

'Is the table laid?' he asked, hanging round her.

'Not yet, but everything's on that tray if you'd like to do it for us.'

Left in peace, she brought the sauce to a successful conclusion and placed it in a makeshift bain-marie to keep warm. By the time Hector returned she was ready with their first course, reloaded the tray, and sent him on ahead.

Tonight she would take her place at his side. They would be partners in life as well as in business, and Kate felt that she was equal to both roles, and had earned them both.

They had dined deliciously, chatted companionably, and were sipping cognac in front of the fire when Hector broached the reason for this particular occasion. His tone was easy. He seemed relaxed. Only Kate, who knew

150

him intimately, recognized signs of tension: a tightening of the manicured hand round the glass, a twitch at the corner of his mouth.

He began by saying how much she meant to him, his appreciation of her as a woman and a former business partner. She listened, lips slightly parted in pleasure, warmed by food and wine and the timbre of his voice.

'I think we're agreed that things can't go on as they have been,' he said, and she nodded. 'We've reached some sort of impasse, and when that happens the only way out is to cut through and be honest.' She nodded again. 'You're in your glorious prime, my dear,' he said, and turned to her and raised his glass to toast the fact, 'but I'm well past mine. No, no, don't protest, Kate. I wouldn't confess it to anyone but you, but it's the truth. I'm something less than I was, whereas you are at your best, and will continue to be so for many years yet...'

A small, cold fear gripped her throat.

'I freely confess that I've been selfish – although you're a little to blame for that.' He kissed her hand, smiling at her. 'You shouldn't be so captivating.'

She could not find her voice, but the apprehension in her eyes made him look away. He kissed her hand once again and laid it in her lap. She stared at it as if his kiss had branded the flesh.

He said, caressingly, 'Kate, you have the best years before you, and the world at your feet. That isn't the case with me. Most of my troubles are due to the fact that I'm not committing myself to either you or my family. It's time that you were free, and I stopped asking for the moon and settled down as a married man should.' Here he waited for a few mistrustful seconds but she said nothing. 'I shall miss you quite horribly, Kate, but I know this is the right thing to do.' He got up and stood by the fireplace.

Her anguish was so great that she feared it might explode from her in some obscene act of birth, and appal them both. Her feast had become a famine.

He continued as if she were going along with him, though he must have known she was not.

'So let's be grateful for some wonderful years. And when you find the man you deserve, my dear, I'll conquer my desire to cut his throat, and dance at your wedding instead. Truly, I shall be very glad – and very sorry. Quite apart from your charms, I treasure your companionship and your abilities. And now, my dear, whilst thanking you for a lovely evening, I must return to duty!'

As she did not reply he finished his cognac and set the glass down with a final little smack.

Voiceless, she stood up and preceded him down the stairs to the narrow hallway. She folded her arms to stop them from shaking. Usually she helped him on with his overcoat; now she watched him shrug it on unaided. Looking past him into the mirror she observed the back of his well-brushed head and the pale oval of her face. She was astonished how calm she seemed – white and stiff, but calm.

He, too, was pale, but his concern was not for her but for himself, and she saw that he was afraid lest she make a scene.

He said, as casually as he could, 'It's a source of some satisfaction to me to know that you have your own house and a good job, and if there's anything I can do for you, at any time, I always will. We'll be seeing each other pretty regularly in any case. And of course we'll be working together on the July concert festival.'

She would have given much to speak, tried, but could not.

He was frightened then and tried to turn fear away with a rough joke.

'Now you're not going to take this too seriously and have a nervous breakdown, are you?'

He had raised Miss Benbow from the shadows, a sorry ghost, and Kate looked on this spectre with terror and new knowledge. She was much the same age Miss Benbow had been when she was paid off and discarded. And he was looking for a new secretary. Perhaps Paula would be set up as his mistress in place of Kate. Perhaps he had found someone even younger, who could be manipulated. She saw a pattern in events, and wondered why she had not recognized it sooner.

'I mean,' said Hector quickly, 'I don't want you to be hurt.'

He tried to put his arms round her but she stepped away from him and her voice returned. It was rather high and tight, but deliberate.

'You flatter yourself, Hector. From what I have seen of marriage I don't want any part in it, so don't expect to be invited to *my* wedding. I have every intention of enjoying – and valuing – my single freedom.'

At the moment freedom was a vast white landscape, with herself as a solitary figure journeying nowhere. She hoped that would change. Meanwhile she opened her front door. She observed the situation dispassionately.

'Your sense of occasion is quite faultless, Hector,' Kate heard her voice say. 'That was a tricky situation to handle. You did it awfully well. Goodnight.'

He tried to say something but she shut the door on him and waited until she heard his footsteps walking away from her down the quiet street. Then she turned to all she had left: her image in the mirror.

'And you did very well yourself,' she told it. 'You went down in style.'

Then she crouched on the tiled floor, cradled her head in her arms, and sobbed without restraint.

Insiders

Rejection

Christmas approached, and the city prepared to don its festive robes. Over the past three months Kate had hidden and carried her burden of pain, while Hector's star rose and shone brighter than ever. The true scale of his plan for the concert festival was now revealed, to the consternation of Shirley, the misery of Kate, and the boundless admiration of the city fathers. What a son was this, they thought, and invited him to switch on the Christmas lights and to be guest of honour at a select sherry party afterwards in the City Hall.

Hector exercised his sense of occasion by sending an invitation to Shirley and revealed the thickness of his hide by including another for Kate. These arrived by the afternoon post while the two women sat in Kate's office, stamping and ticking off the last of four hundred Christmas cards.

'The cold-blooded, black-hearted bastard!' Shirley cried, and threw her invitation into the fire, from which Kate rescued it at the expense of her fingers.

'You have to go,' she said stoically, 'and so

157

have I. It's no use making a fuss.'

Shirley snatched off her wig and cast it down on the carpet.

'Where are my cigarettes?' she demanded.

'You've given up smoking.'

'I'll give it up again tomorrow, but right now I need a whisky and a cigarette.'

'You've given up drinking too, remember.'

'Listen to me, Catriona,' Shirley commanded, pointing a stout forefinger at her assistant. 'First of all, I am very angry because of what he's done to *you*. Secondly, I'm madder than a wet hen because of the trick he's played on *me*. And thirdly, I am bloody furious because I can't do anything about any of it. Now where have you put my whisky and cigarettes?'

Kate fetched them from their hiding places.

'Thank you,' said Shirley. Her dignity was great. She took a long swallow and inhaled deeply. 'Ah! That's better.'

'Remind me to tell you, in ten years' time, just how good this has been for your heart and lungs,' said Kate.

'That's better, too,' said Shirley, approving the dry tone. 'You sound more like your shitty old self.'

She picked up her wig and adjusted it. Then sat frowning and drinking.

'Four or five thousand bloody proles roaming loose round my park!' she said, ruminating. 'Three bloody choirs. Two bloody orchestras. Half a dozen soloists and a fucking conductor.' Her eyes flashed at Kate. 'Did

158

you know about this?' she asked. 'Because if you did, you can clear out now!'

Kate understood her too well to take offence. Her answer was cool and reasonable.

'No, Hector kept it to himself until he'd made sure of the final details. I think he knew that I'd warn you otherwise.'

Shirley returned to the enjoyment of alcohol and nicotine.

'All those fucking trippers, with picnic baskets and deckchairs and kids and cars. And he hands it over to *us*! What are we going to do about the parking?'

'We shall have to open the top and bottom fields, turn the lane into a one-way system, and bring them round by the back of the house.'

Shirley looked at her doubtfully. 'Is that an inspired guess or a practical suggestion?'

'Absolutely practical. I was studying a map of the estate this morning and working it out. We've never done anything as big as this before.'

'And never will again.'

Kate made the best of a rotten bargain. 'Oh, I don't know. It could be a useful rehearsal if we open the house and garden on a permanent basis. We'll rent portable loos and run refreshment stalls this time, but – with your permission – I'd like to have a word with Ronnie about the cost of putting up a permanent toilet block, because if we decide to go into this business professionally we shall need a lunch and tea room too. Later on, if

159

we make a go of it, we can extend the facilities to include a restaurant. I spoke to a friend of mine in the National Trust recently – they do these things so well – and he's sent me all the information. Actually, I've been quite intrigued—'

'Well, let's stick to the concert for the moment,' said Shirley good-naturedly, 'and before you turn my home into a going concern, allow me to remind you that one tycoon in the house is quite enough, thank you, Madam Wing!'

'I take your point, Madam Pringle,' said Kate, smiling, 'but we must always look at least one move ahead – and judging from the house accounts we're coming up to Crunch Time.'

'You sound like bloody Hector.'

'He trained me,' Kate said simply. 'And he's the best in the business.'

Shirley refilled her glass and lit another cigarette. Kate sat and mused, wretched.

'What I really mind,' said Shirley, 'is that he's left me no get-out clause. Are you absolutely sure there's nothing I can do or say?'

'Nothing. He made sure that all the important people knew just before we did, and they're thrilled to bits. Your best bet is to acknowledge the fervent thanks for your generosity and kindness, etcetera, and – if you're feeling mischievous – to suggest ever so subtly that it was your idea in the first place. That will do you even more good, and will certainly annoy Hector, who likes all the

160

credit.'

Shirley raised her eyes to heaven and invoked the god of vengeance.

'May the rain pour down all day and soak the bloody lot of them!' She moved on to the next grievance. 'And the bastard arranged it for the evening, so I've got all the principals on my hands. I'll have to give them tea beforehand and supper afterwards, put them up for the night, and serve breakfast in the morning.'

'It can be done,' said Kate, who would be organizing hospitality. 'And, to give Hector his due, Celebrations aren't mean with their money. You'll be properly compensated – and we do need the cash.'

'Yes, I know, but it's a hell of a disturbance and a heap of hard work.' Then, remembering upon whose shoulders the work would fall, added, 'For you.'

'It's also a valuable experience, which otherwise I shouldn't have had, and the wider the range of organization, the more I'm able to offer in future.'

Shirley looked across at her quickly. 'You're not thinking of leaving me, are you?'

'No. But you may *want* me to go sometime, or I may *have* to go – for whatever reason. We must be practical,' said Kate. 'Everything changes. Nothing remains the same. No one lives for ever.'

Shirley finished her whisky in one long swallow and stubbed out her half-smoked cigarette. 'You sound like Ezra,' she said

161

accusingly.

'I wouldn't know. I have no dealings with the lady.'

'It was Ezra who persuaded me to give up smoking and drinking.'

'So I thought. And how are you doing?'

'God, you are a bitch!'

'You like bitches. They keep your wits sharp.'

Shirley laughed and shook her head. 'I like *you*, at any rate,' she said. 'Here, hide these things away from me. I'll try again tomorrow.' Then, reverting to their former conversation, 'So do I conclude that we watch the bastard switch on the Christmas lights and then go to his fucking sherry party in our best bibs and tuckers with smiles all over our faces?'

'And hatred in our hearts,' Kate added lightly. 'Yes, that's about it.'

She had always held deep reservations about Christmas. As a child, its magical atmosphere had been ruined for her by the need to incorporate Nora's lame ducklings into the ceremonies. There would be a rare feeling of tranquillity on Christmas Eve when the other children were in bed. In harmony for once, Kate and her mother would decorate the tree and lay the parcels beneath it in little glittering piles. In a moment of beauty, when her father switched on the lights the three of them became the family Kate had always wanted. Then some insecure child would have a nightmare, or wander downstairs

162

crying, or be sick, and the whole thing was spoiled. It was the same on Christmas Day when her father carved the first splendid slice of turkey, or her mother carried in the pudding wreathed with flickering blue flames, and Kate wanted to stop the world for a minute or two and contemplate the spectacle. But always came the unbridled shouts of glee, the clamouring cries of, 'Me! Me! Me first! Mam! Dad! I want ... Gimme...' and she could not eat a mouthful with true enjoyment.

I was a healthy child, a pretty child, a bright child, full of spirit, Kate thought. Why wasn't I enough for them?

Still, she went home for Christmas most years because Nora felt the family should be together then. Occasionally Shirley persuaded her to join the house party at Melbury Old Hall, at which Kate worked quite as hard as she played. And in no year could Hector leave his family. So Christmas had always been a matter of duty, and Kate was never given the chance to find out how she would celebrate the occasion if she could choose.

'Oh, by the way,' Shirley began, in the jocular tone that made Kate suspicious, 'I shan't be having a house party this year, so that's one little job less for you.'

'It is indeed. And not so little. Are you going away?'

'No. I've decided to spend Christmas here alone.'

'But you don't like being alone.'

'Well, not exactly alone. Not all the time.' The words came strangely to her lips, embarrassing her. 'I'll be ... communing ... with myself. It's ... it's a form of meditation.'

You're a highly unlikely candidate for meditation, Kate thought.

Aloud, she guessed, 'A Christmas vigil? With Ezra and followers?'

'And anyone else who wants to join us. It sounds very nice from what Ezra told me.' Defensively. 'We're all meeting in the grove a few minutes before midnight, well wrapped-up, each of us carrying a candle, and we meditate from midnight until dawn on Christmas Day.' The idea exalted her. Her broad face was shy and rapt beneath the perky wig.

'You'll be stiff with cold and...' Kate was about to say *boredom* when Shirley's vulnerability stopped her. 'Be careful you don't catch cold,' she finished.

'Ezra doesn't feel the cold, and she doesn't wrap herself up – though she said we should – and she can sit like that for hours.'

Kate quelled an acerbic comment and kept her tone equable. 'She's had a lot of practice. You should take it more easily.'

'I had wondered,' Shirley said, 'whether to offer a few braziers. To stand round us. You know, just to take the chill off the air.'

Kate suppressed her amusement. 'You can try, Shirley, but I think you're expected to transcend the weaknesses of the flesh, as it

164

were. Just wrap yourself up well.'

'I expect you're right.' Downcast for a moment, she brightened again. 'But it'll be a wonderful experience, won't it? The vigil and the candles?'

Kate endeavoured to be sympathetic. 'I'm sure it will. And the grove should look lovely from a distance, as if the trees were full of fireflies.'

'Yes,' said Shirley, whose sense of natural beauty was non-existent. 'Trees full of fireflies. Yes. That'll be nice.'

A magpie for information, Kate had to know more, but she phrased her question tactfully. 'I didn't realize that Ezra was a Christian. She seems more like a Buddhist.'

Grateful to speak of the beloved, Shirley said, 'She's not either of them. She says there's a spirit that's common to all religions and she lives by that. That's her message. And she's working towards an end when everyone stops being prejudiced, and then the world will be united. At least,' Shirley said uncertainly, 'I think that's what she means. It sounds better coming from her.'

'I see,' said Kate thoughtfully. Her sceptical mind added: *An ambitious lady*.

As before, Ezra in person or in absence answered her thought.

Shirley continued, 'She says that her talent for healing is a small thing – mind you, she's very modest and I don't believe that – but Christ was a great healer, and a great religious leader, so we're keeping a vigil to

165

celebrate His birth.'

But the 25th December was originally a pagan festival, Kate thought, and I'm not sure whether Christ's actual date of birth is known.

Aloud, she asked, 'What do you do when the vigil is over?'

'We fast until midnight on Christmas Day.'

'All together? Out there in the cold?'

'Oh no. We go home and fast by ourselves.'

Kate wanted to say, 'You are not going to enjoy this, Shirley!' but she compromised. 'And what happens when you break your fast?'

She could guess: Shirley raiding the midnight larder, praying there was plenty of Christmas provender left, and eating everything she could lay both hands on.

Again she was answered.

'Ezra warned me not to eat too much soon afterwards, so I must be careful.'

'I take it that the staff are allowed to gorge themselves as usual?'

'Oh yes. Christmas turkey, pudding and all.' Shirley was wistful about this. 'But I shall be sticking to a vegetarian diet – will you arrange that with Mrs Bailey? – and as I need to be on my own for three days you can have that time off.'

'Thank you. I suppose we're still giving our usual party on New Year's Eve?'

'Oh yes. I shall have got over the meditation by then.' She referred to this state of grace as if it were a case of measles. 'You go home to

Mum and have a merry old family Christmas.'

'So when do you want me back? The twenty-eighth?'

'Yes, that would be about right. And as I'll be off that diet by the end of the week,' said Shirley, becoming cheerful, 'we can have a slap-up party.'

A rich contralto voice, answering Kate's telephone call, said, 'Hello? This is the flower farm. Hang on a minute, will you? I've got a child here who's— Come out! Come out and bring that dog bowl with you! I know what's going on...'

Kate smiled, sighed, waited until the voice returned to the telephone.

'She'll eat anything,' Nora explained. 'Coal, chalk, dog food. It isn't as if I starved her. Far from it.' She remembered she was speaking to someone. 'Hello? Are you still there? Who is it?'

'It's me, Mother. Kate.'

The voice became warm but wary. 'Hello, love. How are you? You're still coming for lunch on Sunday, aren't you?'

'Yes, I am. And I rang to tell you that I'm free from Christmas Eve to Boxing Day, and I can stay the whole time. We shan't be interrupted for once.'

She was glad to be able to say that. It sounded generous, family-like, the sort of thing Nora wanted to hear. For once she meant to live up to her mother's expectations,

167

however difficult the three days might be. But the expected response was not forthcoming.

Nora temporized. 'Why, what's happened, love? Is Shirley going away?'

Kate felt the incipient chill of rejection. 'No, but she doesn't need me.' She could not help adding, 'I thought you'd be pleased.'

The voice was perplexed. 'I am. Of course I am.' Then, to herself, 'Hmm. What to do?' She again temporised. 'Katie, there's just one fly in the ointment – though not as far as I'm concerned – in fact I'm thrilled, Katie, really thrilled, and it makes no difference to me, because I'd be glad to have you both. But.' A brief pause. 'You see, I know you've found it difficult to get away from Shirley in the past, and then again, it's noisy and untidy here with the children and the dogs, and you like things just so, and you've got a lot of smart friends and he's on his own...' She recollected herself.

'Well, to cut a long story in quarters, I've invited Jack Almond and he's staying with us over the Christmas holiday. I was going to ring you to tell you not to bother about us this year, but I've been so busy one way and the other, and I thought you'd be pleased because it means you can have the sort of Christmas you like instead of mucking in with us, and I know you and Jack don't hit it off.'

'I see,' said Kate. A silence. 'Is he coming on Christmas Eve?'

'No, he's out with Pat Hanna that evening,

but he's coming in the morning on Christmas Day – well, Neville says he'll come when he's sorted out his hangover and it'll be nearer afternoon.' She laughed. 'You know what your father's like.'

Kate made her voice sound bright. 'Never mind. It was only an idea. I won't spoil your arrangements. Look, I tell you what I can do, I'll come for supper on Christmas Eve and bring your presents, and then leave you all to it.'

'But what will you do with yourself over the holiday?' Nora asked, and did mind, but also hoped.

'Take my choice of second-best options,' said Kate gaily. 'There's always so much going on...'

Nora's voice was relieved. 'That's what I thought. "She'll be invited everywhere", I thought.' Her maternal instinct returned. 'But are you sure, Katie? Because you're my daughter and I'm not going to see you turned away for Jack Almond. If you don't mind sharing Christmas with him we can all pull together and have a good time.'

'No, no. Let's leave it as it is.' She made an effort. 'How are you all? I see that the women's page of the *Courier* has published another of Patrick Hanna's features on you this week. They've chosen a good time, too, just before Christmas. Excellent work. Stunning photographs. The trouble is,' Kate made up a story to please her mother, 'you're going to be deluged with orphans!'

169

Nora gave a deep chuckle. Then she said seriously, 'Katie, are you sure you're all right? I don't mean about Christmas. You've had a faraway look for quite a while, as if something had gone wrong. Your father and I were talking about you only last night and we wondered...'

'No, no, I'm fine. Never better.'

'We just thought...' Her maternal instinct was given no time to expand on this theme. Kate heard excited squeals in the background. 'Oh dear me. Not again. I'll have to go, love. Dennis is upsetting the girls. He doesn't mean any harm but he *will* kiss them.'

'OK. Give my love to Dad. See you on Sunday. Bye!'

Kate put down the receiver and rubbed her arms, unable to admit the extent of the shock. She walked down the corridor to Shirley's sitting room and found her sticking a notice on the door with Blu-tack: DO NOT DISTURB.

Kate said airily, in answer to her employer's florid embarrassment, 'Cross my heart and hope to die, I promise not to come near you unless summoned. Does this mean you don't need me this afternoon?'

'That's right. I shall be meditating.'

Kate's tone was blithe. 'Oh. Fine. Everything in the office is up to date. If I'm not wanted, could I do some Christmas shopping?'

Shirley was only too pleased to be rid of her.

'Good idea. See you tomorrow morning.'

The prickle along Kate's spine made her look beyond Shirley. There was no one to be seen but she sensed that Ezra was in the room.

'Enjoy!' Shirley said deeply and closed the door.

Years ago, straggling behind the family group, conscious of her shortcomings and theirs, Kate had wanted to be a grown-up lady with high-heeled shoes and lipstick and shining hair, and they had laughed at her.

She felt as isolated now as she had done then, but at least she had achieved the image. So she took it for an elegant stroll down Broad Street, entering the splendid shops, buying exquisitely appropriate gifts, and finally treating it to the full tea at Mrs Porter's crowded Parlour, because when she got home the evening could only offer solitude and eggs on toast.

Christmas

By eleven o'clock on Christmas Eve pin-points of light were already illuminating the grove. The night was dry and fine and cold.

Driving towards Southgate, on her way back from the flower farm, Kate stopped by the side of the road for a while to watch a procession of the faithful climbing the hill, singly or in little groups, shielding their candles. She imagined Shirley, torn between her devotion to Ezra and her passion for comfort, suffering from arthritic joints – happy to sit near the beloved, but wishing she could stretch out her legs in front of a blazing fire, sip a long, hot whisky toddy and smoke a couple of cigarettes. She wondered what her employer would meditate on throughout the long night: probably the financial success of Porter's Parlours, the financial drain of Melbury Old Hall, and the unavailability of Ezra. Mercifully, she might doze off.

Kate grinned to herself and shook her head. The vagaries of mankind, including her own, never failed to amuse her. For she saw herself clearly, gave herself no quarter, made no excuses, finding that every achievement was

172

followed by another challenge, and every answer by another question.

Nevertheless, the evening at Peddleford Farm had restored her spirits. Nora was more than usually attentive, making sure that her daughter's supper plate was unchipped, her chair dusted, the dogs kept by the hearth, and the usual stray child settled on the sofa out of the way with a picture book. Kate had observed these precautions with a pang, and enquired sympathetically about the progress of the fostering case. She had also re-dressed the Christmas tree and given Nora good advice as she watched her unwrap Kate's presents early.

'I chose these especially for you, Mother, and for no one else. So don't let the children dress up in the kaftan or pee on the herb pillow, or squirt Arpège on the dogs! Understood?'

Nora promised meekly and, unfolding the kaftan said, 'This'll be comfortable. I shall look quite slim in it. Oh, and isn't it lovely?' Smoothing the shimmering rainbow of colours. 'And it's come from the Fashion Cabin! Oh, Katie, you shouldn't go spending your money on me like this!'

'Of course I should,' said Kate, well pleased.

Then she had taken her mother over, first quelling the menagerie with one long, hard look. She brushed Nora's hair and coiled it into a shining knot, made up her face, arrayed her in the kaftan, and scented her lavishly and

173

exquisitely.

'Now, sit down, and I'll finish the supper,' Kate said.

'Not in those nice clothes you won't!'

'They're all washable, and I can put an apron on. Sit down. What's the name of that child?' Pointing to a snub-nosed, round-eyed little girl who was sucking her thumb and watching Kate, overawed.

Nora's voice embraced the child even as she held out her arms, inviting the kaftan and hair to be messed in a good cause.

'This is our Antoinette. We call her Toni for short. And she's spending Christmas with us because her mummy has had to go away.' Over the child's head she mouthed, 'Off with the latest boyfriend and doesn't care tuppence for this dear little soul!'

'I see.'

Kate's tone was ironic but Nora disregarded it, demanding of the world at large, 'So aren't we lucky to have Toni staying with us?'

Kate answered even more ironically, 'I can't imagine anything nicer. Is she one of the little girls whom Dennis kisses?'

The child put one fist in one eye and opened her mouth to howl. But before she could begin, Kate said briskly, 'You should slap Dennis when he teases you, Toni, and say "No!" Like this,' and she picked up the plump little hand and brought it down smartly on her own wrist. 'Kiss? Slap! No! Kiss? Slap! No! He'll soon stop. Try it.'

Neville, coming in at that moment, laughed

174

aloud, and Reggie imitated him even more loudly.

'What a thing to teach a child!' Nora chided, but had to laugh too.

Toni gave up the attempt to cry and giggled instead. She pursed up her lips, smacked a loud kiss to the air, slapped her wrist smartly, and said, 'No!'

She was to repeat this at intervals during the evening. Kiss. Slap! 'No!' Putting her hands over her mouth, tittering through her fingers, rocking with glee.

'I think Dennis's kissing days are over,' Neville remarked. Then, staring at his wife, an empress in her finery, he added, 'Perhaps it's as well or he might start kissing you, Nora!'

So the evening was a great success and, though Kate could not bring herself to cuddle Toni, who was inclined to dribble with affection, she unpinned a taffeta carnation on her jacket that the child had admired, and gave it to her. She patted the dogs and spoke to them kindly, was full of compliments for the supper and the presents her family had chosen, and finally she encouraged Reggie to talk about football, a subject on which he was knowledgeable to the point of tedium. In short, she did her best to please and was so successful that her conscience twinged again.

Her parents were all smiles as they stood on the threshold to see Kate off, and Nora, coming out with the truth, however tactless, said, 'Well, what a lovely evening we've had,

Katie. Why can't you always be like this?'

Neville covered the indiscretion by putting his arm round his daughter's shoulders, saying, 'We can't have special evenings all the time, can we? But this has been one of them. Thank you, love. Have a good Christmas.' And he kissed her as if he knew how bruised and desolate she really was.

Kate kept her lone festival in style and according to tradition. Nora had given her half a dozen new-laid eggs and a home-made loaf. Fortune's Food Hall provided her with a choice poussin and a diminutive pudding, a fillet steak for Boxing Day and a miniature cheeseboard. She bought a selection of organic fruit and vegetables. She chose half bottles of wine and champagne and treated herself to six yellow roses from Charmier's. She selected a dwarf fir tree from the market and decorated it with two boxes of tiny silver and gold baubles from Fairfax's. Beneath it she laid the presents from her family and the envelope containing the usual Christmas cheque from Shirley. This year Hector's gift, usually king of the occasion, was absent, and so was the promise of his presence later on, but she would not think of that. I'm going to spoil myself, she promised.

So she rose late on Christmas morning and took her breakfast back to bed. She looked at her presents again. She cooked and ate her little banquet, and in the afternoon she watched old and new films on television. By ten o'clock, tired of her own company, she drove into town to see how the rest of the world was faring.

The car park was deserted, the grand streets almost empty. A chilly evening breeze set the hanging baskets of flowers in motion. Christmas lights swung and flickered. An illuminated Santa Claus drove his sleigh across the middle of Broad Street. Above and below him chandeliers of coloured bulbs bobbed and twinkled against the night. Devoid of people and purpose, the city had become a noble stage set, an empty theatre, a party that was over.

Occasional huddles of humanity, who had nowhere to go, crouched foetus-fashion in doorways, sheltering themselves from the winter night with newspapers and cardboard boxes. The closed and lighted shops sparkled down on them, their contents as unattainable as the stars. One derelict slept in the warm fragrance of Bentham's Bakery in Groom Street, and had a dog with him that lifted its head as Kate passed and laid it down again without hope. A drunk weaved to and fro on the opposite pavement, and she quickened her pace to avoid him.

Two very young girls, shivering in their smart, cheap costumes, stood on a corner, waiting for custom. A cruising car stopped, swallowed one of them up, and bore her away. Kate remembered Betsy and wondered where she was, and if she was, and could not hope either way. And wherever she looked it seemed that her loneliness was magnified a thousand times, and that wherever she went the city streets would reflect the world's indifference.

In Lower Broad Street a policeman loomed up. He had decided that she was respectable but lost, and addressed her accordingly.

'Can I help you, miss?'

'Oh no, thank you,' Kate replied in a bright voice. 'I was just having a breath of air. Just walking off the Christmas excess.'

Unconvinced, he took charge of her. 'It's not wise to wander round this late at night by yourself, miss. There's drunks and druggies and all sorts hanging about. You could get mugged. Do you live here, or are you visiting?'

'I live here. On the south side. Mulberry Street. Overlooking Dulcie Gardens.'

The address reassured him. He was courteous but firm as he gave his order. 'Well, I should go home if I was you, miss, and I shouldn't walk home, neither. Can I get you a taxi?'

Defeated, annoyed, yet relieved that someone should take care of her, Kate said, 'No, no. Thank you. My car's in Shortlands Street. I'll go there now.'

'Then I'll walk with you, miss,' he said. 'Shortlands Street is on my way.'

It was out of his way, but he knew his duty. He kept up a conversation that sounded friendly and casual but was bent on garnering information. She could tell that he suspected trouble at home: an abusive husband or lover. She adopted a charmingly inconsequential air to convince him that she was the happiest of women and nothing more than a whim had driven her out on Christmas Night. Still, he made sure that she got into her car and started the engine before he left her, and Kate suspected that he memorized her licence number.

Outside the car park she saw him there still, waiting and watching on the corner. He gave her a nod and a brief salute as she turned towards Southgate Bridge.

On Boxing Day she thought of telephoning the family, but that would mean inventing a reason for interrupting the social whirl she was supposed to be enjoying, and then inventing the whirl. She felt capable of telling a good lie in a good cause, but not a string of them in a poor one. So the telephone lay in its cradle, undisturbed, and she ate her steak and opened a half bottle of burgundy and studied her art history books because they were mentally satisfying and emotionally safe.

On the following day the January sales began. She scoured the city shops for bargains and found quite a few, which appeased her for the moment. Spinning out her time she went for an early evening meal at Brown's restaurant on the bridge.

Six years ago the move to Mulberry Street had aroused her parents' concern. They guessed that she could not have provided the house deposit herself, though she spoke vaguely of savings and a loan from the firm, and they suspected her of being involved in a clandestine love affair. Neville said nothing, though his manner was uneasy, but Nora burst out her resentment at Kate's secrecy and her inexplicably single state.

'No boyfriends. No friends as far as I can see – at least *we* haven't been asked to meet them. It's not natural in a girl of your age.'

So she had taken her parents out to dinner at Brown's to mollify them. The meal began badly, with Nora in a belligerent mood. It was unfortunate that a mirror version of their own family was sitting at a nearby table. Mother, father and daughter were in high spirits, and the girl was obviously pregnant.

Nora said bitterly, 'At least *she's* got something to look forward to!'

To which Kate, lashed into reply, answered, 'Yes. Yells, smells, and bondage.'

This evening was peaceful but sad, as if life were bent on reminding Kate of lost opportunities and failed ambitions.

The adjoining table was full of students celebrating someone's eighteenth birthday. The girls wore tight, short, sleeveless, low-cut dresses, and very little else as far as Kate could judge – lovely arms and shoulders, radiant faces, a glimpse of firm young breasts. The boys, abashed by their closeness and sensuality, were attempting to be offhand and worldly wise. All of them ate heartily of the set menu and drank carafes of red house wine. Flowering in the company of their equals, briefly secure in the charmed circle of college years, dreaming of an illustrious future, they were privileged, and Kate envied them.

I would have read art history, Kate thought, and then I would have travelled. Worked and travelled for a year before deciding what to do. Found out who I was. Because I'm not sure who I am. Is this Old Hall dogsbody really me? This discarded mistress? This unwanted woman?

She had been so proud of making her own way, of seizing the moment, of creating her public image. But now her self-taught knowledge seemed ponderous, her way of living second-rate.

If I'd had their opportunities, Kate thought, watching the students, I would never have been taken in by a charlatan like Hector. Never have needed him. If I were young again I would do so much better.

Yet the youngsters, glancing idly at her as she summoned the waitress and gave her order, envied her self-possession, her air of independence, and wondered what it must be like to have enough money to order Brown's chef's special and half a bottle of fine claret.

A Chill

The Christmas break, though sad, had at least been restful. Back on duty at the Old Hall, Kate found its lady sitting up in bed, red-nosed, dry-lipped, hoarse and deflated. Shirley hailed her with relief.

'Am I glad to see you! I nearly sent for you to come back early. Katie, I've been desperate. Did you know that my darling old Dr Beardsall had retired? You did? Last summer? Why didn't you tell me? Oh, you did tell me. Well, I'd forgotten. And I've got this new-fangled person – Dr Simpson – who is most unsympathetic. He says it's only a cold, but it has to be more serious than that. He doesn't know how bad I feel. And he won't give me anything for it, either. I need tonics and antibiotics and things, but he says the most sensible prescription is to stay in bed, drink plenty of liquids, take aspirin, and build up my strength.'

'Which you are doing, I see,' Kate replied, observing whisky, lemon, honey and hot

182

water to hand, and the remains of a large and excellent cooked breakfast.

She liked the sound of Dr Simpson, but summoned up the sympathy required.

'Poor old Shirley. What a Christmas you must have had. How did the vigil go?'

Sitting on the end of the bed, immaculate and smiling, no one would have known that her own Christmas had been abysmal. She would have died rather than let anyone know.

'Oh, blow the vigil!' said Shirley snappishly. She recollected what was due to Ezra and corrected herself. 'Mind you, it was a wonderful experience. Wonderful.' She returned to important matters. 'Katie, I think you'll have to cancel the party on New Year's Eve.'

Kate raised her eyebrows and smiled. 'I agree. I'll do that first. By phone, fax, email and letter. Breathing sorrow and promising tremendous future junketing to make up for the present disappointment. Right?'

A weak smile from Shirley turned into a tremendous sneeze.

'Oh God!' she whimpered. 'I feel terrible. How do I look?'

'Not exactly at your best.'

'You'd better keep your distance,' Shirley advised. 'We don't want you down with it, too.' She brooded. 'Do I look really awful? Am I fit to be visited?'

'No. It wouldn't be fair on anyone.'

'Why are you always so bloody truthful?' Shirley asked pettishly.

'It saves time in the long run.' Impishly.

Shirley was not amused. 'You don't give a damn about me, do you? So long as you're all right the rest of the world can go hang, can't it? Give me that mirror!'

Kate stopped smiling and became formal. Early in their partnership, vowing never to be patronized, she had brought offended pauses to a fine art.

'Please,' Shirley added.

Kate complied, and waited for the next burst of anguish.

'Oh God!' Shirley snivelled at the scarlet, puffy visage. 'Why should anyone care about an ugly old woman like me?'

She cast the mirror down.

'Have a medicinal Scotch,' Kate advised.

Shirley had probably been drinking medicinal Scotch all morning because she gave way to the truth and maudlin tears.

'Oh, Katie, I did my best with that vigil. I really did. Katie, I stayed there all bloody night in the freezing cold. It took three of those travellers to get me on my feet again. You could hear my joints cracking a mile away. And Ezra never said a word. Didn't ask me how I was. Didn't come home with me to make sure I was all right. And I was limping, Katie. *Limping.* When Mrs Bailey saw me she nearly had a fit. Made me have a hot bath and go straight to bed. She switched the electric blanket on, but I couldn't get warm. So I had to give up the vegetarian diet. Mrs Bailey wouldn't hear of it anyway. She cooked me a plate of ham and eggs and put whisky in my tea, and I slept all Christmas Day. Worst Christmas I've ever spent. And I'd run out of cigarettes. Then on Boxing Day I woke up with a temperature of a hundred and two and Mrs Bailey sent for the doctor and it was this new chap.'

Kate opened a fresh box of Kleenex and passed it over.

'What exactly did he say?' she asked, guessing how forthright he had been.

Shirley hiccuped and sobbed. 'He reminded me how old I was – looked it up in his notes, if you please! – and said what did I expect at my time of life, after sitting outside in the cold all night? The rudeness! The insensitivity! I mean, what am I paying him for? I could be insulted for nothing on the NHS!'

Kate laughed, and Shirley gave a ghostly chuckle.

'Yes, I suppose it would be funny if I didn't feel so bad,' she said, and lapsed into a sombre mood. 'Oh, Katie...' Here comes the confession, Kate thought. 'Katie, I think the world of Ezra. I've never felt like this about anyone else. Honestly. I'd do anything for her. Follow her anywhere. And she doesn't even ask how I am.'

'Does she know you're ill?'

'Oh yes. I sent her a note, thanking her for the wonderful experience, and mentioning that I was in bed with a severe chill. And she sent a verbal message back – by that miserable little twerp, Joel – that I was in her prayers.'

185

Kate waited for the whimper.

'But I don't want to be in her prayers, Katie.' Lips trembling. 'I want her to come here and ask how I'm feeling, and heal me and comfort me.'

Kate sighed, and watched her pluck at the sheets like some female Falstaff.

Shyly. Coaxing. 'Katie, I don't want her to think I'm a nuisance, so I can't write to her again, but do you think you could have a word with her – as if it was coming from you? Couldn't you go and have one of your clever, tactful little talks with her? Only, don't mention the bacon and the whisky because I'm going to give them up again when I'm better. Please, Katie?'

Kate said soberly, kindly, 'You're going to be hurt if you try to force this relationship. You're going to be hurt anyway, because it will never work out as you want it to. Ezra's way of life isn't yours, and you'll only be miserable if you try to change yourself to please her.'

Shirley heard without listening. 'I just wanted to see her. That's all. I'm not asking for anything more.'

Kate sighed again. She knew the lies that lovers told, the excuses they made, the promises they didn't keep, the ridiculous hopes they cherished. Resigned, she said, 'All right. I'll give it a try. Have you any idea where and when I can find her?'

Shirley's red face shone with hope and pleasure.

186

'She meditates in the grove every day until twelve o'clock. Rain or shine. Then she goes back to the hut for their midday meal.' A further worry beset her. 'Katie! I'm sure it's not healthy to live on a handful of rice and vegetables twice a day.'

'Ezra seems to thrive on it, and – to be perfectly frank – she isn't the one who's in bed with a bad cold, is she?'

'That's very unkind,' said Shirley automatically. 'Oh, and while you're out, take the car and get me some ciggies, will you? Just one little packet.'

'Not – on – your – sweet – life,' said Kate. Sweetly.

The day was bitter, the ground frozen, and Ezra was wearing one of Shirley's soft white blankets round her shoulders. The back turned to Kate was arrow-straight, and she sat at the edge of the lime tree grove, a hand resting on each knee, palm facing upwards, finger and thumb closed in a circle.

Kate glanced at her watch and decided to wait. Her winter coat was thick enough to withstand the cold. She sat down on a tree stump, some distance away, pulled her scarf over her head, and stuck her gloved hands in her pockets. She was revising and polishing the speech she would make to Ezra, but no amount of polish could hide the meaning beneath the words. It was a shriek of longing and despair from an unloved lover, and she knew that Ezra would understand what was meant rather than what was said.

Kate began to compose possible replies and to revise the speech to answer them, but the stillness of that small figure, sitting down below, was hushing the words that chattered and nattered in her mind like fretful children.

Oh, what the hell does it matter? Kate thought.

Gradually Ezra's quietness quietened her. The wound dealt by Hector ceased to ache. Kate let go the bonds that tied her to her mother, the irritations of Shirley, the feeling that she put far more into her work than she ever got out of it. She watched familiar faces and places assemble in her mind, and let them go again. Finally nothing came, no one disturbed her, and she drifted out on a placid sea.

Some time later she returned to find Ezra standing beside her.

Kate was about to make some light observation that both excused and explained her presence. Instead, she heard herself say peacefully, 'I was in a good place.'

Ezra held out her hand to help Kate to rise. The hand was cool and small, bird-boned. 'Yes, it is a good place,' she answered.

They walked together without further words until they reached the hut. Then Ezra turned to her and said, 'I am giving my time to those who are really ill and who truly need me. Tell Shirley I have not forgotten her. I am sending her healing thoughts and I shall come to see her as soon as I can.'

The interview was over without Kate's speech being delivered. Ezra looked directly at her and said, 'You ask no healing for yourself?'

Kate's independence reared its wilful head. 'Why? Do you think I need it?'

Ezra smiled. 'That is not for me to say.'

Kate relaxed. 'Oh. Well. Thank you, anyway,' she said, quite awkwardly for her.

Now what was I thanking her for? she wondered on the way back. For dealing so easily with the Shirley problem, or for thinking of me? And how is Shirley going to take the news that Ezra is giving her time to those who are *really* ill and *truly* need her? No, I won't say that. I'll give great emphasis to the healing thoughts, and put the message in a general way. Not lying. Just misleading. I'll mention, in passing, that there's a gastric bug going round the travellers' camp – there usually is! I'll say that Ezra's been fully occupied. Give Shirley a half-truth and let her make a false connection. After all...'

Thoughts chattered through her head once more, like demanding children.

Crises

The new year began badly. Snow, heavier than usual, blanketed the outlying country-side, blocked major roads and closed minor ones. Telephone and power lines came down. Villages were isolated. Within the city the roof tops remained white and beautiful, but in the streets below pedestrians trudged on pavements grey with slush, or mounted grimed banks of snow in order to cross from one side to the other, while public and private transport crawled between.

In their bright breakfast room on Holden Crescent, Hector and Jocelyn Mordant were dealing with a family crisis and making a poor job of it. Unable to command the situation, Hector was laying the blame elsewhere, while Jocelyn distanced herself as far from the problem as possible.

'This is the school's responsibility, not mine,' Hector cried. 'They're supposed to be in charge. Why should I pay extortionate fees, if not to know that the children are in safe hands? God knows I've got enough to worry about, providing for you all.' He found a scapegoat. 'And it's your job to bring them up

190

properly. Judging from these two letters you seem to have fallen down rather badly!'

Driven into the open, Jocelyn became nettled. 'It's hardly my fault that Toby was caught smoking cannabis or that Hermione shinned down a drainpipe at midnight dressed for a party. I can assure you they didn't learn that sort of thing from me. My boarding school was fearfully strict. We never had the chance to do anything more exciting than a midnight feast.'

He ignored her, crying, 'Why, oh why – if they *had* to do something disreputable – couldn't they cover their tracks? Are they totally devoid of self-protection?'

Jocelyn could see herself being blamed for this, too. In a conciliatory tone she asked, 'What are you going to do about it, darling?'

'Why should *I* have to deal with it?'

'Darling, because you're so clever at making people do what you want.'

'So are you.' Bluntly.

She pouted, smiled, turned the accusation into a compliment. 'Darling, only little trifling things. You use your influence in a big way.'

Slightly pacified, he reread the letter.

'They say they're not thinking of expulsion – as yet. Apparently, Toby was sharing a joint with eight others, so they won't want to lose all those fees at one blow! And Hermione said her exploit was a dare and she was going to shin straight back up the drainpipe as soon as she'd reached the ground – which I don't believe for a minute and I shouldn't think they do either. They've both pleaded first offence, which has been accepted, but this letter is a shot across the bows.'

Jocelyn, admiring the mirrors of her frost-pink nails said, 'Yes, darling. Positively grim.'

Hector made a bridge of his fingers and tapped his lips, thinking.

'Personally, I think both of them are telling lies. I suspect they've been smoking joints and shinning down drainpipes long before this, and I'm going to give them hell. So telephone the school this morning on our behalf. Tell them how shocked and saddened we are. Pay them a compliment on the way that they've handled the situation, promise our full co-operation in whatever measures they intend to take, and arrange for us both to go up this weekend. We'll drive there on Saturday, see the head teacher, take the kids out to tea – if we're allowed – give them a damned good ticking off, and stay overnight at the Falcon...'

'Oh, I *love* staying at the Falcon! If we went up on Friday evening and came back late on Sunday, we could make a real weekend of it.'

'Just book Saturday night. This isn't a frivolous jaunt in the country. We have a job to do.'

'Of course we have, darling. Only we shan't be with the children for more than an hour or two, and you need a break. You work too hard.'

She followed him into the hallway. She

192

brushed a non-existent speck from his overcoat and kissed his cheek. 'We'll sort it all out, so don't worry,' she said, as softly as if she cared for him.

He grunted, unimpressed.

'Will you be home to dinner, darling?'

'Most probably.'

'Then we'll have a bottle of champers to cheer us up. And pheasant?'

They both knew he was being persuaded into taking her away for the whole weekend, and would eventually do so.

Hector stood on the doorstep and sniffed the cold air appreciatively. The news of his children was disturbing, but he had managed to deal with life on his own terms so far and intended to continue.

If I can't sort out a fusty old head teacher and two idiotic adolescents I ought to resign, he thought.

The consultant's room on the first floor of a house off Westgate was also warm and bright, and its long windows overlooked the winter grace of Adelaide Park, but Jocelyn shivered as she sat on the edge of her chair and, though she stared out at the park, she did not see it. Expensively dressed and perfumed, relying on charm and prettiness for support, she entreated the man opposite in her soft, crooning voice.

'Surely it isn't as serious as all that, Mr Bradley?'

He answered factually, 'You really should

193

have consulted your doctor months ago, Mrs Mordant.'

She evaded him by saying, 'I just needed time to think things over.'

But he pursued her. 'You've no more time to waste. The only solution is surgery.'

Jocelyn conceded a point and asked, 'Keyhole surgery?'

'No. A complete mastectomy.'

Her face, which had displayed a range of feelings from fear and apprehension to sadness and disbelief, now set in resolution.

'No,' she said. 'I don't accept that. There must be another way out.'

'If you were my wife,' he said earnestly, 'you'd be in hospital tonight, and in the operating theatre tomorrow morning.'

She was silent, fingering her gloves.

'I understand that you find this news difficult to deal with alone. If you had brought your husband with you for moral support—'

She interrupted him, crying, 'My husband doesn't know! He mustn't know.'

'But he'll have to know.'

Cornered, Jocelyn became obstinate.

'No,' she repeated. 'No, I don't intend to worry him.' She collected herself, put on her social front. 'He's so awfully busy, you see.'

The consultant ignored this. 'I can operate on Monday. If you come into the hospital on Sunday evening...'

Smiling, light of heart and voice, Jocelyn cried, 'Oh, I'm afraid we shall be away this weekend.' She glanced at her wristwatch.

'Goodness, how late it is!'

'Mrs Mordant, you are risking your life with every day of procrastination.'

Graciously, she said, 'Thank you, Mr Bradley. I do understand. I just need a little more time to think things over.'

He stood up and held open the door for her. The last of the winter sun came in and lit the room most beautifully, but she did not notice, passing by him as if he were not there or she were blind.

Kate and Patrick

The snow disappeared grudgingly, growing dirtier as it melted, but the winter did not lose its grip. Temperatures plummeted and a bitter wind turned the streets into funnels of cold. The inhabitants emerged from icy houses booted, hatted and gloved: shapeless bundles negotiating the treacheries of glassy pavements. And, as if this were not enough, a virulent influenza struck down its first victims, spread rapidly and became an epidemic. The city was in a state of siege.

The local radio station mounted a Help Your Neighbour campaign and gave hourly bulletins on both weather and virus. The radio doctor advised bed rest, warmth, aspirins and plenty of fluids, and asked the afflicted to look after themselves as far as possible. In the surgeries an answering service related the same message, and only those at risk were treated. Patients overflowed into the hospital corridors. Even Hector was afflicted and retired to bed for three days, after which he recovered sufficiently to run Celebrations from home while he convalesced. Meanwhile a steady core of untouchables supported the sufferers.

In the outlying districts immunity reigned as long as they remained away from the city. The Flower Farm at this desolate time of year was a fortress because no one needed to stir beyond it. Kate, level-headed as usual, telephoned regularly but stayed away to avoid carrying infection. Jack, with unthinking devotion, visited the family to see how they were and took the plague with him. At the Old Hall, Shirley, barely recovered from her Christmas chilling, went down with it badly. Her only comfort lay in Ezra, whose visits were necessarily infrequent.

She was a bad patient at any time, but in her anxiety to prove Ezra's capabilities she did both of them a disservice by overreacting. Staggering from her bed after a healing session she would cry, 'Cured! Cured!' and an hour later would stagger back again with renewed symptoms. Kate, having weathered similar physical and emotional crises before, kept the wheels of house and business turning and silently damned her employer.

Nora was so ill that the doctor called an ambulance and moved her to the City Hospital immediately, leaving Neville and Reggie to nurse each other at home.

'We can manage all right, Katie,' Neville said hoarsely over the telephone, 'but there's no one to visit your mother and she's really bad.'

Kate's reply was cheerful as she added Nora's name to a growing list of casualties.

'Don't worry. I'll visit her every day and give you a report every evening.' A note of tenderness crept into her voice. 'Now are you sure you're all right, Da?'

'Oh yes. We're managing. But poor little Toni's gone down with it and she's none too good. It's the short neck that does it.'

'Who's little Toni?'

'Antoinette. The little lass you met on Christmas Eve.'

'She isn't still staying at the farm, is she?'

'No, not now. She's back at home, poor little lass. I hope they're looking after her because the mother thinks nothing of her, and the boyfriend can't abide her. That's why Nora has her here so much. But don't tell Nora that, because she'll only fret, and if she asks you...' He stopped, unsure of instructions. Kate finished the sentence for him.

'I'll tell a whopping great lie.'

Neville chuckled, which made him cough. When he had recovered he said, 'That's my girl. Take care of yourself, love.'

'And you take care of yourself, dear Da.

Oh,' remembering, 'and Reggie, too.'

But as time wore on, and wore her out, Kate became tired of other people's problems, tired of the sick, tired of being everyone's drogue anchor, and extremely tired of Shirley. Stealing an hour for herself after a hospital visit to Nora, she avoided the enticements of Mrs Porter's Parlour and chose a place unlikely to be frequented by any of her acquaintances. Someone had mentioned it at some time, and the name stayed in her retentive memory: Mulligan's in River Street, near the university.

Mulligan's was a dark little bar down a flight of stairs: the perfect retreat for secret assignations and shady deals. Lights were dim. Bamboo chairs and round brown tables were tucked away in the shadows. Its licensing hours seemed to be elastic and its owner apparently managed with a minimum of sleep. Open at most times of day and night, it was frequented mainly by students who felt they were living dangerously, but also by a small hard core of those who did. These were tolerated by the owner, provided that they did not misbehave openly and kept any undercover operations well under cover. Even the police, maintaining a watchful eye on certain customers, never raided the bar publicly but had a private word with Mulligan first. Then, dressed in plain clothes, they mingled with the crowd and arrested his dodgier customers unobtrusively.

Mulligan was a devoted husband and

father. His family lived above the premises and under his fierce protection. Severe on his fellow men, chivalrous towards women, his passion in life was boxing. He acted as his own bouncer while employing extra help at the bar, and had the reputation of packing a mean punch. The sepia prints on the walls, if anyone cared to hold up a light in order to see them, were all of the Fancy: deceased Fancies, to judge from the names. Gentleman Jim Fairchild. The Newgate Knock-out. Charlie Stonefist. And so on. Huge men with bulging muscles and menacing fists, dressed in long johns.

'They fought to the death then,' Mulligan would say, 'and they fought hungry. None of your rich lads with padded gloves and Queensbury rules. Bare knuckles, battle and blood.'

At this time of the day, and in the middle of an influenza epidemic, the bar was peaceful and almost empty. Kate ordered her drink in a subdued voice and was served with quiet respect. Peering into the gloom she chose a table furthest from the entrance and hid herself there thankfully until the voice of Patrick Hanna hailed her from a neighbouring cavern.

'And what is good Kate and bonnie Kate and sometimes Kate the shrew doing in a place like this?'

She jumped slightly, frowned involuntarily, cursed inwardly. She now remembered who had spun this wonderful yarn about

199

Mulligan's, and called herself a fool. She did not bother to make a cordial reply. He knew her opinion of him and, as far as she was concerned, he could lump it.

'Looking for privacy,' she said abruptly.

'And what are you looking for, Patrick?' he asked himself, unperturbed. And answered, 'What are you ever looking for but news and company?' He carried his glass over to her table and smiled his crooked smile. 'And what might you be sip-sip-sipping, all by yourself, Kate, at three o'clock on a winter's afternoon?'

'Malt whisky,' she answered through her teeth.

'I'd have sworn that China tea in a Dresden cup was more your line. Life must be tough.'

'It is.'

'And how is the Lady Shirley?'

'She has the flu. So has my mother, who is in the City Hospital, and my father and my stepbrother, and anyone else you care to mention.'

He was serious in an instant. 'Now, I'm sorry to hear about Nora. She's a grand woman. One of the best.' He took out his notebook. 'Give me the name of the ward and I'll drop in on my way home to cheer her up.'

Reluctantly she gave him the name and the visiting hours.

'Ah, you needn't bother about them,' he said cheerfully. 'Nora's pleased to see me any old time.'

'The ward sister might not be.'

'I've never had trouble with ward sisters before.'

'I'm surprised to hear it.'

He surveyed her, smiling. 'It isn't privacy you want, it's a fight, isn't it?' he said comfortably. 'I know the symptoms.'

She answered coolly, though she was raw with rage. 'Do *you* want a fight?'

'Always prepared to oblige a lady.'

Kate closed her eyes in an effort to control her temper. Today he was life's final insult. She stood up, poured her malt whisky over his head, and prepared to walk out. Unfortunately the light was so dim that she wasn't quick enough to evade him, and he caught her arm as she passed. His manner was easy, but the grip was not.

'Let – go – of – me!'

'Not until you've finished the round,' he said. 'Cutting and running the minute you've landed the first blow – what sort of sporting behaviour is that?'

'Mr Mulligan!' Kate called in desperation. 'This man is annoying me.'

Mulligan's pale round face loomed through the gloaming. He walked towards them, flexing his fingers and looking hard at Patrick.

'Now what are you up to? Take your hands off the lady.'

Patrick let go of Kate's arm and mopped his face and head.

'I'm up to nothing at all, Seamus. She poured her drink over me.'

'She's a lady of spirit,' said Mulligan, drawing his own conclusions, 'and you're a mongrel. I admire her for doing it.'

Close to tears, Kate said in a high, controlled voice, 'I simply wanted to sit here quietly by myself, but he insisted on joining me.'

'Do you know the lady?' Mulligan asked him.

'Not as well as I'd like to.'

Mulligan reproved him. 'You know I won't have that sort of behaviour here, don't you? It isn't the first time you've pushed your luck. One day you'll go too far and then me or somebody else'll give you a smack in the snout such as you won't forget.'

'Which has happened,' Patrick admitted humbly, indicating his broken nose, 'more than once.'

The situation was becoming farcical.

'The lady wants to sit by herself,' Mulligan explained to him, as to a child. 'Now I'm going to bring her another drink and chalk it up to you, and you're going to sit over there and behave yourself. And unless the lady gives you permission to talk to her you don't say a word. Is that understood?'

'With all the pleasure in life.' In an aside to Kate, Patrick said, 'This is just his fun. He's a great lady's man.' Mulligan's brawny arm shot out. His thick forefinger pointed. 'Over there!' he ordered.

'And when you bring the lady's glass would you be kind enough to fetch me another drink, Seamus?'

'Over there!' Mulligan repeated.

Patrick went.

Kate's anger had simmered down and she was feeling slightly silly.

'You're very kind, Mr Mulligan. I'm sure there'll be no more trouble.'

'I wasn't trying to chat her up,' Patrick said amiably, from his former cavern. 'I've got news for her, and I thought we could have a profitable talk.'

'You just stay where you are. I want any lady on her own to feel safe here,' said Mulligan portentously. 'Remember that.'

He nodded once or twice for emphasis and walked away.

'Are you trying to make out that this is a respectable place, Seamus?' Patrick called after him.

'It always has been,' Mulligan replied over his shoulder. 'Some of the customers aren't.'

In the brief and blessed silence that followed, Kate began to relax, to feel sorry that she had made a fuss, but she was so glad of a respite that her conscience soon ceased to trouble her.

'Your whisky, madam,' said Mulligan, returning soft-voiced and light-footed. And to Patrick, 'Here's yours, and don't make a hog of yourself over it.'

Silence once more washed over them. Mulligan stood guard in the background, polishing spotless glasses, holding them up to the bar lights, squinting at them judiciously. Patrick scribbled in his notebook. Kate

203

leaned against the wall, let the whisky warm her and closed her eyes. Peace reigned. Outside, the city froze.

In a while – she did not know how long – Kate said conversationally to the writer in the shadows, 'Did you really have some news for me?'

He answered without rancour, 'I did indeed, but I'm not about to shout it out from here.'

Kate hesitated, glanced at Mulligan, and conceded. 'I should like to hear it,' she said, and gestured him to join her.

Patrick stood up and addressed Mulligan, 'Now before you start knocking me about, are you happy with that?' And as the man nodded, 'Then we'll have another whisky apiece and pour one for yourself – though you don't deserve it.'

For the second time he made his way over to her table and sat opposite. His eyes courted her.

'You're a woman of discretion, so what I'm telling you is for your ears alone.'

'And why should you confide in me personally?' Unimpressed.

He lowered his voice. 'Because it concerns your job and involves Shirley.'

'I see. Were you going to tell me anyway, or simply because I happened to walk in here?'

There was a pause during which she wondered if he might take himself and his drink off for good, and he evidently thought about it for a few moments. Then he grinned, settled back in his chair, and said, 'Even when I most dislike you I have to respect you.'

She compressed her lips, felt lonely, – and probably looked lonely because he relented.

'No, Kate, I was going to tell you anyway. You're a tough, smart woman. You know your own mind and do your job well. I like that.'

She was touched and stung at once. His description of her did not match the picture she had of herself, but it sounded bleakly familiar. Like the late Miss Benbow, in fact. The image depressed her.

She replied stiffly, 'You can trust me not to repeat any confidences.'

He nodded and lowered his voice still further.

'Your household saint is making waves in the city's high places. They've put pressure on the *Courier* to discredit her and the job's been given to me. Ezra carries no clout, so the operation would be reasonably simple, except for Shirley, who is being all kinds of a fool. Word has spread that one of her bottom fields is full of penniless travellers. The city fathers don't want them but they can't evict them, because it's her property. Then there's the rumour of a pagan celebration being held sometime in the spring, to which other un- desirables may come. Have you heard any- thing about that?'

'No. Nothing at all. Shirley and I had a row about the bottom field being used, so I don't hear anything nowadays, and shan't do until she needs me to clear up the mess.'

He raised his black brows in silent comment, and resumed his tale. 'Now, as you know from long experience, an official festival that attracts respectable tourists and fills the city coffers is good business...'

This was a slap at her work for Celebrations.

'...but a free festival for life's losers is not. And as our mutual friend Hector Mordant might say, charity not only begins but also ends at home...'

A glint in his eye told her that he knew all about herself and Hector and she detested him for it. One more crack like that, her expression said, and I walk out. Patrick's glint disappeared. His tone became conversational.

'Shirley's been useful to the city fathers so far, but if they have to ditch her in order to get rid of Ezra they will, and they won't mind how they do it either – you get my drift? Scandalous hints about Shirley's sexual preferences, tied up with Ezra living rent-free on her estate, could kill two birds with one stone. On top of this, everyone knows that her grand estate is swallowing the Parlours' profits whole, and that can't go on for ever. So, unless she recants, turfs out the travellers and hands Ezra over to the wolves, the Lady Shirley of Melbury Old Hall will no longer be allowed to play with the big boys. She's a stubborn old bird and she'll survive somehow, but you'll lose your job, my girl, and – if you're not careful – your personal and

206

professional reputation, too. When mud's thrown it not only sticks to the victim, it spatters anyone standing by. My advice would be to look about you, and to go while you have a choice.'

Staring at her glass, fingering the rim, Kate did not reply, and he watched her, serious for once. Then she looked up.

'That conclusion presupposes that you discover something dubious about Ezra,' she said. 'Do you think you will?'

He put one long finger at the side of his crooked nose. 'This tells me I shall. I don't believe in amateur saints. Do you?'

Kate shook her head. 'No, I don't. And I've advised Shirley against this business from the beginning. So far, I must admit, Ezra's stuck to her principles and seems sincere, but I'm suspicious about something – I don't quite know what – the followers, for instance.'

'Ah yes!' said Patrick in an appreciative tone. 'I've had my eye on those two jokers from the start. They're tomorrow's news in the *Courier*, but keep this under your hat, too. By the grace of the good god who protects snooping journalists I happened to catch sight of them in a pie shop, at the wrong end of town, a couple of weeks ago.'

'No-o-o!' Kate cried, intrigued.

'Oh yes. And not a vegetarian pie shop, either – if there is such a thing. Many a gallant porker has turned up his trotters to supply the filling for these pies. Lambs have been slaughtered, probably inhumanely, in

207

their cause...'

Kate could tell that he was quoting almost verbatim from the article he had written, and suppressed a smile.

'Battery chickens have been battered and innocent mushrooms gathered in the flower of their youth. Portions of beef, perhaps best un-named, have been cruelly minced and served up with fried onion. Mention an animal, moisten it with gravy, cap it with crust, and you have not only a good, tasty midday meal but Temptation before you, spelled with a capital T. And, as Oscar Wilde advised, the followers never resist temptation. I call them Batty and Basher – which is self-explanatory, I take it?'

Kate laughed aloud, upon which Mulligan marvelled at the changeable nature of women.

Warmed by her appreciation, Patrick flowered.

'I discounted Batty, who must blow as the wind blows, whatever company he's in, but I was pretty certain that Basher's done time, and with the aid of a photo kit and a pal in the police department, I found him. Beginning in the primary school of borstal, he has committed a long series of offences. Petty crimes. Not a master criminal. But he could be a useful recruit in a bigger scheme. Anyway, having this background knowledge I started to keep tabs on them.

'I found out that they come into the city three or four times a week on the old begging-bowl lark, and after the pie shop episode I followed them. First of all they paraded down Broad Street, chanting, to let everyone know that they were here on a holy errand. Then they branched out, keeping to the wealthy quarter, and visited various greengrocers and health food shops. Batty did the begging and Basher carried the loot. That's the legitimate side. Then they disappeared to the wrong end of town, where presumably nobody knew or cared about them, and doubled in and out of those back streets like a pair of rabbits.

'They lost me for half an hour, but the luck of the Irish was with me, and I finally caught sight of the pair of them, tucked away in a quiet corner of the wharf. Chilling out, as you might say. And the smell of fish and chips in newspaper with vinegar (the only way to eat them, in my humble opinion) wafted towards me, that had eaten nothing since half past ten the night before. When they'd upended their cans of beer Basher sat back and smoked a cigarette and Batty dipped into a bag of toffees. Then they got rid of the evidence and presumably headed for home.

'Now where, I asked myself, had they found the money to pay for all this? Actual begging takes too long to be viable, and they couldn't risk being caught at it because of their supposed principles. So, knowing our Basher, a little quiet pocket-picking suggested itself. A purse lifted out of a shopping basket. A wallet from a back pocket. Nothing too ambitious.

And in that garb they could get away with a lot. No one suspects a monk – except me, and you, perhaps.'

He said this ironically, and Kate made a grimace of acknowledgement.

'But I needed proof. So I recruited my good friend Jack Almond and we spent a profitable Saturday afternoon following them around. Tomorrow's *Courier* is opening the anti-Ezra campaign with a centre-page fold on her un-likely lads. Nothing unpleasant. No reference to Basher's record or Batty's intelligence. Just a giggle about the frailties of the flesh, backed by photographs of them legitimately visiting a charitable greengrocer, unofficially buying pies and chips, and then swilling beer and smoking fags in their cosy on the wharf.'

He finished his whisky and waited for her reaction.

'Well – I'm – damned,' said Kate slowly.

Ezra meant nothing to her, and frauds deserved to be exposed, but the politics behind the exposure were undoubtedly sus-pect. She moved to safe ground.

'Then after tomorrow I prophesy that you're likely to be bad news at the Old Hall for quite a while,' she said plainly. 'Shirley will be furious with them for letting Ezra down, and with you for finding them out.'

He nodded. 'I can wear that. Hopefully there'll be worse to come.'

'You'll probably never be invited again.'

He grinned at her. 'Would you like another whisky?'

'No, thank you. I don't want to be found drunk and disorderly in the car park.'

'Ah, I can tell you're feeling better.' With a twinkle.

'Yes,' she said, smiling. 'Yes, I am.' In her usual ironic tone. 'Revived by drink and gossip as you might say.'

He was serious. 'Mind now, I'm trusting you.'

The history of his life was in his face – a long hard fight for crusades real or imagined, armed with wit, leavened by humour. For once he seemed real to her, and she liked him.

'You can trust me absolutely,' Kate replied. Rising, preparing to join the parade again, she smiled down on him. 'I'd be interested to know why you really confided in me.'

He said easily, 'I suppose it's because most people are fools and you're a realist, like myself. I'd be sorry to see you go down the pan with the rest of them.'

She was touched and delighted, but careful not to show it.

'This knowledge puts me in an invidious position, you know,' she reminded herself rather than him.

'You've been in invidious positions ever since I've known you. So what's new?'

Hector's ghost rose again. She lifted her eyebrows, gave a rueful nod, shrugged, took a deep breath.

'Yes, I've been a fool myself, in my time,' she said. 'But I believe I do learn.' Slowly.

'Thanks for the drink. Oh, and for the conversation. I must go now.' As she passed the bar she flashed a bright smile at the owner and said, 'Thank you, Mr Mulligan. You're a star.'

'All part of the service, madam. I hope we shall see you here again,' he replied.

'Remember my words,' Patrick called after her, 'and start looking after yourself.'

Kate paused, and her smile this time was personal. 'You, too,' she replied, and stepped out into the freezing street.

The encounter with Patrick Hanna left a warm glow that lasted until the following morning, when Shirley brought her back to cold reality. Kate twice reminded herself not to be a fool before she rang Patrick Hanna from her office telephone. She kept her voice light and humorous.

'The top of the morning to you, Patrick. This is Kate. Shirley is outraged – her own word – by your article, and she wants a word with you and Jack. I'm warning you, it won't be a gracious one.'

Patrick's smile came down the telephone. He replied in kind. 'Tell the lady to come up and see me sometime.'

'Sorry. Not good enough. She wants you both here as soon as possible, first of all to be carpeted, and then to interview Ezra while Jack takes beautiful photographs of her, to give the caring public her side of the case.'

'Ah, you're only trying to scare me. And me

having taken the pledge again, with a bottle of whisky in the bottom drawer of the desk in case I can't resist temptation.' More seriously, 'Does Ezra want this publicity?'

'I don't think she's even been asked. Shirley wants it. On Ezra's behalf.'

'Ah, but I have a cynical editor who only deals with people direct, and the gossip has to be hot. We aren't in this game for charity.'

'And as he's been ordered to gun Ezra down, he won't do it anyway.'

'No, now. Tuck in those claws. Shirley's affairs of the heart – unless she chooses to reveal all – are not sufficient reason to write a chatty feature about one of her little friends.'

'That's what I told her – but more tactfully.'

Patrick was breezy. 'Then tell her again from me like a good pal, will you?'

'I'm not your pal, good or otherwise,' said Kate, though she smiled in spite of herself. 'But I'll give her the message.'

'Stay a while, mavourneen. I've heard a couple of other things that might interest you. Suppose we talk over another whisky or three? Would you be free this evening?'

Kate hesitated.

'Yes, it *is* information,' he said, and again she could hear the smile in his voice. 'But, my nature being what it is, and you the proud beauty that you are, I might have to make a pass at you as well.'

She laughed. 'Forget the pass but I'd like the information. Where and at that time?'

'Six thirty at Mulligan's? He'll act as chaperone.'

'Both those arrangements will suit me fine.'

'You'll have no difficulty recognizing me. I'll be the tall, dark, handsome feller wearing a red carnation.'

'I'm glad you told me. I should have walked right past you,' said Kate, laughed again, and hung up.

Meetings

February

The erring disciples were in disgrace with everyone except the person they had betrayed. Despite Shirley's outrage, Ezra remained philosophical.

'They are human and this is a hard path to follow.'

'But surely they must be punished,' Shirley demanded.

As one who fell frequently at the religious wayside she was doubly critical of other people's lapses. Ezra's smile accepted this fault too. She was reasonable in her argument.

'They are being punished. They were gaining self-respect. Now they have lost it.'

Fine points of morality always escaped Shirley.

'Well, that's not enough in my opinion. They've dragged us all into the mud with them. Made us a laughing stock. They've even cast doubts on *you*.'

Ezra considered this with deplorable calm. 'I have no doubts about myself. Have you?'

Shirley blustered, defended herself, encountered no opposition, could think of no solutions, and returned to her original attack.

'Well, I think you should throw them out.'

Ezra's eyes looked deeply into hers.

'For a while,' Shirley added uncomfortably. 'A few weeks, say.' She tried to raise the level of her conversation. 'We should send them into the wilderness,' she explained. 'Like we did with Christ.' She ended lamely, 'And when they've repented they can come back.'

Ezra said, hiding a smile, 'But Christ went of His own accord, and for meditation, not repentance. Perhaps you are thinking of another who was driven out into the wilderness. The scapegoat. To carry away the sins of the people. And he did not come back.'

'Oh well. You know what I mean...' Trailing off.

But Ezra would not let her get away with this. Her tone was forthright. She held Shirley's gaze.

'Simeon and Joel were tempted and they fell – as they will again – as we all do. Have you never failed in your intentions, Shirley?' No answer. 'Please to excuse me now. I begin

215

a healing session soon and I need to prepare myself.'

Dumbfounded in the dock of her conscience, Shirley attempted a jaunty reply. 'Oh. Righty-ho. Yes. Well. I'll be off then. Ta-ta for now.'

She felt those clear grey eyes on her back all the way to the door of the hut and hurried home across the field to Kate, for she needed worldly company.

As she scrambled over the stile, and swore at it, she caught sight of a tall, slim woman making her way to the hut from the lane. For a moment, without her glasses, she thought it was Kate, and the notion that she was being double-crossed rose from its murky depths. Then as the woman came nearer she saw that the easy elegance belonged to someone else: Jocelyn Mordant.

'Well I'm blessed!' said Shirley, which was not true. 'I must tell Kate.'

Earlier that same week, Hector's appearance at No 11 Mulberry Street on a dank evening had been unexpected and unwelcome, and he knew it.

'Kate, I wouldn't disturb you without good reason,' he said quickly, 'but could I just come in for a few minutes? I need your confidential advice – and it *is* very important.'

He brought in a gust of memories that stirred her senses: the subtle scent of shaving lotion, the roughness of his tweed overcoat, the timbre of his voice, the presence of a man

216

in a wholly feminine house. With renewed pain she preceded him upstairs to the sitting room and offered him a drink.

'My favourite whisky,' he said appreciatively.

The thought that the bottle had been bought specially for him hung between them. Briskly she dispelled it. 'Mine too,' said Kate.

He was unusually self-conscious and chose his next words carefully.

'I've come here, rather than to the Old Hall, because – in a way – this concerns Shirley, and I don't want her to know.'

Another of them, Kate thought, and asked in her pleasant, neutral voice, 'And how can I help you?'

'It concerns, in part, your ... resident healer,' he began hesitantly.

Kate poured two handsome slugs of whisky and sat opposite him. 'You mean Ezra? She isn't my healer, and I have very little to do with her.'

'No, I suppose not. I should imagine your opinion of her is similar to mine.'

Would you indeed? Kate thought, but said nothing.

'This ... Ezra,' he began again. He cast round. 'You know, of course, or may have guessed, that her presence has become increasingly unwelcome in the city.'

'Yes, I do know.'

'And that Shirley's indulgence of her whims is now casting doubts on Shirley's own usefulness and reliability?'

'Yes.'

With some of his old bullying friendliness, Hector said, 'Then in that case I hope you're not clinging to any false notions of loyalty. Your first duty is to yourself.'

'Just – one – moment,' said Kate, holding up a hand to silence him. 'We're not talking about me. My life is my own business and I do take care of myself. Now, what exactly have you come to ask me?'

He reverted to humility and said, 'It's about Jocelyn.'

Wild notions of Jocelyn suing him for divorce, and citing Kate rather late in the day, rose to her mind. Nostalgia left her and she was angry.

Their thoughts were on the same wavelength, but he misread them, thinking that she still hoped for marriage. He blurted out the truth.

'No, no. It's nothing to do with us. It's herself. She's ... she's suffering from cancer of the breast.'

Kate felt her face go cold. She neither liked nor respected Jocelyn, but at that moment she became a sister in that particular female hell. To be gnawed by fear and pain, to be mutilated in the hope of cure, to wake up daily to the threat of death, and then to wait out the years because hope is not certainty.

'Dear God!' said Kate to herself.

'She's known this for a few months, apparently, but didn't want to tell me. She didn't consult our doctor until it was well advanced. So much valuable time wasted. She's now seen a specialist and he wants to operate. At once. But she still won't consider it. She's been going in for this macrobiotic diet nonsense. That's when she had to tell me. I could hardly sit at one end of the dining table eating pheasant without noticing that she had a bowl of birdseed, or whatever it is.'

He finished the whisky in one gulp, and in his distress got up and strode the little room from end to end, running his hands through his hair, talking at rather than to Kate. She had seen him like this often in the past, but now her heart no longer ached with remembrance.

'This last month has been ... horrific. We – her doctor, the specialist and I – have all tried to persuade her to do the sensible thing, but she's panicking. She's trying anything that promises to cure her. Fringe medicine. Crystals. Charms. You name it, she's tried it. Kate!' Turning and facing her, distraught. 'Kate, I never knew how many crazy people there were in the world. And don't imagine that these quacks do it out of charity. They prey on people's fears and demand hard cash. Recently, she paid fifty pounds for a box of pills that stank to high heaven and made her vomit. I threw them into the fire. And now this latest idiocy of hers seems to have superseded the others, though I have to admit that it's free...'

Kate, enlightened, lifted her hand to stop the flood and said, 'Ah! Now I understand.

She's gone to Ezra to be healed.'

He stopped and sat down abruptly. She poured him another whisky and he thanked her absently, sipped it, and sat back in his chair.

'Yes. She's gone to Ezra. In spite of everything I could say to stop her.'

'And of course this puts you in a very difficult position, city-wise.'

'Yes, of course it does. I'm trying to get rid of the blasted woman, and my wife takes her seriously and espouses her cause.'

'Is Jocelyn's condition improving?' Kate asked, curious to know.

He shrugged. 'She says it is. She says the lump's no bigger and she feels hopeful.'

Kate was silent for a while, thinking, then said, 'What advice can I give you?'

He sipped his whisky and stared bleakly ahead of him. 'I don't know,' he said tiredly, 'but I value your judgement. Tell me your thoughts on the situation first of all.'

Kate said outright, 'I think Jocelyn's playing with fire – but so is Ezra. Because if this healing doesn't work then Jocelyn will die, and Ezra's reputation will suffer. At worst she could be seen as a party to Jocelyn's death.'

His face changed for an instant, and she saw him thinking that this would solve both problems. Then he was ashamed of the thought and asked her humbly, 'What do you think I should do?'

'Do everything in your power to persuade Jocelyn to have surgery. If she's determined not to, and Ezra's healing seems to help her, then the kindest thing is to go along with it. And I should call off the *witch-hunt*,' and she emphasized the word, 'unless you want to be publicly embarrassed.'

There was no more advice to give. He thanked her and finished his drink.

In the hall, shrugging on his overcoat, he said, 'You've no idea what an appalling time we've had. Her birthday's this month. It was a nightmare. I'd bought her a set of lingerie ... lovely stuff ... handmade – silk and lace. That was when she first broke down. Sat on the floor and cried and cried. Scared me sick. Jocelyn never cries. I thought she was upset about the kids. They're giving us a lot of trouble. But it wasn't that. I see it now. She was frightened of being ugly, of dying. She was crying for herself.'

In that moment Kate and Hector were closer than they had ever been, but they had no future together, only a past.

Kate held out her hand and he clasped it in both of his.

'Take care of yourself,' he said.

'You too – and take care of Jocelyn.'

She closed the door behind him and rested her forehead on the cold glossy panel, and saw Hector's wife sitting on the floor, clutching the lingerie, sobbing for a Jocelyn who had been healthy, beautiful and whole.

'Guess who I've just seen!' Shirley cried, bursting into Kate's office.

221

'Ezra?'

'Oh, will you stop saying Ezra down your nose like that – as if she was a bad smell – well, yes, I have been to see her as it happens, but that's not what I meant. She was waiting for someone to come for a healing session, and as I turned round to get over that bloody stile – I'll have it replaced with a gate – I saw Jocelyn Mordant on her way to the hut. What do you think of that?'

'Nothing much. What do *you* think of it?'

'Well, what could be wrong with her? It must be something serious for her to have defied Hector – he's so prejudiced about spiritual things.'

'Didn't you tell me, when you came back from the Paupers Day lunch in the autumn, that she had a friend who was ill and lived a long way away, and she asked you if Ezra could heal from a distance?'

'Oh yes,' Shirley remembered, disappointed. 'So she did – and Hector was very disagreeable about it and shut her up. I'd forgotten about that.'

'I'm not an expert,' Kate continued smoothly, 'but Jocelyn might be taking some personal possession to Ezra, such as her friend's watch or a bracelet, so that Ezra can use her healing through it.' She began to fold letters and slip them into their envelopes to show she was busy. 'Psychometry they call it. Sounds idiotic to me, but then I'm an unbeliever.'

Shirley hovered from one large foot to the

other, wanting to gossip.

'Do you suppose that Hector knows she's doing this?'

'I've no idea. It isn't of any importance to us, is it?'

'No, I suppose not. No. Oh, well.'

Shirley trailed over to the door and then turned back.

'It's just that I suspected something when she asked me that question at the Paupers lunch. You know how people say "a friend" when they really mean themselves? I wondered then, and I'm wondering even more now.'

Kate did not answer, apparently preoccupied. Shirley watched her for a moment or two, and started again.

'Oh, and I went to see Ezra about those two miserable little dependants of hers, and gave her some good advice. Send them packing, I said. Because if she lets them get away with this she's got bigger problems ahead of her. But she's not going to do anything about them. What do you think of that?'

Kate swung round in her chair and confronted her employer.

'Look, Shirley, if we're going to talk about anyone's problems, let's discuss your own – Ezra being Number One. She's becoming a cult figure among the travellers, and more and more of them are coming here to be healed and counselled. So far most of them are passing through – which is fine – but some stay on, and the number of our residents, *our* residents, is growing.

'Since they took down part of that fence in the bottom field, they've gradually encroached on your property, and the gap in the fence has been widened to take more vehicles. Quite apart from the fact that you can no longer use the field, and it looks like an old junkyard, we shall need it as a car park for the Music Festival at the beginning of July. So we want them out by the end of May at the latest. I can't see them going quietly, but we'll face that problem when we come to it. In the meantime, what happens if we get so many that they need to extend their territory? Another field – or fields? Just where and when exactly do you intend to draw the line?'

Shirley drew herself up in what Kate privately called her 'Christian soldier' posture. 'I regard Mike as a personal friend, and the rest of them seem to be well behaved. They haven't damaged the fence, just taken it down and stacked the wood. If I choose to go along with that it's nobody else's business.'

'Agreed. But we don't provide facilities for resident travellers. So they all use the services provided by the council for Marchfield, which are now seriously overstretched. I can't see the local council or the city fathers overlooking that little item, and amazing though it may seem to a charitable lady like yourself, you have enemies. Enemies employ spies. Spies tell nasty tales. So I'd advise you to equip your bottom field – or fields – with water and sanitation, or risk an official complaint.'

When Shirley was afraid, she blustered. 'Oh, don't be ridiculous, Catriona. Equip a field, indeed! A few more travellers here or there won't matter to the council.'

'A few? Do you know how many people are on your property? I thought not! Nearly fifty. Forty-seven at the last count.'

'How do you know that?' Swelling.

'As your assistant I make it my business to know. I walk down there once a week to find out what's going on and how and what they're doing. I'm astonished that you don't do likewise. And have you heard about an unofficial pagan-cum-healing event, to be held in the grove in April?'

'Idle rumours! I always ignore rumours, Catriona.'

'Rumours nothing. I've made it my business to find out about that, too. Apparently Jack Almond, who has no more sense than a child, was researching pagan festivals, and came up with a popular spring celebration that might possibly – *possibly*, mark you! – have been held in the grove. So he told Ezra, who thought it would be a lovely idea, and between them – God knows how! – they've arrived at April the fifteenth. Ezra will be conducting a healing ceremony early in the afternoon and inviting the travellers to attend. That would be bad enough if it was just *our* travellers, but word of the event is buzzing along the cranks' grapevine. Now if you're not very firm about this with Ezra, and you don't make your position very clear, you'll be the unauthorized bus and caravan park for an unknown number of weird people. It could be hundreds.'

All the colour left Shirley's florid face. She made a final attempt to carry off the conversation with a high hand.

'That is a very material and unsympathetic point of view, Catriona. How would *you* like to live in an old bus and try to feed your children on charity?'

Kate said, 'We're talking about you, not them, but let's take this point to its logical conclusion. Are you really going to bestow all your goods to feed the poor? Will you hand over the Old Hall to the travellers, and keep them on the profits of Porter's Parlours? Is it bankruptcy that you're aiming for?'

'You can be really nasty!' Shirley said. 'And in your present mood, Catriona, there is no point in continuing this conversation.'

And with that she swept out.

Kate and Jack

On a wet and windy Saturday morning in March, Jack sat in the window of Leatherhead's, the city's largest bookshop, signing paperbacks of *The Sacred Grove*.

The hardback had become something of a handbook among the moneyed faithful, and its jacket had been evocative and beautiful, since the publisher used one of Jack's photographs at dawn with first light breaking through the trees. But the paperback cover was a sensational illustration of hooded figures hovering over an altar in the clearing of an ominous forest, giving the impression of human sacrifice. And now that the casual reader could afford a copy, many would be persuaded to buy, lured by the promise of abominable revelations.

Jack had voiced his uneasiness about this idea, but was taken out of his depth by professional sales talk and left adrift. Still his conscience would not allow him to sign a copy without issuing a personal warning that the contents were mysterious rather than titillating. Fortunately for everyone's bank balance the word *mysterious* simply whetted the potential buyer's appetite and the paperbacks were selling well.

Towards noon interest had waned and he was thinking about lunch when a long, pale hand proffered a copy for his signature. He looked up to see a familiar face he had not expected.

'Hell-o!' Jack said, surprised out of his usual awkwardness in Kate's presence. 'What are *you* doing here? Shirley's got a signed complimentary hardback.'

'I know. I read it for her,' Kate replied crisply. 'This one is for my mother. She's only made murmurs about *The Sacred Grove* so far, but if I give her a copy she'll read it and be fascinated. She has a good brain, you know, despite being festooned with other people's children, and I thought I'd pay tribute to her intelligence for a change.'

'All I know is that she's a wonderful human being,' said Jack sturdily, penning a loving message to Nora. He added, 'I offered her a copy when we first met but she refused. She said that she had one on order and was expecting it any time.'

'Well, she was telling you little white lies,' said Kate smoothly. 'Glad the book's going so well, by the way. I thought it was excellent – quite potty, but excellent!'

Jack laughed, even though her flippancy annoyed him.

'That's more or less what Pat Hanna said about it.'

'He's a cynical rogue. Anyway, thank you,

Jack. Nora will love this – and it will keep her off her feet while she convalesces. Dad...' The humble name slipped out inadvertently and she corrected it. 'My father can't keep an eye on her as much as he'd like to – nor can I – and she doesn't rest enough.'

Jack asked, though he guessed the answer, 'Any luck with the adoption?'

Kate's laugh was ironic rather than amused. 'None whatsoever. And she did hope, this time, because she'd lost weight with the flu. But they made her take a medical test, and quite frankly the results weren't good. In fact, Dad and I are very worried. Poor Mum!' Again the homely names escaped her. She recovered herself. 'Still, I mustn't natter on. I'm holding up the queue.'

Something about her aroused Jack's compassion. Outwardly she seemed as chic and cool and competent as ever. Inwardly, she was suffering. Life had scraped her raw. And there was no queue, only one lugubrious man hovering, and he could wait another couple of minutes.

'I'm stopping for lunch at one,' Jack said. 'How about joining me for a...' No, she wasn't the ale and pie type. 'A glass of wine and a sandwich?'

Kate noted that he had more confidence than usual, and was looking tidier. Success must have broadened his horizon. Anyway, the rest of her day was free and this would be better than lunching at Mulberry Street alone.

'I'd like to,' said Kate, to his surprise. 'Where shall we meet?'

He discounted his own choice of the Wheatsheaf in Cornmarket.

'How about Nibbles?'

He had judged her perfectly. Nibbles was both casual and smart.

'That would be fine.'

For the first time she smiled at him as if he were a friend instead of an unsatisfactory acquaintance. Then she thanked him nicely and left.

'Sorry to have kept you waiting,' Jack said, turning to the lugubrious man who was leafing through a copy of *The Sacred Grove*. 'Would you like me to write your name in this?'

'Oh, I don't want to buy it,' said the lugubrious man. 'I thought it'd be a juicy read, judging from the cover, but I can tell it's not in my line.' He replaced it on top of the pile and leaned forward confidentially. 'I like a book with a bit more go in it. To tell you the truth I came in to buy the new Dick Francis. You should take a tip from him if you want to get on,' he advised. 'Ginger your plot up. There didn't seem to be much of a plot.' Then he looked round and asked, 'Do you know where they keep the crime novels here?'

Kate giggled when Jack related this.

'I know I should throw up my hands and register shock,' she said, 'but I've dealt with too many people to be surprised by any sort of rudeness.'

Charmed by the giggle, Jack expanded. 'It reminded me of the days when I was sweeping Adelaide Park. It was as if people labelled me "Peasant" and believed it was all right to patronize me or order me about. They'd even criticize me for something the council had done.' He imitated the gobble of a bossy woman. '"You've ruined the Beech Walk, you know!" Or they'd praise my work from a great height.' He became an ex-army officer. '"Good for you, my man!" They'd talk to me as if I was the village idiot or walk past me as if I didn't exist. I got far more respect as a professional photographer, but even then I was patronized. People think because they've bought your services they've bought *you*.'

'You're not alone,' said Kate, amused. 'I'm patronized too, but in a different way. "Oh, isn't she wonderful?" they gush, as I play Figaro to Shirley. "Whatever would you do without her?" And you can see them thinking, "Thank God I haven't got *her* job!"'

At one o'clock Nibbles was almost full, but they found a small table at the window where they could look out on the people passing by. This was one of the newer businesses, geared to the city's pace, full of light and noise and huge wall mirrors that made it appear endless.

Nibbles specialized in fast, upmarket food of all kinds. You were served at a long, glass-fronted counter and began with sandwiches –

the sort of sandwiches that are served with a decorative garnish and have to be eaten with a knife and fork – went on to imaginative salads and desserts, and wound up at hot and cold drinks. On the far wall was a wine bar. The tables and chairs were of Scandinavian simplicity. They could seat fifty people already and were converting the cellar to accommodate more. At the moment the owner-manager lived above the premises, but if business boomed he would find himself a flat and use these rooms too.

Whereas Mrs Porter's Parlour catered for the wives and families of those who had arrived and could linger enjoyably, Nibbles had become a meeting place for those on their way up: the under-thirty-fives with sophisticated tastes, not enough money to indulge them, and little time to spare.

Kate said, 'This is a luscious sandwich!' and made a note of its contents. 'I do like Nibbles,' she added. 'It moves at my pace!' she laughed.

His choice of venue being approved, Jack relaxed.

'Excuse us,' said one couple, squeezing past Kate. They were riding high in their relationship. Elated. Even sitting together in a public place with a table between them was heaven.

Kate absorbed a sigh and asked Jack, 'Tell me, are you going to write another book?'

'I shouldn't think so. I'm not a real writer. This book happened because of the subject matter. I've said all I want to say about the grove, and I'm not interested in anywhere else. And yet...'

'And yet?' Kate prompted, because she could be the perfect listener.

'I did enjoy sitting there by myself, in another world, writing.' She smiled encouragingly. He expanded. 'It was the first time I'd lived by myself. My parents had died, you see. Not that I had much in common with them.' He added honestly, 'I hadn't *anything* in common with them.' He took a deeper plunge. 'I'm not even sure now that I loved them. I think I needed to love them, but whether I did or not is a mystery.'

Kate began to regard him with interest.

'I changed the house completely in one weekend,' Jack said. 'Shut some of the rooms up and shut most of the furniture away in them. Made the front room what I wanted it to be.' He paused, fork in hand, bearing aloft its sprig of rocket. 'Yes,' he said, 'I became myself then.' He ate the sprig.

'I know the feeling,' said Kate. 'My first bedsit was a little world of peace after the chaos of Peddleford Farm.'

He was thinking ahead of her. 'Ah, but you're lucky. You can respect your parents.' A lift of her eyebrows emboldened him. 'You see, I couldn't even respect mine. My mother was a decent, well-meaning little woman and I was sorry for her, but pity isn't respect. And my father was a ... well, he was a lackey – a family tyrant who grovelled in front of everyone except us. Most of the time I disliked him

You're supposed to honour your parents, but I can't, and yet the need is still there. So where does that leave me?'

'On your own?' Kate suggested lightly.

His pleasant face was solemn. A well-fleshed man in his mid-thirties, with silky, butter-coloured hair and fresh complexion, he lounged in his chair, staring ahead of him. His presence was immensely comforting, and yet he remained uncomforted. Kate sensed that if anyone was in trouble they could turn to Jack. He was safe harbour. She could well imagine some lonely, troubled woman – though not herself, of course – crying, 'Oh, *there* you are!' Casting herself on that broad warm chest, feeling those strong arms shielding her and conveying the message that she was loved and all was well.

On the other hand, Kate reminded herself abruptly, he was hopelessly naive; he trusted people and thought the best of them instead of discriminating. And, of course, it nettled her pride that he loved Nora for her generosity of body and spirit, and preferred Kate's family to Kate herself.

He was saying, 'No, I couldn't respect my parents and I don't think I loved them, but when I told Ezra she only smiled, as if she didn't believe it. And that made me think again – not that I've come to any conclusion.'

Kate was instantly dismissive. 'Ezra? Our live-in saint? Oh dear. Are you another faithful follower?'

Her tone made him stiffen. Had she criticized him he would not have defended himself, but for Ezra he went on the attack.

'No, I'm not a follower,' he said sternly, 'but I *am* a decent photographer, and if you come home with me I'll show you studies of Ezra that will make you think twice before you speak about her like that again.'

Unrepentant, Kate replied, 'You're asking me up to see your etchings?'

He lost his temper with her. 'Oh, don't be so damned fatuous. To hear you talk no one would think you had a brain in your head or a decent feeling in your heart.'

They were both taken aback by his vehemence, and he hurried to make amends.

'I'm sorry, I shouldn't have said that, but Ezra's a great woman and so often you sound like a shallow one. I'm sorry, I shouldn't have said that either, but it's the impression you give most of the time.' He was red with exasperation and self-reproach. 'Oh, Christ! Sorry again! What I really meant to say was that I'd like you to see Ezra from another angle.'

Kate swallowed her anger and an indigestible amount of pride, and answered ironically, 'There's nothing like having your failings aired over lunch. Speaking seriously, I should like to come back with you and see the studies.'

He regretted then that he had asked her and launched into further apologies. 'I'm afraid my home isn't up to your standard. It's not the Old Hall – or your place – not that I've

235

seen your place, but Nora says it's a little gem. Knowing you, I'm sure it is. In fact – to be frank – my place is a bloody shambles.'

Kate's humour surfaced. 'I'll risk it,' she said with a smile.

He smiled back, relieved, and remembered his duties as a host. 'Are you sure you've had enough to eat?'

'Quite sure, thank you – and I've really enjoyed it.'

He said, 'I can drive you there and back but my car's a bit on the shabby side.'

She was in control of both herself and him now. 'You don't have to. My car's in the Shortlands Street multi-storey. If we liaise, I can follow you. Where's yours?'

'Same place. We'll have to walk a bit.'

'After a Nibbles sandwich we need all the exercise we can get.'

He gave her a final warning. 'I live in the less salubrious suburbs of the city.'

She answered demurely, 'I'll try to overlook that fault.'

At his ease again, Jack laughed. 'Come on!' he said heartily, and took her arm.

Good God, he thought, I've taken Kate Wing's arm as if she were an ordinary woman. I don't believe this!

They walked briskly, amiably, up to Shortlands Street.

44 Markham Terrace would have benefited from a severe scrape-down and several coats of paint. And even then, Kate thought, would

236

it be worth the effort and expense? A snob about buildings, she loathed this place the moment she saw it, for her parents' farmhouse had character and history, and Mulberry Street was perfect of its kind. How could he live here? she wondered. He wasn't poor. In fact he must be reasonably affluent, with his book selling well and his reputation as a photographer established. So why didn't he move? Appearances were so important to her that she could not imagine anyone being unaware of them.

Entering proved to be the first problem. The Yale lock was stiff and the frame swollen. Jack's confidence ebbed. Finally he wrenched the key round and kicked the front door open.

They walked into a place that managed to convey both emptiness and muddle. Kate felt instantly depressed, and Jack sank still lower in his own estimation.

'There's only one decent room,' he said defensively, and ushered her into his sanctum.

Then Kate smiled because this room, clean and white and bare of all but essentials, made sense.

'Oh, bloody hell,' Jack muttered to himself, 'I'd forgotten.' Aloud to Kate he said, 'I'm afraid the photographs are in my darkroom upstairs. If you'll wait here I'll sort them out and bring them down.'

'No, no,' she said, unthinking. 'I should like to see your darkroom.' For it sounded a professional place.

The stairs were uncarpeted. As they ascended hollowly, Jack explained, 'The carpet had holes in it. Dangerous. I threw it away.'

'Very sensible,' said Kate, avoiding the banisters, which were thick with dust.

She caught a glimpse of an unmade bed through a half-open door as they reached the landing, and a pair of boxer shorts thrown to the floor.

'My storeroom,' said Jack grandly, pointing to the boxroom door. 'And here we are.' Ushering her into the bathroom.

A row of photographs, pegged out on a line across the bath, had dripped themselves dry. The bath had a ring round the inside and a wet grey flannel dropped over the taps. The wash basin needed a good scrub and so did the towels. There was one domestic point in his favour: the lavatory smelled of disinfectant. But his work transcended the surroundings, for here was Ezra in a dozen moods and places.

Jack was talking as he unpegged and showed the pictures to Kate.

'Some people suggest colour to me. I'd photograph you in colour, for instance. You're an autumnal woman, like your mother. Ezra is at her best in black and white. I took this one from the slope above, so she's sitting at the edge of the grove looking down into the valley. I used the trees on either side as a frame and the countryside opens out below her. I aimed for a panoramic landscape and one small grey figure.'

Ezra was sitting deep in meditation with her back to the camera, captured in an inspired moment on a wintry day in the grove.

'Oh, that's exactly how I saw her once,' said Kate, remembering. 'Shirley had sent me with a message, and I didn't want to interrupt her, so I sat on a tree stump a few yards behind and waited.'

Jack said, amazed, 'Do you know, I actually *stood* on that stump to get a more dramatic viewpoint.'

Kate remembered that while she waited everything became peaceful and still, and then she had woken up, or come to, or whatever it was, to find Ezra standing beside her, and she had said, 'I've been in a good place.'

But she did not tell Jack.

He was saying, 'She was completely un-aware of me. It was as if she'd stopped the world and got off. Now look at this one. Full face. The eyes – those astonishing eyes. So deep you could drown in them, and yet they're full of light. And this one, laughing. She's got a lovely sense of humour, you know. People don't realize. I suppose they're so preoccupied with themselves and their problems that they treat her like a Delphic oracle instead of a person. But she and I had a long chat about why I was there and what I was doing. She wasn't keen on being photo-graphed at first. She said, "But I don't want this." And quick as a flash I said, "No. But I do!" And when she laughed I pushed my luck and said, "I'm doing this just for selfish old me." Joking, but meaning it. And she said. "Then I mustn't be selfish, too." Teasing me, and yet understanding me.'

'They're extremely good,' said Kate unwillingly, still nursing her prejudices.

He was not listening to her. 'What about this study of the hands? Healing hands. Oh, and I like these others, too. Taken down at Marchfield with the travellers. Not so studied. More like snapshots. And these, inside the hut with those two boneheads she carts round with her...'

'Oh, aren't they the *pits*?' cried Kate.

'Here's a picture of them by themselves. I wasn't interested in them, but Ezra asked me to do it. What a pair they are! Pat calls them Batty and Basher.'

She saw them in their sorry truth, and said wryly, 'Yes, I know. And he's right.'

'I call them B & B, for short.'

'Basher looks just like Desperate Dan!'

'But mean, instead of well-meaning.'

Studying Joel's round, childish eyes and half-open mouth, Kate said idly, 'Batty really should be in care, you know.'

She had offended him again.

'He *is* in care – her care,' Jack replied curtly. 'He couldn't be safer or happier than he is with her. It's Basher who's the odd man out, and he influences poor old Batty when they're on the loose.'

Kate held her tongue.

Am I mellowing, she wondered, or is it a mixture of being curious about Jack's way of life, fed up with Shirley, and afraid of going home to that empty house?

Jack recovered his good-natured self.

'I'm being bloody rude, and I don't mean to be,' he said. 'I'm not annoyed with you. I'm angry with myself. Pat's article in the *Courier* about B & B's escapade really hurt Ezra – not for her sake, for theirs. Shirley was furious and stomped all over us. I didn't think at the time. It was simply a lark with Pat, prowling after those two idiots like a couple of naughty schoolboys. We had a pint afterwards and laughed ourselves silly. Pat still thinks it's funny, but I don't like hurting people, so I called in later to make my peace with Ezra.

'The three of them were sitting cross-legged on the floor of the hut, having their midday meal. I'm not surprised that B & B snatch a pork pie on the side. How they keep body and soul together on those rations I don't know. But she asked me to sit down and share it with them. I could see that the two boneheads were worried in case I accepted. I didn't, of course. I made a handsome apology and started to clear off. But Ezra looked straight through me and smiled. Then she got up and came over to me, and ran her hands very lightly over my neck and shoulders. She can touch you without embarrassing you. If anyone else did that I'd feel a complete fool. And she said, "You have pain here?"' I tend to crunch myself together when

241

I'm concentrating, you see. Holding the camera, and so on. And sometimes I ache like hell.

'She told the others to eat, and made me sit on the one chair they have. She keeps it for visitors. Then she stood behind me and arched her hands a few inches above my head, and I felt the heat as if she'd turned on an electric fire. She went all over me with her hands from head to foot – never touching me – and the heat came with her. It took several minutes. "Tell me what you feel," she kept saying.

'Suddenly something clicked in my neck and I fairly shouted out, "Oh!", as if she'd punched me, and I felt quite sick. She said, "Good. Now I'm drawing out the pain."

'When she'd finished she made a rinsing motion, like a doctor washing his hands after examining a patient, and said, "How do you feel now?" I felt as if she'd wrapped me up in a big comfortable shawl and apart from being a bit dazed I was fine, and I could move my neck easily. She asked me about my work, and recommended a few simple exercises to counteract the everyday strains. And I thanked her.

'She smiled and put her hands together and bowed. So I sort of bowed, too. Then she sat down on the floor and picked up her bowl, and B & B picked up theirs – they'd waited for her, I'll say that much for them – and I left them eating their rice and vegetables. I've been her liegeman ever since, in a manner of

242

speaking, and when I'm satisfied with these,' touching the photographs, 'I'm going to present her with a set. It's my way of saying I'm sorry.'

He had effectively stopped further conversation.

After a pause Kate said humbly, 'They're extremely beautiful and I'm sure she'll love them. Thank you for showing them to me, and for the lunch. I must be getting back now. No need to show me the way. I can remember it.'

Scrutinizing his ankle boots, large and unpolished, Jack said, 'I could make you a cup of tea first.'

Guessing the state of his kitchen she answered, 'Oh no, thank you.'

Still they both lingered. Then Jack looked straight at her and said, 'Aren't Saturday afternoons a bugger when you're on your own?'

She was moved by his honesty, and the bleakness of the statement.

'But I suppose you don't feel that, being so organized,' he said quickly. 'I expect you run your life in the same way you run your job.'

'I try to, but it doesn't always work,' she admitted. 'I was at a loose end this morning when I came into the bookshop.'

'You were?' Astounded. 'You didn't seem to be. You never seem to be. You always look very ... together.'

'I'm quite good at keeping up appearances.'

He shuffled his boots, noticed their state of

dimness, and polished one stealthily against his trouser leg. 'I suppose you're not at a loose end now, are you?'

She hesitated. In his innocence he was asking too much of her pride. But Jack had no inhibitions and came out with the truth.

'Pat Hanna and I knock about together when we're both free but he's gone off somewhere this weekend. Wouldn't give me details, so he's up to some skulduggery for the *Courier*. And I've got no plans. We could ... go for a walk, or see a film or...' Imagination failed him. In desperation he admitted, 'I'm useless at organizing anything but my work. I can see that things are wrong but I don't know how to put them right.' He gestured all about him. 'I knew I should never have asked you to come here in the first place. I knew you'd hate it. I can't think why I'm bothering you anyway...'

Intrigued, Kate began to laugh. She put one hand on his arm and gave it a friendly shake. 'Oh, do shut up, Jack. You sound, as Nora would say, like a dying duck in a thunderstorm. What in God's name do you want to organize? Just tell me.'

Though flustered by her proximity, his sense of humour came uppermost. 'My life?' he suggested.

They both laughed.

His arm was warm and strongly muscled. She would have liked to move into its circle, to be held close, just for a comforting minute. To be held. To be close. To shut out the world

244

and be alive.

Oh, don't be an idiot, she thought. You're just sex-starved. She released him, while continuing to smile and banter.

'What part of your life would you like me to organize first?'

'Well, my domestic side, for a start. I mean, if this were your house what would you do with it?'

Burn it down and collect the insurance, she thought, but asked, 'In what way? So that you could enjoy living in it? So that you could sell it and buy something else?'

'I hadn't thought of moving,' said Jack slowly.

'I wasn't suggesting...'

'No, no. I mean, I'd never thought of it. But it's a good idea. It's a wonderful idea. Yes, tell me what I have to do to make the house decent enough to sell.'

Mocking, serious, Kate said, 'That's a tall order, but I never could resist a challenge, and I've tackled worse. The Old Hall versus Shirley for a start! I shall have to look round, of course.'

Embarrassed, he said, 'I'll just tidy up my bedroom first.'

'Yes, yes. Whatever. And if you'll find me a few sheets of paper and let me borrow your writing table, your house will be organized by – what's the time? Three o'clock? – let's say five o'clock. It will take me only two hours to change your life. That isn't bad going, you must admit.'

The atmosphere became cordial and relaxed.

'I'll make us some tea after all, and I think I've got a cake somewhere,' said Jack. As she hesitated, he said, 'I know I'm untidy but I'm not dirty. The cups are clean and the milk's fresh – so long as you don't mind tea bags...'

She was reminded of Nora, trying to please a difficult daughter. 'No, not a bit. But I like my tea weak.'

Outside, the March wind blew the rain against the windows.

They were both immensely happy.

Reparations

'Surely not Hector?' Kate asked herself as she heard the triple knock at her front door. It was more urgent and less confident than his usual rat-tat-TAT.

She went over to the bedroom window and looked down into the street. Could the sound have misled her after all these years – was she hallucinating? No, there he was. She saw the thinning top of his grey-blond head and as she looked he knocked again.

Jocelyn she guessed, and ran down the stairs.

He came in with a stammered apology,

246

brushing his hair back nervously.

'Kate, I'm terribly sorry to disturb you.' He registered her dressing gown and towelled head. 'Were you having an early night?'

'No. Just a shower and shampoo at the end of a long day.'

He burst out his news. 'Jocelyn collapsed at home this morning. I was away in London. Fortunately the cleaning woman was there, and telephoned for an ambulance. They took her to the City Hospital. When I got home half an hour ago I found a message on the phone. Apparently she's very bad. It's obvious that I ought to go there.' He hesitated, ashamed but desperate. 'Kate, it sounds appalling, but I don't want to see her in this state. I'm no good at this sort of thing. I don't know what to do.'

He walked through to the kitchen and slumped down at the table, head in hands. Kate followed him, feeling out the situation, handling it warily.

'Hector,' she said carefully, explaining the situation to him, 'Jocelyn will need you to be with her.'

He shook his head. 'Can't,' he said. 'Can't bear it. I loathe hospitals and sickness and death. And apparently she's been begging to see Ezra. But that quack's done enough damage already. I won't allow it.'

This isn't about you, she thought, suddenly angered. This is about Jocelyn – a child facing the dark.

The evening was coming in wild and wet,

247

and the sky over the city darkened with the approaching storm.

'Hector,' said Kate, feeling her way round the situation, 'I do understand how you feel, but Jocelyn should have everything and everyone she needs now, so you must let Ezra come. And above all you must see your wife.' She paused in order to find the right tone: neither pushing nor patronizing him, simply using friendly persuasion. 'Let me help you. I'll do anything I can. Just tell me what you want me to do,' she said.

He looked up quickly, seeing a way out for himself.

'You go,' he said. 'You go, Kate, and – yes – get hold of Ezra, too, if you think that's appropriate. And then I can ... I can come along later.'

He stared round the warm, bright kitchen as if seeing it for the first time, and focused on a bowl of daffodils glowing in the window.

'Yes,' he said decisively. 'I'll stay here and collect myself for an hour or so. You come back and tell me how she is.'

She reassembled her argument. 'I think we should go together *now*. Jocelyn needs you, not me. She only knows me on social terms. I'm nothing to her. Give me half an hour to sort myself out and I'll come with you. I can stay in the background for moral support as long as you like. Have you sent for the children?' He shook his head. 'She may want to see them. Has she asked for them?'

'I'm not sure.'

'They should be told anyway.' He buried his face in his hands and seemed not to hear. 'Hector, she's their mother.'

He lifted his head and cried, 'She won't admit how ill she is. She's been visiting this Ezra instead of dealing with the ... the ... trouble properly. I did as you advised. I played along with the healing nonsense, both of us pretending she was getting better, and knowing she was getting worse. I'd have that blasted charlatan tarred and feathered and run out of town on a rail if I could. The last few months have been hell on earth. Oh, Christ Almighty, death is an ugly business.'

Kate made up her mind and, hopefully, his. 'I'll dry my hair and dress, and we'll go together.'

He had buried his face in his hands again by the time she came back.

'Up you get, Hector,' she said, keeping her tone matter-of-fact. She grasped his arm and half-helped, half-pulled him to his feet. 'Would you like a stiff whisky first, and I'll drive us there in my car?' she asked.

He shook his head and made an effort.

'No, no. I'm all right. I can drive. It's the rest that I can't manage.'

'You'll manage beautifully. You always do. Do you want me to contact Ezra, and the children, and anyone else who needs to know? All right, I'll do that. And I'll stay as long as you need me, and disappear when you want me to. All we have to remember is that Jocelyn is the important person in this

249

situation. You and I don't matter, whatever it costs us. Only Jocelyn matters.'

Hector nodded. He had placed himself in Kate's care.

'Shirley, this is Kate. *Kate,* love! Yes, Kate! You sound confused.'

A faint chink, as of a glass colliding with the receiver, and a mumbled excuse.

Kate sighed, and answered, 'Yes, it must be the line.' She spoke clearly and slowly. 'Shirley, this is important. I'm ringing from the City Hospital. Jocelyn Mordant is dying. Dying. Yes. And she's asking for Ezra. I know it's late at night, but this is an emergency.'

So for God's sake pull yourself together and make yourself useful!

'Could you send someone down to the hut to get Ezra, and put her in a taxi and send her here? Ring me back when you've done that – this is the ward number. And tell her to come to the Tower block. I'll be waiting for her in reception. Yes, Hector's here and I'm giving him moral support.' With some asperity, 'No, Shirley, that's all over between us, and it isn't necessary for you to involve yourself in any way, apart from giving Ezra the news and sending her here. She won't have any money so I'll pay for the taxi – oh, all right then, *you* pay if you insist. I don't mind either way. No, don't come with her. Jocelyn isn't allowed visitors and Hector isn't in any state to talk to friends. The kindest thing you can do is to

250

stay at home.'

She divined hurt feelings but had no time to soothe them.

'Sorry if I sound abrupt, but I've got a list of people whom I need to contact and I'm working my way down it, so I must go. Yes, it does seem sudden, but apparently she's been ill for a long time. I'll tell you all about it when I see you.'

Those are maudlin whisky tears that I hear at the other end of the line, she thought. Jocelyn meant no more to you than she means to me, but death invests us all with distinction.

'Truly I must go now. Bless you, Shirley. You're a star!'

She cut the conversation short, waited a moment, and then dialled the boarding school number.

Kate was staging a Victorian deathbed, with everyone assembled for the farewell performance, and her organization was impeccable, but unfortunately the leading lady refused to play her part. Jocelyn decided not to die just yet and lingered for a week or two, heavily sedated. Occasionally she surfaced in mild surprise, finding herself surrounded by flowers and cards, and often with some friend, relative or social acquaintance watching solemnly over her. On each of these visitors she spent her scraps of strength in explaining that she had suffered a nervous breakdown.

'Too much to do, darling!' she would confide, with charming dishonesty. And lest anyone wonder what she did do, apart from spending her husband's money and entertaining their friends, she would add, 'Hector relies on me so.'

Only to Ezra did she admit the truth, and then only in part.

'I'm very ill. Have you come to make me better?' she asked, as Ezra placed cool brown hands on hers.

'I have come to give you rest and peace of mind,' said Ezra gently, 'but I can promise you nothing else.'

'That's right,' Jocelyn would say, bypassing the deeper implication. 'I've had too much on my mind. But you've come to heal me so I shall soon be better.'

Jocelyn's two youngsters, whisked home on the heels of Kate's announcement, now sat by their mother's bed for half an hour every morning and evening, and then hung aimlessly round the house on Holden Crescent, lost and frightened. The sight of their mother, drugged and often insensible, silenced them. But when she was conscious they did not know what to say to her, nor she to them.

'What are you two doing here? Shouldn't you should be in school? You haven't been naughty again, have you?' she would ask each time, knitting her brows.

'No, Mummy. Oh no.'

'That's my darlings. Are you on holiday already?'

After a little hesitation they decided to go along with the charade and answered, 'Yes, Mummy.'

Jocelyn's parents and sister arrived in the city speedily, put the Mordants' housekeeper to a vast amount of trouble for a couple of days, and returned home immediately when no one could tell them how long the wait might be.

Hector had done all he could, which was to move his wife to a private room and to engage another specialist to examine her, though he could only confirm the verdict.

Kate, as she put it later, 'stood by'. This involved doing her own work and remaining available for anything or anyone at all times. Hector's patience with personal affairs being minimal, and the Music Festival just over three months away, he soon absented himself, leaving her to cope. Without the presence of Jack in the background she would have been ill herself, but he kept watch over her, turning up when she was exhausted, taking her out for a meal or a walk, listening to her, giving good advice, and delivering her back refreshed and ready for another punishing round.

Patrick also took care of her in his own way. His humour rendered even this major trauma a matter of temporary inconvenience. He would take her out for a drink, and retail the latest gossip with relish. They would eat late and casually, and rarely in the same place: a snack at a pie stall, a visit to a transport café, a take-away to be enjoyed at Mulberry Street.

Nora was also allowed to be a stalwart supporter at this time, and the crisis suited her. It meant that her daughter was dependent on her, needed her. 'Come home whenever you can, love. Night or day. Any time,' said Nora. Her care was a lifesaver, though her running commentaries infuriated Kate.

'Well, I can't understand why you're doing it,' Nora would say, making her daughter a late-night bacon sandwich. 'It's beyond me! A woman of your capabilities and intelligence, who could command a high salary anywhere with the best of companies, hanging about for years at Melbury Old Hall with that drunken old Shirley, and running to and fro for this Hector Mordant as if you were his office girl. Mind you, I always thought there was a lot more going on in that quarter than I was ever told! And though your father says that I do too much for everybody, and he wished I had your common sense, if you start taking on other people's problems and letting them push you around you're no more sensible than I am.'

'The girl's doing what she thinks is right, and she's tired out,' Kate's father would say gently. 'Leave her be, Nora. Leave her be.'

And Kate, warmed and fed and spent, would lean against him on the sofa and rest her head on his shoulder and fall asleep, while Nora continued to half-praise and half-chastise her.

And when Kate enquired of herself why she

254

was doing all this she was dismayed by the lack of logic in her answers.

Because if I didn't, Hector would stay away from Jocelyn, using his work as an excuse, whereas knowing that you're there he daren't run away.

Why do this for Jocelyn, who means nothing to you if you are to be honest, and surely to God, honesty is all you have left?

No human being should die friendless and alone.

But his presence there is a pretence. She knows it and he knows it.

They need to keep up appearances and they'll take comfort from this. Besides, he must set an example for the children.

You don't even like the children.

No, but I'm sorry for them. Their mother is dying.

She was an indifferent mother.

Yes, but she was all they knew, and the bond is strong despite her failings.

In the end what will you get out of this?

It isn't about me.

In the third week Jocelyn stopped pretending. Her pretty gestures and mannerisms left her. She slept her drugged sleep, or lay there with weary eyes, and lived only for the time that Ezra spent with her.

Small and grey and quiet, the healer came and went in her own hours and by her own means. Heaven knows how she got there and back but she did. In the minds of many she had attained the status of wise woman. Her net was cast far and deep and her friends were many. She might arrive in a limousine or in a lorry. Once she was forced to catch a bus, and though she had no money the conductor knew of her and charged no fare. When Hector protested at her continued visits Kate quelled him effectively.

'Oh, all right, all right!' he would cry irritably, waving his arms as if to rid himself of a gadfly. 'I suppose Jocelyn needs the damned swindler. Just keep her out of my sight.'

As if she knew this, Ezra's visits never coincided with his.

The nurses accepted that her unorthodox presence soothed their patient and grew used to her appearing at odd hours. With the dark, dry humour of nurses, the ward nurse quipped, 'You're as good as a dose of morphine, Ezra!'

And she did take away pain, but not for long, and she could not conquer it.

'She's making me better,' Jocelyn would gasp. 'I'll soon be better. Then I can go home.'

They tried to teach her to control the pain herself, but she refused to acknowledge the need so they instead controlled it for her.

Kate, directing this deadly circus from behind the scenes, appearing upfront only in her role as chauffeur, was surprised when Jocelyn addressed her one evening in a ghost of her former manner.

'It's Kate, isn't it? Kate Wing? Didn't you used to work for Hector at one time? Yes, I thought so. I tend to forget things these days. Would you be good enough to stay with me for a few minutes?'

Kate, recognizing and resenting the tone of kindly employer's wife to lowly employee, gritted her teeth as she complied.

Still in her society hostess mode, Jocelyn said, 'You seem to have been awfully busy on my behalf. I just wanted to say how terribly grateful I am.'

Kate answered drily, 'You're welcome.'

Jocelyn scrutinized her as she would have scrutinized a strange specimen under a microscope. She spoke derisively. 'I suppose you're doing this for Hector? I knew, of course, that you were his mistress. Perhaps you still are. I lose track of his mistresses.'

Kate answered coldly, 'You're wrong. That's all over. For good.'

'Then why should you?'

'I don't know. I suppose because I must. Call it common decency.'

Jocelyn's expression changed. There was a short silence while she reflected. Then she confided in quite a different tone, 'I'm going to die soon.'

Involuntarily, Kate clasped her hand. Her apology was also a confession.

'I'm sorry if I hurt you. I was young and selfish. If I considered you at all I told myself you didn't care.'

Jocelyn replied candidly, voice dying, 'If I did care, I expect it was only pride. Hector and I didn't have much of a marriage. I cheated, too.'

She closed her eyes but they continued to hold hands, no longer needing to accuse or explain.

When Jocelyn finally lapsed into a coma Kate was advised to contact Hector, but he was away in London and she left a message at his hotel. Then she and Ezra kept a vigil, sitting in peaceful silence together. The nurses came and went, observing each change in the patient's condition. A doctor looked in before he went home. Lights went out in the adjoining ward and the night nurse put her head round the door to tell them she was available if needed.

'If you want a cup of tea later on, just let me know,' she said. 'And if you get hungry we generally have a snack halfway through the shift and you're welcome to join us.'

Ezra said, 'I shall need nothing, but you go, Kate.' And as Kate hesitated, because she had missed out on supper, Ezra added, 'Jocelyn won't die yet. She clings to life.'

So at three o'clock in the morning Kate joined a group of nurses in the kitchen and ate corned beef sandwiches and piccalilli and drank strong tea, and marvelled at the normality and strangeness of their night world. They accepted sickness and death, talked of bargains at the superstore, their children, their husbands or boyfriends, high prices and low wages. One old woman in the ward had been whimpering for a home perm she couldn't afford. 'Poor old body!' And they were starting a collection for her, but when Kate wanted to contribute a five-pound note she was refused. 'No, we all give the same. That's only fair,' they said, and she subscribed her pound coin like the rest of them.

Subdued and exalted, she reported back to Ezra.

'I thought I'd met everybody and seen everything,' Kate ended, 'but I haven't even scratched the surface. It's a revelation.' And then, looking at the wasted form on the bed, 'How is she?'

'She is working her way across,' said Ezra, 'but she knows that we are with her.'

The atmosphere was serene, and time of no consequence.

At one point Kate said, 'I feel I should warn you that you have enemies on the council who will use any evidence they can find against you – who will twist evidence if necessary – and Jocelyn's husband is foremost among them.'

Ezra nodded, and gave the slightest shrug of one shoulder.

Kate insisted, 'They intend to get rid of you, Ezra. They're very powerful. They'll put pressure on you to leave.'

'I shall stay.'

'But what will you do if they make life unbearable?'

Ezra answered, 'Nothing.'

Then I can't do anything either, Kate thought, but at least I've told her.

Jocelyn was making reparation. She frowned and muttered. Her fingers were restless. But the drugs did their work, and left her to do hers. And Kate sat in peace, as she had sat on the tree stump in the winter of that year, and waited with Ezra.

At six o'clock in the morning, as the hospital began to stir awake and light came greyly through the window, Jocelyn opened her eyes and looked round for the last time. Her expression was remote. She seemed about to speak. One hand lifted an inch or so as if in acknowledgement. Then she was no longer with them.

Hector met them as they were leaving. He had arrived too late and was ashamed, enraged, and relieved. Someone must be blamed. He turned on Ezra, loudly, passionately.

'I shall hold you to account for the loss of my wife, and you will pay for it.'

Kate, distanced from him by the long watch and lack of sleep, observed that he spoke of Jocelyn's death in financial terms.

Ezra said, without emotion, 'I told your wife from the beginning that I could not cure her, but she preferred to hope.'

'So that's your version of events, is it?' Hector cried. 'Well it's not good enough. People are checking up on you, and what they find might not be very savoury. We'll see what you have to say when the facts come out. But let me tell you this – facts or no facts, you're

260

finished as a local tin god, and the best thing you can do is to clear off right now. Go on. Get out!'

He advanced on her, waving his arms. Kate's command halted him mid-step.

'Hector!'

She moved in front of Ezra. She motioned advancing nurses away. She took his arm and spoke to him soothingly, firmly.

'You've had a terrible shock,' Kate said. 'Come with me and I'll take you home.'

He went with her, like a child.

In Council

The council was being held in private.

On an April afternoon, in the grandeur of the city council chamber, the chairman rose to offer condolences to Hector Mordant, one of their most valued colleagues, and to thank him for attending the meeting so soon after his tragic loss. The warmth of the room coaxed a delicate fragrance from the bowls of hyacinths, and an aroma of beeswax from the polished mahogany. Both were extremely pleasant, and every member sniffed their approval, and silently thanked God they were still alive.

The first item on the agenda was entitled

'Unofficial Ceremony on Grove Hill' and as this was Hector's special province he was invited to begin.

He looked older and greyer, had lost some of his ebullience but none of his authority. He received the committee's sympathy with dignity and went straight to the heart of the issue.

'I should like, briefly, to refresh our memories with regard to the possible ceremony on Grove Hill. So far the council has kept a low profile, since we received only rumours that this meeting was contemplated. There was no advertising, no attempt to organize such an event, and no one approached us to ascertain official opinion. We did not know the exact date, nor how many people might attend, nor what arrangements – if any – had been made to accommodate them. All we could do was to keep an eye on future developments. In fact, up to now, this meeting could be regarded in much the same light as a school picnic.'

Subdued agreement.

'However...' He paused momentarily and they straightened up. 'I now have positive information that it will take place on the fifteenth of this month in the early afternoon. That a large number of new-age travellers are expected to attend it and are already gathering – not only in Marchfield but in a neighbouring property, where I presume the owner has given them permission to stay. I am also told that no provisions have been made to look after them, which means that they will be a nuisance to the local community and a burden on Marchfield. In fact, this whole ridiculous enterprise,' his voice became hard, 'has – been – left – entirely – to – chance.'

Rumbles of indignation.

His tone lightened, became satirical. 'I know that you share my feelings with regard to what we might call "The Grove Hill Mob"...'

Some amusement.

'...and I have a personal grievance with the major troublemaker.'

A general murmur of understanding. A few members, who neither admired nor were afraid of Hector, looked ironic and remained silent.

'But I have put personal feelings aside,' said Hector, who had not. 'Our concern as a city council is with the broader issues and we must remain mindful always of our first and greatest duty, which is to the public.'

Most relished this picture of themselves and there were cries of 'Hear, hear!' One member said 'Cant!' very quietly. But Hector was in rabble-rousing mode.

'Such an unorganized gathering would encourage theft and damage to public and private property, violence, drug-dealing, and other unlawful behaviour.'

Rumbles of 'Youngsters taking ecstasy...', 'Indulging in disgusting sexual practices...', 'Shocking publicity...', 'All over the damned papers...', 'Get rid of the travellers!', 'Get rid

263

of that woman!', 'Ban it!'

Hector lifted one hand for silence, got it, and spoke persuasively.

'It would be sensible of the estate owner – even so late in the day – to realize what might be involved and at least to mention the matter to someone in authority. Let's hope that she does. Meanwhile, I suggest we wait and see.' A murmur of surprise and disappointment. Hector held up one manicured hand to indicate that he had not yet finished. 'I can understand your reaction, but let's think before we act. Remember that this event will not take place in our backyard. Grove Hill is outside the city, so we shan't be disturbed personally – that will be Peddleford's problem. And I would point out that the Grove Hill Mob...'

No amusement now.

'...do attract respectable cranks as well as disreputable vagrants, which gives us further reason for restraint. If this ceremony passes off without major incident and turns out to be a success, let's not be seen as the ones who condemned it. Let us rather make use of the occasion by taking it over as an annual event.' Confusion. He toughened. 'With regard to the chief offender, my decision remains the same. We must cut out the...' The words *cancer in our midst* hovered over the meeting and for a moment even Hector faltered. Rooting out a metaphorical cancer, he had forgotten the personal one. There was a shocked pause, but for only a few seconds, then he recovered himself and spoke as smoothly as ever. '…the evil that besets us. If the meeting takes place and fails then we punish the major offenders and punish them heavily!'

Approval. They were with him now.

Hector addressed them with all his former impudence and charm. 'But if it happens to be a success we take it over.'

Laughter and one or two claps.

'And if you feel inclined to ask Celebrations to organize it, I'm sure they could be persuaded!'

Laughing applause, punctuated by one doubting Thomas.

'But this Ezra is the star attraction in this particular circus. How could we manage it without her?'

Hector brushed him aside. 'We shall provide safer entertainments. Turn it into a pagan celebration. Dig up some history about it – real or imagined. Get everyone to dress up for the occasion. But let me make one thing clear: Ezra must go.'

They were very quiet now, listening to him.

'Fellow members of the council, I vote that we do nothing at the moment – apart from providing the rope with which they can hang themselves!'

The motion was carried unanimously.

He looked round, smiling, having the last word as always.

'Meanwhile, there is one sweetener to offer. I am reliably informed that most of the
265

hotels, lodging houses and bed and breakfast places in the city are already fully booked. I cannot think that this is only to be attributed to the forthcoming Easter holiday. We should be grateful for even the smallest mercies.'

They all laughed.

Rebellion

Shirley began her meditations with the aid of a cigarette and a double whisky to put her in the right frame of mind, but she was to be disturbed on this April morning by her assistant knocking peremptorily at the door and entering without permission. Kate was in what Nora would have described as 'a right paddy'.

'Shirley, we've reached crisis point. I've just been down to Marchfield, only to find that yet another lot of travellers has arrived, and taken down a *second* fence and moved into *another* field. This time they aren't stacking the wood – they're using it to make fires. The council's water and sanitation facilities were already inadequate, and these people are now using water from the stream for washing and drinking, and digging holes in the ground for earth closets. We've got a civic problem and a major health hazard on our hands.'

Shirley was possibly more unhappy than she had ever been, and in no mood to have her hidden terrors realized.

'You know very well, Catriona, that I'm not to be disturbed during meditation.' ('Oh, meditation – balls!' said Kate under her breath.) 'The travellers have come in time to attend Ezra's healing ceremony, that's all. There may be one or two problems at first, but the situation is only temporary and they're used to roughing it. I'll have a word with our good friend Mike and I'm sure he'll see that the whole enterprise is conducted in an orderly fashion.' Afraid of hearing more, she added caustically, 'And now, if you'll grant me half an hour's peace and quiet...'

Kate was not to be disposed of so easily.

'If you actually went there yourself to assess the situation – as I've just done! – you'll find that "our good friend Mike" is being metaphorically trampled underfoot by the ongoing hordes. As well as using your property they've packed Marchfield from side to side. This is a question of basic survival, Shirley, and you must do something about it before they start fighting each other.'

Her employer's temper flared.

'What's wrong with you these days, for God's sake? You used to be so helpful and level-headed and now you're running round like a hysterical hen, worrying me with every little problem. Nobody's asked *you* to deal with the arrangements for the ceremony – perhaps that's what bothers you? You always

267

have to be boss-man, don't you? I repeat that Mike will sort this out. Now go away.'

Furious, Kate let her tongue talk for her.

'What arrangements are you talking about? There *are* no arrangements. That's my point. And I have it on excellent authority –' Patrick, the previous evening, over a drink at Mulligan's – 'that the city council is deliberately holding back and waiting for this affair to blow up in your face. Then they're going to drop on Ezra, and on you, and finish the pair of you.'

She had disclosed more than she meant to, and inwardly cursed herself. In a more conciliatory tone she said, 'Shirley, we don't want trouble with the authorities. We should have persuaded Ezra to go to them a long time ago when this ceremony was just an idea, instead of allowing it to happen and hoping for the best. I know it's late in the day, and we've got all kinds of difficulties, but we can at least minimize them. An event of this sort can't be left to chance.'

'I suppose you have some kind of master plan with which to impress us all!' Shirley said loftily.

'I have a sensible suggestion to make. You can't stop this love-fest – or whatever it is – so deal with it. Organize the damned thing – as Hector would. After all, we're catering officially for a few thousand in July, so we can treat two or three hundred as a trial run. Hire Portaloos and bring in water. Make it clear to these newcomers that this is only temporary, and everybody goes as soon as the show's over. We can still get away with it. I know the ropes and I'll do the work. It's going to be expensive, of course, but that can't be helped.'

'Oh, money, money, money!' Shirley fretted. 'Why are you always nagging me about money?'

'Because more is going out than coming in, and it's in very short supply.'

Kate's tone was also very short and Shirley came to attention. Sobered, she looked everywhere but at her assistant. Finding no escape route, she attacked her. 'You don't pull the wool over my eyes, you know. All this criticizing and bossing people about is pure envy. *Envy* – the meanest sin of the lot. You're not afraid that this meeting will fail; you're afraid it'll succeed and put Ezra on top. You know she's a better person than you'll ever be. You've always hated her.'

'I don't hate her,' said Kate, shocked. 'Indeed, I do not. On the contrary...'

Shirley became dramatic, and historically inaccurate, in her cups.

'As the disciple said of Christ, you're not fit to black her boots. Ezra would give you the food off her plate and the clothes off her back if you needed them. She never counts the cost to herself.' Her own demons beset her. She spoke through them. 'But you won't do anything for anybody unless the price is right and they fit into your scheme of things...'

Kate said in a high, tight voice, 'I've come

269

to like and admire Ezra, and I am not for a moment questioning her sincerity. What I *am* saying is that she's a political innocent who has no idea of the trouble she's brewing up for herself and others...'

Higher and more volubly, Shirley cut across her, crying, 'And that's why you can't make a decent relationship or keep a close friend. You think you know it all, but what exactly have you got? A little bitty house that Hector Mordant put you in for his own convenience so that the finger couldn't be pointed at him, and a job he made up so that you could still work for him while being paid by me. I'm not a fool. I know that the pair of you have been using me. And on top of that you've altered *my home* to suit yourselves, in the name of good taste. And who are you, I might ask, to be held up as a model of good taste? And why should one thing be in better taste than another? I liked that blackamoor holding the tray, but oh no, it wasn't good enough for Hector, so it had to go. And when all's said and done, my lady, you're no more than a collection of designer labels and pretty party manners and he's a con man. Oh, you make a lovely couple.'

Kate's white silence frightened her. She poured another whisky to steady her nerves, and tried to turn the tirade into a mere grumble.

'I've got nothing against a self-made woman. I'm one myself. And I appreciate all that you've done and we've been good

270

friends. But I won't have you poking round my property, inspecting fences, and talking behind my back with your informant, whoever he is...' Her words tailed off. She tipped the whisky round and round her glass, observing its movement closely so that she didn't have to look at Kate. She could not manage without her and was wondering how to pave the way to reconciliation when Kate made up her mind.

'In that case I suggest you find someone to take my place, because I'm giving you a month's notice according to our original agreement,' she said. And walked out, leaving Shirley shocked into sobriety.

Two Kates sat at her desk in the next half-hour: one rejoicing in that moment of truth, relishing that flash of freedom, the other bedevilled by practical considerations and regret at the loss of a job she had created. As she strove between them, Patrick walked in unannounced.

'I gave Walter a tip for the two thirty at Cheltenham tomorrow, and told him I was expected,' said Patrick, grinning. 'So he let me in.'

It was as if a light had been switched on. Kate felt suddenly carefree.

'I don't see an appointment here,' she said, pretending to consult the diary. 'What might I do for you, Mr ... er...'

'Ah, now, don't be like that. Come out to tea,' said Patrick, wheedling. 'Let me show you what a civilized man I am. I can eat cucumber sandwiches without dropping crumbs on the floor. I know the difference between a napkin and a handkerchief. I can even drink tea out of a cup and crook my little finger with the best of them.'

'Where were you planning to take me?' Kate asked, trying not to smile.

'Where is there, in this fair city of ours, to compare with Mrs Porter's Parlour? Oh, I know it's like offering a bottle of beer to a brewer. I dare say you and the Lady Pringle nip and sip dainties there at four every afternoon, but then you don't have me with you to liven things up.'

'Actually, I haven't been to the Parlour for ages. The only sipping is done here, by Shirley, and she finds whisky far more welcome than tea.'

'Sour!' Patrick chided.

'But true.'

He held out both hands and she allowed him to pull her to her feet. He was wearing an expression she had never seen before: humble, vulnerable. Usually he gave the impression of being ageless. Now he looked every one of his forty-five years and Kate felt suddenly young again. She became the child who had been denied, the outsider seeing how insiders lived, nose pressed against the window, coveting delicacies she would not be offered and could not afford.

'Yes, please,' she said. 'I would like you to take me out to tea at the Parlour. Let's make it a good one – to hell with healthy eating.'

'Oh, I never trouble myself about that,' said Patrick truthfully.

'I had noticed,' said Kate, acerbic. Then, contrite, 'Oh, why am I being nasty when you're being so nice to me? Patrick, I've just taken your advice and given Shirley a month's notice. But that,' seeing his eyes light up, his broken nose twitch, 'is strictly confidential. Strictly.'

'Just get your bonnet and shawl on, and stop being disrespectful to your elders and worsers,' said Patrick, grinning. 'Did you think I was going to write a scurrilous article about it? *Immorality at the Old Hall. One of our most notable public figures, Shirley Pringle, has lost her assistant. Glamorous Kate Wing, who has left her employer for undisclosed reasons, told the* Courier, *"Let us say that suggestions were made that I found offensive. I come from a respectable home and value my good name."* Oh, the vanity of the woman!'

'Oh, shut up!' said Kate, printing a notice that said: GONE OUT FOR TEA. BACK TOMORROW MORNING. She stuck it on her door with Blu-tack.

'I know you're not to be trusted with any item of news, however small,' she remarked. 'And instead of standing there talking nonsense I might remind you that it's usual to help a lady on with her coat.'

'Lovely as Sheba and wise as Solomon!' said Patrick as she handed it to him. 'Now tell me, do you like vanilla slices? Because I can't

273

resist them.'

They went out together, arm in arm, laughing.

At the Parlour he was on top form, courting the waitress and making them giggle, drawing the attention of the county ladies who had been whiling away a dull afternoon and now found entertainment in their midst.

'I know there must be some point to this invitation,' said Kate, through a mouthful of cinnamon toast, 'but don't get to it until I've finished making an absolute pig of myself.'

'Ah, that's what I like about you. Always the perfect lady.'

Finally, relaxed, replete, content, she smiled on him and round at the Parlour.

'This is a good place to be on a cold afternoon,' she said. She remembered another cold afternoon, sitting in the grove behind Ezra. 'A good *secular* place to be,' she added, and laughed, and didn't share the joke. 'So what's the news?'

'It's personal.'

'You're pregnant and looking for good advice?' she suggested unkindly.

'Ah, what a cynical young woman you are, to be sure. No, I was wondering...' His expression was uncertain, but his tone remained breezy. 'I was wondering what you really thought of me.'

Taken aback, Kate said, 'I regard you as a real friend.' She brightened the words by adding, 'And an extremely likeable rogue.'

274

'But do you think,' Patrick said confidentially, leaning forward, 'that I'm an *attractive* rogue – what I mean is, could you fancy me?'

She checked a smart retort, and answered teasingly. 'I think you're eminently fanciable.'

'I'm being serious, on one of the very rare occasions in my life.'

'I'm listening seriously.'

'For a start, I'm thinking of going freelance. What's your opinion of that?'

Puzzled, she said, 'I'm sure you could do it. In fact, I think it might suit you better than working for someone else.'

His tone was flippant, but he was in earnest. 'I can't remember how long I've been on the *Courier* – but it's longer than I've stayed anywhere else. It's time to move on. And now you're leaving Shirley, you're as free as I am.' He hesitated on the brink, then plunged in style. 'So I was thinking, Katie, mavourneen, how about thumbing our noses at the lot of them, wiping the city dust from our feet, and running away together?'

She sat in dumbfounded silence.

'I've fancied you for quite a while, Kate, as well as liking and respecting you,' he said humbly, 'and you're the only woman I've ever been able to call a friend.'

She said slowly, 'Patrick, I do appreciate what you're saying, but attraction, liking and respect aren't enough to make that sort of commitment.' She smiled then, judging the expression that flitted across his face. 'You don't like the word *commitment*, do you? But

275

from my point of view, finding a new job in a new place, making a new life with you, and leaving behind everything and everyone I've ever known would be an enormous commitment.'

He dodging the answer by mocking her. 'Ah! You're still in love with Celebration Hector. Now that's a fine suit of clothes, if you like, on a fine cardboard figure of a man.'

He had stung her and she stung back. 'Having finished one cardboard relationship I'm not about to take on another.'

They had raised their voices above the acceptable level of Mrs Porter's Parlour. Smart heads turned. A waitress appeared, smiling anxiously, to ask if everything was all right.

'No, it bloody well isn't!' Patrick cried, pushing back his chair.

'Thank you,' said Kate, smiling back at her, ignoring him. 'I should like another pot of lemon tea, but this gentleman is going.'

Which he did, in high dudgeon, leaving her to pay the bill.

She had three telephone calls that evening. The first was from Hector, sounding so urbane that she knew he was worried.

'Hell-o, Kate. This is Hector. How *are* you, my dear?'

Dry but pleasant, she answered, 'Never better. How are you?'

'Oh...' He had to milk sympathy. 'Finding the house an empty place without poor Jocelyn. It will take some time to get used

276

to that.'

She ignored this hypocrisy. 'And how are your two youngsters?'

'Oh...' He had to think. 'They're staying with my parents at the moment. I believe they're coming along pretty well. Pretty well. All things considered.'

She waited, not prepared to play his game. He came at once to the point.

'Kate, I've heard some disturbing news, which I hope isn't true. I know how Shirley exaggerates and – speaking frankly, my dear – I'm beginning to think she has a serious drink problem. She sounded incoherent when she spoke to me. But in the midst of her ramblings she told me that you'd left her. Is that true?'

'Yes.'

'You mean, for good?'

'Yes.'

A short pause while he gauged her mood. 'This is rather sudden, isn't it?'

'Not as sudden as all that,' said Kate, enjoying herself. 'I've put up with her nonsense for a long time.'

He dropped his easy manner and became the man of business she knew.

'What the hell's got into you, Kate? You know perfectly well that she can't replace you at this stage in the proceedings. What's going to happen to the Celebrations festival in July?'

'That won't be my problem,' said Kate sweetly.

Aghast, he tackled her from another angle. 'Do I presume you have another job to go to?'

She dodged him. 'There's an offer in the wind. Nothing settled – as yet.'

He lost his temper. 'You're a damned fool, Kate, and you're playing outside your field. If you're going to let me down like this you needn't think you'll get a reference from me – and I'll make sure you don't get one from Shirley either.'

Kate's answer came of itself, laconic, rousing her admiration, appalling her.

'I shan't need fine words from either of you. The offer comes from someone who knows my work well, and has known me for some time, so a refusal to back me would merely be regarded as petty jealousy on both your parts.'

Now what on earth persuaded me to leap into the unknown? she wondered.

Hector's short silence was also appalled. When he spoke again he had smoothed his tone, changed tactics and become the kindly friend.

'I shouldn't like you to be hoodwinked by Needham, or Stuyvesant, or anyone of that ilk. People like that can promise the earth but they rarely deliver.'

He believes me, Kate thought, incredulous. He actually believes me. He's checking rivals and enemies in his mind for a possible poacher. Well, what the hell, I can always run away with Patrick if the worst comes to the worst.

278

She proffered further bait. 'It's no one you know, Hector.'

And no one I know either.

'The suggestion came out of the blue. I've plenty of time in which to consider it.'

All the time in the world, since there's nothing to consider.

'I see.' He was now the good-humoured coaxer. 'Look, Kate, you've got me over a barrel on this. I don't blame you for looking out for yourself, and jolly good luck to you. As for Shirley, I don't give a damn about her. She can drink herself into a rehab centre as far as I'm concerned, let the Old Hall fall about her ears, and go bankrupt – which she will if she doesn't pull herself together – but the July event *must* go on and you're the only one who can do it.'

As she waited for him to entangle himself further, Kate thought: Why shouldn't I look round seriously for another job? Even outside the city. Why let the city decide my boundaries?

Hector was urgent. 'How much time have you got, in which to decide?'

She answered easily, 'Two or three months,' and this time she was not afraid of her adventurous self.

Hector's relief was evident. 'Then please, please, will you see me through, my dear? I do realize that working for Shirley has limitations that you have long since outgrown, and no one will be more delighted than me when you find the job you deserve. But stay with

279

me until this show's over, will you, Kate? Please!'

She had already decided that she needed more time and money while she found her mythical job. She made a show of capitulating gracefully.

'All right, Hector. I'll extend my notice to the end of July and see Celebrations through. Will you do something for me in return?'

'Anything,' he said recklessly, relying on her good sense and integrity.

'You've never given me more than thanks for the work I've done on behalf of Celebrations at the Old Hall. I think this final business favour deserves a fee.'

There was a short pause while he swallowed, recognizing his own teaching, then he said coldly, 'How much?'

'I leave that to you.' Knowing that his pride would not allow him to undervalue her services.

'Very well.' Very grim. 'Anything else?'

'I'd be most grateful if you would ring Shirley and tell her that you persuaded me to change my mind. I don't want her to think I'm doing her a favour.'

Hector was a gracious loser. He chuckled. 'I always thought you were a clever woman, Kate, but I underestimated you. Look, Kate, how would you like to come back to Celebrations as my assistant? On generous terms? Whatever you've been offered elsewhere, I'll better it.'

'What about your latest secretary?'

280

'She'll have four months' notice and a good reference. Nothing to grumble about. You start at the beginning of August. Say yes, Kate!'

She would have liked to tell him exactly what she thought about him and this idea, but left the answer to her new, dark self.

'I'll think about it, Hector. Goodnight.'

The second call came from Jack, who knew nothing of what had happened, would never be up front with the news, and was seemingly incapable of a devious word or thought. The background noises sounded like the Lamb and Child in full swing. His voice told her that he had worked hard all day, was exhausted, and had realized that the world was a lonely place.

'Hello, Kate. Have I rung at a good time?'

'Never better.' Dry and pleasant.

Then he surprised her. 'You sound as if you've been in the wars. Did you win?'

She laughed then. 'Yes. Three good battles so far. But the war goes on. I'll have to stay vigilant.'

He chuckled, conveying pride in her prowess. 'Who've you been battering this time, Kate?'

'Shirley and Hector – oh, and Patrick Hanna.'

'The big guns. Am I next in the firing line?'

'No. I've nothing against you, Jack, and I've had enough fighting for one day.'

He had forgotten himself and was thinking

of her.

'Have you eaten?'

'Not yet.'

'Well then,' he said, and she could picture him: genial face alight, butter-coloured hair flopping on his forehead, finding the solution to his empty evening and hers, 'how about coming out to Choy's for a meal?' He added, 'Or the Bombay Palace? Or something posher?'

He was the answer to a larder that contained eggs and cheese, and a cupboard full of tinned meat and fish.

She said, 'There's a wonderful new restaurant down in Eastgate, which only opened three months ago. They're an Italian family and everyone works there, down to the grandmother who prepares the vegetables. They're going be featured in the May edition of *In the City Today*. In a few months they'll be fashionable and more expensive. At the moment they're cheap and absolutely brilliant.'

'You're like Pat. You always know everything before it happens,' he marvelled.

'Do you enjoy Italian food?'

'I enjoy anything you enjoy.'

'That's not an answer. Though very charming.'

Again he surprised her. 'You're in a bullying mood, Kate, but there's no need to bully me. I'm easy to please, my girl. I just want to please *you*. I live on rubbish food, as you know. A decent meal of any sort is always welcome.'

She laughed again, all the tensions of the day and evening draining away.

'Then Paolo's will please us both,' Kate said, at her nicest.

She got home before midnight, smiling and well-fed, to see the red message light winking and winking, to hear the telephone ringing and ringing. Before she lifted the receiver she knew who it was, and who had rung and rung before.

'Yes, Patrick? Yes, I've only just come in. No, no need to apologize for this afternoon. You were angry. Understandably. And so was I. No, there's no need to reimburse me for the tea. I ate more than you, anyway. No, I have not changed my mind about running away with you. Running away is for the young and foolish. No, I'm not being cynical.

'Patrick, I think we should continue this conversation when you aren't drunk. You're not drunk? All right, then, in your cups, merry, tipsy, well-oiled, slightly intoxicated, whatever. You tell me what state you're in and I'll go along with it.'

And be it moon, or sun, or what you please, henceforth it shall be so for me, she thought. Only I don't mean that. Oh dear, he's wanting the answer that he wants and no other. Well, it will be the other, whether he wants it or not.

'Patrick, love, listen to me. I'm not running away anywhere or with anyone. If I choose to

283

spend my life with a man I'll *walk* off with him, having made up my mind thoroughly first. No, I'm not angry with you. No, I don't hate you. Yes, I'll see you soon. But for now let's say goodnight, shall we? A kind goodnight.'

Kate and Nora

On the following Saturday afternoon, mother and daughter sat in the farmhouse kitchen with their feet on the hearth. Nora never let the range go out because it was a core of warmth for the house, supplying hot water, drying washing and offering four ovens ready to cook her bounteous meals at all times. In high summer the kitchen could become uncomfortably hot, but in April the weather was still cold and they were glad to sit by the sultry ovens and drink tea and talk.

Kate was wearing her trouser suit and a thick wool sweater. Fresh from a visit to Shearers, her hair had been cut to a shorter, smarter length and gleamed like an October chestnut. Nora, who never dressed for any occasion, was comfortable in her usual uniform of loose skirt and smock: peacock-blue splashed with orange and scarlet leaves. That morning, while her daughter was being coiffured, she had wound her hair into a thick knot and anchored it with a comb. Already a strand or two was drifting down.

They had paused in the conversation while Nora absorbed Kate's news. Then she spoke out.

'I always thought you were like your father,' she began, 'and so you are in your ways. You keep yourself in trim, and you think before you speak, and you don't fly off the handle like I do. But that's as far as it goes. Underneath, where it counts, my girl,' tapping Kate's knee, 'you're like me. You're one of life's willing horses, and you know what they say about a willing horse. Oh yes.

'I've watched you for years, being short-changed by that Hector Mordant – I'm not prying into your private life, but I wasn't born yesterday. I can guess what went on, and when it stopped. He's used you all the way along. And that Shirley's been just as bad in a different way...' A shift in her daughter's position stopped her in mid-speech. 'Now, let me finish before you start explaining...'

'I'm not going to explain anything,' said Kate shortly. 'Carry on.'

Nora did. 'I dare say you've learned a lot from the experience, that it's been valuable in its way, but you've paid a high price for it, my girl. A very high price. And what have you got to show for it? You're a good-looking young woman who can earn a good living, and that's important, but...'

A round beseeching face appeared at her

285

side, doll clutched to its chest.

'Oh, not now, Jessie ... Oh well, all right then, you can come on my lap. Wherever have you been? The coal hole? Now sit there nice and quietly and don't interrupt because I'm talking to your Auntie Katie...'

Kate reminded her drily, 'I am not that child's aunt.'

'We must give and take,' said Nora peaceably. 'She only understands who people are by calling them auntie and uncle.'

'And who is this one, and why is she here on a Saturday afternoon when you're supposed to have the weekend off?'

'Why, this is our Jessie!' Nora cried in a voice of delight, 'and we're always pleased to have Jessie, aren't we?'

The child crowed appreciation and cuddled up.

Nora mouthed silently over her head, 'The parents are wonderful, but they need time to themselves. I'm looking after this one while they go away for a few days.'

Kate would have liked to laugh, and to cry. She took a deep breath and said, 'Point taken. Crash on, Nora!'

The big woman cradled one child and nodded at the other.

'Your father and I were just the same as you once. We were young and full of ideas and fine dreams but our vision of life was more ambitious than yours. You just wanted to change *your* world, and that's possible, and you've done it. But we wanted to change the

286

entire world, which is ridiculous when you come to think. But we came to terms with it in the end. What I'm trying to say, and making a poor job of it, is that we understand more than you think, Katie. We do, love.

'I've guessed – and I want you to forgive me for what I'm going to say –' Nora took a fresh grip of the child on her lap – 'but I've guessed that you saw yourself as Mrs Hector Mordant. well, that sort of man never divorces his wife, because she acts as a shield so that he can play without paying. And even if he had married you it wouldn't have worked, love. He'd have used you as his wife and as his business partner, and he'd have cheated on you, too. You'd have been stuck in a double trap.'

Kate bent her head in acknowledgement, but couldn't speak.

Conscience-stricken, Nora said, 'Katie, I wouldn't hurt you for the world. I know I have done many a time, but I never meant to. You wouldn't let me near you, you see, and I've been worried about you all these years and not able to say anything. Don't be vexed with me, love.'

Kate said, looking down so that her mother could not see that she was full of tears, 'It's all right. I've been at fault, too. I know my faults.'

The child sat in Nora's mattress of a lap and pillowed her head on Nora's breasts, doll clutched to her chest, eyes round, thumb in mouth, watching and listening without comprehension. Gradually her eyes began to close.

Nora patted the dirty little knees thoughtfully and went on, 'Your father and I were just like you. We had to scale our dreams down. When I knew you were on the way it sort of woke us up. And Neville's parents and my mother were very generous, very good. Not that we gave them credit for it at the time. We thought it was our right to change our minds again and come home. The prodigal son and daughter feasting on the fatted calf.

'I held my mother off, just like you held me off, because I felt I knew how to live life better and I didn't want her to interfere. What I should have reckoned was that we were all different. Neither better nor worse than each other, just different. I've been glad, looking back, that you and Grandma were so fond of each other. You were what she wanted me to be, and I wish she could have lived to see you now. She would have been so proud.' A pause. 'No, you don't realize when you're young. I've thought about it since, and been sorry many a time at the way I took her for granted. I always took her a nice bunch of flowers when I saw her, but a kind word would have meant more. And when it came to her funeral I made up a carpet of flowers that covered the coffin, and everyone said how lovely it was. But it didn't salve my conscience, because flowers are for the living, not the dead, and I knew I should have given her a bit more understanding while she was alive.'

288

Kate got up and put her arms as far round Nora and Jessie as they would reach, and kissed her mother's cheek. When the child protested Kate gave a laugh that was half a sob, and drew back.

'Yes, you're right, Jessie,' said Nora, wiping her eyes on her apron. 'It's time for you to lie down and have a proper nap while we make tea for Grandpa.'

Kate recovered her irony. 'Grandpa?' she queried. 'Are you Grandma, then?'

Nora lifted her head and answered simply, 'Oh yes. What goes around comes around. I'm Grandma now.'

Preparations

On her own initiative, Kate contacted the local district council, who were very curt. It was difficult, she discovered, to explain that a friendly gathering (something like an over-sized picnic) might turn into a mass meeting. That this in turn could lead to complications, though there again there might be none. And no, she was not responsible for the event itself; this was Ezra's idea. Ezra the healer – they had heard of her? – a very good woman but not worldly. The possible complications would not occur to her. She had simply

issued an open invitation to a healing ceremony by word of mouth, and did not realize
what was involved – what might be involved –
indeed there might be nothing involved at all.

No, she was not speaking for Ezra, she was
Miss Pringle's assistant at the Old Hall. The
estate abutted Grove Hill and Marchfield,
and they had been making arrangements for
travellers who had come for the event. How
many travellers? Well, possibly a hundred.
So far. They were parking in two of Miss
Pringle's fields. Temporarily, of course, and
there had been no trouble. So far. And as the
facilities at Marchfield were limited, Miss
Pringle was providing water and sanitation
for those on her property. But she had felt
that the situation should be mentioned, in
case any laws were infringed and she was held
responsible.

Coldly, they replied that what Miss Pringle
did with her own property was her business,
but that she would indeed be held responsible
if her travellers caused damage to or placed
undue demands upon council property. Furthermore, she was not licensed as a caravan
or camping park, and therefore she should
make sure that her temporary visitors left the
premises immediately this event was over.
The health department would be inspecting
Marchfield immediately afterwards, and they
thought it wise for Kate to inform the local
police department of the situation and her
concerns. They added that this seemed to be
an extraordinary muddle, which should have

290

been brought to their attention far earlier.

Having apologized all round, and been grudgingly excused, she then faced a similar interview with a desk sergeant, who was kinder and more helpful. He suggested that a discreet police presence near the entrance to the site should be sufficient for any ordinary occasion, but gave her a telephone number to call if anything untoward materialized.

All this she kept from her employer, while cursing her silently, soundly, and often.

Meanwhile, even Shirley, in the throes of unrequited love, could not imagine the healer bringing in a few friends for lunch after the meeting, but she guessed that it would draw people from all sections of the community. Like the council, she only tolerated travellers as proof of her goodwill. Interesting members of the middle class, hoping to heal and enlighten themselves, were a different proposition. She felt that they would welcome a little civilized hospitality, particularly after spending hours in a crowd on Grove Hill, and then, surely, Ezra was bound to come with them.

She did not give full rein to her imagination with Kate, who would be sceptical, but tried out the idea on her.

'Just casual refreshments. Nothing elaborate. A sandwich, a glass of wine.' She remembered Ezra. 'Or lemonade. What do you think?'

Kate knew that Shirley's mind was made

up, guessed why, and did not intend to waste time trying to change it. Her answer was frank.

'Do whatever you feel is right, but if you're expecting me to organize it I must refuse. I'm up to my eyes with arrangements for our travellers. Printing notices and trying to hire Portaloos a fortnight before Easter is no joke.'

'Oh, of course, I wasn't going to bother *you* with it,' said Shirley, dashed. Then she thought again. This meant that she had a free hand, and no critic in the background. She became Shirley the Hostess. 'You can leave it entirely to me and Mrs Bailey, Catriona. As I say, it's only a sip and a snack for anyone who happens to drop in.'

Left to her own devices Shirley flung herself and the housekeeper into an elaborate entertainment. Two large cold collations were to be prepared: one vegetarian, the other for carnivores. Alcoholic and non-alcoholic drinks, tea and coffee would be offered. 'And some good hot soup,' said Shirley. 'Vegetable soup. If the weather continues to be as cold as this, people will be glad of a cup of hot soup.'

Mrs Bailey prompted her. 'For how many, madam?'

'I don't know exactly how many or when they'll come. Let's say ... shall we say ... we'd better say ... forty!'

Her imagination leaped again. She saw Ezra, exhausted after the long day, accepting an invitation to spend the night in the Queen's Room.

'The meeting may last until the late afternoon, even early evening. We must be prepared for all contingencies. Someone may even stay overnight.'

Inwardly sighing for Kate, who was specific and understood exactly what would be involved, Mrs Bailey prompted her employer again. 'You would like a guest room made ready, madam? Which one?'

Again Shirley's imagination roamed. Important people from afar, impressed by the hospitality of Melbury Old Hall, eager to extend the visit.

'Well, come to that, there may be more than one person staying overnight. Two or three, perhaps. Oh, I don't know ... do *all* the rooms,' said Shirley.

Mud

15th April

Up at the Old Hall on the cold grey morning of the day, while fires were being lit, beds made up, and the kitchen became bedlam, Shirley arrayed herself as Ezra's disciple.

In the cause of simplicity and spirituality she left off her jolly red wig and wore a long white pleated silk gown. Her make-up was pale and discreet. She gave up the idea of jewellery but wore her gold wristwatch. During the Christmas Eve vigil it had helped her to check the endless time and divide it into possible units. Only seven, six, five, four, three hours left – though occasionally she had been inclined to wonder if the bloody thing had stopped.

In contrast to her employer, Kate turned up for work dressed as for a visit to Peddleford Farm. The two women eyed each other uncertainly. Having survived their recent confrontation they were careful with each other. Shirley spoke first, turning round slowly to show off her angelic robes.

'Well, what do you think?'

Formerly Kate would have answered in teasing mode, but in the present situation she said, 'It looks like a Fortuny gown. Lovely material.' She could not resist adding, 'Only, do wear something warm underneath, Shirley. You mustn't catch another chill.'

At that moment the grey sky opened and rain assaulted the windows.

'God damn it,' cried Shirley, 'I shall have to wear a bloody mackintosh.'

She'll look as if the house had caught fire and she'd rushed out in her nightie, Kate thought, but said tactfully, 'The meeting won't begin for ages yet. The rain may stop before too long.'

Unimpressed by Kate's thick wool sweater, slacks and green wellingtons, Shirley asked, 'Are you going home to change or are you changing here?'

'I'm not changing at all. I have to keep an eye on things, be prepared to go anywhere and do anything.' To soften this brusque retort, Kate added, 'Remember I'm only ground staff in this event.'

'But you won't leave me before my guests arrive.'

'No, I won't leave before then.'

'And you'll be with me to meet them and eat with us afterwards? Oh, do join us. Mrs Bailey's doing a wonderful spread. She persuaded me to have an ongoing buffet. Then people can come when they like and stay for as long as they like. She even thought it would be wise to make up a few beds. Just in case.'

Kate heard this news with foreboding. The arrangements had been transformed from a casual sip and snack to a banquet and overnight visitors. She indicated her working self. 'But as you see, I'm not dressed for a social occasion.'

'Exactly. So why don't you pop home now and bring back one of your pretty frocks and an overnight bag? You can sleep here.'

'You're very kind,' said Kate automatically. 'Naturally I'll be around as long as you need me, but then I prefer to go home.' She forestalled further persuasion by saying, 'Shirley, I really shall have to dash. I need to check the state of affairs at Marchfield and the grove.'

Slightly piqued, Shirley complained, 'But you checked everything yesterday. What are you worrying about now?'

Kate murmured, 'Portaloos!' and left.

'Fuss, fuss, fuss,' Shirley said to herself when her assistant was out of earshot. 'Portaloos indeed. The only thing to worry about is this weather. And how does she expect me to manage a houseful of guests without her? Selfish.'

Outside the rain had changed from common assault to heavy battery.

Kate took three raincoats and an umbrella from the garden room before tramping to the shepherd's hut. There she found Ezra serene, Simeon disgruntled, and Joel miserable. They had just finished their midday bowls of rice and vegetables.

'I thought I'd bring these,' said Kate, 'in case you hadn't anything quite up to the weather outside.'

The rain beat against the windows: all noise and slanting wet.

'That is kind of you,' said Ezra. 'We shall be glad of them.'

Simeon grunted. Joel cringed. The two men looked as if they could do with a pork pie and a bottle of beer apiece. Kate wondered, as always, why they had come to Ezra and why they stayed.

'What time do you start?' Kate asked convivially, as if this were a garden party to be opened by a local celebrity.

'We shall go soon,' said Ezra.

She conveyed the idea that there was an

appointed moment that would announce itself.

'Right!' said Kate, unconvinced. 'Then I'll be off. I'm just checking that everything's in place and working.'

This is bloody bizarre, she thought. Nothing organized, except by me. Shirley looking like an elderly fairy at the top of a Christmas tree. God knows how many fools plodding up the hill, planning to be enlightened. Patrick on the prowl for news of the worst sort. Jack taking photographs to back him up. How shall we all emerge, I wonder, and in what shape?

Her mind wandered away from imponderables.

Oh, I do hope the other three Portaloos have arrived, she thought.

Jack, confronted by a middle-aged hippie said, 'I didn't recognize you for a moment.'

The broken nose and twinkling eyes were the same, but Patrick's shabby conservative clothes had been replaced by a long shapeless sweater, faded jeans, Dr Martens and a dirty anorak. A red and blue band was strapped round his head, an inch above his eyebrows.

'You look even more dissipated than usual,' Jack remarked bluntly.

'This is what you should be wearing yourself,' said Patrick. 'I blend in with the crowd. You stick out like the fuzz. Anyone seeing you would know you'd been planted here to take incriminating photographs.'

'I thought I was being employed by a reputable paper to record a local event.' Stiffly.

'Always look below the surface – and on this occasion, well below it!' Patrick advised. 'What do you think of this mess for a start?'

Paupers Ground, now known as Marchfield, though bleak of name and aspect and furnished with concrete utility buildings, was quite attractive in other ways. Hedges and stone walls to west and south made its boundaries seem rural; the eastern entrance was agreeably disguised by trees, and Shirley's neat fencing and peaceful pastures on the north side afforded a pleasant prospect.

Recent incomers had changed all this. Walls had been broken down to gain access to the highway, and hedges showed gaps where short cuts had been forced through. Unlike the considerate travellers of early days, these temporary visitors had no respect for property. They regarded landowners as an injustice that should be punished, and Shirley's domain was suffering. Her fences were being uprooted and chopped into fuel, her fields invaded, her stream fouled.

Kate's efforts over the past fortnight had only been able to produce three Portaloos – already filthy and full – half a dozen water barrels and a modest pile of logs. Her notices had been torn down, or flapped forlornly in the wind. The weather was a final insult and did worse damage by turning grassland into liquid mud.

'Unless this was supposed to be a rain festival,' said Patrick, pulling up the hood of his anorak, 'I think old Ezra's got her spells mixed up.'

Jack, too, was wearing his hood. It came down to the top of his glasses and gave him the appearance of a trapped owl. His camera sported its own raincoat. He began to record civic destruction and defacement.

'Get a picture of that group over there,' said Patrick, suddenly alert. 'I'll bet it's a drugs sale.'

'What makes you think that?'

'It looks suspicious. I'll check it out. Meanwhile, use your camera. This is the sort of story the paper wants.'

'Are you sure,' said Jack, clicking steadily, 'that you have the right approach? I mean, this mess has nothing to do with Ezra – and Mike's lot are OK...' He had to speak loudly to overcome the sound of the rain beating on the roofs of ancient vehicles, pattering on leaves, splashing on walls, tattooing an incessant rhythm on himself and his camera. The sky was livid, the weather in surly mood. The two men stood on the edge of chaos. Mud sucked at their boots.

Patrick was factual. Given his brief he could not have been more pleased with the conditions. 'We're here to report news, not to make moral judgements. Get the overall picture. Anything exciting. Fights. Deals. Destruction. See you when the ceremony starts – it could get ugly – and turn yourself into background. We don't want them to know we're watching.'

He slouched off, hands in pockets. Jack sighed.

A hundred yards further on Patrick was approached by a pasty-faced lad with bleached hair, who asked if he had anything to sell.

'I'm looking for some myself, man,' said Patrick. 'Let me know if you find it.'

The lad drifted away.

Mud, mud, mud.

Kate's green wellingtons squelched from top to bottom of the estate. Hands in raincoat pockets, rain hat jammed well down, she made mental notes and despaired. The lower fields, crowded with old buses and caravans, meant that she had been unable to provide parking space.

'Fingers crossed!' she said to herself as glistening cars began to line up on the grass verge at the side of the road below. And, 'Oh, Christ!' as she saw the state of the stream and the clogged Portaloos.

In the temporary camp she made civil enquiries, gave tactful advice, and received sulky answers. Pretending not to notice their hostility she plodded on to the Marchfield site where the atmosphere was more friendly, though subdued.

'Ah, here's the gaffer!' Mike cried with false cheerfulness. 'All right then, Kate?'

'Not entirely. We're still short of drinking

300

water and the new people aren't respecting the facilities as they should. I've spoken to them about it, and it's in their own interests, but they seem to think I'm interfering.' They had, in fact, told her to fuck off.

Mike said nothing. His wife gave a scornful little laugh.

'Is it my imagination,' Kate asked, 'or are they less neighbourly than your group?'

Mike said uneasily that it took all sorts.

'They did strike me as being here for the hell of it rather than for the healing.'

He did not answer. Kate gave up.

'Anyway, camp conduct isn't my business. I'm simply here to provide supplies. So I'll leave you to it, Mike. You're the man in charge.'

The compliment was also a reminder. He looked uncomfortable and did not reply.

'I'll be off then,' she said, defeated.

On her way back to the grove a hand caught her by the arm and an intimate voice muttered, 'Do you want to buy some smack, lady?'

She turned indignantly to find Patrick's face grinning into hers.

'Oh, it's you. Playing the fool again. You look disgusting,' she replied coldly, turning her back on him and squelching forward.

'It's all part of the disguise,' he answered, matching his pace to hers.

'What disguise? A drug-pusher?'

'I'm not selling. I'm buying. Are you interested?' Proffering a small packet. 'It's genuine.'

'Don't be ridiculous! Suppose someone catches you with it?'

'I'll be turning it over to the police as evidence, together with relevant photographs,' said Patrick. 'Old Jack's not far behind me.'

A motley group of travellers was plodding ahead of them up the hill, a straggling chattering procession of sparrows, augmented and infiltrated by human crows anxious for pickings. Other disciples and visitors trudged after them. In the rear came the middle-class devotees, well-fed and clothed, puzzled by the company in which they found themselves.

Kate looked over her shoulder and saw Jack several yards away, a large wet owl bobbing above the crowd. She stopped to get breath and deliver her verdict.

'Patrick, you bring out the worst in Jack. Together, you're no better than a pair of naughty schoolboys. I'm off.'

'Now are you sure you don't want some smack? It might sweeten your temper.'

'Oh ... smack off!' said Kate, and headed for her chosen vantage point at the top of the grove, from which she could keep an eye on the proceedings.

Now how is Ezra going to conduct this? Kate wondered. Because it's a far cry from meditating with a few followers and healing a few people. Has she any idea how to control a crowd? If she intends to speak, will her voice carry, and what exactly will she say? Does she realize what sort of impression Simeon and Joel make? And look at those

302

ranks of faces – every type of face, every expression from sincere to stupid, and showing every emotion from reverence to scepticism. Scepticism. So there are disbelievers here. Well, I'm not surprised. Patrick is a disbeliever, for one. Jack isn't a disbeliever but he's acting like one. And talking of stupid, look at Shirley simpering on the front row. Yes, that does look like a nightie under the mackintosh!

The assembly went well at first. The rain stopped. A watery and uncertain sun came out, and Ezra's appearance, flanked by disciples Simeon and Joel, was greeted with a hum of pleasure and a spatter of applause. A dark, diminutive figure in a long grey robe, she looked the part of the prophet. Standing for a few moments in silence, she put her hands together and bowed her head in greeting. Then she began to speak.

Within minutes, murmurs of reverence changed to mumbles of discontent as people asked each other what she was saying, and tried first stealthily and then more aggressively to find better places at the front.

Ezra had not experienced the impact of a large audience. She had imagined a small, quiet body of people, waiting for a blessing. Instead she faced a public speaker's nightmare, unable to command their attention.

She held out her arms in welcome. She spoke, and heard her disembodied voice, gentle and barely audible, fading out over the

303

assembly. She called on those who needed healing to approach her, and those who could hear surged forward like the sea. Simeon attempted to marshal them into some sort of order, hindered by Joel, who was trying to help him.

For the first time since Ezra had accepted her new way of life she felt a loss of power. Summoning her beliefs, she tried to concentrate, but was slipping out of focus with herself. A row of beseeching faces brought her momentarily back. She walked down the row, legs shaking, and passed her hands over their heads. Nothing was coming through and time was running away, leaving her without hope or purpose.

Automatically, she motioned them to kneel down, and knelt with them. The chilled ground shocked her flesh and she realized with deeper shock that she had asked these people to muddy themselves for nothing.

The noise rose. Pushes turned to punches and brawls started at the back. The meeting was getting out of control. Simeon was fighting, Joel standing speechless, arms hanging by his side, mouth open. They were moving out of her orbit, the one growing ugly, rough; the other terrified, anchorless. She tried to call everyone to order, but a sudden gust of wind swept her words away. The struggles at the far side of the crowd turned into serious confrontations. And then the rain returned in cold and deadly earnest.

It was at this stage of the proceedings that

Kate pulled out her mobile and dialled the local police station. From her vantage point on the tree stump she saw Patrick, indistinguishable from the hippies except by those who knew him, pushing blithely through the throng. From time to time he joined in some fracas, always ready for a scrap in whatever cause, but on the whole he kept his fists to himself and filled his head with reportable facts. Kate did not worry about him anyway. She need never worry about Patrick. He would survive all but the last enemy.

She looked for Jack and spotted him caught up in the fray, shielding his camera as if it were a lover in peril, which of course it was, because he had been spotted by those who didn't want to be photographed. Luckily his height and bulk favoured him, and though he was a peaceable man by nature, self-preservation came first. He butted, punched, kneed and kicked with the best of them, and at last retreated at a lumbering trot, camera intact, to the comparative safety of Shirley's adjoining field. Kate sighed with relief.

Below her, Simeon had abandoned any attempt at restraint and was using his fists and feet without mercy, and though Kate could not hear the words his mouth was making blasphemous shapes.

Joel, helpless in the clamour, was being carried to and fro by the movement of the crowd. A wave of people engulfed him. He went under without a struggle, seemingly without protest. So far he had been a figure of fun, a subject for mockery to Kate. Now she felt concern for him. He was a child, needing shelter. His only hope was to fall among friends. His only strength and safety was in Ezra.

The horde changed direction yet again. Emerging from the morass, covered from head to foot in mud, Joel raised his arms to heaven as if asking for help. From Shirley's field, Jack, glancing over his shoulder, instantly turned round and caught the moment on his camera, then blundered on.

Someone knocked Joel down again. Instinctively he lay there, motionless, until they had moved away, then began a cautious crabwise crawl towards his protector.

The fray was at its height when Kate heard the approaching sirens.

'Here comes the cavalry!' she said to cheer herself, and drew breath quickly to catch a sob of relief.

At the bottom of the hill a little forest of blue lights was flashing, dark-blue figures were advancing. Two police vans and an ambulance were standing by.

Wrongdoers, catching sight of the law, thrashed their way to freedom. Innocent people, hesitating, bewildered, were struck down or thrust aside by those who needed to escape. Travellers with families caught up small children, urged older ones to hold on to them, and began to struggle homewards, heads down against the onslaught. In the grove those about to be healed scrambled to their feet, staring this way and that, wondering what to do.

Wrenched from her peaceful inner world, Ezra was in the grip of an old instinct: the desire to survive at any cost. It urged her to run and run, but her mission held her back. She exerted enough control over herself to cry out to those she was healing that they should leave. Then, remembering what and how she should be, she said that they should go peaceably, giving thought to themselves and others. And as Joel reached her with a gulp of gratitude and clung to her skirts for protection, she bent down and put her small cold hands one on each side of his face to calm him. For a few moments they formed a tableau of peace in the turmoil: Ezra thinking only of him, he safe in her. Simeon, punching his way towards them both, had no such fine feelings. Impatiently he shoved Joel aside, caught hold of Ezra's arm and began to propel her to safety.

Seeing his two companions hurrying away from him, Joel scrambled to his feet and tottered after them.

The tide of folk had turned again and were ebbing down the hill. The uproar receded into the distance. The tumult became a motion picture, something to be watched that was happening at a safe distance. Cautiously, Kate left her tree stump and floundered down to view the situation.

Shirley, slung to the ground in the urgency of the retreat, lay there in her dirty white gown and torn red mackintosh, too petrified to move.

'Oh, Jack, where are you?' Kate whispered to herself, needing his masculine strength and bulk to come to the rescue and give her reassurance. But there was no one to help her so she slogged forward and, by dint of coaxing, tugging and bullying, raised the fallen angel to its feet: filthy, lamentable, and lamenting.

Leaning heavily on Kate all the way to the house, Shirley whimpered over and over again, 'Why, oh why, Katie? Where did it all go wrong?'

'If you can't guess,' said Kate bitterly, 'how can I possibly explain it to you?'

An Unwanted Banquet

And now for the reckoning, Kate thought, as she piloted Shirley into the house.

The main hall had been dressed for an occasion that no longer existed. Around the walls a line of chairs waited for guests who would not arrive. In the centre stood the waiting banquet: a tribute to Mrs Bailey's art and Shirley's fancy.

308

As they stood there, trembling and exhausted, an odour rose in the warmth, rank and dank as of ancient marshes. They had brought it in with them. Their clothes reeked.

Faced by general consternation, Kate soothed one person at a time.

'No need to worry, Mrs Bailey. I don't think Miss Pringle's hurt, just shocked and bruised.'

'Doctor,' Shirley whimpered.

Kate sighed and said, 'But we'd better make sure, so please will you call the doctor, Walter? Oh, thank you,' as he removed their sodden raincoats.

His hands were courteous. His expression fastidious. The housekeeper came forward to help him. Kate continued to speak to both of them in turn.

'I'm afraid your wonderful buffet party won't take place, Mrs Bailey. Such a pity. It looks absolutely delicious and you've gone to so much trouble...'

'Walter, if you'll hold Miss Pringle up for a moment I can take my boots off, and her shoes...'

'Yes, Mrs Bailey. A hot bath would be an excellent idea...' Then in quite a different voice, she cried, 'Oh, Jack, thank God!' as he strode into the hall, saying simultaneously, 'Thank God you're safe, Kate. I've been worried to death. It's murder and mayhem out there.'

Impishly, the rain stopped. A ray of sun sparkled on the crystal tumblers round the punchbowl.

Shirley saw it and whispered, 'Whisky.'

Jack, sizing up the situation, said, 'I could use a drink, myself. No, stay where you are, Walter,' seeing that the man was supporting his employer, 'I can look after us. How about you, Kate?'

'A whisky would save my life but Shirley and I are too dirty to sit down. Better change first.'

The whisper was urgent. 'Whisky. Now.'

Mrs Bailey, adjusting to this new situation, said, 'I'll lay some newspapers on the chairs, madam, and while you're resting I can draw the baths.'

Shirley gulped her whisky standing, held it out for a refill before her housekeeper could protect the chairs, and collapsed into one of them.

'Take the weight off your feet and drink up, Kate,' said Jack.

Walter approached with a plate of smoked salmon sandwiches, but they shook their heads, and Kate said, 'We just need to sit for a while, Walter. I'll call you if we need anything.'

So he left them to it.

The three of them sat in silence for several minutes, sipping and musing. Then Jack burst out, 'What a bloody shambles! What a bloody shame!'

Kate, bemused by exhaustion and alcohol, answered from a long way off. 'Oh, this is only the beginning. There'll be such a reckoning. Oh, Jack, those poor travellers were trying to protect their children, and poor old Mike was trying to defend the entire group. People will have been injured out there. Pray God no one was seriously hurt. There'll be endless questions asked. Inspections and interviews and inquiries. Certainly court appearances. Scandal on a broad scale. The *Courier*'s bound to make a song and dance about it. Even national newspapers could pick it up. You name it, we're in for it.' She attempted to infuse her tone with irony but only sounded bleak. 'And guess who'll be put out front, as usual.'

Jack put one big warm hand on hers. 'You know I'll do anything I can to help you, Kate. Any time.'

She nodded, but did not look at him. The two of them talked together quietly, intimately, as if they were alone. Shirley sat in soggy silence.

'I knew you'd gone and yet I was literally *praying* for you to turn up out there, Jack. Hauling Shirley back home was no picnic. I had to keep stopping to rest. She did nothing to help herself. She was a dead weight.'

An aggrieved snivel at her side.

'I'm sorry,' Jack said. 'I was pretty frantic about you, but I didn't know where you were. I just about saved my own skin – and the camera.'

'I know. I saw you. Hitting your way out and escaping across the field. I was standing on the tree stump behind Ezra. I saw everything. Where did you go?'

'Through the estate and down to the main road, to photograph the clash with the police. It was rough. Scary.'

They were silent again. From Kate's side a plump and dirty hand trembled forth, holding out an empty tumbler.

'Right you are, Shirley,' said Jack good-naturedly, and refilled all their glasses. 'What happened to Ezra?' he asked.

'She was hustled off the scene by Simeon, who'd been punching and shoving in a most irreligious manner to get to her.' Kate giggled. 'More like a bodyguard than a follower!' Then in acid answer to the scandalized hiss at her side. 'Well, he's not exactly a saint, is he, Shirley?'

Another silence. Kate brooded over her glass, looking at no one, staring into her future.

'But I am absolutely certain about one thing,' she said. 'I made the right decision to leave this place, this job, and this way of life.' A muffled moan roused her to add, 'Oh, don't worry, Shirley. I'll see Hector's festival through. Then I'm off. I've had enough, and more than enough.'

The moan was repeated, but less woefully. The hand held out its glass for a fourth refill.

Jack said, 'The answer is no, Shirley. You've had enough, too.' He turned to Kate. 'I've got to go. I just wanted to make sure you were safe. I have to find Patrick and compare notes. We need to get the story in, in time for tomorrow's edition, so I'll have to develop the pictures, but I should be free by this evening and I'll ring you. Why don't you stay here and take it easy?'

'No. I'm going home as soon as I've had a bath and found my sea legs again.'

'Then I'll ring you at your place, pick you up when the furore's died down, take you out to Paolo's and we'll—'

Before he could finish his sentence Mrs Bailey announced that the baths were drawn. Simultaneously, the front doorbell rang and Walter ushered in a doctor and two policemen.

'Forget the arrangements. Here comes the reckoning,' said Kate.

It was to be longer and more complicated than she could ever have imagined.

The Reckoning

Kate was sitting up in bed with a breakfast tray when the telephone rang late the following morning.

'Kate? It's Jack. I hope I didn't wake you up.'

'Not exactly. I'm steaming my eyelids open over a pot of tea.'

'Sorry I couldn't get back to you yesterday. When I phoned the Hall just now Walter said you'd been there until midnight and wouldn't be coming in until ten o'clock. How are you?'

'Dazed. I had to mediate between the police and Shirley – who became hysterical, of course – and when they'd finished with her they wanted to interview Ezra. For some reason I felt protective and went with them. I needn't have done. They got absolutely nowhere with her. It did strike me, though, that she was different in some way. Like a sleeper woken up too suddenly. She'd lost her air of detachment. I felt she was playing the part of Ezra, rather than being Ezra.'

Jack's silence stopped her.

'Oh, take no notice of me,' said Kate airily. 'I'm still light-headed after last night's shenanigans. And truly she was superb. She explained the whole affair in spiritual terms. By the time she'd finished they didn't know whether she was mad or they were. The constable kept rereading his notes in disbelief.'

Jack chuckled then, and Kate smiled to herself.

'They wanted to interview Simeon and Joel, too, but Simeon had disappeared and Joel was too terrified to talk. So that's a jolly treat to come. I think I'll leave Ezra to it next time. What happened to you and Patrick?'

'We've been up most of the night, toing and froing between Marchfield and the city. We gave in Pat's story and my photographs.

Haven't you seen the front page of the *Courier*?'

'Not yet. It was sitting on the doormat, face down, but I'm afraid I crept past it. Sorry about that. No offence intended. I'm only just coming to life. Are you and Patrick the *Courier*'s morning stars?'

Jack chuckled again. 'Oh, I don't know about that, but we've got a terrific spread, and this is only the beginning.' He was exultant. 'We had a hunch that the trouble wasn't over, so we went back. A group of hooligans had joined the party, and they didn't want the fun to die down. There were some ugly fights between them and the travellers – until they were arrested. One of the buses was set on fire with four kids and a cat sleeping inside. We got the kids and cat out, but we couldn't save the bus, and it was right under the trees and *they* caught fire. God, what a nightmare! Dogs yelping. Kids screaming. Broken bottles. Iron bars. Casualties. Ambulances. Sirens. The fire brigade and the police earned their living twice over, yesterday.

'And talk about damage! They tipped your precious Portaloos over – I won't go into details. And the stream's so silted up that it looks like part of the field – all mud and litter. Shirley won't be too pleased when she sees that mess. The council won't be thrilled either. The rowdies trashed Marchfield. Wash basins broken, dustbins turned over, notices torn down. Oh, and I shot rolls of film. Got some marvellous pictures...' He was high with excitement, hoarse with exhaustion, talking on.

'This story will run and run. Marcus Bray's thrilled to bits with us. He's told Pat and me to follow it all up. Pat's heard a rumour that all the travellers are to be moved on. Not only Shirley's lot, but poor old Mike and co. as well. Not just yet, of course. There'll be a breathing space while everyone's interviewed, and it takes a day to obtain a possession order, but then comes the crunch. I'm not surprised. They say the cost of repairs will be sky-high. Anyway, it was all quiet by six o'clock and we had breakfast at a truck-drivers' caff outside Peddleford. Very decent grub, too.'

Kate roused herself, though her tone was dry. 'Good for you. I'm glad someone is benefiting from the disaster.'

Jack had no more to say, apart from, 'Oh well, I'd better be off to bed now. What are you doing today?'

'Further interviews with the police. And Mr Reeve, Ronnie Baxstead and I will be tramping round the estate, assessing the damage.'

A short silence.

'I'll take you out for that meal this evening, then, shall I?' Jack asked gently.

'That would be lovely.' Smiling into the mouthpiece.

He was smiling back. 'Dare I say ... have a nice day?'

316

Her reply was sardonic. 'You must be joking,' said Kate.

Patrick's report, illustrated with Jack's photographs, was the *Courier*'s front-page news.

PROPHET AND LOSS

This city reckons to provide everything that its citizens and visitors could desire, but yesterday our local prophet topped the bill with an impromptu meeting on the old pagan site of Grove Hill.

Ezra, as she likes to be called, is a healer and a spiritual adviser of no particular denomination. Reports of her ability vary. Some patients are completely relieved of physical aches and pains. Others improve for a while and then relapse. One case ended tragically.

Ezra lives on charity. A local lady, well-known for her community spirit, has made sure that the prophet is comfortably if modestly housed, and Ezra's two followers sustain the three of them by begging for food. She seems content to live on rice, fruit and vegetables but sometimes her disciples lapse.

To be fair to them it must be a dismal life, walking forever in the shadow of a religious figure. Even Christ's apostles had faults and I am not surprised. But Ezra thrives on her self-inflicted sainthood, and had been busy building up her reputation until she felt she could hold a public meeting. The height of Christ's career was the Sermon on the Mount. Was this, I wonder, what she meant the Grove Hill assembly to be? Unfortunately for her and many others it became Armageddon.

Her audience was a mixed bag of middle-aged eccentrics, misguided scholars, students (always game for adventure and a laugh), travellers and their children, the old, the ugly, the unloved, the weird and wonderful in all their guises. There must have been two or three hundred people present, braving the winds and wet.

Ezra is a small woman dressed in grey garments, with a small grey voice to match. She really should take lessons in public speaking if she plans to call other meetings, because only those in the front row could hear her. As so often happens these days there was a group of aggressive youths bent on mischief who began scuffles just for the hell of it. Then the wind came up and the rain came down and the mood turned nasty.

Wet, muddy, bewildered and thoroughly miserable by this time, the halt, the lame and the blind – or their modern equivalents – besieged Ezra. I will say this for the lady, she takes no notice of circumstances. She carried on as if everyone was happy and the sun was shining. Incredibly, she indicated that those nearest should kneel down in front of her, and

318

kneel down they did. Dry-cleaners will be in great demand today. Then she walked along the row, passing her hands over each head while her lips moved, in prayer or incantation.

After a couple of minutes, which should have been devout and silent but were noisy and distracted, she brought them to their feet again, and summoned the next contingent. I squeezed between jostling shoulders to ask the chosen ones whether they felt better for the healing. They said they didn't know yet, and their main concern was to get away quickly and clean themselves up.

Meanwhile our photographer, looking as always for good pictures, found two or three extremely interesting subjects. Apparently other prophets were abroad, offering a quick trip to heaven, though not for free. I am told that there was a regular market in family bliss: big brothers heroin and cocaine, little sisters ecstasy and cannabis. Why do all that tedious work on your soul when you can smoke, swallow, sniff or inject your way to paradise in an instant...

There was more, in the same, droll vein, but Kate was in no mood to read the rest. Patrick was relishing his role as a spectator, which was easy. She, on the other hand, would be picking up the pieces, which was painful.

The most impressive of Jack's photographs

became a symbol of the event and was re-printed in a number of national newspapers. It was of Joel. His fouled robe clung to his meagre body. He raised muddy arms to the sky as if begging for mercy. His face was a white triangle of terror. Behind him the mob, caught in the moment's violence, were thrusting each other this way and that. The caption beneath asked SAVED?

Kate reached the Old Hall in time for morning coffee.

'I'm afraid you'll find Madam rather shaky after all the upset, Miss Wing,' said the house-keeper, laying an extra cup and saucer on the tray.

'She'll be shakier still when she reads this,' said Kate, tucking the *Courier* under one arm, accepting the tray.

Shirley, sitting up in bed, wigless, cried, 'Katie, I've been awake all night, meditating, and I've come to the conclusion that this is a punishment for our sins!'

Kate, suffering from lack of sleep and too many fools, snapped, 'Oh, balls! It's a punishment for sheer spinelessness on all our parts. Ezra thought God would protect her. Mike and co. thought you would look after them. You left it to me to sort everything out. And I did nothing until it was too late. That's what went wrong, Shirley. Too many people dodging personal responsibility. I'm not a religious person but if I were God I'd think we deserved all we got!'

Shirley would have liked to spread a

320

spiritual shawl over this heresy but was too dejected to argue.

'And here, to cheer you up,' said Kate unkindly, 'is the morning paper, with Patrick's juicy article about yesterday's fiasco.'

Shirley said loftily, 'I'm not going to read that hack's rubbish, and as you're so thick with him these days you can tell him that he is no longer welcome here.'

'Right!' said Kate, unmoved.

The telephone rang. A confident, self-satisfied voice rang out.

'Good morning, Shirley. This is Hector. Have you read Hanna's article in the *Courier*?'

Her tone was stately. 'I've just told Kate that I don't read scurrilous rags, Hector.'

'You should read this one. Everyone else will.'

Speechless, Shirley held the receiver out so that Kate could hear.

'And speaking of rags, Shirley, I advise you to get rid of your own rag, tag and bobtail before you sit in judgement on the *Courier*. Don't imagine that this latest outrage can be swept quietly under the Old Hall carpet.'

He paused for a moment, and Kate could picture him, freshly shaved and fragrant with toilet water, firing each arrow into the heart of its target.

'And that's not all. One of Ezra's sidekicks has disappeared, and I believe there are doubts about both their backgrounds. Harbouring criminals is a serious offence. When and where she picked them both up, I don't know, but that Irish bloodhound Hanna is on their trail and he'll find out. The *Courier* has a big story here. They're going to milk it dry.'

As she maintained an appalled silence he continued, 'To be quite frank, Shirley, if I were not in over the head with the concert festival I wouldn't dream of staging it at the Old Hall...'

She recovered herself sufficiently to cry, 'I was doing you a favour to have it here in the first place. And don't you forget it!'

Hector glided past the remark, saying, 'Well, you're unlikely to be troubled again by me or anyone else until you clean up your act.' He applied bully-boy tactics. 'And if you imperil the concert festival in any way I'll sue you.'

He paused to let her feel the full weight of his words.

'We're old friends, Shirley, and I'm sorry to have to speak so frankly. But I won't risk my money and damage my reputation because of your sentimental entanglement with a spiritual fraud. And others will feel the same way.'

Shirley's bottom lip quivered. She handed the telephone to Kate, wordless. Hector's voice floated on the air between them.

'Just a friendly warning,' he said unctuously.

Kate answered, light and sweet.

'Thank you so much, Hector. It's always good to know who your friends are. It's also as well to remember that I'm organizing the concert and Shirley's providing the venue. So it's best not to antagonize either of us. Have a nice day.' And she set down the receiver with a little smack.

'I need a whisky,' said Shirley hoarsely. Her eyes avoided Kate. Her aspect was timid.

Without speaking, Kate brought a bottle and glass and a packet of cigarettes, and set them down on the bedside table.

'Just a sip and a ciggy,' Shirley explained, 'to settle my nerves.'

Kate said, 'I've got a lot to do, Shirley. Is there anything else before I go?'

'No, no.' She fingered the bedspread. 'Except ... how are things over at the hut?'

Kate noticed that she did not mention Ezra by name.

'Chaotic. Like everywhere else. Which piece of bad news do you want first?'

Shirley looked beseechingly at Kate, who looked coldly back. Seeing that she was not about to volunteer information, Shirley said heavily, 'Katie, love, I think we must close the fields and put the fences up again. I know that some of Mike's friends are in there, as well as those other travellers, but the best thing they can do is to leave. They've caused me a lot of trouble. All I did was to allow them to stay on my land as a temporary measure. It's a funny old world when you're punished for an act of kindness.'

Here she reached for the box of Kleenex, and while applying it to her eyes and blowing her nose, maundered on about how much she had done for everybody.

Coming back to the point she said, 'But I don't want to expose you to any danger, and that new lot do seem to be very rough, so if you could drop a word in Mike's ear – you do it so tactfully – and ask him to set things in motion...'

Kate translated abruptly, 'You want me to play the axe-man?'

Shirley sniffed, wiped her eyes and nose, and nodded. Then justified herself.

'But with regard to Ezra, I'm prepared to stand my ground. I'm not going to turn her out of the hut or anything like that, but I think it's best if we don't see each other. Perhaps you could hint that if she feels she should go, and she needs any help to set her up somewhere else...'

'Oh really, Shirley. What help? She likes it here and she's living rent-free.'

'Yes, of course. But if you could you drop in and see how she is, and have a friendly word?'

'What a very pleasant morning I have ahead of me,' Kate remarked to the bed curtains.

'Well I'm sorry about that, too. Of course I am. But what can I do? Oh, and, Katie love, if anyone else wants to ask me any questions could you answer for me? You know far more about it than I do, and you're so good at dealing with people.'

But the police were not prepared to take Shirley's evidence through Kate, and the thoroughness of their investigations further undermined her. Demoralized, Shirley announced that she would stay in bed until it was all over.

'And give me the Parlour accounts books,' she said. 'I've let things slide recently. Time to pull myself together.'

Kate heard a note of sorrow in the voice, but also a certain firmness.

Goodbye, Ezra, she thought. Your days as a favourite are numbered. Ingrid and co. come forth!

For the next three weeks the citizens and their *Courier*, though professing to be shocked and saddened by the turn of events, revelled in every scandalous detail of what became known as the *Grove Riots*.

The effects were far-reaching and diverse. Peddleford Cottage Hospital was full of minor casualties – the cuts and bruises brigade as Patrick called them. A few serious cases, fractures and broken bones, were sent to the City Hospital. One elderly man who had suffered a heart attack was pronounced dead on arrival, and a second case was in intensive care.

Busy solicitors looked grave, sounded solemn, and zestfully launched a series of claims for their clients that would trickle on for months and even years.

The innocent were caught up with the guilty, and though they were excused and discharged, the interviews and enquiries ate up their time and nervous energy.

At the best possible season of the year for

tourism, the grove had to be closed to the public while it was restored it to its former state. The clean-up operation on this site and on Marchfield would amount to tens of thousands of pounds. The city council endeavoured to recoup this by transferring responsibility to someone else. As it was useless to sue Ezra, they laid the blame on Shirley, who had sheltered the guilty parties. Lawyers were engaged for both sides – a vast expense which in the end would either burden the rate-payers or bankrupt Shirley, who had her own estate to clean up.

Most of the travellers had left before eviction notices could be served, but the regulars put up a stand, led by Mike. He argued that they had lived in their allotted quarters peaceably for over a year and in that time they had settled down. The community had become, if not enamoured of them, used to them. Their children attended Peddleford Primary School. The adults made themselves available for fruit and potato picking and other seasonal jobs. All of them had respected council property and committed no offence.

Privately, farmers round about might have disagreed with him on the latter point. Chickens and eggs had gone missing, but not in sufficient quantities to constitute an official complaint. Other sources of supply had been tapped: to be classed as a nuisance but not a crime. Even the Wings' flower farm had contributed a modest quota to the aesthetically minded, and many a jam jar in a bus window sported its bunch of Peddleford pinks.

Bereft of Shirley's patronage and Ezra's counsel, this site was all that the travellers had by way of a home and they decided to fight for it. When the police arrived at five o'clock on a fine summer Sunday morning they found the entrance to Marchfield choked by concrete road blocks and a barrier of big stones. Behind it Mike and his company shouted defiance, though they knew they could not win.

The obstruction took several hours to remove and caused a great deal of inconvenience to passing traffic, but finally the way was clear. The police moved in, throwing a cordon round the sorry collection of vehicles. Mike had given orders to his group that there should be no violence. This was partly in deference to Ezra's teaching, but mostly because the police were well-equipped to deal with insurrection and the travellers were not. So, around the time that people with houses were having tea in the garden, the travellers climbed into their cabs, praying that they would start, and having started would take them to some resting place before nightfall. Then they waited, sullen and impassive, for orders.

Immediately the tension slackened. The police became helpful, turned into advisers, marshals and traffic wardens. There were even one or two jokes as they eased the convoy out on to the main road. Coughing and spluttering like consumptives, the engines finally barked to life. The travellers looked for the last time on the place that had been home. Children pressed their faces to the windows, some waved. Then Mike, at the head of the column, gave the signal to start and they moved on to nowhere.

Ezra, who should have borne the burden of the complaint, seemed impossible to punish. Forbidden access to the grove, she circumvented this order by finding a quiet spot under the trees in the field above the hut and making that her meditation centre. Her visitors were rare these days, though people still came to her occasionally, surreptitiously, for healing. She had lost Simeon, who protected her, and must care for Joel, who depended on her. Still, she survived, and the council feared that when the grove was reopened she would establish herself there once again.

Meanwhile the authorities had to dig deep into their pockets for materials and workmen, and made no secret of the fact. Public opinion, once inclined to admire, ignore or be amused by Ezra, now saw her in terms of lost civic revenue and turned against her.

Simeon had disappeared for good. Questioned yet again by the police, Ezra was frank about his past.

Yes, she knew of his prison record. He had just come out of prison when she met him outside Birmingham.

No, Simeon was not his given name. She had chosen it for him. It meant 'hearkening'. No, she had not renamed him in order to conceal his identity. He had heard her speaking. He had *hearkened* to her.

Yes, she knew his real name. Was it important?

Why had he joined her?

Lacking family and home and purpose he had decided to try her way of life.

The police were sceptical. *Had she not been suspicious of his motives in this dramatic change?*

No. What motive could he have?

Here they suggested stealing money, under the guise of being a religious mendicant, and then making a getaway.

But Ezra pointed out that they had travelled together for over a year. He had always been free to go.

Then why did he leave now?

'He was afraid of you,' said Ezra. 'He had a prison record. He knew you would not believe him.'

This could not be denied.

They turned their attention to Joel next, interested in his identity. Since he was crouching in the corner of the hut, face to the wall, arms clasped over his head, they could not question him and so confined their enquiries to Ezra. She replied patiently that she had found him lost and penniless, and had taken him along with her. Perhaps – she was not good at remembering length of time – eighteen months ago. Yes, she knew his name. He had not been happy under that name. She had called him Joel after the prophet. In the Book of Joel, she explained, there was a plague of locusts that leaves the land bare. But in the end the land is healed by love and brought back to life. He had liked that story.

The policemen were unimpressed but Joel lifted his head and looked hopeful.

And you presumably changed your name, too? No need to explain the meaning of it. What was your given name?

She told them, adding, 'You must understand that to change a name brings new life, helps us to begin again.'

They made a note of that, too. Suspiciously.

Outsiders

Exposure

The city fathers did not always welcome the controversial offerings of Patrick Hanna, but the story that he brought back from his most recent investigations delighted them.

OH! MARY MAGDALENE!
Or is the name Shani Jenkins, Slim-fingered Sally, Fancy Nancy? Take your pick. This lady has had many names, nicknames, guises and occupations. There is no vice she has not practised.

Let me give you the brief, sad biography. Born to a prostitute, father unknown. Taken into care at the age of five because of abuse and neglect. Described by a children's home as 'aggressive and unlikeable' and 'a bad influence'. Ran away as often as she could, and finally made it on to the Cardiff streets to practise her mother's profession at the age of fourteen. You name it, she experienced it. Illegal abortion, treatment for sexual diseases, drug-taking to get away from it, drug-carrying to get out of it, and caught with the goods on her first trip.

Prison. Here she had further instruction in crime, but they couldn't teach her a thing about vice. Once out again, she was down to the sea to find ships. A light-hearted foray into picking up sailors, drugging them and taking their wallets. Petty theft, confidence tricks, a talent for picking the wrong company, an overdose – whether accidental or deliberate no one knows. Finally hospital, where she was found to be suffering from alcoholism and malnutrition.

At this point our National Health Service, which can keep law-abiding citizens waiting months and years for necessary minor operations, but will always find the odd million to spend on spectacular surgery or resuscitating a social outcast, saved her life. In the Nelly Kindersley ward of a north-country hospital, Magdalene was given the best of medical and psychiatric help. They would probably have sent her to convalesce in Lanzarote had there not been an outcry against such trips at the time.

Dried-out and cold-turkeyed, Magdalene was ready to face the world again. But the million-dollar question had to be asked: once freed, would she go straight? The authorities need not have worried. This is where the miracle begins.

Conveniently for everyone, she was granted the vision of an angel standing at the foot of her bed in the Nelly Kindersley ward. The angel – name and sex unspecified – painted a picture of the world as it could be, if everyone was loving and unselfish. Then it bestowed the gift of healing upon her and bade her go forth to bring glad tidings of great joy.

Released into the community, Magdalene wandered about the country for a few years, preaching sweetness and light, taking away people's aches and pains, and relying on their kindness and generosity. Travel certainly broadens the mind, but as an indefinite prospect it can become tedious. Understandably, she found a place she could call home, and a benefactor who provided shelter, and settled down with a couple of social misfits to be a boon and a blessing to all. In medieval terms she became the local saintly hermit.

The two disciples who lived with her were also of doubtful origin. One man had a criminal record and needed to keep a low profile. The other apostle was sprung, if I may use the expression, from a mental home where he was undergoing treatment.

Now, I am not questioning Magdalene's good intentions, but she lacks that rare virtue known as common sense. Probably light-headed with success, possibly in an effort to consolidate her position, she held a so-called healing ceremony to which all were welcomed. Unfortunately, she didn't think of informing the authorities, who were not visited by an angel but did understand such mundane matters as the provision of water, sanitation, accommodation and crowd control. In fact, practical preparations were left to Chance, and we all know what a false friend Chance can be.

I am told on good authority that the city council had heard rumours of this event and had been greatly concerned, but as they were told nothing, and nothing could be proven, they were powerless to act. In fact, they had to stand by, hoping for the best and prepared for the worst.

I may, like them, deplore the outcome, but I must say that I admire the internal organization of this festival. Apparently the invitations were transmitted by word of mouth, in which case Magdalene could teach the town hall a thing or two about communication. Two or three hundred Seekers after Truth turned up without a clerk being employed, a sheet of paper printed, or a single telephone call made. But when the weather turned nasty, so did the Seekers. The police had to be called in, extensive property was damaged, one elderly gentleman died of a heart attack, and several people suffered injuries ranging from cuts and bruises to bone fractures and subsequent hospitalization.

Now I agree that we should all look into

our hearts and save our souls, and with this purpose in mind the authorities have provided places of worship for all sects. In the public library you will also find a list of groups that cater for fringe religions. None of these groups – I have checked my facts – has ever been responsible for a riot or cost us one pence. All of them pay rent for their accommodation, and many goodly citizens can testify to the spiritual comfort and fellowship they offer. So, surely to God we can find consolation in what we've got already without looking elsewhere?

This whim on the part of our local Magdalene will cost the council (that is, ourselves as rate-payers) a small fortune and has harmed her benefactor, among others. I am not questioning her sincerity, but I am asking – can we afford her?

I won't beat about the bush and be coy about her identity any longer.

Ezra, take your message elsewhere, will you, sweetheart? Pack your blanket and begging bowl and move on!

The first voice on Patrick's answering service was furious.

'Patrick! Jack Almond speaking. This will be a long message because I've got a lot to say. So you'll probably only get half of it. You've been my friend, and a good friend, for a long time, but – that – is – over – pal – as – from – now!

337

'I want you to know exactly how I feel about your character assassination of Ezra. I quote at random, because I'm so bloody mad that I can't think straight. "Law-abiding citizens" you say – a phrase that will warm the cockles of thousands of so-called law-abiding readers and make them feel great. Since when did you give a fuck about the law, or even keep one or two rules? But that sort of hypocrisy and sycophancy is just another way of boosting the sales, isn't it?

'Shall I tell you how I, and probably a few thousand others, felt when we read your jaunty little mud-slinger? We felt dirty. Dirty. The facts may be true. I correct myself. Knowing you, they *will* be true. You'll have letters and notes and tapes and the rest of the fucking evidence to prove it. But it's not the real truth. Reading between the lines, Ezra had a raw deal. I'd say more. She never stood a fucking chance until they took her off the streets half-dead—'

'...This is me again. Jack Almond. I hadn't finished, so I'm leaving a second message. With regard to my last comment I can hear you saying that lots of people have a raw deal, and they don't get involved with prostitution and drugs and the like. But some of us are just too bloody sensitive and too bloody unlucky to cope with it. So we sin. Now there's a good old-fashioned word. I'm surprised you didn't use it! Ezra *sinned*, and as Patrick Hanna is a model of propriety, he's the right man to see that she's punished.

'You miserable, scurrilous bastard! You know damned well that she can't fight back – that she *won't* fight back. She'll take it all. Accept it all. Probably forgive you, you scum. Well I don't, and won't, and can't. I've had my doubts about you from time to time. There was that poor old soak you found dead in the doorway. I've always wondered whether he'd actually gone, or whether you could have saved him if you hadn't been so keen on getting a good story. But I never thought you'd have stooped to hitting someone who can't hit back—'

'...This is Jack Almond for the last time. Your message service is too short. Let me tell you something else. Ezra may not have contacts in high places, but she's not short of one good friend – and that's me. I'll help her in any way I can, whatever anyone says or thinks or does. But as far as you're concerned you can count me out. So goodbye and – as you would say – the back of my hand to you!'

The next voice was smooth and rich.

'Patrick? This is Hector Mordant speaking. I've just read your article on Ezra, and I want to congratulate you on a particularly fine piece of work. We never expect anything but the best from you, as far as journalism goes, but this time you've done the city a social service as well, and I think you'll find you've made a lot of valuable friends in the process. I know we've had our differences in the past, but I want to wish you all the best. Perhaps we can have a drink together sometime?'

A voice of dry ice.

'Patrick? This is Kate speaking. I've no doubt that your article on Ezra has raised great waves everywhere, but none greater than at Melbury Old Hall. We've had a charming afternoon here, chock full of amusing little incidents, and all thanks to you.

'You've frightened Shirley to death and she's been busy knocking hell out of a bottle of whisky, telling the heavens she's been woefully deceived, and asking God what should she do. He seems to be ignoring her and who could blame Him?

'She hasn't quite screwed herself up enough to turn Ezra out, but she will do. Through me, of course. So you've proved that the pen is mightier than the sword, and a hell of a lot more sordid. I will just make a few cryptic remarks before I go.

'First: you're wasting your time on a reputable local paper. You should be grubbing for dirt on a national tabloid.

'Second: our supper this evening – and every other evening, come to that – is cancelled. I'm delighted to say that you'll miss an excellent meal.

'Third: all ties of friendship are severed as from now and for ever.

'Fourth: you *shit*!'

★　★　★

340

There were several assorted messages on Patrick's answering service when he drifted in from Mulligan's at six o'clock. In fact, the tape ran out on a particularly abusive one. He had, he realized, impressed his enemies and alienated his friends. Always a loner, he was now truly alone, which, he realized too late, is not quite the same thing. He had forfeited the respect of those he liked, and been left with admirers he did not admire.

'Fuck the bloody lot of them!' he said sorrowfully.

He could foretell his future: the *Courier's* postbag full of readers' letters both for and against him, the congratulations of his editor, the envy of his colleagues, the general indifference to Ezra, who had now ceased to be a person and become a succulent item of news.

His heart was sorest at the loss of Jack and Kate. He had been looking forward to seeing Kate that evening – eating and drinking and talking at Mulberry Street, being laughed at and approved, coming home in the small hours on top of the world. In the present circumstances he felt disinclined to go out at all.

His cupboard only held a packet of corn-flakes and half a dozen tins of food. He opened the door of the refrigerator and looked for inspiration. There was none.

He set out a bottle of whisky and a deep tumbler. He began to drink.

'Kate? This is Jack speaking. Sorry to badger you the moment you get home. I tried to get you at work, but Shirley said you'd just left. Yes, I know, you're knackered too, but I need to talk to you ... OK, yes, get yourself a drink first.'

He tapped his work table nervously, waiting. He knew by the sound of her voice that she was weary to the bones from bearing the day's burdens. He was sad for her, and yet needed her and must talk.

'Ah, Kate. Have you got a glass in hand? Good. God bless you, girl. What a bloody day it's been. Look, it's about Pat Hanna's article. I'm sick to the stomach with the bastard. If he'd had to do it under orders, so's to speak, I'd still despise him but I'd understand his situation. Know what I mean? As it is, I happen to know that he was just as keen on the idea as the rest of them, and he's been ferreting round for months. So I've finished with him.'

'So have I.'

'And I've told him so.'

'So have I.'

'Good.'

Silence. Kate was too tired to fill in the pause, and Jack less versatile than she at doing so. Finally she said, 'Jack. I'm exhausted. I've got to go.'

'Let me take you out for a meal.'

'I'm too damned tired to go out. I'd fall asleep at the table. I'm going to make myself tea and toast and go to bed.'

'Tea and toast isn't enough at the end of a hard day. Let me bring a parcel of fish and chips over to your place.'

She wondered why her friends' suggestions were always less satisfactory than her own. How could fish and chips compare with her three-course menu? She summoned up the necessary energy.

'No need. I've got a meal ready here. Patrick was coming to supper. I cancelled on him. I was going to put it in the freezer. It only has to be heated up.'

Jack hesitated, unwilling to coerce her, and said, 'No, no. It's all right. We can leave this until tomorrow. You have your tea and toast and go to bed.'

His consideration proved to be his open sesame. Kate made a final effort.

'You may as well come over and eat Patrick's supper.'

Again he hesitated, but he knew Kate's suppers. Appetite overcame solicitude.

'Don't move hand or foot,' he said. 'I'll be round in ten minutes to help.'

Automatically, she began to psyche herself into a sociable mood, to make sure that the meal and she were at their best. Then, like a benediction, she remembered that this was Jack, who asked nothing of her except that she be herself, and would appreciate the smallest effort. For the first time that day she felt that she need not be on guard, need not fight, need not extract from herself the last drop of energy and courage. The evening could be a pleasure, a relaxation, even a form of healing.

Smiling to herself for the first time that long, hard day, she began to lay the table.

Consequences

The other apostle was sprung, if I may use the expression, from a mental home where he was undergoing treatment.

That mischievous sentence in Patrick's report revived enquiries in the police department. Was this the truth? they asked him. Patrick proved that it was by giving them the information they required, though without his usual relish. The vision of Joel rising from the mud and flinging his arms to heaven was clear in his mind. He guessed what would happen to the poor little sod, and regretted that he was the means of exposing him. Though Kate's edict had been unmistakable, he felt he must do what he could. He lifted the telephone and dialled her number at the Old Hall. As her voice came across the wires, bright and cordial, the thought of further alienation made him wince. He kept his approach simple.

'Kate. It's Patrick speaking. Now don't, for God's sake, put the phone down on me. This concerns Ezra and it's a crisis. The police have only just left me. They were interested in my reference to Joel escaping from a mental home.'

The voice was no longer cordial. 'Go on.'

'They'll be coming to the Old Hall to inter-view Ezra about him, and alerting the social services...'

She heard him out. She answered coldly, 'So you've stirred up the mud yet again. What do you expect me to do about it?'

'You can speak up for the pair of them. Tell them that he's better off with Ezra. I've seen the home. I've been there. You wouldn't want it for yourself. The inmates are all daft and, short of cruelty, that's the way they're treated – if that is short of cruelty.'

A pause. Kate sighed. 'I expect they'll take the poor little devil back anyway, whatever I say.'

'All right, then, but at least you can help Ezra.'

'Why are you so concerned about her suddenly?'

'She got him away from there. I'm not clear how. He said something to me about climbing a wall. But I know for a fact that she took him off with her.'

'Did you tell the police that?'

'No. I had to give them the address of the so-called home, but I said the rest was just my blarney – to add a bit of colour to the article.'

'How very restrained of you. And how did you find out about his escape? Or is that information classified?'

Patrick hesitated, but as he was damned already he might as well be damned for the blackest deed of the lot.

'I've been on this story for a long time, and I always go to the source. Joel's fond of sweets. I saw the two of them on their usual begging round in the city a while ago. I gave Simeon a fiver to buy whatever he liked and keep away for an hour, and I took Joel for a walk. A friendly arm about the shoulders, a friendly voice, and a pound of chocolate fudge gave me all the facts I needed. I just hope he wasn't sick later.' He waited humbly for the sky to fall on him.

A sound as of an indrawn breath.

'You are the lowest sort of thing that crawls,' said Kate emphatically. 'In fact, I am insulting the lowest thing that crawls by saying so.'

Even more humbly. 'I'd agree with that. But I'm trying to make up for it.'

A pause. She was thinking. Her tone was not friendly but the sting had left it.

'Well, they won't get any information out of Joel. The poor little mutt will be incoherent. So if Ezra keeps her mouth shut about her part in the affair they can't accuse her of kidnapping – or whatever.'

'Ah, but you can't rely on her for that,' said Patrick. 'She has this problem about telling the truth.'

Kate's mind was made up. 'All right,' she said. 'Now if you'll promise me, on whatever honour is left in you, to tell no one else what you've told me, I'll go down and do my best to keep her out of trouble – even if I can't do anything for Joel.'

'You're a fine upstanding lass and I thank you for that.'

'I won't say you're welcome, but I'm glad you asked me,' said Kate, and put down the receiver.

The two of them were sitting in meditation when Kate knocked softly at the door of the hut and entered. At least, Ezra was meditating. Joel was winking at his fingers and making shapes with his mouth to pass the time. He smiled wetly on Kate, regarding her as a welcome interruption.

'I beg your pardon,' she whispered to Ezra, and sat on the floor with them, cross-legged, to wait.

In the tranquillity of silence, and the summer sunlight, she thought how very different this was from Shirley's idea of meditation, which bore a strong resemblance to that of Joel: something to be got through as best one could. But he had no such consolations as alcohol and nicotine. Not even a toffee to suck, she thought, remembering Joel's sweet tooth. She wished she had one to give him. For herself, she was glad to rest and forget her daily duties. So she closed her eyes and flowed silently out on the tide with Ezra.

A general movement brought her back to shore. Ezra rose, smiling, and held out one hand to help Kate to her feet. Joel scrambled up clumsily and stood to attention, arms at his sides, watching his carer soulfully. As often happened Kate's thought had been anticipated. Ezra drifted over to a jar on the windowsill, took out two striped humbugs, and bestowed them on him.

To Kate's amazement she said, 'It is too hard for anyone to give up everything at first. Joel does his best. This is a little help along the way.'

Busy with his sweets, Joel was as near heaven as he would ever get.

Jocelyn's death had brought them closer, but now the two women communicated face to face for the first time.

Kate asked, smiling, 'Did Simeon have a little help, too?'

'Of course, but not from me. He could look after himself. Here, in the hut, he kept the rules. Outside...' She spread her thin dark hands in a little gesture of dismissal. 'To what happened outside I turned the blind eye. It was a sin of omission on my part, but it helped him.'

Then she unburdened herself.

'I never concealed the life I had led from Simeon. Our friendship was based on mutual understanding. He tried to find the same peace and purpose that I had found. But he soon realized that he could not give up the world as I did. His struggles were unknown to anyone but myself. They were heroic, and unrewarded. He was bound, sooner or later, to return to his old life. And he is not clever. He will make mistakes and be punished for them. Sometimes he will try to be good, and still make mistakes, and curse himself for being a fool. But perhaps, from time to time, he will remember how we were and take strength from it.'

Kate was silenced but Ezra needed to explain, to defend.

'You are going to say that he must have stolen the beer and the pies, or stolen money to pay for them? But he had a personal code. He would not steal from those who could not afford the loss. I know this because some-times – not every time – he would tell me what he had done. He did try to remake his life.'

Kate was modifying her opinion of Simeon. A rough-hewn product still, but the roughness concealed a tender spot.

'I was brought up as a Catholic,' Ezra continued. 'The confessional is a cleansing process. You put the offence behind you, and you walk on. So after confession he would not steal again – for a while – and he could walk on.'

Kate found her voice, but made only a modest observation. '"Walk on!" is a Buddhist injunction.'

'I take wisdom from wherever I find it. It does not need a name.'

Still Kate had to test the truth of these confidences.

'Forgive me for being so direct, but where

do you get the money to buy toffees?'

Ezra's smile lit up, amused by the implication.

'I need no money. I ask at the sweet shop in Peddleford. I do not ask for much. They know me. I give them healing. They give me perhaps half a pound of sweets a week. They are very kind, very understanding.'

Kate shook her head and gave a little laugh of admiration and disbelief. Then the reason for her visit sobered her.

'Ezra, I'm sorry to be the bearer of bad news...' She hesitated, looking at Joel.

'Come outside for a while,' said Ezra. Her smile faded. Her air of tranquillity left her.

Outside, the sun shone serenely on the Old Hall field and on the sunlit lime grove from which all litter had been cleared.

Ezra folded her hands in her sleeves. It was a self-protective gesture and Kate wished she were not the cause of it. She began, 'I'm afraid Patrick Hanna's article has done you harm.'

'He wrote the truth.' Stoically.

Behind the gentleness, the soft speech, Kate saw the face of a woman who had survived a brutal life.

She hurried on. 'I'm afraid there's more trouble in store. There were enquiries about the article. Patrick had to give the police the address of the mental home where Joel was being treated. They'll be interviewing you any time now. They may bring someone from the home to identify him. Possibly to take him back.'

A long silence.

'There's another thing,' said Kate. 'They'll question you, too. They may suspect you had something to do with his escape.'

'I helped to free him. Yes. He could not have freed himself.'

'It would go badly with you if you admitted that.'

Ezra said, 'If they take poor Joel that is the greatest harm they can do to him or to me.' Suddenly she put her hands over her face, desolated.

Kate felt as helpless and sorry as she did when Nora was finally denied Pearl.

'But they could put you in prison.'

Ezra made a sound that was half a laugh, half a sigh. 'I have been in prison. There is nothing there that I have not experienced before, and I am stronger now. And sometime they will have to let me out. Prison is not the worst. Taking Joel is the worst.'

'But wouldn't it be simpler to say nothing...' Kate began, when Ezra stopped her with an upraised hand.

'Kate, you wish me well. And I thank you. I shall answer any question they ask. I tell you, they cannot hurt me except through Joel.'

I've wasted my bloody time, Kate thought, but had to admire her.

'I respect your judgement,' she said.

There was nothing more to do or say. So she went.

★ ★ ★

351

'Kate? It's Jack. I rang you earlier but you weren't home. Have you kicked off your sandals and sipped something that cheers and definitely inebriates?'

Tired as she was, padding round the kitchen in her bare feet, reaching for a glass from the cupboard, she said almost flippantly, 'You're right about the sandals, and I'm just going to open the wine.'

'How's things?'

'They have been better. In fact, far better. I had to stand by and watch, this afternoon, while a social worker took poor little Joel away.' She burst out, 'It's so stupid. It's just the same situation that Nora was in with Pearl, and we've had exactly the same result. Some bloody pettifogging rule takes precedence over kindness and common sense.'

'Poor little bugger. How's Ezra?'

'Riven. It's the first time I've seen her beaten.' Kate became garrulous in her distress. 'It's so difficult to be a saint. No one can do anything for you. Can't make you a cup of tea or offer material comfort. Can't get past the suffering. In the end I put my arm round her and held her hand and we sat together for a while. I couldn't think of anything else to do.'

Jack said, 'You did all anyone could.'

'The police were there simply as a formality. I don't suppose they thought Ezra would make a scene, and of course she didn't, and of course she told them the truth. Apparently he'd climbed a tree and was

352

trying to get on to the wall. She shinned up and helped him over. But the police are not – to quote them – "pursuing the matter further". Oh, Jack, it was gruesome. Joel was demented. He clung like a leech to Ezra. Crying and begging. She offered him sweets and he threw them away, angrily, like a child would. She stroked his hair and tried to persuade him to go quietly, and she promised to come and see him. But they had to prise his fingers off her. He was screaming, Jack. Thin little screams.'

Her head drooped. She said, 'Oh, Jack, I've had enough. Of everything. And life keeps adding to the load. With all the work for Hector's Music Festival, and the catastrophes from Ezra's meeting, I haven't been able to deal with my own problem. I should have been applying for jobs and having interviews by now. I should have my future in mind. And I haven't, Jack. I haven't.'

Ezra had neither sought nor wanted publicity. In finding the grove and her patron she simply felt that she had come home, and from there could use her gifts of insight and healing to help people. Though streetwise from her youth, she was still a political innocent. Rapt in her inner life, asking nothing of this outer world, she had assumed it would not trouble her. Instead, she had aroused controversy of the bitterest kind, done great harm to those who supported her, and could make no reparation.

Public failure and disgrace attract the compassion of some, the curiosity of many, and in a few the desire to inflict further hurt and humiliation.

Late one May evening three youths, to whom the words 'Temporarily Closed to the Public' denoted a challenge to their manhood, and the warning 'Trespassers Will Be Prosecuted!' a final inducement, sidled up Grove Hill in search of adventure. There was none. Frustrated, they looked all around them and spied a small grey figure sitting in meditation in the adjoining field. For a few moments they watched it, puzzled, then the ringleader guessed its identity.

'It's that religious smack-head, Ezra, what was in the paper!' he said.

Their eyes lit up. Their body language became aggressive. They swaggered over to the fence that divided Shirley's property from Grove Hill, to get a closer look.

'She were a slag,' he remarked.

One of the others had taken a smooth flat stone and was turning it over and over between his fingers, as a card sharper turns a card.

'Bet you can't hit her from here.'

In reply the lad aimed and skimmed the stone skilfully, but the range was too great and it fell at Ezra's feet. Motionless, absorbed, she did not notice.

They watched her for a few moments and, seeing she remained oblivious to their presence, they climbed the fence. Whispering, sniggering, they hunted here and there for stones until they had collected a small pile of ammunition. Then, judging their distance, they launched the first fusillade at her.

The attack was even more horrifying than they realized. Shocked out of deep meditation, suddenly aware of stinging pain and hostile intent, Ezra scrambled to her feet and shielded her face with her arms.

Elated, they shouted abuse as they hurled their missiles and as she began to run towards the hut they ran after her. Impeded by terror and her loose robe, she stumbled and fell, and they were on her, cursing, punching, their savagery intensified by her helplessness and their joint strength. She tried to speak, to communicate with them, but the leader struck her across the mouth.

'Fucking Paki,' he said, and kicked her in the ribs.

Then her will to survive came uppermost, and Ezra fought back. They were bored adolescents, reared on a diet of television violence and playground bullying, imagining themselves as tough men. But Ezra had lived harder, sunk lower, clambered out of deeper pits, seen and suffered genuine pain, and she fought tooth and claw like the street brat she once was.

Still, it was three to one, and the outcome might have been tragic had Shirley's builder, Ronnie Baxstead, not been on his way home to high tea. A burly man, he charged to the rescue with zeal and used his fists without compunction. Within minutes the youths had struggled out of his clutches and were running as fast as they could for freedom and home.

'I know who you are,' he shouted after them. 'I'll have you prosecuted!' He bent over Ezra and helped her to rise. 'Local hooligans,' he remarked. 'Nothing to do but make mischief.' She felt like a little heap of bones in his hands and he was afraid. 'Can you walk, miss?'

She nodded once, a little jerk of assent.

'Let's get you up the Hall, then, and they'll phone for help.'

'No,' she whispered. 'Not ... the Hall. I have brought ... enough trouble ... on Shirley.'

He hesitated, but his cottage was not far off. 'Come on home wi' me, then,' he said, 'and the wife'll make you a cup of tea and patch you up a bit until we can get you to the hospital.'

'You are ... very kind.'

But she could not walk, though she tried, and Mrs Baxstead was shortly astonished to see her husband carrying a small grey bundle of clothes in his arms, and crying, 'Phone 999, Edna. We need an ambulance right away.'

Atonement

When Patrick felt vulnerable he presented an impervious face, when guilty he looked baby-innocent, and when distressed he adopted a buoyant air.

The Mary Gilchrist ward at Peddleford Cottage Hospital was warm and white, and cosy with subdued chatter. Through the delicate scent of flowers drifted a whiff of antiseptic. It was peopled by women in every stage of illness, from convalescents sitting up in fancy bedjackets to those asleep or lying listless after operations. One, screened from this small world, was presumably working her passage into the next. It was a quiet time of day, just after visiting time. Fresh fruit was being chosen from bedside bowls, new bottles of squash opened and poured. Near the doorway two nurses stood talking, with their backs to him.

He slipped an arm round one neat and one stout waist, and winked at each of them as at a pair of allies.

'You know me. Patrick Hanna of the *Courier*,' he purred, 'come to make the pair of you famous as nurses of the year.'

His reputation had long since gone before him. The older woman raised her eyebrows and drew down the corners of her mouth. The younger one giggled.

'Oh no, you haven't, Patrick.'

'And keep your hands to yourself, you naughty boy, or we'll be in trouble with the sister. What are you after this time?'

Patrick's smile was wide and friendly, his eyes shrewdly assessed them.

'I'm not after anything. I've come to visit the lady Ezra. By appointment,' he added untruthfully.

They both laughed in disbelief.

'I know the lady personally,' he purred. 'She's by way of being a friend of mine.'

They were unimpressed. 'I doubt it,' said the stout nurse, stoutly.

'Ah, come on now. Where are you hiding her?'

'We're not supposed to say, and any visitor has to be vetted.'

He decided to be improbable. 'Did you not know that I'm a long-lost relative of hers?'

The older nurse pursed her lips, the younger one giggled again.

'Sure I am. I'm her cousin come all the way from Donegal,' said Patrick, grinning, squeezing.

'Oh no, you're not,' said the stout nurse. 'You wrote a very nasty article about her, and let me tell you this – having nursed the poor woman I don't believe a word of it. She's a really sweet little person.'

'Are you going to write another nasty article about her, Patrick?' asked the younger one pertly.

Soft swift squeaks announced the approach of rubber-heeled shoes.

'What's happening?' a pleasant but imperious voice demanded.

'Nothing, Sister! This gentleman was just making an enquiry, Sister!' the nurses chorused, and hurried away.

Patrick measured his opponent and decided that charm would be useless. He became frank and respectful.

'I'm Patrick Hanna of the *Courier*, Sister, but I'm here in a private capacity. I wrote an article about Ezra that caused her a lot of trouble. Let me say that I was doing my job with blinkers on, and I'm sorry for it.'

She inclined her head but continued to watch him.

'Ezra is a good woman. I wish her no harm. Others do. But right now the person who can harm her most is herself. She should leave this place entirely, but she's the sort of woman that sticks to her principles, and she'll not budge.'

Sister gave the briefest of nods.

He considered a compliment to the still-handsome face before him, and wisely discarded the idea.

'Speaking between the two of us, I'm not of a mind to let her be killed in the line of what she sees as her duty. I've been thinking how I could help her, how I could save her – if you'll excuse the hyperbole. Now, if you were to let me see her for ten minutes I've a feeling I could talk her round. You might not believe it,' said Patrick disarmingly, 'but I could talk the hind leg off a donkey and never hurt it!'

Sister permitted herself a little smile. 'I can well believe *that*, Mr Hanna.'

'Then would you let me try, Sister?'

She summed him up, and decided in his favour. 'I'll give you ten minutes and not a second longer. She's better than she has been, but she's still weak and shocked and mustn't be tired. As soon as I think you should go I shall turn you out. Is that understood?'

Honestly, he said, 'Thank you. One flick of the eyelid and I'll come like a lamb.'

'She's in a private room. We thought it best, in view of the circumstances. Come this way, Mr Hanna.'

Ezra did not waste words, but turned her bandaged head and looked at him, and Patrick sat down at the side of her bed and confessed, as he would have confessed to the priest in his boyhood.

'I've come to say I'm sorry for the article I wrote, and I'm sorry it harmed you.'

She smiled slightly, for Patrick in a penitential mood was a droll spectacle.

'I want you to know that I've been thinking seriously about your –' he hesitated for once, seeking the right word – 'your bond with the grove.'

A flicker of interest in the clear eyes.

360

'Because of what you've done, and above all of what you are, I've been studying different religions and beliefs, in a manner of speaking. I can't claim to be an expert on the subject. I've only just skimmed the surface. But I get the general picture, and I've had an idea that I'd like you to consider.'

Ezra said slowly, 'It is difficult to speak, but I am listening.'

'And your eyes are windows to your soul,' said Patrick gallantly, sincerely.

He saw the shadow of a frown.

'And right you are to ask me to stick to the subject without paying compliments – though that compliment was nothing but the truth.'

She touched the back of his hand gently.

'I take your point,' said Patrick, and launched forth. 'Now, spiritually speaking, before we can begin to improve ourselves – to whatever degree – we have to go through an experience known as the dark night of the soul. Is that right?'

She smiled a little then, and formed the words, 'Many times.'

'And I'm sure you'd do that with a good heart, over and over again, though from what I've read of it, once would be more than enough for me. Then we come out of that stage into enlightenment.' He read her expression. 'Or some degree of enlightenment. We know more than we did, at any rate. But this still isn't enough. We have to go on improving. And, human nature being what it is, the tendency is to slide back, and then the

361

devil in us – or the dark side, or whatever you like to call it – sees what we're about and begins to deceive us.'

Her gaze was attentive.

'Now you've given up all your worldly goods. Right? Yes, you've done that, and more than that. You've given yourself as well. Right? You can say to me, "I've only got my begging bowl and blanket and the clothes I stand up in." Which is to your heavenly credit. Right? Furthermore, you love everybody – even, possibly, the bastards that harmed you most. Am I right? Yes, I was afraid I would be.' He digressed for a moment. 'You can take it from me, Ezra, that a swift punch to the jaw would do them more good than any amount of forgiveness, and that includes myself!' He came back. 'But there's one last little thing that I think you missed – what the Buddha called "attachment" – meaning, in your case, the grove.'

A spasm contracted her face.

'Are you in pain?' he asked, contrite.

'Yes,' said Ezra, very slowly. 'Because ... I know ... what you are about ... to tell me.'

He was sorry to continue, but must.

'Attachment creeps up on you from behind, and comes in many guises. It pretends to be a way to help others, a solution, a goal, even a well-deserved reward. And it's nothing of the sort. It's another temptation to forsake the road.'

Her lips parted, and a sound that came from the bottom of her heart, the softest of moans, escaped them.

Patrick put both of his hands tenderly on hers. 'Forgive me,' he said.

The bandaged head moved forward clumsily in a nod.

He rose, in obedience to the sound of Sister's shoes squeaking softly towards them.

'We understand each other. I'll say no more, but leave you to think about it. This is a private matter between the two of us. There'll never be a word about this in print. The decision is yours and I'll abide by it. Just remember that I'm there for you, and if you decide to move on, wherever you want to go, then I'll take you there and wish you God speed.'

Two single tears slid down her cheeks.

'I know,' said Patrick. 'I know.'

She said, out of her trouble, 'You are ... a good man.'

Patrick replied nonchalantly, to cover his own emotion, 'Now you'll find out you're wrong about that, but when they consign me to hell will you drop an onion down on a string and pull me up again?'

She nodded, wiped her eyes clumsily with the back of her hand, and smiled.

'Remember,' she said, 'not to push away ... the other needy souls ... who will also reach ... for salvation.'

'I'll stand back like the gentleman I am, and hope for the best. God bless the both of us,' he said. And then, as his watcher loomed tall and white beside him, 'I'm leaving this

363

minute, Sister. You can put that horsewhip away!'

And left the ward twice as jauntily, because he was in pain himself.

The late spring was cool. A log fire had been lit in the main hall and Shirley was warming her knees in front of it, legs spread well apart, sipping whisky, when Kate knocked and came in, full of portent.

Shirley had changed in the last few weeks. Her face wore the old hard handsome look, her air was businesslike, her wig seemed redder, her stance sturdier. She had consigned the disciple's white robe to the dustbin and reverted to well-cut mannish tweeds. She no longer apologized for anything she ate, smoked or drank. At the moment she was busy playing Hector and the council at their own legal game, and with considerable relish. She had taken up the reins of Mrs Porter's Parlours with her former zeal, combed through the accounts, galvanized the manageresses, and was planning a royal tour of the tea shops in the autumn. Somehow she would scrape through this present crisis. Her relationship with Kate was brisk and friendly but not as close as before. Mentally she had cast Ezra out.

'Don't say a word until you've poured yourself a drink and taken a seat,' she said to Kate. 'You've got NEWS written all over your face, though I'm not sure whether I want to hear it.'

She did not speak for a while after Kate had repeated Patrick's tale, but continued to sip and warm herself. Then she reached for a cigarette, lit it, and spoke honestly.

'I'm sorry she's decided to go, but to be quite honest I'm relieved. I didn't know what the hell I was going to do about her if she insisted on staying. Feelings were running high. Being beaten up was bad enough, but it could have been worse. Someone might have burned the hut down, with Ezra in it. And I couldn't have brought her up to the Hall, because that would only transfer the problem to me, and my position is difficult enough as it is.' Her eyes narrowed. 'Though I'll fix those bastards yet!'

Kate was silent and sad.

'Let's get real,' said Shirley frankly. 'Anyone who champions Ezra is in deep trouble. She's bad luck, and I don't want my business or my reputation to suffer. It's all very well being loved by the poor and humble, but they can't help you. The action lies with the haves, not the have-nots.' She glanced sideways at Kate, and accused her. 'I know what you're thinking. You think I ought to stand by her, come what may. But I'm being practical.'

'And you must take care of your own interests,' Kate remarked.

Her comment held no sting. It was just a comment, but Shirley flared up.

'Well, what else *can* I do?'

There was no point in discussing the matter further.

'How about thanking Patrick for sorting it all out?' said Kate lightly.

'Oh, he's back in favour, is he?' Sourly. 'Part of the three musketeers once again? You amuse me, Kate, you really do, with your unsuitable men.'

Kate ignored this dig and began her news. 'I came to tell you about Ezra. Jack and Patrick and I felt we must take care of her as far as possible. She's leaving hospital on Friday, and she's got nowhere to go apart from the hut – which is quite unsuitable. She reckons she'll be well enough to travel on Sunday. I don't agree. I think she must convalesce for a week or two. After all, she'll be going off into the blue, living on a handful of food and sleeping rough.'

Shirley said hardily, 'Ezra is Ezra. She'll act as she thinks best. But she's a fool to trust Pat Hanna, and so are you. He's only doing this to get a good story for his newspaper. I'll bet you a fiver that he's told Jack Almond to follow them at a safe distance and take photographs.'

'Indeed he hasn't,' said Kate indignantly, 'and Jack would refuse. He'd consider it a form of betrayal.'

'Then both those leopards have changed their spots!' said Shirley. 'I should have thought they were too fond of publicity to miss an opportunity like that.'

Unconvinced, she poured herself another whisky. She was embarrassed, knowing that morally she should offer Ezra shelter at the

Hall. There was a time when Kate would have let her continue to feel guilty, but now she had mercy on the weakness.

'It's no longer your problem, Shirley. I'm going to ask Ezra to stay with me. She won't attract any attention in Mulberry Street and the move will be made discreetly. No one knows when she's leaving hospital. Jack's going to pick her up from the back entrance. And Patrick is keeping his mouth – and column – shut. So the three of us will manage it between us. There's no need to involve you.'

Momentarily, Shirley was ashamed. Slipping back into their former comradeship, she said warmly, 'That's good of you, Katie. I didn't know what to do.' She hesitated. 'I suppose I ought to see her. Wish her well.'

Reading her mind, Kate said, 'It would be better for both sides if you didn't. I can take a message.'

Then Shirley spoke sincerely. 'I'm sorry it had to come to this, Katie. Sorry I can't stand by her. She's a good person and she deserves it. But we can only do what we can do, and be what we are. She said that herself once, only she put it better. Give her ... give her my love ... and tell her how sorry I am – and that I wish her all the best. And ... thank her for the good things she did. Say ... I'm grateful.'

'She won't blame you, you know. She does understand.'

Shirley nodded, fingering the rim of her glass, staring into the fire. The flames struck glancing lights from the crystal tumbler, giving her cheeks an unbecoming flush and revealing a snail-trail of tears. 'I did truly try to change, Katie.'

'Indeed you did. And you were very generous to her. Everything she's had here, and everything she's accomplished, was only possible because you provided her with a home. She knows that. Now, as she'd say to you herself, walk on.' She finished her drink and set the glass down.

'Well, I must get back to work on Hector's Music Festival. When I die they'll find the word Portaloo carved on my heart!'

An Unobtrusive Guest

A Sunday evening

To take Ezra into her home had been a costly decision on Kate's part because the house was her sanctuary, but Ezra turned out to be an unobtrusive guest and a model convalescent at No. 11 Mulberry Street.

Both women were frank with each other from the beginning. Each stated her own needs, and tried to anticipate the other's wishes. Solitude was the most important concern, meaning restoration for Kate, meditation for Ezra. So they arranged a signal to indicate when they wanted to be alone: a card on a string hung on the door handle. No card meant that company was welcome. Their dissimilar lives flowed on quietly side by side.

At first, being weak, Ezra dozed or rested in the spare bedroom most of the time, making her own frugal meals during the day, accepting unfamiliar comforts. Then, as she gained strength, she concerned herself with the private life of her hostess.

Nora, whilst grumbling about her daughter's increasing tendency to sustain the weak and be exploited by the strong, was endeavouring to help her. From her weekly visits Kate brought back new-laid eggs, home-baked bread, an armful of flowers, and a fund of good advice that constantly missed its target.

Arriving home late on one such evening, Kate poured herself a glass of wine and sat at the kitchen table, head in hands, so tired that she forgot to hang out her card. Hearing Ezra's soft step outside she suffered a spasm of anger, and glared at the wine bottle. For God's sake let me be, she thought.

'I'm sorry,' she said to the intruder, as agreeably as she could, 'but I'm feeling antisocial. I've been at Peddleford all day and I'm exhausted.' She indicated the bounty. 'From my mother,' she explained, sighing, smiling.

'She is a good woman,' said Ezra, putting

the flowers in water.

'She's a very good woman. It's just that she drives me mad.'

Ezra did not answer. She put the rest of the contributions away, then stood behind Kate and placed thin brown hands on her shoulders.

'Sit back and I will give you a massage,' she said. 'Then I leave you alone to drink your wine in peace.'

Her small-boned hands were surprisingly strong and Kate felt the day's tensions gradually being kneaded away. Relaxing, watching a patch of sunlight on the kitchen wall turn a darker shade of gold, she drifted on the quiet flow of Ezra's conversation.

'Today I have been so obedient. The hospital would be pleased with me. They told me that I must eat more protein and more fat for the sake of my health. So far I could not – and meat and fish, never. But today I had a boiled egg with brown bread and butter cut into fingers.'

Kate was amused by her earnestness. 'Did you enjoy it?'

Ezra mocked herself. 'Ye-es, but that is not important. The obedience is important. As they would say in the hospital, "Tha-a-at's a good girl!" Everything changes,' she continued in a different tone. 'When I was young I used to dream of food. For a while, I forget when, I must have been a very young child, I had foster-parents. I forget their names and faces, too. It was a long time ago. The foster-mother was a kind woman, like your mother. Every day she gave me a fresh boiled egg for breakfast and bread and butter fingers – she called them soldiers. But I was bad to her. I always had to be bad. And they took me away. I didn't miss the foster-mother, but I missed the egg. The egg was magic food.'

'What did you usually eat that made a boiled egg magical?'

'As a child? No food. Poor food. Institution food. As an adolescent on the streets? Anything I could get. All served with the sharpest sauce of all – hunger. Once, when I was washing up in a café kitchen, I was so hungry that I ate what people had left on their plates instead of scraping it into the bin. I would hunt through the restaurant bins for scraps to take home.'

Kate listened, giving little grunts of pleasure as her aches were eased.

'I smoked, too, when I could. I picked stub ends from the pavements. To smoke was to feel less hungry. But to take drugs was best of all because that was to forget hunger. And hunger was always there, like a bad companion.'

The sides of Ezra's hard little hands batted swiftly from left to right of Kate's shoulders and back again. Giving herself up to the massage, Kate wondered if this dialogue was in the nature of a confession, and Ezra answered the thought.

'I do not ask you to be sorry for me. There is no need. I am talking aloud to myself. Like you, I have come to the end of an old road. Before I set foot on the new road I must fit the pieces of my life together to see how they look. I am making a picture of my life with words.' She mocked herself again. 'It is a change for me to talk and for someone else to listen.'

Her hands glided along the released muscles in one long final stroke, stopped, pressed, and gave them a little pat of farewell.

'Now how do you feel?' she asked, knowing the answer.

'Blissful!'

'Would you like me to leave you?'

'No, not just yet. I'm feeling friendly now. I wish you drank wine. We could have a glass together. Draw up a chair and talk on, if it helps.'

'You will be my counsellor?' Ezra asked, smiling.

'I wouldn't know how to begin counselling you.'

'That is not true. You have already decided what I should do next. You and Patrick the Wanderer and Jack the Giver. You have all counselled me.'

'You're more than welcome,' Kate said automatically, but she was thinking of the descriptions that Ezra had used. 'Patrick the Wanderer and Jack the Giver,' she repeated. 'What am I?'

'You would like me to tell you how I see you?'

'Please.'

'You are Kate the Warrior, fighting the worst enemy of all: fear.'

The last of the sun left the kitchen wall, and Kate's warm feeling vanished with it. Shaken, she managed a composed reply. 'Fear? Of what?'

'You are afraid of making a mistake.'

Kate remained silent.

'I face a new road,' said Ezra. 'That is hard, but I know where I am going, and my road lies straight ahead, so that is simple. You stand at a crossroads, which could go either way, and that is far more difficult. You are saying to yourself, "Suppose, whatever choice I make, I am trapped again? Suppose I become that child again, looking in shop windows at a world I cannot share? Suppose I choose the wrong man, the wrong job?" Am I right?'

Kate nodded, and poured herself a second glass of wine to dull the fear.

Ezra said, 'Yes, you need a little anaesthetic. Metamorphosis is painful.'

Kate said, 'I've worked so hard, tried so hard, and gone wrong somewhere.' Her demons besieged her. 'Shirley told me I was nothing but a collection of designer labels and pretty party manners, and that Hector was a con man, and that we made a lovely couple.'

Ezra said, smiling, 'That was the whisky talking. She was probably angry about something else and had to blame you for it.'

'She was right about me and Hector,' said Kate, and looked up quickly, shyly at Ezra.

'We all make mistakes. Why can you not forgive yourself for making yours?'

Kate was silent again, knowing this was true.

Ezra continued, 'Tell me what else has been said about you.'

'Patrick did say that he respected me even though he disliked me, and that I was a tough, smart woman with a mind of her own, who did her job well.'

Ezra chuckled. 'But that was before you became friends. He likes you very much now.'

Kate nodded. 'Yes, but the description is too near the bone for comfort. And once, when I made a flippant remark, Jack told me I was fatuous. He said no one would think I had a brain in my head or a decent feeling in my heart. He said I gave the impression of being shallow – although he did add that he thought I wasn't.'

Ezra laughed outright. 'And now he is your best friend.'

'Yes,' Kate said, and smiled. 'Yes, he is. My best friend. And it's childish to mind so much about being criticized. To remember it and still feel the sting.'

'Especially when it is no longer true.'

'Yes, especially then.'

They sat in quiet contentment for a few moments, then Ezra said, 'So Patrick and Jack are forgiven. Now you should come to terms with your sternest critic, who never changes her mind or relents in the slightest. Yourself.'

Kate thought again. 'Yes, you're right.'

The atmosphere was tranquil once more.

'I shall leave you now, not by yourself but with your Self,' said Ezra. 'Think of her as a separate being, a sister. Instead of driving her, tormenting her, finding fault with her, you should ask her what she needs. And when the right moment comes – jump!' She smiled again and said, 'Goodnight, dear Kate.'

A Proposal

Patrick, feeling that he had saved Ezra's life, knowing that he would be the one to see her on her way, regarded her as his personal property and confidante. He visited her sometimes when Kate was away, and made such a nuisance of himself, without meaning to, that Kate concocted a PLEASE DO NOT DISTURB notice to hang on the front door-knob. But on the occasions when the notice was absent, and Ezra felt herself fit to be a counsellor, he poured forth the story of his life and his feelings for Kate, and when finally reduced to silence by his own loquacity, he listened. Then, being Patrick, he adjusted her advice to suit his own purposes and believed that he was acting according to her guidance.

In their conversation, Ezra had said to Kate, 'The wandering Patrick will not commit himself. He does not walk on. He makes sure always that he can walk away.'

A few days later, over a second sumptuous tea at Mrs Porter's Parlour, Patrick said, 'This is to make up for past sins, and the treat's on me.' He adopted his most beguiling tone. 'Now you remember what we talked about last time?'

'Oh dear,' Kate sighed, but smiled.

He ignored her. He had solved a problem. He would not be interrupted. 'I was asking you to make a commitment, you said, and I was making none. Well, I've thought about it since, and you were right, and now I'm prepared to do it.'

'Patrick...'

'One minute of your valuable time. I've thought it all out. Now, no doubt you have a little nest egg put by...'

'Patrick, I haven't a job to go to at the moment. Any nest egg...'

'I understand you. Think no more about it. I'll provide the nest egg.' He considered this rash statement. 'Not that I've got anything at the moment, but my credit must be good for something.'

'Patrick...'

'Supposing that we commit ourselves to a life partnership in love and business. Now what do you say to that?'

This stopped her short. She stared at him in appalled wonder. He soared away, in the grip of his dream.

'Neither of us needs to give up anything we
376

have already. We could set up a business here in the city. There's a grand house on the market in Charlotte Street...'

Mentally, Kate reviewed Charlotte Street, whose grand days were long since over, whose great houses had become students' flats, whose stately facades concealed hideous ills and would incur even more hideous expense to remedy them.

'I can't believe you're serious,' she said drily.

'Listen to me. I've thought it all out. I know the place needs a lick or two of paint, but you've had first-hand experience of old houses and how to restore them – look what you've done for Shirley at the Old Hall...'

She flagged him down. 'Shirley has spent a fortune – *her* fortune – on Melbury Old Hall, and the best thing that can happen to her is to find a rich and foolish buyer.'

'She's selling up?' Patrick enquired. He switched plans. 'Now, how much would she want for it, I wonder?'

Kate caught hold of both his hands and made him look at her, which he was reluctant to do because the dream was so splendid. But the contact pleased him, and he squeezed her fingers and kissed them.

Kate said incisively, 'Patrick. You're talking in terms of hundreds of thousands of pounds.'

'All right then,' he conceded instantly. 'We'll forget the Old Hall. Charlotte Street it is.'

377

Kate laughed aloud. She pulled her hands away gently and sat back in her chair, resigned. 'All right then,' she repeated. 'Tell me the rest of the plan.'

'We buy the grand house in Charlotte Street. I haven't looked round it yet. I've left that to you. You're the expert. But I know that the two of us could turn it into a wonderful hotel. You'd be in charge, of course...'

'I rather thought I might be.'

'...and I, as your humble servant, will be at your command.'

'I won't bore you,' said Kate, smiling to herself, 'by running through a list of what must be done before we can open this mythical hotel.'

'No, that's right,' he said, carried away, 'we'll not be bothered with the details. It's the main scheme that matters.'

She brought him back from his vision. 'So we'll assume that we've found the money from somewhere and I've wrought a miracle of restoration in my spare time, that the hotel is ready to open, and I'm in charge. I understand. So far. What happens next?'

'We take out a licence. Find a good chef. Run a place that will end up as one of the brightest jewels in the city's crown. And live happily ever after on all the money we're going to make.'

'I like the last bit best.' Ironically.

'Well, I know we shan't make it pay for a year or two, but I can be earning for the both of us until then. And you can manage the

378

money,' he added, infused with generosity. 'I'll be handing everything over to you, including me.'

'How could I ask for more?' said Kate, beginning to enjoy herself.

She observed the suit that needed dry-cleaning, the disgraceful shirt and tie, the wild hair, and reflected that this was only his appearance. Years of heavy drinking, spasmodic eating and bouts of insomnia must have wreaked havoc with his constitution. As well as these drawbacks there was the reckless spirit of the man to consider, the wayward moods and quarrelsome nature.

'And when I've retired,' he continued, 'my time is all yours.'

'Patrick,' she said, very kindly, 'when that exalted day arrives and you can take part in the business – and I'm sure I shall be extremely glad to have a little help by that time – what exactly will you be *doing*?'

He cast about for a suitable answer but his vision did not extend to practical matters. 'I could run the bar in the evenings,' he answered.

She smothered a laugh and watched him come down to earth. He gave her a sheepish grin, knowing himself as well as she did. When she began to laugh he joined her. They laughed until they were spent, blowing the dream of Charlotte Street away.

When they were both quiet, he said in his old style, 'Ah, it's all my nonsense, but I had to give it a try.'

'Patrick, what I am about to say is of no more use to you than the Charlotte Street house but I have to say it. I really, truly *love* you!'

For Sale

Jack also visited No. 11 Mulberry Street when Kate was not there, under the impression that he was in some way looking after Ezra. He did not know that *he* needed *her* counsel, and understanding this, smiling to herself, she waited for him to pour out his doubts and hopes.

Afterwards he turned their conversation over and over in his mind until he had absorbed it. But, having no confidence in himself, he did nothing. Fortunately for him fate intervened.

Since that windy afternoon in March, when Kate outlined a plan of what must be done to sell his house, Jack had carried it into action. Kate had suggested workmen, inspected the work when it was completed, given her approval, and found an estate agent. Such a property was beneath the notice of Hussif and Fedor, but a local agency by the name of B.J. Jackson & Son was prepared to put it on their books.

A FOR SALE notice was planted in what Jack called his front garden – a patch of threadbare grass bordered by a ribbon of earth, in which a privet hedge struggled to survive. A key was left with the agent, and there were two or three lacklustre enquiries, but no offers. Then one Saturday morning Jack rang Kate with a shout for help.

'A Mr and Mrs Hindley are coming round this afternoon at four o'clock to view the house. Bill Jackson thinks it's a good possibility but I must be prepared to drop the price if necessary. What do I do? That cleaning lady you found for me came yesterday, so the place is clean and tidy – well, relatively tidy – there's only a line of prints drying over the bath and I'm going to make the bed. Should I offer these people tea and cakes? They sell packets of cakes at the corner shop. I could nip out and get some. And my mother had tray cloths somewhere, but I don't know where they've gone – or the tray. Should I buy flowers—'

'Jack!' Kate commanded. 'Jack! Calm down!'

He said humbly, 'This is the first real bite, and Bill Jackson says it gives a better impression if the tenant's at home. More personal. I do my best, but you know me, I'm frightened of messing things up.'

Mentally, Kate cancelled what had been a hard-won free day. 'I'll be there in just over an hour, bringing a picnic lunch and whatever else I think we need. And I should offer them coffee, if I were you.'

'But four o'clock is teatime...'

'Tea doesn't smell wonderful. Coffee does. And you simply say you have coffee and cake in the afternoon – it's a German custom.'

'I've never been to Germany...'

'Well, never mind that. Anyway, I'll set it all out, and when everything's done and dusted, and a tray laid, I'll disappear.'

'Oh, God bless you, Kate. But, Kate, don't disappear. Stay with me. You know me. I'm a shambles. If I can mess it up I will. Please stay with me, Kate, and tonight I'll take you to the best restaurant you can think of. I'll take you to –' he sought for inspiration, and with his usual ineptness hit on the one restaurant that Kate would never go to again – 'Lamprey's!'

'I get the message,' said Kate. 'I'll stay. And I accept the offer of dinner, but not at Lamprey's, thank you very much.'

Putting the receiver down, laughing, exasperated, she made her complaint to Ezra, who was studying an atlas and mapping out her route.

'It's quite incredible. I've worked all week to get this day to myself, and look what happens!'

'But this is how you are, and this is how Jack is,' said Ezra, unsurprised, 'so it will always happen. And the thought of putting Jack and Jack's house in order pleases your nature, so I shall not sympathize.'

'Thanks a million!' said Kate.

She hummed to herself as she hunted

382

through the kitchen cupboards and drawers for necessary items. Her step was light as she bought flowers, fresh ground coffee, smoked ham, home-made cakes and bread and, as an afterthought, fresh milk and butter. She was glowing as she drew up outside 44 Markham Terrace with a loaded car and saw Jack hovering on the threshold like an agitated bear.

'Ah, you're marvellous!' he cried, hugging her.

'Don't touch anything,' said Kate crisply. 'In your present mood you'd be sure to drop it. I'll unpack and we'll have lunch before we start.'

The Hindleys came from London, and had two school-age children whom they had left behind with grandparents in Surrey. Mr Hindley was a practical man, looking for a soundly built property in the city suburbs. Mrs Hindley, dazzled by the prospect of moving to the West Country, was nourishing the dream of a family-sized cottage in a pretty village.

'It's my husband's job,' Mrs Hindley confided to Kate. 'His firm's taking up this new idea of working in the country. Cheaper properties, you see. Far cheaper. We were amazed when we heard what our house was worth.' She preened herself, thinking of its superior value. 'The price of property in London. Even in the outer suburbs. You wouldn't believe.'

'Oh yes, I would,' said Kate, divining the

dream and treading on it. 'But it does depend what properties you're looking at down here. The West Country is very popular for second homes. Terraced cottages on the main road in Peddleford Village, a few miles from here, are asking a hundred thousand and getting it. If you want the picture-postcard variety with three or four bedrooms and a big garden you're looking at a quarter of a million.'

Mrs Hindley's face fell.

Kate stretched the distance of Peddleford. 'And Peddleford – I give that as an example, because I know it well – is several miles away, and only has village amenities.'

She telescoped the distance from Markham Street to the city. 'Whereas you could walk into the city centre from here, or the forty-five bus from the corner will take you in minutes. And then you have such a wide choice of schools and shops and so on.'

'Besides,' said Mr Hindley, unsympathetic to his wife's idyll, 'if our sale goes through and we buy cheaper here we'll have money left for luxuries.'

As Jack stood there, hands in pockets, smiling amiably and saying nothing, Kate asked, 'Would you like Mr Almond to show you round?'

Jack came to life. 'No, you do that, Kate. You're better at this sort of thing than I am.'

'Your husband seems very nice,' said Mrs Hindley as they went up the newly carpeted stairs (a bargain in Fairfax's sale). 'Though shy.'

'He's very nice indeed, but he's not my husband. We're just friends.'

'Oh.'

'He lives here by himself since his mother died.'

'Ah.'

Kate had added finishing touches to the cleaning lady's efforts. Jack's mother would have been astonished and delighted. Her furniture was polished and rearranged to the best advantage. The rooms, except for Jack's sanctuary, were graced with clean curtains and fresh flowers. Sash windows, screeching and complaining in an alarming manner, had been raised a few inches to let in the summer air.

'He keeps it very nice, anyhow,' said Mrs Hindley.

Kate raised her eyebrows to herself.

'But very plain.' Looking critically at the newly painted pastel walls and white paint-work. 'I prefer a bit of colour and pattern myself.'

Her husband spoke up then, with tolerant good humour. 'You mean you'd want me to redecorate, don't you?'

Kate laughed obligingly and led them downstairs to the kitchen where the aroma of coffee invited them and a tray was laid with her best china cups and saucers. Jack, feeling he should be helpful, had put on the cleaning lady's apron and was watching the coffee percolate.

'Just see what Mr Almond's done, George,'

said Mrs Hindley, indicating the shining sink, the gleaming gas oven, the hospitable tray. 'Some lady's going to be very lucky, Mr Almond. I was saying to your ... to this lady here that you keep the house very nice.'

'I do my best,' said Jack, beaming.

Kate transfixed him with a look, and said, 'There's one more room to show you, which would be your front parlour,' and led them into the stark white beauty of Jack's study.

Jack followed them.

After a very long pause Mrs Hindley said to her husband, 'We'd have to redo this from top to bottom, George.'

He smoothed his chin, assessing the workload.

'Do come and have some coffee,' said Kate.

Behind her she heard Mrs Hindley whispering, 'Like a monk's cell, and there was a nice flock wallpaper under all that white emulsion ...'

And he whispered back, 'But it's got all the basics ...'

Jack whispered to Kate, 'Should I offer to drop the price now?'

'No. Don't rush things.'

Replete with coffee, cake and polite conversation, the Hindleys left, saying, 'We'll be in touch when we've thought it over.'

Kate kicked off her shoes, sat in one kitchen chair, put her feet up on another, and accepted a reviving whisky.

'I think you might have a sale,' she said. 'Mrs Hindley has dropped the idea of a

386

country manor, and Mr H. knows this is a good buy. They can move in without incurring major repairs or alterations, and with the sale of their own house they'll have extra money for what Mr H. calls "luxuries".'

She saw that Jack was pensive. 'Cheer up! It was a good trial run if nothing else. Even if they don't make an offer we know what to do next time.' No response. 'Have you been looking round for somewhere you'd like to live?'

Jack said in a full voice, 'I didn't *like* those people.'

'Nor did I. Does it matter?'

'Yes,' he said. 'It does.'

She swung her feet to the floor and stared at him, astounded. He was distended with rage.

'It matters to me that they're going to come here and take my study over and change it, and put their beastly things in it. They saw nothing. They mean nothing. They are nothing. And they'll turn my study into nothing ...'

'Oh dear,' Kate said to herself, momentarily sorry. She had discounted the personal value of Jack's haven.

'Everything I've done in this house that's worthwhile has been done in that room,' he went on. He paced up and down, the glass of whisky lost in his paw, his blond hair flopping into his eyes, his face red with trouble. He still wore the apron. 'I never thought,' he continued, 'what it meant to me. I went along with your ideas. With *you*.' He pointed the

387

whisky glass accusingly at Kate. 'I went along with that plan you drew up. Redecoration. Furniture brought out. Rooms opened. The cleaning lady.' He was breathless with injury.

Kate's concern for him turned into fury for herself, her wasted time, her lost Saturday. 'Tell me more,' she said, so coolly that he should have been warned.

But his wounds chafed him. He strode up and down, agonizing. 'I liked it as it was. All right, it wasn't the House Beautiful, it wasn't the Gracious Life, but I *liked* living here by myself. I enjoyed a friend like Patrick dropping in from time to time. Someone who didn't want to change me, who understood what I was about. I didn't want to be tidied up and sold up and sent somewhere else. And where would I go, anyway? Have you asked yourself that? Where would I go?'

Kate answered in her deceptively cool voice, 'Do you mean that you haven't been looking round at all, at anything?'

'Looking round?' he roared, and for the first time she saw the passion behind his good-humoured passivity. 'Where in hell's name would I look? What would I look *for*? I had everything I needed *here*.'

Kate jumped to her feet and began to pack the tea things, unwashed as they were, into their cardboard box. Two small cakes were left. She set them fastidiously on the table. She emptied Mrs Almond's imitation cut-glass vase and stood it in the sink. She clutched the flowers in one shaking hand and faced him.

'Now I find myself practically homeless...' Jack was declaiming.

'Just – one – minute!' Kate demanded, biting off each word as it came.

He stopped in his tracks, aware that the tide had turned.

She said with icy pleasantry, 'May I jog your faulty memory before I go? Three months ago you asked me for my advice. "Tell me what I have to do to make the house decent enough to sell," you said. So I spent an afternoon, when – like today – I could have been doing a hundred other pleasant things' – she knew that afternoon had been empty and she glad to fill it, but chose to ignore the fact – 'working out a complete plan of conversion. Please don't interrupt!' Imperiously holding up the free hand while the other gripped the flowers as if they were his neck. 'Since then I have – while in the midst of the biggest bloody crisis in the whole of my life – been at your beck and call.' Unfair again, but she swept it away in her rage. 'I found a cleaning lady for you – and God knows the place needed one, and I practically had to bribe her to take the job on. I suggested a reliable firm of workmen who could repair and decorate the damned place. When it was finished I inspected it to make sure they had done a good job, and also found an estate agent to handle the sale. On top of that, on a Saturday morning, a Saturday that I had carved out – carved out! – for myself, you ring up and scream for help because you have a buyer coming in the afternoon.

'So what do I do? I'll tell you what I *should* have done, I should have told you to sod off, and gone out by myself and enjoyed a day's holiday. Because, strangely enough, I like my own life and my own company just as much as you like yours! But no. Oh no. Instead of that, I think of all the things that might help to create the right atmosphere for a buyer, and I pack up my best china and go shopping for you. Finally I come here, bringing our lunch with me, and work all afternoon, and show those *pits* of humanity round. And what do you do? You put an apron on, to look as if you'd done everything yourself, and accept that stupid woman's compliments...' Here she paused, because she was breathless, as Jack had been, with the injustice of it all. But she would finish. 'And when everything goes well you turn round and accuse me of bullying you into doing something you didn't want. Well, I'll tell you what I think of your lies and ingratitude. I think...'

She did not know what to think. She flung the flowers in his face.

Jack, never at his brightest in an argument, said foolishly, 'But I've booked a table at Paolo's for tonight.'

'Why not ask *Patrick* to join you?' said Kate, savouring the last word. 'He's the sort of friend you prefer. Someone who knows what you're about – whatever that is! Someone who doesn't want to change you – but I wasn't trying to change you, I was trying to *help* you. No, on second thoughts, cancel Paolo's. It's too civilized for either of you. Ask your good friend Patrick to bring a crate of beer round, and get sozzled!'

Then she picked up her basket and left him festooned with carnations.

Jack rang early that evening, and as she refused to answer the telephone or to speak to him he sent a message by Ezra, who had been given Kate's story in bitter detail.

'I will tell her,' said Ezra.

She put down the receiver and turned to Kate, who was standing, arms folded, in the doorway of the kitchen.

'The people who came to see Jack's house this afternoon are interested and have made an offer, but it is less than the price he is asking. The agent has told them that Jack will think about it, and hinted that other people were interested. But he told Jack that they were the only people who had been interested and he should think seriously about accepting a lower price.' Having delivered this speech she added, 'I am glad I have no house to buy or sell. People would be happier if life was more simple.'

'I agree,' said Kate, 'but it isn't. And did the prime procrastinator share his thoughts on the subject?'

'He did not say. He did not seem to know. I think he needs your advice.'

'Tough luck.'

Ezra began to laugh. 'How strange you are,

391

you lucky ones! Millions of people are hungry and homeless and friendless. They have cause for complaint. But you and Jack have everything you need – and you quarrel. Why? Simply because you are required to change your lives, and you are afraid. God must shake His head,' said Ezra, and shook hers.

Kate felt both ashamed and annoyed.

'Well, what do you think I should do?'

'It is not my problem. What do *you* think you should do?'

Kate cried in despair, 'But Jack's made no effort to find anywhere else. Not – one – single – effort. All he cares about is his workroom.'

Ezra was inexorable. 'As you care about your pretty house?'

Kate was silent for a few moments, but her sense of fairness forced her to answer. 'Oh, I do see why he cares. Of course I do. But he could find somewhere else, and make another workroom, and be far more comfortable. And, after all, he was the one who asked me how he could sell the house.'

Ezra would not let go. 'Have you thought why he asked you?'

Kate was silent again.

'Did he ask you because he felt his house was not up to your high standards, and he wanted to be worthy of your friendship?'

Frowning, arms folded, Kate walked the little hall as Jack had walked his kitchen an hour or so ago. 'That's not fair,' she cried. 'That puts the responsibility on to me.'

'You invite responsibility.'

Kate wrestled with that one, too, but still burst out in her own defence. 'I'm responsible for myself. Jack should be responsible for himself. He should take charge of his own life.'

'But he did,' said Ezra, not allowing her to escape. 'He locked away the sad memories in his house and created a room where he could live fully and be himself. Here he worked and became a success in the eyes of the world. But once he had made friends with you this was not enough. He wanted to be a success in your eyes also.'

'I respect his talents. He knows that.'

Ezra saw the effect of her argument, and pursued it. 'Jack is not like you, Kate. He does not care where he lives, what he wears, what he eats. By himself in his own room, or out with his camera, or laughing with Patrick the Wanderer, he is content. But you expected more of him. And he did his best to please you.'

'Oh, don't!' Kate said, wrung by memory. 'That bloody apron...'

'You did not like the way he lived or *where* he lived, so he asked you how he could change this. Not to please himself, because he did not care, but to please you. And suddenly everything he knew, and the one thing he valued, has gone. He is left in a void and he is afraid, like a child in the dark. But you are strong and confident and sure that you are right. So instead of listening to him, and

393

understanding him, you throw your flowers at him and walk out.'

Kate did not answer, head bent.

'Jack rang you up this evening to make amends because he needs you and cares for you. That is the meaning of his conversation. It has nothing to do with the agent and the buyers and the house. You have only to say "Sell" or "Don't sell" and he will do it. But no, you choose to make him suffer. So where is poor Jack? Lost in a wilderness of his making and yours.'

'Oh God!'

'Leave God out of this,' Ezra advised, unconsciously quoting Kate's injunction to Shirley. 'It has nothing to do with God, but with you.'

'Then tell me,' Kate begged. 'Tell me what to do.'

Ezra produced the verdict much as Moses must have produced the tablets from the Mount.

'You have three choices. You advise him to stay where he is, and live as he does. Or you find him a new house so that he can make another room for himself. Or you make a home for him – the sort of home you like, and he will like because you like it! – and give him a room of his own. But if you desert him now, without help or counsel, you will have disrupted his life to no purpose, and the consequences will be your responsibility, whether you acknowledge them or not.'

Kate went to the telephone.

'Jack. This is Kate. Have you still got that table at Paolo's?'

Reconciliation

There was a pause at Jack's end of the telephone, and then he answered, in a voice clogged with resentment, 'No, I haven't. I cancelled it half an hour ago.'

'Oh!' Kate said, momentarily stalled.

Ezra passed behind her and went quietly up the stairs to her room. Her exit told Kate that she was now on her own.

Jack cleared his throat and spoke in a more vigorous tone. 'You made your feelings about me perfectly clear, so there was no reason to keep it.' He added, with some satisfaction, 'And as it's Saturday night they were full, with people on the waiting list. So they thanked me for letting them know. The table's gone.'

Then he waited. The ball was in Kate's court and apparently he intended to leave it there until she returned it or walked away.

She had expected him to be grateful for reconciliation, to fall in with her plans and be soothed back into their former relationship. But he continued to wait, and she knew that if she did not answer he would say goodbye and ring off. This was a new turn of events, and she did not know how to deal with it.

'I suppose you've asked Patrick over?' Casually.

She knew how to cope with either a yes or a no.

The new Jack said, 'Why?' which she had not anticipated. Some kind of apology was in order.

Kate said, 'Jack, I'm sorry if you're angry with me, but you must admit that I had good reason to act as I did. I'd gone out of my way to help you, and you accused me of interference.'

No response. She tried again.

'I've been thinking things over and although, as I said, I tried to help you, the truth is that I didn't fully appreciate how you felt. I took you at your word instead of finding out what you really wanted. So let's say we both got it wrong, shall we? A misunderstanding. We don't have to quarrel about it.'

He did not reply. He could be silent with resentment or, knowing Jack, silent because he couldn't think what to say. She gave him the benefit of the doubt and ended the conversation with dignity.

'Let's leave it at that, shall we? If you feel like getting in touch I'll be pleased to hear from you. Goodnight, Jack.'

Ezra had gone, so there was no one to talk to, no one to take the sting away. She stood for a few moments, hands on hips, staring down at the telephone, and then shook herself physically and mentally.

'No good sitting at home moping,' she told herself. 'Better to distract myself. Go out. See a film.' Still she brooded over the conversation. 'I never thought he could behave like that,' she told herself.

His patience and good nature had seemed endless.

A film of Jack unrolled before her. She could see him clearly in her mind: humming to himself as he walked and stopped and walked again, looking for a good picture, camera slung over his shoulder, utterly happy. She remembered the support and comfort that he always gave her, the unflagging admiration.

She saw him drinking tea with Nora, face alight with affection, steadying one passing child, not noticing that another was dribbling chocolate on his shirt front. She heard him laughing with Patrick, shaking his head with pleasure at the wit and gossip. And though his hair flopped over his forehead, his glasses were awry, and he was congenitally untidy, he had tried to please her. Had let her have her own way, until now. And through it all shone the honesty and integrity of the man.

Kate lifted the receiver, and then slowly set it down again. She had come upon the hard core of him, the part that would not be changed, and she must come to terms with it or lose him.

'Better have something to eat,' Kate said to herself.

She hung Ezra's notice on the front doorknob and went out.

The summer night was hot and airless when she drove into the city centre. Over the years, with and without Hector, she had become used to being on her own. She made a ritual of it: buying an evening paper with news of what was on, sauntering up and down the splendid streets, looking in restaurant windows, reading their menus, deciding which one to choose.

The city was about its evening business. Long, slow, patient queues of vehicles at traffic lights. Drivers tapping a tattoo of impatience on the wheel. Buses blundering past. Cars swerving recklessly or arrogantly into the occasional parking space. Ceaseless movement and noise.

Holiday couples in striped T-shirts and white cotton trousers lingered, hand in hand, staring at the sights.

Youngsters from abroad with maps, rucksacks, and not much money, looked for a cheap place to stay, a cheap meal.

Late shoppers hurried home, laden like packhorses with bags of food from Waitrose.

Students in sweltering kitchens eked out their meagre allowances by performing the most menial jobs.

Old men in long, fusty coats, trousers folding round their ankles, shambled along without hope: drunken, foolish and garrulous. Strangers to the world and themselves.

We've all lost our way, Kate thought. We're all strangers.

Finally, having walked herself tired, she turned into the Swithin Street Wine Bar. Years ago Hector had taken Shirley there in order to find out her plans for the future, and to lay down his own. The wine bar, with its hushed atmosphere and polished brass and mahogany, was originally a meeting place for professional gentlemen. Then gradually it had enlarged its scope to accommodate professional women, though retaining the Victorian air and decor.

This evening, she was shaken to see that it had changed hands since she last went there. The new owners had replaced the male staff with young black women whose perfect figures were dressed in black skin-tight suits. Instead of the usual English snacks there was a long and exotic menu of tapas. The room, restyled, looked lighter, brighter, shinier. The hush was a noisy hum. The clientele no longer had an air of privilege. Even in a few months this long-established venue had turned into something else. Time had moved on yet again.

Kate found a small table, so squeezed into a corner that it only had one chair. All the windows were open to the night, but in the crush of people the atmosphere was stifling. She ordered a glass of chenin blanc and chose a fish tapas: kalamata olives, calamari in chilli oil, taramasalata and olive bread.

Warned that as they were busy there would

399

be some delay, she said it didn't matter, and turned to the entertainments page. But the words conveyed nothing to her. She sipped her wine, her mind on the conversation with Jack.

A ravaged woman, sitting at the opposite table with two men, was telling them a dream. She smoked as she talked, inhaling deeply, staring past them. Her voice, roughened by years of alcohol and nicotine, cut through Kate's thoughts, and the shield of her evening paper.

'...and in this dream I'm running and running and going nowhere. Keeping on running and running and finding myself in the same place. I've lived by myself ever since I was eighteen. I'm used to taking care of myself. But this dream scares me. I'm scared. I wake up at night. Scared.'

The men sat in uncomfortable silence. Kate got the impression that they knew each other but did not know her very well. They were taking her out for the evening, and yet there was nothing sexual in the relationship. They could be distant relatives, friends of friends, doing a kindness. The woman talked on, oblivious of them except as listeners.

'The other bedsits on my landing are empty at the moment, and I don't like that. Don't like being alone on the landing. I feel safer when there's somebody around. With a man around I feel safe.' She ground her cigarette into the tray. Ground it to an acrid mash.

One of her companions laughed uneasily.

The other said, 'Cheer up, Bee, have another drink.'

'Thanks. I will. And that's another thing ... I use alcohol as a way to get to sleep. I've become used to it. So I have to take it. It's a safety net.' She lit a fresh cigarette.

'Do you want something to eat?'

'No, thanks. Just keep the wine coming...'

The woman's years had gone and left nothing behind. The smoke from her cigarette trickled across to Kate's table, and brought all her anxieties to the surface. Kate's throat filled. She could not breathe. She needed to do something active, to get up, get out, get away. She caught her waitress by one elegant black arm, as the girl glided past, and tried to cancel her order.

'I'm afraid it's on the way,' the girl drawled.

Kate pushed a ten-pound note into her hand and said, 'Keep it!'

Back in the summer streets, walking and walking to walk the panic away, she did not know what to do. She must go somewhere else or back to the car park. As she hesitated her mind was made up for her.

The evening light turned a dirty olive-green. The atmosphere was stretched silk, suddenly to be ripped apart by a blinding flash and crack. Ominous rumbles were followed by further cracks and flashes. Kate ran to her car and huddled inside, breathing rapidly, heart racing. She had heard it was safe inside. Outside was certainly unsafe. Buckets of rain were being flung against the

401

windows. People were running for cover, holding evening papers over their heads as frail protection, thin clothes already sticking to their bodies with wet. Drivers around her, jumping into cars, began to start their engines, to move out. They were going home.

Having nowhere else to go, Kate followed them on to the thoroughfare and headed for Southgate Bridge. Windscreen wipers, flicking madly to and fro, failed to dispel the streaming rain. The darkened sky made visibility poor. At the traffic lights she braked gingerly, aware that the road had turned into a skating rink. Showers of spray shot up on either side as she moved on. She peered desperately at street signs, only deciphering them in the moment of passing. The tarmac glistened with treachery. She gripped the driving wheel and concentrated, possessed now by the fear of disaster even as she had been seized by the terror of loneliness. Still, some stubborn streak prevented her from panicking outright. She reached Mulberry Street alive and whole. Turning the corner at last with an exclamation of relief, she saw that the street was full of parked cars, and someone had drawn up in her space.

'Now that,' said Kate aloud, 'is the final bloody straw in a bloody day!'

Her house in that early Victorian terrace, overlooking a little square known as Dulcie Gardens, had never failed to charm her, but now it seemed to stand apart, keeping its charm to itself, and the wind was ripping a clematis from its trellised porch. For over a hundred and fifty years, No. 11 must have enchanted each of its owners, seen them come, watched them go, and regarded all of them with serene indifference. The house was not an extension of Kate, but itself. In this hour of crisis it could offer her no comfort other than that of shelter.

Furious, she drove up on to the pavement outside Dulcie Gardens and got out. She could not see the car properly in the poor light and driving rain, but some idiot was sitting in it and she meant to give them hell. In the few moments it took her to run across, her thin summer dress was saturated. A further crack and flash brought her temper to boiling point.

'Excuse me!' she cried, hammering on the driver's window. 'This is *my* parking space!'

In the instant of hammering and accusing, she recognized Jack, and stepped back, ashamed and afraid.

He wound the window down, saying awkwardly, 'I was waiting for you.'

She managed to say, 'You'd better come in, then!' and ran to the front door, trying to open it with trembling fingers and a slippery key.

He followed her, hands jammed in pockets, coat collar pulled up round his ears, blond hair streaked with rain, equally ill at ease.

Kate closed the door and stood in the hall, speechless and shivering, staring down at her soaked sandals.

'I phoned you twice,' Jack said, 'but I only got the answering service. I thought you might be in – just not answering the phone – so I drove over. Then I read Ezra's notice and realized you'd gone out. I've been sitting in the car, waiting. I was worried about you. What a night!'

Outside, the storm whipped round the terrace, carrying with it a cargo of rolling dustbins. Discarded newspapers flattened themselves against the railings. Trees tossed and swayed. Flowers were flattened.

'Let's go into the kitchen,' said Kate. 'It's warmer there.'

'You ought to change.'

'Yes.' Kicking off her sandals. 'But I need hot coffee first. You, too?'

He nodded, standing there in his wet rain-coat, hands hanging by his sides. In silence, she helped him out of the coat, hung it up, and said, 'Sit down, Jack.'

He sat down.

Kate measured out coffee, filled the machine, switched it on, and a certain peace descended on them. They knew that his presence and her acceptance of it was a form of reconciliation. Putting the situation into words would take a little longer, and they were exhausted with emotion. They drank their coffee. Unheeded, the storm flashed its warning over the terrace and cracked its whip, the wind whiffled down the chimney, the rain beat and beat against the windows.

Jack said, crowding his words together, 'I

was out of order. About the house. I did ask you to sell it. You did all the work. I know how much responsibility you're carrying at the moment. The doubts and difficulties. Then me and my problems on top of it all. I should be taken by the scruff of the neck and kicked round the block and back again.' He glanced at her, and away, unsure how she would take this.

Kate, concentrating her gaze on her coffee mug, answered as lightly as she could, 'You might not want to sell. Not just at the moment. Perhaps not at all. You didn't like the Hindleys. Why should you drop the price for them? The house is comfortable now.' Honesty compelled her to augment that statement. 'Comfortable enough to carry on as you are. You have a good cleaning lady, and you work well there. Unless you're certain that you know what you want – don't jump.'

But Jack did. 'All I want,' he said simply, 'is to please you.'

Kate sat up, flushed up, stared at him, transfixed.

'I may as well have my say,' said Jack, with the air and tone of a man who is about to be executed. 'I don't want to be friends with you, Kate. I can't be friends. Friends isn't enough. I didn't come here to make up some piffling sort of quarrel. Who cares about a quarrel? I want more than that. Much much more. I want you. I want you any way you want to be wanted. Married, not married, an open marriage – whatever that is – keeping

405

your own surname, taking mine, both of us choosing another surname, not bothering either way...'

He had pushed back his chair and risen to his feet as he spoke, and in his present eloquence he harangued rather than courted her. And again Kate stared into the core of the man and was amazed.

Jack thumped the table and the mugs jingled in protest.

'You say it. I'll do it. Sell the house. Keep the house. Stay here. Go abroad. Have a full-blown career of your own. Don't have a career at all. I'll support us both, gladly. Gladly. Kate, I want to love you, take care of you, protect you, punch anyone in the nose who hurts you. I want...' His eloquence deserted him suddenly, and he sat down just as suddenly, saying in a subdued voice, 'I know it all sounds very old-fashioned, but I love you, Kate.'

She whispered, 'Oh, Jack!' Full of tears.

He blundered to his feet again, jolting the table, and his mug overturned and rolled to the edge. Kate began to laugh and cry at once. He tried to mop up the trickling coffee with a clean tea towel, talking all the time. The mug fell to the floor and broke.

'Oh God, oh God, I am a blundering fool. Don't cry, Kate. There's no need to be sorry for me. I know you don't feel the same way and I don't blame you. I'm a walking disaster.' He threw the stained tea towel towards the sink, and missed.

'I only making things worse. It's all right, Kate. I'm going. I'm going.'

He was trying to tug his raincoat off the hanger and the hanger spun across the kitchen like a boomerang. He cursed it roundly, apologized, and began to say, 'Just one more thing before I go...'

In a breath and a sob Kate pulled herself together and cried, 'Oh, do shut up, Jack!' Then she put her arms round his neck and laid her wet cheek against his. 'Oh, my dear Jack, I love you, too. God help me!'

Jack dropped the raincoat on the floor and held her to him very gently, dazed, amazed. Then tightened his clasp, exultant, and kissed the top of her head. Kate could not see the expression on his face, but Ezra looking on her angel would have shown no greater wonder or delight.

Coming Home

Because Ezra was staying in Mulberry Street they decided to use 44 Markham Terrace for their meetings, and made love in the double bed in Jack's parent's room. Whether its sad ghosts were so outraged that they left in high dudgeon, or were laid to rest by their son's happiness, was not known, but they never troubled Kate and Jack.

No one was specifically informed that their relationship had changed, though it was obvious to those closest to them. Kate's sensitivity and Jack's shyness being well known, no comment was made, but henceforth they were treated as a couple.

Nora, strongly cautioned by Neville, kept her exultation to herself, and behaved with commendable tact. She permitted herself only one indulgence. Telephoning Kate, she said they quite understood that she might not want to come to lunch every Sunday, but that if she did she must bring Jack. Kate's reply was also commendable, though she volunteered no information. She accepted the invitation for both of them that coming weekend.

Only Shirley, locked within herself, noticed nothing. And Patrick was too preoccupied with his own future to concern himself about anyone else.

Looking back, Kate saw that time in their lives as a little centre of calm and beauty in the midst of chaos.

Jack, keeping his options open, refused the Hindleys' offer but left his house on the market. Now and again someone came to view it in a desultory sort of way, and then Kate was galvanized into action while Jack learned minor social skills without the use of an apron. Nothing came of their efforts, apart from making a fresh pot of coffee when the visitors had gone, and comparing notes, and each occasion ended in bed.

'One good thing about me,' Jack said, early in their alliance, 'is I'm not clumsy in bed.'

Kate repressed a giggle and answered, straight-faced, 'Yes, I was relieved to find that out!' Then in fairness she added, 'You're a lovely lover. Where and how did you learn, if I might ask?'

He answered honestly, 'From Patrick's girls. They weren't exactly promiscuous but they were very experienced, and they didn't mind who you were so long as you were...' seeking the right word, 'hygienic. Just jolly girls, you know, not...'

'Not prostitutes?'

'No, no!' Shocked. 'Certainly not. They were a product of their time. Liberated. They didn't want to take you seriously. You were just another man, and they liked men. All they asked was a good time. I called them the good-time girls.'

'Well, I'm obliged to them,' said Kate.

Hector's love-making had been like Hector: a further demonstration of his magnetism and authority. He domineered. She submitted. He gave. She accepted. Coming to him as a virgin she had no former knowledge by which to gauge him. So he gratified himself and Kate had what was left. But Jack brought in a new dimension: herself. Considerate, loving and imaginative, he made Kate the centre of their love-making. She responded, blossomed.

'We're learning each other,' said Jack, on one especially delicious Sunday afternoon.

For once she had no reply, smiling through the kiss she gave him.

Shirley, having studied her accounts in discouraging detail, postponed her plans for a new Mrs Porter's Parlour in the Midlands and put Melbury Old Hall on the market. A surprising number of people were interested and, Shirley's hospitality being part of her nature, she offered them refreshments according to the time of their visit: morning coffee, afternoon tea, evening drinks. Sunday was a particularly favoured day, and became a regular entertainment in which Kate flatly refused to take part and Mrs Bailey lost her afternoon off. Despite the interest aroused, no one seemed prepared to buy it. After a while Kate pointed out, rather unkindly, that they were simply amusing themselves.

'It's just something to do!' she said. 'It would cost them quite a lot to go round a National Trust property and use the restaurant. Whereas they can have a free tour and a free tea here. So why not? Sunday is a dull day.' Then she thought, 'Except...'

Nora was told bluntly by her doctor at the health centre that she could either diet or shorten her life.

'Your heart and lungs were both affected by the influenza,' he said, having examined the voluptuous landscape of Nora's body. 'You

410

don't smoke, I hope?' Peering at her sternly over the top of his glasses. 'Good. That's something. But you have very high blood pressure and are grossly overweight. Now we find you have diabetes as well – which doesn't surprise me. Mrs Wing, we can't let this state of affairs continue, now can we?'

Nora shook her head. He scribbled hieroglyphics.

'This is a new prescription for your blood pressure, and on your way out the nurse will give you a diet sheet, which you *must* follow to the letter. Diabetes is not a minor ailment. Very unpleasant things can happen if you let it get out of hand. Ulcers. Gangrene. Blindness. Loss of limbs...'

He was not being harsh. He knew his patient. Only the most alarming verdict would impress – might impress – that agreeable lady.

'We'll help you all we can,' he continued. 'Weigh you regularly and monitor your progress. And we'll give you a good start with a week in hospital for observation and further tests.' Seeing that her fingers trembled as they buttoned up her smock, he sweetened his sentence. 'Why, in six months' time you'll be a new woman!' he said cheerfully.

With no waif in the background to make deprivation worthwhile, Nora took this ultimatum very hard indeed. She began the new regime in her usual way the following Monday, when she kept strictly to the diet. Tuesday was almost as good. On Wednesday she slipped a little. On Thursday she slipped still more. On Friday she was so upset by her failures that she ate a large bar of chocolate to cheer herself up. On Saturday she received news from the City Hospital, and decided to make up for all the food she had missed and was going to miss. Late that evening she telephoned Kate, sounding euphoric.

'And I can't tell you how much I'm looking forward to it, Katie. All I've ever needed is a little help. They reckon I shall lose the best part of a stone while I'm in there. That'll give me a good start.'

They had been over this ground many times before. Dutifully, Kate trod it yet again. 'You have been following the diet, haven't you?'

'Oh yes. Yes. Oh yes.' Conscience made her add, 'Mostly.'

The diet sheet, pinned on a kitchen wall near an open window, was at this moment blowing gently in the summer breeze. Long before autumn it would be brown, tattered, and still ignored.

'Your father's been helping me to stick to it.'

Neville had, that morning, caught Nora putting sugar in the teapot so that she would not be detected, and poured the contents down the sink. They had had what Nora called 'words'.

'That's good. Is there something wrong with your telephone line? Now and again you sound muffled.'

'Oh, it's only...' Defiantly. 'Well, if you must know, I'm finishing up a pot of strawberry jam and a few scones that were left over from tea. It seemed a pity to waste them. Now make sure that you and Jack come to lunch tomorrow, because we're having a really grand spread. After that, of course, I'll be on a very strict diet...'

Marcus Bray, whose father, though rich, believed that his sons should learn to stand on their own feet, gave them all an excellent education and then threw them out into the world. Marcus began his career as a junior reporter on a small provincial paper and worked his way up to news editor. Whereupon his father advanced him a handsome loan and the young man bought a local paper called the *City Courier*, then at the lowest ebb of an undistinguished career. Over the next few years he trnasformed this indifferent rag into the distinguished *Courier*.

Today, his excellent instinct divined that Patrick Hanna was restless, rootless, and ready to move on. This, Marcus could not allow. So he sent for Patrick on a pretext, took him out on a drinking spree, and persuaded him – without difficulty – to talk. Sensibly, he did not believe half what Patrick told him, but deduced that the Irishman had tried to settle down and been thwarted by a fair cruel maid. Patrick further confided that his soul – an article that Marcus regarded with some doubt – had been gravely troubled and he felt he should listen to its complaint.

Marcus put these ramblings down to the

male menopause but did not say so. Instead he painted a marvellous picture of Patrick as the flaming torch in the *Courier*'s stalwart hand: the light of its wise eyes, the blood of its brave heart, its radiant spirit of truth.

He ventured further. He depicted Patrick older, greyer, wiser, even more deeply loved and respected. He retailed the story of an illustrious journalist in Marcus's youth (a figment of Marcus's imagination) who had become the father figure of his paper, refusing to retire from his post and actually dying there on the accomplishment of his last and greatest crusade.

Marcus wiped his eyes at this point, overcome by his own eloquence, and Patrick's emotion was such that only more whisky could help him through it. When he finally fell asleep with his head on the table Marcus called a taxi and took charge of him.

Waking the next morning with an appalling headache, the *Courier*'s brightest star found himself lying on a sofa in the Brays' living room, being surveyed by a row of handsome young adolescents. He had at last, in a metaphorical sense, come home.

Departure

Interest in the Grove Riots had died down for a very good reason. The brutal attack on Ezra sobered Patrick, the *Courier*, and the city council. Public reputation was a fragile thing. Hector, who would not have hesitated to employ any devious method to be rid of Ezra, had scruples when it came to open violence. No one in high places wanted to be associated with the assault or to be accused of causing it, so they had a quiet word with influential people.

In consequence the *Courier* gave discreet coverage to the incident, which, the paper said, was deeply regretted by all concerned. The public could rest reassured that police were handling the inquiry with their usual efficiency, that justice would be done and the perpetrators caught and punished. Fortunately, they added, Ezra's condition, though serious, was not life-threatening. The hospital reported her to be 'comfortable'. Every possible care would be taken of her, but in the meantime, rest and privacy were essential.

The *Peddleford Advertiser*, which would have preferred to make front-page news of a local scandal, grudgingly followed suit. A week later both papers reported that Ezra was well on the road to recovery, and local youths were helping the police with their enquiries.

No further reference was ever made to the affair.

No one was ever charged with the assault.

At six o'clock on a fine June morning, Ezra, Jack and Patrick ate a farewell breakfast given by Kate, who celebrated it with a battery of cereals, a clutch of boiled eggs, and a stack of toast. Croissants, jam and marmalade were offered, as well as stewed fruit salad, coffee, tea and fresh orange juice. She also packed a robust vegetarian lunch and supper, in case Ezra failed to find a sympathetic host that evening.

'Do not worry. Wherever I am there will be a kind farmer with a barn,' Ezra murmured, as Kate tried to pin her down to time and place. 'People are very good to each other when there is no money involved.' She added, smiling, 'There is enough food here for two days. How like your mother you are.'

'Despite that inflammatory remark I shall miss you.'

'No, Kate, don't miss me, keep me in your mind. I shall take you with me.' She turned to the others, holding out her hands. 'I shall take all of you with me, and think of you, and wish you well.'

'And we all wish you had a forwarding address,' said Kate very drily, determined not to be sentimental.

'Dear Kate. It is not necessary.'

416

Jack said, as if the words were torn from him, 'You've changed all our lives.'

'No.' Gently. 'You have changed them.'

Jack hesitated. 'I wondered,' he said, 'knowing how much you liked my book, whether you'd care to take a copy with you? It's in paperback. Doesn't take up much room. Very light.'

She smiled and shook her head. 'I thank you, but no. Your book has done its work. When I meditate, I am in the grove. And now,' as they stood mutely, sadly, around, 'it is time to go.'

Patrick's old Ford had been through the car wash, an experience that must have astonished it. He had put a cushion on Ezra's seat because the springing was not too good. He had also cleaned the inside after a fashion, removing numerous cigarette ends and empty cardboard cartons, and finding, like a surprise present, an unopened tin of something that had lost its label. This he gave to Kate, who consigned it to the dustbin when he had gone.

'Ah, there's not enough room for all that luggage,' he remarked of the bowl, blanket and rucksack. 'You'll have to send some of it on.'

Smiling at him, Ezra climbed into the car.

Jack had brought his camera with him. Kate still has the photograph. Patrick is standing by the battered Ford, arms akimbo, grinning like a cat. Ezra, already away from them in her mind, sits mouse-grey and silent in the

417

front seat, eyes fixed on the road.

The car did not want to start at first, and then jerked forward suddenly and percolated down Mulberry Street. Reaching the corner it burbled out of sight.

Jack wiped his eyes and said, 'I wonder if we'll ever see her again.'

Kate said, 'I just hope that heap of rust gets as far as the border. I'm sure it can't have passed its MOT.'

Then they turned to each other, transferring the emotion they felt to themselves and their central world.

'The house is all ours now,' said Kate.

'And it's very early,' said Jack. 'Let's go back to bed.'

It was not a long journey to the border, and the two travellers were silent for most of the way. The West Country was quiet at that time in the morning, mild and beautiful. They saw only tractors trundling from place to place, harvesters at work in the fields, and the cars and caravans of visitors who had driven through the night and parked in side bays to sleep. Later, traffic would become busy, later still congested, but for now Ezra and Patrick had the place almost to themselves. And the road wound ahead of them, up and over the green downs, like an illustration in a fairy tale.

'You've got a fine day for walking,' Patrick said at last.

She smiled and nodded.

418

'Will you...' He hesitated out of delicacy, but his need for information overcame him. 'Will you be seeing Joel?'

She answered containedly, 'No. It would be cruel. I can do nothing for him.' Then, surprising him with the emotion in her voice, 'It would break my heart and his if we had to part again.'

'I'm sorry. I shouldn't have asked.'

He was instantly repentant, but a few moments later his curiosity got the better of him. 'Ezra, did you really see an angel at the foot of the bed?'

Then she laughed at him. 'But I have never said I saw an angel at the foot of the bed. You said that.'

'I did?'

'You wrote that in your article. What I saw was a vision. That was the best way I could describe it, because it was not a human form but an experience. A radiance. A knowledge of all being well. And it was not at the foot of the bed, but all around me and within me. I wanted to stay there for ever. That is what I am seeking, and sometimes finding, and always seeking.'

'This vision. Did it not tell you to ... mend your ways or anything like that?'

'No, Patrick. There were no words or instructions – except from yourself. That was not what I said, but what you wrote.'

'I did?'

'I expect,' said Ezra charitably, 'you were explaining it in a way that you and your

419

readers could understand.'

He did not speak again until they reached the sign that marked the end of one county and the beginning of another.

'Well, here we are,' he said, reluctant to part with her.

She was tremendously important to him, though for the life of him he did not know why. He was not in love with her. As a regular companion she would bore him. There was no way he could have adopted her beliefs, nor even, like Shirley, have attempted to adopt them. But he needed something that she was, that she was taking with her.

Ezra stepped out into the road. The sadness at Joel, the amusement at Patrick had left her. Tranquil, she was ready to walk on. She held out her hand. 'Goodbye, Patrick. I thank you for all you have done. You will be in my heart.'

He kissed the thin dark fingers fervently, then hugged her hard and held her to him for a moment. Her fragility worried him.

'Now you'll send us a postcard from time to time to tell us how you are, won't you?' he said jauntily, releasing her.

She shook her head, looking kindly at him.

'It's goodbye for good then?' he said, crestfallen.

She smiled and nodded, and began to turn away.

'No, don't go just yet,' he cried desperately. 'I've something important to ask you, something that gnaws at me, something I can't find the answer to...'

She stopped and turned.

'It's something ... it's just that...'

His tone changed. He spread out his hands, speaking in his most beguiling manner. 'Ah, there's no real harm in me. No harm at all. A bit of mischief, yes, but we can't be serious all the time.'

Patiently, she waited.

He exchanged charm for sincerity. 'But there's nothing great about me either, not like there is in you, and there never will be. I was brought up a Catholic, and though I lapsed long since and never gave it a thought for years, it comes to me as I get older that it's about values.'

He placed both hands upon his chest.

'Now, what's the value of *me*? I'm not worth much. Sometimes worth nothing at all. I see life as an entertainment and me as one of the entertainers. And I feel I should be more than that, better than that, but I can't change how I am.'

As she remained silent he put in a good word for himself. 'Surely that's not entirely my fault. Isn't that the way God made me?'

She nodded, still waited, still smiled.

'So why,' said Patrick, in deadly earnest, 'why did He do it? What's the reason for me, as far as He's concerned?'

She came forward then, and with the utmost tenderness laid her hands on his.

'*You* are the reason,' said Ezra. 'Eternity is timeless. The way is hard. The suffering often unbearable. Sometimes ... God likes to make a joke.'

He watched the figure growing smaller and smaller until it vanished over the brow of the hill, then got into the car, exalted, and tried to start it. Minutes later he was still swearing and jabbing the starter when the answer came to him.

'Laughing at me again, are You?' he cried to the heavens.

Capriciously, the engine leapt to life.

Postscript

Festival

Nora had truly intended to keep the event clear of children.

Weeks ago Neville had said, 'Just for once, let's you and me and Reggie have a treat by ourselves. The children aren't supposed to come on a Saturday, but I know you and them. They'll sneak in if they can and you'll let them!'

Nora agreed, but her resolution failed her when Toni's mother planned to go to Spain with her boyfriend just before the concert festival, and asked Nora if the child could stay until they got back.

'It'll only be our Toni,' Nora explained.

Then the child boasted of her future evening out to the others, who went home in tears and returned with little notes asking if they could come too. Nora temporised, explaining that the children would be out very late.

No one minded.

She said she doubted they could get tickets

425

at this late date. One of the fathers, who worked for Celebrations, explained the situation piteously to Hector, who liked to be known as a benefactor and was still intent on courting Kate. He sent free tickets for the entire party, enclosed in a charming note to Nora, and insisted on refunding money for the tickets they had already bought.

'So you see, it's not going to cost us anything,' said Nora to her husband, hoping to be pardoned.

'Isn't it? Who's providing the picnic?' Neville asked, unimpressed.

'Oh, I'll be doing that.' Flustered. 'It'll be easier than the children bringing sandwiches and lemonade.'

'Have the parents offered to pay their share of the food?'

Nora said brightly, 'How about us having a pot of tea?'

Inexorable. 'Are the parents providing transport?'

Evasive. 'No one's mentioned anything about that. I'll put the kettle on.'

'Which means that they're coming with us, doesn't it?'

'Well, we'd have to take the truck anyway, love, wouldn't we?'

'Right,' said Neville, his mind made up. 'Then as we're doing the catering and ferrying, it'll be three pounds a head.'

Nora was shocked. 'You're never charging them for a bit of food and a ride in the truck?'

'Yes, I am. And cheap at the price.'

426

'But what about Marianne? Her father got us the tickets.'

'We'll let her off. The rest must pay.'

'And Toni...'

'We'll deal with that later. I'm going to have a word with Toni's mother about present and future arrangements anyway.'

'Oh, Neville...' Woefully.

But he was adamant.

'As from now I'm laying down a few ground rules, without which no one goes anywhere, free tickets or not. Apart from Toni, no child is staying with us beforehand or overnight. The parents must make sure that each child has a good afternoon nap, that they bring them here at half past five, and collect them at eleven. We should be home well before then but it gives us a bit of leeway in case the traffic's bad. Finally, and most importantly, *any* deviation from these rules means that the child automatically forfeits its place in the nursery group. No excuses, no exceptions. Understood?'

He meant every word and Nora knew it.

'Whatever you say, Neville.'

'And just in case they try to get round you – which they will – I'm ringing up every parent personally and delivering that message straight.'

Her plans scattered, Nora said, 'Oh, Neville, you mustn't. You'll upset them. You'll hurt their feelings.'

'Tough luck,' said Neville.

* * *

427

All the parents said they understood perfectly, would follow his instructions to the
letter and be delighted to pay such a modest
sum for the privilege. They also thanked him
and Nora, and said how much they
appreciated their generosity.

'I should have done that long since,' said
Neville with quiet satisfaction. 'I'm sick of
people taking advantage of your good nature.
If you can't take care of yourself, Nora, I shall
have to do it for you. And another thing – I
don't want to see you wearing an old mackintosh over your working clothes because
you've been thinking of everyone else and
haven't had time to change. I want to see you
dressed up and looking like a queen.'

Her fire drawn, Nora said mildly, 'You
sound like our Kate.'

'Our Kate's a sensible lass. And mind what
I say – stop work at some stage and spend an
hour on yourself.'

'Oh, Neville,' said Nora mournfully, but
could not help feeling beloved, and was heard
to sing as she punched her pannikin of dough
into shape.

A week beforehand, Neville printed a large
cardboard notice saying: CLOSED FROM 2 P.M.
NEXT SATURDAY. OPEN AS USUAL 8 TILL 8
MONDAY AND ALL WEEK. and nailed it to the
bottom gate.

This was the busiest time of the year for the
Flower Farm, so on the day of the festival
Neville and Reggie started work as soon as it

428

was light.

Nora gave her men what she described as 'a scratch lunch' at noon, meaning last night's leftovers fried up, and put out a cut-and-come-again cake and some serious sandwiches at four o'clock lest they go hungry. Otherwise she concetrated on producing the picnic of a lifetime, which filled two old wash baskets. Then she whiled away a luxurious hour in the bathroom, with shampoo and essences supplied by Kate, and came down in her silk kaftan: an empress.

This splendid image was somewhat lessened by the arrival of her small dependants, one of whom was sick with excitement the moment he crossed the threshold and another wet her knickers. But the occasion bore them all up, and when Neville and Reggie appeared in their best suits, bathed and shaven, the festivities began.

The concert didn't start until eight o'clock that evening, but the Wing family planned to leave home at six, bent on arriving early and finding a good place. Reggie had cleaned out the truck, fitted it with a bench on either side, and fixed ropes from end to end to hold the children in. He had also been volunteered to sit with them to make sure they were safe, though Nora had protested that they were her responsibility and she should look after them.

'What you need is a comfortable ride up front with me, not swaying about on a hard seat at the back,' said Neville. For Nora's diets never seemed to work, and she was a little heavier than she had been.

'Besides,' he added, to comfort her, 'it'll make Reggie feel important.'

So the children were roped in, giggling, and regarded this as part of the great adventure.

The moment they arrived at the gates of the Old Hall, Neville realized that they weren't early enough. The top car park was full and they had to join a host of cars in the bottom fields and toil up the side lane laden like packhorses. But Neville parked the lorry in a place he could leave quickly. Knowing the estate pretty well he had a plan in mind to make their return journey easier.

They had brought everything Nora could think of: two cold roast chickens, a chiller box full of mixed salads, a jar of mayonnaise, three loaves sliced and buttered and put together again, the contents of the strawberry patch, a ponderous fruit cake, two bottles of Chardonnay that Kate had given them for Christmas, a flask of milky coffee and another of strong tea, a plastic container of home-made lemon and barley water for the children, soft peppermints to suck if they felt sick, damp facecloths, extra pairs of knickers, paper napkins, Kleenex, cutlery, china, glasses, plastic mugs, folding chairs, two travel rugs, a first-aid kit and a mound of cushions.

Neville, having settled his family, nipped off again and impudently moved the truck up to the staff's personal car park behind the house. They would be among the first to leave.

The weather had done its best for the concert festival and towards the end of this July day the atmosphere was one of high holiday. An evening sun slanted through surrounding trees, turning the Old Hall's stonework to the colour of honey. A deliciously bland breeze carried mingled scents of herbs and flowers. The green sward, freshly mowed, had become a picnic area for over four thousand people. Sitting in canvas chairs or on rugs, each family claimed its patch of grass. Kate's long row of Portaloos were placed discreetly behind the trees at the back of the crowd, and to left and right stood stalls selling refreshments, programmes and local art and craft products.

With his son and daughter on either side, Hector strolled through the crowd, nodding affably to acquaintances, having a few special words with important personages, smiling on all.

'That's Hector Mordant from Celebrations, and his youngsters – sad for the children, losing their mother – but there's nothing la-di-dah about them,' people said. 'They're dressed no different from us.'

This was Hector's intention, though the material and the cut of their casual clothes made all the difference.

They were a highly presentable trio, the children tall and fair like Hector, fine-featured like Jocelyn. Signs of mourning were

431

restrained and in excellent taste. A black silk handkerchief peered above the top pocket of the widower's cream linen jacket. Hermione wore a narrow jet ribbon round her throat, as aptly and prettily as Jocelyn would have done. And their housekeeper had stitched a discreet ebony triangle on the sleeve of Toby's T-shirt.

Hector had ordered his youngsters to behave themselves, and they did – two pieces of human property fit to be introduced to suitable people at the proper time. Their feelings they kept to themselves. Toby had taken his mother's death harder than anyone, and endured the double wound of adoring and losing her without having known her very well. His sister, cast in a harder mould, had already realized that if she did not look after herself no one else would, and resolved to leave both home and school as soon as the opportunity came. Had Hector noted his daughter's wilful eyes, and the suffering line of his son's mouth, he might not have been so complacent, but he never delved below the surface. Satisfied with outward show, his mind moved on to the festival arrangements.

'Pretty good. Pretty good. Twelve Portaloos aren't sufficient for this number of people. The parking arrangements could be better, and there aren't enough signposts. Must have a word with Kate, ready for next time.'

For he did not believe she meant what she said, and in the end he always had his own way. Look at the weather, for instance. In spite of an indifferent summer the day was perfect.

'Kate! Kate!' he called, for she was walking towards a motley group that he recognized as being her parents and a number of retarded children. He would have to meet them sometime, when Kate became Mrs Hector Mordant, but certainly not now. He resolved to make the acquaintance brief, and subsequent meetings few.

So he called, 'Kate! Kate!' and held up a commanding arm to attract her attention.

Since she also didn't want to confuse the day with introductions, though for different reasons, she changed course and came towards him.

'Hello, how are you both?' she asked the youngsters, smiling.

They responded with a warmth that surprised and pleased Hector. Evidently there would be no difficulty in introducing her as their stepmother. Since this was another problem solved he sent them away.

'Here, you two, here's a tenner apiece. Off with you and spend it!' Delighted with the impression he must be making as a kindly father, he took Kate's arm and said, 'Not quite enough Portaloos, my dear...'

'No. I realize that.' Crisply. 'This is our first effort, remember.'

'Of course. Anyway, they'll manage somehow. What I should have said first was – what wonderful hospitality! Everyone's talking about it. Shirley's an idiot, but you're a jewel, Kate.'

'I'm glad you realize that.' Tongue in cheek. 'Semi-precious or precious?'

'A twenty-four-carat diamond.'

He led her under the shade of a fine cedar tree. Around them the festival was gathering momentum, heightening the effect of their intimacy. She remained unmoved but he was in the grip of his latest and most wonderful idea.

'Kate, let's be together again. You know what you've always meant to me.'

'Indeed I have.' Smiling. 'At every stage in our long relationship.'

He was not a fool. He changed tack effortlessly. 'Of course, I had to stick to Jocelyn, because of her ... illness.' He could not say *cancer*. Disease and death were too real to be acceptable.

Kate was silent.

He supplied the answer to what she was thinking.

'And before that – oh, for heaven's sake, Kate, help me out – you must know the reasons. The children. The responsibility. Jocelyn would never have managed on her own. There was nothing to her, God rest her soul. Unlike you, she couldn't have made a life for herself. You do understand, don't you, that I couldn't leave them?' Seeing that no help was forthcoming he hurried on. 'But things are different now. And the youngsters like you, respect you. You were good to them at an appalling time. You were good to us all, Kate.'

She said, taking pity on him, 'Hector, I did what had to be done, and I'm glad I did, but don't read too much into it.'

He could never let go of a good idea. He assumed his most engaging tone. 'Kate! Dearest Kate. I'm asking you to marry me.'

'I do wish you wouldn't,' she answered in quiet desperation, because he had once meant so much to her and she didn't want him to spoil that.

He rode on. 'It won't be a marriage such as I had with poor Jocelyn. It will be a full partnership. You can join me in Celebrations...'

Kate's thought was acerbic. *An invaluable unpaid assistant.*

'Together we'll be matchless. Don't you see? It's all going for us.'

Her silence and uneasiness discomposed him.

'We can find another house, if that's what you're worrying about. You can make it over to suit yourself – and me, of course. There'll be no family photographs on display to remind you of the past. No second-wife nonsense. No stepmother trouble. It will all be yours. To do as you will. And to have me as you want me.' A long pause. 'Kate?'

When she did answer, out of mercy to him, she sounded sadder and older than he had ever heard her. 'Oh, my dear. You should have said that a long time ago. To a very different Kate. I do truly thank you for all the good and wonderful times, Hector, and for

435

the most generous of offers. But, no, thank you.'

'And why are you looking like a dying duck in a thunderstorm?' Nora demanded as Kate returned. She rescued the butter before Dennis could tread in it. 'You've done all the work and done it well. Can't that Hector Mordant let you enjoy yourself for five minutes? What did he want?'

Neville and Kate looked at each other with complete understanding. She had never told him anything about her love life but he had always understood.

'Just sorting out final details,' said Kate. 'Winding up the job.' Then on an impulse she bent forward and kissed her mother on the cheek. 'What a very handsome lady you look,' said Kate.

'That's nice,' said Nora, pleased and touched. But before she had time to savour the tribute she had to cry, 'Harri! Stop it. Neville, pick that child up. She'll be as sick as a cat. She's eating grass...' Then to her daughter, 'Katie, when does this concert start?'

'Not until eight. That gives you plenty of time to eat, drink and be merry. So enjoy yourselves.'

'And where's Jack? I thought that he and Patrick would have been here, reporting an event like this for the *Courier.*'

'No, it's social column material. Freda Wilde's here with her camera.'

'Well, I should have thought Jack would be

here, anyway.' Meaningfully. 'Judging from what a little bird's been saying.'

'And what busy little bird is that? Patrick the Prattler?'

Nora looked both pleased and coy. 'Never you mind. Only,' a shadow crossed her broad good-natured face, 'I'd have expected you to tell *us* first.'

'I haven't had a minute to tell you anything yet. I obviously can't talk now. And anything you've heard so far is pure speculation. But Jack and I are coming for lunch tomorrow, and as we've got lots of news – and it's important – I'd be extremely grateful if we could be by ourselves for once.' She appealed to her father. 'Da, will you see to it?'

'Don't you worry,' said Neville grimly. 'I'm in charge of a new regime. We'll be by ourselves all right, even if I have to farm Toni out for the day.'

She hugged him very hard. Then, turning to Nora, she said, 'Until then, whenever any little bird opens its beak – shut it!'

'Nora,' said Neville, before she could react, 'these children are getting restless and I don't blame them. Let's feed the multitude, shall we?'

Recalled to duty, Nora began to tuck napkins into necklines and to set out the contents of the first wash basket.

'I must have a blow,' said Shirley, casting her flowered hat to the carpet, sinking into an armchair, reaching for a cigarette. 'I've been on my feet all afternoon and these shoes are murder.' She kicked them off. 'My face aches with smiling and I'm hoarse from chatting to people. And after the concert we've got to start feeding the principals and putting them up for the night, and giving them breakfast tomorrow. I could kill bloody Hector.'

Kate poured her a double whisky without being asked.

Shirley looked wistful. 'Are you really going to leave me at the end of this month?' she asked.

'Shirley, you know I am. We've been over this a hundred times already. I shan't change my mind.'

'And where are you going?'

'France, for a start. For a good long holiday.' She made an effort to sound casual. 'Jack and I decided that we'd earned a break, so we're going together.'

'So it *is* true about you and Jack Almond,' said Shirley thoughtfully. 'I didn't believe it when Patrick told me.'

'Yes, it is true, and I wish Patrick would mind his own damned business.'

She talked on, trying to cover embarrassment.

'We're going in my car because it's more reliable, but taking it in turns to drive. My French is pretty fluent, so if we have any real problems I can cope with them. We shall go anywhere we fancy, and stop when we want to. No pressures, no alarm clocks, no must do this and that. Just the way on.

'If we find a place that particularly appeals to us we might decide to sell our houses here, and buy a property over there. At the moment Jack only knows enough French to get by, but he'll learn. He's very bright. He'll do it. I don't think his ear's as good as mine but, unlike me, he doesn't mind making a fool of himself. And people always respond to him and want to help him. From me they expect perfect service, and wait until I produce the goods. But that's part of our package. That's how we are.'

Shirley stared at her inquisitively. 'I never thought you'd fall for Jack Almond,' she remarked. 'Oh, I like him, of course. Everybody likes Jack. But I shouldn't have thought he was sophisticated enough for you.'

'Hector cured me of a liking for sophisticated men. And I haven't *fallen* for Jack. I've grown into him. A much more important proposition.'

Shirley mulled this over, but was not enlightened. 'You've said nothing about a new job, so far. I take it that you have a job somewhere along the line.'

'Not as yet.'

Shirley sipped and smoked, thinking aloud. 'It's not like you to be without a plan. You always wanted everything to be cut and dried. Too much so, at times.' Remembering their quarrel over the new-age travellers and putting the blame for that on Kate.

Kate read her mind, but didn't care who Shirley blamed.

'I'm trying this way for a change, and I must say I'm looking forward to it.'

'So everybody's leaving me,' Shirley mused, bringing the subject back to herself.

Kate laughed. 'I think that's a tad dramatic. As long as you're at the Old Hall you have a devoted staff. And if you sell up...'

'I should be so lucky! But I keep trying.'

'Oh, someone will buy the Old Hall. She's a siren, and she's looking remarkably beautiful at the moment. Some reckless adventurer with lots of money and a big dream will make an offer for her.'

'And then what's left for *me*? Where shall *I* go?' Shirley accused her. Whisky always had the effect of making her maudlin.

'You have a chain of tea shops to run – also furnished with devoted staff – and with the money from the sale of this property you can live in a very smart flat in the city centre. After all, Shirley, the Old Hall's worth much more now than it was when you bought it. Or,' as an idea occurred to her, 'you could turn it into a country retreat for tired city dwellers. You'd need a first-class manageress, of course, but then you're good at finding the right people.'

Shirley's eyes narrowed over the smoke from her cigarette.

'That's quite an idea, Katie. Keep the Old Hall and run it as a business concern. I suppose you wouldn't like to...'

'No, thank you, but you're welcome to the idea.'

440

Shirley observed her assistant closely. She did not believe in simple solutions.

'I wonder what you'll do in the end? I mean, when you and Jack have got fed up with wandering around holding hands, looking at the scenery and drinking French wine.'

'I've no idea. He's a photographer first and foremost, but he might fall in love with some foreign standing stones and write another book.'

'And you?'

'I make things work,' said Kate. 'There are plenty of opportunities for people like me in the world.'

Shirley struggled with her curiosity, her incomprehension, but finally gave in and asked, 'Katie. Don't be offended. I mean, I'm really fond of Jack. In his homespun way he's a bit of a star. But what's the attraction?'

'He loves me,' said Kate. 'He's a miles better person than I am, and he loves me more than anyone else in the world. He makes me feel special. To him I *am* special. That sounds egocentric – perhaps it is – but that's the reason.'

'And do you...' Shirley could not use the world *love*. 'Do you feel the same about him?'

'I hope I love him just as much, but in a different way.' She considered this statement. 'I know I should be empty if he left me. I should be empty again.'

'But that could happen,' said Shirley, ever tactless. 'I mean ... it happens to all of us in the end ... he could die.'

441

Kate finished her cup of tea and stood up. It was time to go.

'I hope, by then, that I shall have been loved sufficiently to learn to stand alone. And now, Shirley my dear, I think we should both return to the fray.'

Outside, mouths were being wiped, picnic baskets being packed, litter collected tidily into plastic bags, and crumbs shaken from rugs and cushions.

Within its big black hood the orchestra was tuning up.

The programme had been designed to cope with a wide range of ages and tastes and to cope with most contingencies. For instance, complete silence was impossible. Some child would always cry or call out, some dog would always bark. So they were to be introduced to Johann Strauss, wooed by Vaughan Williams' English folk songs, whirled round by Borodin in the Polotsvian Dances, joined in a meditation of Finlandia with Sibelius, enraptured by Schubert's lieder, and bidden farewell by Tchaikovsky.

A twenty-minute interval was allowed between the two halves of the programme, to allow visits to the Portaloos, and reviving swigs of wine and pop.

The players paused momentarily on the edge. The conductor gave the signal and they plunged into a glorious parade. Within minutes the audience was clapping in time to the

Radesky March.

Children who had never listened to music before now stood up, or demanded to be held up, so that they could stare and stare at the giant hood full of little figures making charmed sounds with magical instruments. Lights glinted on heraldic brass, white arms gleamed over bows, legs straddled, fingers plucked, heads moved in emotional time, and occasionally from his own rostrum at the back of the orchestra the timpani player would mark a moment.

Years later some of the young watchers would choose to play a flute, a cello, a violin, beat a drum, blow a horn, because of this evening. Now they simply watched and listened, enraptured.

Kate and Jack stood, arms round each other's waists, and dreamed a life together. Nora and Neville dreamed the life that had been. Shirley dreamed of what had never been, and never would be. Hector did not dream at all, believing that he had broken and saddled destiny and made it trot to his measure. Patrick, having no musical ear, was at present sitting in Mulligan's drinking his supper.

The orchestra was surging to victory with the 1812 Overture. Guns fired a triumphant salute in Moscow. A flash of lightning and a crack of thunder shook the night sky as a salvo of rockets roared up and instantly burst into giant gold dahlias.

'A-a-ah!' they all cried.

Children, clapping their hands over their ears or mouths, shrieked with delight, laughing round at their parents.

The dahlias lingered for a moment. Their petals drifted gently down. Falling stars. Children lifted unavailing arms to capture them. Another blast and blaze.

'A-a-a-ah!'

The music rode exultantly on. Guns, bells. Noise, light, sound. Fountains of fireworks soared and exploded. The sky was incandescent with glittering drops of gold. A hail of brilliant arrows. A shower of jewels. The upturned faces of children, marvelling.

A final crescendo.

A spellbound silence.

Very soon the applause would begin, deafening any sound made so far, but for a few moments everyone had become part of the music.